D0350937

THE DARK CLOUDS SHINING

Books by David Downing

The John Russell series
Zoo Station
Silesian Station
Stettin Station
Potsdam Station
Lehrter Station
Masaryk Station

The Jack McColl series
Jack of Spies
One Man's Flag
Lenin's Roller Coaster
The Dark Clouds Shining

Other titles
The Red Eagles

THE DARK CLOUDS SHINING

DAVID DOWNING

SOHO
CRIME

Published in the United States by

Soho Press, Inc.
853 Broadway
New York, NY 10003

Library of Congress Cataloging-in-Publication Data

Downing, David, 1946–
Title: Dark clouds shining / David Downing.
A Jack McColl novel

ISBN 978-1-61695-606-6
eISBN 978-1-61695-607-3

1. Intelligence officers—Great Britain—Fiction. 2.Women
journalists—Great Britain—Fiction. 3. Espionage, British—Fiction. I. Title
PR6054.O868 D37 2018 823'.914—dc23 2017029033

Interior design by Janine Agro, Soho Press, Inc.

Printed in the United States of America

10 9 8 7 6 5 4 3 2 1

There's a silver lining,
Through the dark clouds shining,
Turn the dark cloud inside out
Till the boys come home.
(from "Keep The Home Fires Burning,"
lyrics by Lena Ford, 1914)

A curtain was lifted, a light briefly shone,
a swift shadow fell down the wall and was gone.
(Vladislav Khodasevich, 1922)

THE DARK CLOUDS SHINING

March 1921

A Simple Act of Violence

The Harrow courtroom was in a shabby condition; like so much else it was still waiting for a postwar recovery. The large expanses of wood paneling looked like they hadn't been polished for years, which was somewhat surprising given the number of people outside yearning for gainful employment.

The railing in front of Jack McColl was shiny enough, presumably greased by the sweating palms of previous defendants. It wasn't the first time he'd stood in a dock, but he'd never been alone in one before, and for some reason the experience felt less stressful. Perhaps because he had only himself to worry about.

He was glad his mother hadn't come down from Scotland. She had visited him in Pentonville a week or so earlier, and he had obviously convinced her that there was little point. He had refused her offer to pay for a better lawyer for much the same reason. Moral support was always nice, but she didn't have that much money to spare, and both of them knew it would have been wasted.

The mere fact that the authorities had gone for a jury trial suggested, at least to McColl, that the outcome was a foregone conclusion, and that the Crown's chief concern was to maximize his sentence. The jury, of course, might prove awkward, but nothing in the faces of its members suggested any sympathy with his case. The judge, a white-haired man in his sixties, had been palpably hostile from the outset. According to one newspaper that McColl had seen, the judge was known as "the Met's best friend," some accolade when London's police force was clearly spoiled for choice in that regard.

And some choice when the alleged crime concerned the serious injuring of a policeman. The officer, PC Owen Standfast—even the name seemed like an accusation—was still, ten weeks later, in too frail a state to attend the court. Or so it was claimed. McColl had his doubts, but admitted he might be doing the man an injustice. It was, after all, his instant aversion to PC Standfast that had set his fist on its face-bound trajectory.

The police constable had been well enough to recall and describe the events in question, and the middle-aged detective inspector now entering the witness box was armed with the interview transcript. He began by explaining the reasons for PC Standfast's nonappearance, and then announced, apropos of nothing, that the constable had decided on doctor's advice to take early retirement. When McColl's state-provided counsel protested that this statement might be prejudicial, the judge reluctantly agreed, and advised the jury to forget they had heard the offending words.

The inspector started reading Standfast's testimony, his voice rather loud for the mostly empty courtroom, his tone suggesting a penchant for amateur dramatics. PC Standfast had first observed the vehicle—a Ford Model T—coming toward him on Preston Road at around four o'clock in the afternoon. It had been traveling in the center of the highway at what he considered an excessive speed. Only a few seconds later it had abruptly swerved to the left and crashed through the plate-glass window of number 146, the Eternal Rest Funeral Parlour. PC Standfast had hurried toward the scene—a distance of about a hundred yards—worried that someone might be badly hurt, but on reaching the spot had found two men in the automobile's front seats laughing hysterically. The man behind the wheel, half of whose face was covered by one of those tin masks commonly worn by soldiers who'd suffered facial disfigurement in the war, was so taken by the humor of the situation that he was rhythmically beating his hands on the steering wheel.

All true, McColl thought, aware of the stares of several jurors. His and Nate Simon's sudden confrontation with a window display of coffins had, at the time, seemed a joke of almost cosmic proportions.

"I see you still find this amusing," the judge commented, noticing McColl's involuntary smile.

"You had to be there," McColl replied.

The judge gave him a contemptuous look and invited the inspector to continue. According to PC Standfast, he had been about to order the two men out of the automobile when he noticed that the driver, Nathaniel Simon, had no legs. The vehicle had been adapted for his use, hand levers bolted to the foot pedals in what appeared a highly slapdash manner.

"Mr. Simon chose to end his own life in police custody, I believe," the judge noted.

"Yes, m'lud," the inspector said.

"One might consider him the second victim," the judge went on, looking at the jury.

One could if one wanted to influence the verdict, McColl thought. Though only a fool would deny that Nate had been a victim.

Thinking it unlikely that a man with no legs would step out of the car, PC Standfast had asked the man in the passenger seat to do so.

"The defendant, Jack McColl?"

"Yes, m'lud."

PC Standfast had then asked Mr. McColl to help him get the driver out of the car. At which point Mr. McColl had punched PC Standfast in the face, causing him to fall backward and—as he discovered much later—to hit his head on the edge of the roadside curb. "PC Standfast was in a coma for five weeks," the detective added helpfully.

He was dismissed with fulsome thanks and the lack of any opportunity for the defense to question or challenge the absent witness blithely noted. Two other witnesses were duly heard and confirmed the basic outlines of the incident—neither had been close enough to hear the exchange of words. By the time the second man left the stand, it was almost noon, and the judge was apparently hungry. The case for the defense would be heard that afternoon.

McCOLL WAS ESCORTED BACK DOWN to the basement for his own feast—a chunk of yesterday's bread with a slice of ham, washed down with a decent mug of tea. It was an improvement on the fare at Pentonville, to which he assumed he would soon be returning. He was resigned to a lengthy sentence, and much of the time was inclined to think he deserved one, if not for this particular crime. He had the feeling that things were finally catching up with him, that his ham-fisted search for atonement had been finally deemed insufficient by some nebulous higher authority.

As was often the case at such moments, his thoughts went back to that day in Moscow, almost three years before. The anguished look on the young boy's face when McColl had told him he couldn't take him to England. Eleven-year-old Fedya, whom McColl had chanced across in a far-off village while on his way to Moscow, and whom he'd taken with him partly for the camouflage that a child in tow would provide. Fedya, who had refused to take no for an answer, followed McColl from the orphanage, and then been caught in the middle when Cheka agents chasing McColl had recklessly opened fire. His old enemy Aidan Brady, then serving with the Moscow Cheka, had probably fired the fatal shot, but McColl had felt responsible. He had brought the boy to Moscow and stupidly put him at risk.

That heartbreaking day in the summer of 1918 had been only the first of several—in the months that followed his brother Jed had been taken by the Spanish flu, and Caitlin Hanley, the Irish-American love of McColl's life, had decided that the Russian Revolution meant more to her than he did. Her decision to stay on in Moscow had effectively ended their long on-off affair, and a subsequent letter had formalized the break. His career with the Secret Service had already ended after he'd sabotaged a plot by the Service's Russian allies to poison Moscow's food supply.

McColl and his mother had helped each other through their months of grief over Jed. In truth, she'd been in much better shape than McColl had, and her continued immersion in the postwar radical politics of Glasgow's Clydeside had provided a focus that his own life lacked. Then in the spring of 1919, he'd received a letter from London. Long before the war, in what seemed another age, McColl had met and married Evelyn Athelbury, and gone on to work for her brother Tim, a designer and manufacturer of luxury automobiles. It was the opportunities implicit in hawking these vehicles around the world that had first persuaded Mansfield Cumming, the head of Britain's new Secret Service, to enlist McColl as a part-time spy.

Already aware that Evelyn had died in the postwar flu epidemic, he had learned from the letter that her brother had recently succumbed to one of the more aggressive cancers. Before dying, Tim had advised his younger sister Eileen—the letter's author and his sole beneficiary—that she should seek McColl's advice on the future of the firm. Would he be willing to visit her in London and do as her brother had suggested?

McColl had been reluctant, but his mother had persuaded him that the change would do him good. Eileen, an attractive widow in her late thirties with a traumatized eleven-year-old son, had asked him if he could take a week or two to decide on which was the sensible course—selling the firm outright or finding a new man to manage it for her. The business, as McColl soon realized, was nothing like its prewar self—the days of small automobile manufacturers were rapidly drawing to an end, and Athelbury's was now little more than an upscale garage that specialized in servicing luxury cars. But the buildings were sound, the equipment mostly up-to-date, and the Swiss Cottage location a good one for the trade in question.

McColl had taken on its renaissance, hiring a one-armed mechanic named Sid whose skills were far greater than his own and making his home on the premises. He liked Eileen, and when she suggested they share the office cot, his body didn't get the argument that it probably should have. Over the next six months, they made love once or twice a week, and it was only when she suggested marriage that he realized how serious she was about him.

He couldn't face the responsibility, for her or her son, who sometimes even looked like Fedya, if only in McColl's imagination.

He had built her a thriving business, and she let him go without any rancor. McColl had learned a lot from the one-armed mechanic and soon found another job at a garage in Wembley. With someone else doing all the paper work, he had more time for the disabled veterans' group, which Sid had introduced him to, and spent much of his spare time ferrying men with missing limbs around London. On several occasions his passengers were bound for demonstrations outside Parliament or one of the ministries, and twice he found himself involved in skirmishes with the police.

Waiting for a passenger on one occasion, it occurred to him that a car could be adapted for disabled use. He arranged to meet Sid for lunch at a pub on the Finchley Road, and the two of them had enjoyed a long and liquid discussion of the possibilities. In the eight months since, they'd experimented with all sorts of bespoke adaptions for the myriad forms of maiming suffered in the war, often in vain but sometimes with heartwarming success. The vehicle that Nate Simon had driven through the funeral parlor window had been one of their simpler jobs, and McColl was still at a loss as to what had gone wrong. He suspected that Nate—not the sanest of men since losing half his face and limbs—had done it deliberately, but now he would never know. Nate was beyond questioning, by McColl or the jury upstairs.

"I WOULD LIKE TO TAKE you through Police Constable Standfast's statement to the police," the defense attorney began.

McColl nodded.

"He said that the car was traveling at excessive speed in the middle of the road. Do you agree?"

"In the middle of the road, perhaps. There was, as far as I remember, no other vehicle in sight. At excessive speed? I would guess we were traveling at around twenty-five miles per hour, which few drivers would consider excessive in this day and age."

"I think we can agree that the automobile took a sudden turn to the left, before mounting the pavement and crashing into the funeral parlor?"

"Yes."

"Can you explain why that happened?"

"It certainly had nothing to do with the modifications we had made to the car. They were still in perfect working order."

"How do you know that?" his counsel asked.

"I used them myself to drive the constable to hospital."

"So what do you think happened?"

McColl hesitated. He was reluctant to point the finger at Nate Simon, because of how it might reflect on other disabled drivers, but the truth was the truth. "I think Nate—Mr. Simon—had a moment of madness. He saw the sign above the funeral home—'the best care for your loved ones'—and something just snapped."

"Were you 'laughing hysterically' when PC Standfast arrived on the scene?"

"We were. It just seemed so appropriate somehow, after everything that happened in the war, to find ourselves literally in death's lap. It wasn't as if anyone had been hurt."

"Quite. So what happened next?"

"Mr. Simon took off his mask, something he often did when confronted by figures of authority."

"With the intention of upsetting the person in question," the judge interjected, with only the slightest hint of inquiry.

McColl took it in his stride. "He liked to make people aware of the sacrifices he and others had made for their country."

"But a provocative act, nonetheless," the judge insisted.

"If you say so," McColl said dryly.

The judge considered another verbal intervention, but opted instead for simply shaking his head.

"How did PC Standfast react?" the defense counsel asked McColl.

"He blanched. Which was not an unusual reaction—Mr. Simon's face was quite shocking at first sight."

"And did he ask you to help him get Mr. Simon out of the automobile?"

"In a manner of speaking. He said: 'Get this monster out of the car.'"

"Those were the exact words he used?"

"Yes."

"And what happened next?"

"I punched him," McColl admitted.

"Because of what he called your friend?"

"Yes," McColl said, more hesitantly than was sensible. How could he explain the years of pent-up anger and anguish that had gone into that punch?

"And when you saw that the constable had struck his head on the curb, and was probably seriously hurt, what did you do?"

"I drove him to Harrow Cottage Hospital."

"Did Mr. Simon accompany you?"

"Yes, I helped him into the passenger seat."

"Was he upset?"

"I think so. He refused to put his mask back on."

"One last question, Mr. McColl. If PC Standfast was unconscious, what was to stop you simply driving away and leaving him and avoiding the situation in which you now find yourself?"

"Humanity, I suppose. It didn't occur to me. I never had any intention of seriously hurting the constable, and I certainly didn't want his death on my conscience."

"Thank you, Mr. McColl."

The prosecution counsel was already on his feet. "Just a few questions, Mr. McColl. First, we have only your word for it that PC Standfast used such an ugly term to describe Mr. Simon. That is true, is it not?"

"The only other person there was Mr. Simon. And as far as I know, he never spoke again."

"And yet one might assume that a person so insulted might make some sort of protest?"

"Perhaps Mr. Simon had a better idea than you do of how effective such a protest might prove."

"Perhaps. But this uncorroborated insult provides you with a most convenient line of defense, does it not? Without it, you're just someone with a hatred of authority, a very short temper, and a disposition to violence."

McColl smiled at that. "That would be true if I were making it up. But I'm not."

The prosecution counsel shrugged his disbelief. "As a matter of fact, we have only your uncorroborated word that Mr. Simon took off his mask when you said he did. Neither of the witnesses saw him do so."

"They were still fifty yards away, and he had his back to them."

"Indeed, but still . . . And I suppose in the end it doesn't matter, because even if PC Standfast is being reticent with the truth, and everything happened exactly the way you say it happened, the fact remains that you struck a policeman in the course of performing his duties, and came remarkably close to killing him. And that no matter how offensive the alleged remark, there can be no excuse for what you did."

The judge didn't say he agreed, but the jury was left in no doubt of his expectations. McColl was barely back in the basement before being recalled; the eleven men and lone woman had taken less time than it took to smoke a cigarette. The guilty verdict was unanimous, and none of them looked in the slightest bit doubtful about its rightness.

"Jack McColl," the judge began, "you have, as the learned member for the prosecution pointed out, an obvious affinity for violence. PC Owen Standfast was the victim in this instance, but two other police officers—as I am only now allowed to reveal—have suffered at your hands in the last eighteen months. Both in political demonstrations which, accidentally or not, descended into violence. Neither man suffered serious injuries, but perhaps they were simply more fortunate than PC Standfast.

"The disabled and disfigured veterans of the war have been a feature of this trial. They, and the treatment they receive from a mostly grateful society, are obviously of enormous importance, but this trial has not been about them. A simple act of violence—that is what this trial has been about, and you, Jack McColl, have been found guilty of committing it. In some ways you are a very lucky man, because if Owen Standfast had died, you would now be facing a probable life sentence, or even an appointment with His Majesty's hangman. I was minded to give you ten years in prison, but have decided on reflection to reduce that by three, on account of your driving the victim to hospital. Take him down."

With one last glare at McColl, the judge rose to his feet and headed for his chambers. McColl felt hands encasing both his arms, and allowed himself to be led from the dock and onto the stairs. He was vaguely surprised and somewhat aggrieved by the length of the sentence, but realized, with something of a shock, that his strongest feeling was one of relief.

Waifs and Strays

Sergei Piatakov had hoped that the Red Army train wouldn't stop in the town where he'd grown up, because these days the past was something he mostly tried to forget. But here he was staring across at the old familiar platform and the snow-draped buildings that lay beyond. A short walk away, hidden by the curve of the main street, was the school where he'd taught. A verst beyond that, the house by the river where his family had lived.

The urge to see the place again was surprisingly strong, but the train would probably soon be on its way. And anyway, what would be the point? Everyone was gone, and all would be different. He certainly was.

Five years had passed since he'd left from that platform on another late winter afternoon. He, his mother, and Olesya had waited to say their teary good-byes under the canopy, watching the snow floating down to the tracks. The wall poster proclaiming that THE KINGDOM OF THE PROLETARIAT SHALL NEVER END certainly hadn't been there that day, and the soldiers hadn't been wearing caps with gleaming red stars. On the contrary, if memory served him right, a couple of priests had been telling a group of doomed young conscripts how lucky they were to be serving the beloved czar. Before, no doubt, scuttling home to the warmth and safety of their church.

He remembered Olesya making sure the top button of his navy greatcoat was securely fastened before she kissed him good-bye. He remembered his mother's pale face and feverish eyes, and the brave smile she had just about managed to keep in place.

It was the last time he'd seen either of them. Now one was dead, the other in exile, God only knew where.

The train jerked into motion, stanching the flow of memories, blurring the picture inside his head. They were gone, he reminded himself, as the station slipped from sight. That world was gone.

And what had been put in its place? To say that the last five years had seen their ups and downs felt like the mother of understatements. The horror and despair of the czar's war against the Central Powers had dissolved in the joyful hopes of the October Revolution, but they in turn had been all but swallowed up by the horrors of civil war. When that had been finally won the previous winter, the winners had found themselves deeply at odds with one another over how to proceed. And now, this very week, the sailors at the Kronstadt naval base—whom many had thought the heart, soul, and fist of the revolution—had come out against Lenin's government.

Piatakov was no longer a sailor—these days the regime's enemies were almost all on land—but he, his father, and his brother had all been stationed at Kronstadt at some time or other. He had traveled to and fro between the base and nearby Petrograd in the autumn of 1917, and been lucky enough to take part in the storming of the Winter Palace. He knew these men, and if they said the revolution had lost its way, he was inclined to believe them.

He certainly had no desire to fight them, and when the regiment had received its marching orders the previous evening, that distinct possibility had filled him with dread. But on reaching Velikiye Luki their train from the Polish border had continued eastward on the line to Moscow rather than north toward Petrograd, and soon thereafter new orders had been divulged. The rebellion in Tambov province, which they'd fought to subdue in the months before Christmas, was apparently still alive, and the regiment was headed back for a second tour of duty.

Which had to be better than fighting old comrades, but still seemed a less than inviting prospect. Piatakov had no sympathy for the mostly peasant rebels, who had no hope of victory, and whose barbaric depredations he had seen at first hand. His own side had often behaved just as badly, but who could afford bourgeois scruples when the towns were starving for lack of grain?

The things he had seen and done in his twenty-five years. Things he would have found unimaginable when he left for war that day. Things you did because the bastards clung to power and privilege like limpets, and had to be loosed, finger by finger, until they fell away.

He suddenly realized how hard he was gripping the corridor handrail.

Outside, the countryside was growing dark. They should be arriving in Moscow sometime tomorrow and, if the past was any guide, would probably not be setting off again for at least another twenty-four hours. He found himself hoping that the train would just keep going, because Moscow meant his wife, and these days he found his comrades-in-arms a much more comfortable fit. He still loved her, but he was far from sure that she still loved him or, indeed, ever had, at least in the way he'd once hoped for. These days they barely ever talked politics because both of them knew it would end in a row. And the problems they had in bed—the problems he had—certainly hadn't helped.

He told himself that he was being foolish, that it would be good to see her, and that, anyway, it wouldn't be for long.

Once he had only his own reflection to look at, he made his way back to the crowded compartment. With the windows shut against the cold, the tobacco fug grew ever thicker, but at least they could hear one another talk, and soon the usual debate was underway. Piatakov's regiment had more than its fair share of revolutionary veterans, and not for the first time, abuses of power and position were the principal topic under discussion. Some thought the increasing stratification, and the uneven distribution of goods and privilege that went with it, were only teething troubles—that once the economy was back on its feet the party would find a way to restore the simple egalitarianism of the early years. Others were convinced that the revolution had been betrayed, as much by the party leadership as by the specialists they'd hired in such numbers, and that these new bosses would soon resemble the old unless the lower ranks fought back.

What neither side disputed was the proliferation of double standards. Several other men had noticed the train that Piatakov had spotted in Polotsk station, with its luxury saloon for Lenin's beloved specialists and overcrowded, run-down coaching stock for everyone else. Those specialists were the bourgeois gentlemen that Lenin had promised he would first squeeze dry and then cast aside. They hadn't looked squeezed or fearful for their future.

Many soldiers had similar tales to tell. There was the brand-new workers' sanatorium in Odessa, which had no worker patients, but was proudly shown to any visiting bigwigs. There were the dachas of long-vanished nobles in the woods around Moscow, which the government had confiscated in the name of the people, before erecting taller fences and gates. While in Petrograd, one of the soldiers had visited the Smolny Institute, where the October Revolution had been organized, and found himself in the midst of a bitter conflict over different canteens for different grades of party membership.

The general accord as to what had gone wrong didn't extend to how things could or should be put right. Ever since the first revolution, stepping onto a train had usually also meant stepping into a highly animated discussion of political rights and wrongs. But in those early days, the debates would usually remain good-natured— people were genuinely intrigued by other possibilities, and not inclined to dismiss all opponents as merely self-interested. These days an argument was more likely to end in a brawl, as this one looked likely to do before an unscheduled stop gave everyone the chance to literally cool down.

Walking up the platform, Piatakov found himself with the teller of the sanatorium story. They knew each other by sight, but had never spoken before. The other man said he already knew Piatakov's name, and that he was Vladimir Fyodorovich Sharapov.

"Are you really as pessimistic as you sounded?" Piatakov asked him.

Sharapov laughed. "I sometimes wonder that myself. I do think it will get a lot worse before it gets better. The Kronstadt sailors have seen to that."

Piatakov was taken aback. "You think they're wrong?"

"They're right, and everyone knows they are, but our leaders can't admit it. So they'll make an example of them."

"Will they find troops willing to go up against them?"

"Oh yes. The only ones that won't are older regiments like ours." His smile was bitter. "And look which way we're heading."

"But there must be another solution," Piatakov said, hoping it was true. The acute sense of loss he was feeling suggested otherwise.

Sharapov just shrugged. "You know the party's Tenth Congress is happening in Moscow?"

"Of course."

"Well, the leadership will be announcing a new economic policy in a few days' time. People will be free to trade again."

Piatakov was more shocked than surprised. "How do you know this?" he asked, hoping it might be no more than a rumor.

"My brother works in the Economic Commissariat. They've been drafting the new regulations for weeks."

Piatakov took a few moments to take this in. "But that sounds like they're reintroducing capitalism," he said eventually.

"That's exactly what they're doing."

"But . . ."

"They think that as long as the party retains absolute political control, they can afford to lessen their economic grip. Give the bourgeoisie enough economic freedom to get everything moving again, but don't let them get their hands on any political levers. A breathing space, a period of transition. That's what they say we need."

"You don't believe it."

"I don't doubt that's what they're thinking. I don't even question their good intentions. I do fear the consequences."

"Dictatorship."

"Of course. The more economic freedom you offer, the less you can risk any real democracy. We've seen it whittled away: the banning of other parties, even those with whom we shared a lot. Now there's talk of banning factions in our own. Democracy's like virginity—once it's gone it's gone. Can you imagine Lenin and the other leaders meeting a few years from now and deciding that powers should be handed back to the soviets or the unions or anyone else? It's a fantasy. There won't be any going back from this."

Piatakov shook his head, but couldn't deny a terrible sense of foreboding. "Is it really that hopeless?"

"Sometimes I think so, sometimes not. We can keep on arguing until they actually shut us up, and who knows? Miracles happen. We might even convince the men who matter. If we can't . . ." He shrugged. "I have a wife and son to think about."

Ten minutes later their train was on the move again, and this time running on a decent stretch of track. Piatakov arranged his body for sleep as best he could in the cramped space, and then went through his usual ritual of mentally reliving one of the many horrors he'd witnessed over the last two years. He chose the moment that he and a comrade had come across the commissar tied to the post, his eyes still showing signs of life, his entrails hanging out of his stomach, which was stuffed with the grain he'd been sent to requisition. This was the memory that often woke him screaming, and over the last few months he had convinced himself that reliving the experience while he was still awake made it less likely to haunt the sleep that followed.

THE VIEW FROM THE SMALL office window was surprisingly evocative, a wide expanse of grass sloping down toward the river, and the monastery sat on the bank beyond, white walls and golden domes set against the wall of birches, all beneath a pure blue sky. Moscow's ragged streets seemed a world away, not a handful of versts.

The manager's assistant, a woman of no more than thirty, was clearly unnerved by Yuri Komarov's presence. This didn't surprise the M-Cheka's deputy chairman—few people instinctively reached for the samovar when the Bolshevik security police came to call. Most, in Komarov's experience, were too busy trying to guess which of their activities had brought such dangerous visitors to their door.

The four men he had brought along looked almost as unhappy. They were standing around in the yard outside, smoking and staring moodily into space, all in their trademark leather coats. When he'd called them in that morning to explain the task at hand, the looks on their faces had suggested he'd lost his mind. When he had pointed out that higher authority had decreed that the Cheka take responsibility for Moscow's large and ever-rising population of young waifs and strays, they'd rolled their eyes and offered muttered doubts about the Orgbureau's collective parentage. Komarov had just smiled at them. He liked the idea of softening the Cheka's image.

"I want to examine the facility," he told the woman.

"All of it?" she asked.

Komarov nodded.

"I'd prefer the manager to be here."

"So would I. But he isn't, and we don't have all day. So . . ."

She hesitated, failed to find a counterargument, and reached for a heavy bunch of iron keys.

"They're locked in," Komarov murmured as they crossed the hall. It wasn't a question.

"Of course."

"For how long each day?" he asked as they ascended the staircase.

"All but an hour. Each child is allowed a full hour's exercise."

"Like a prison," Komarov said blithely.

The look on her face suggested she didn't know how to take that comment. Most people would have considered it a statement of disapproval. But from a high-ranking Chekist? "We don't have the staff to offer any more," she said—unable was always a better excuse than unwilling. "If we let them out without sufficient supervision, they'd just disappear. And you'd have more gangs on the street to deal with."

She unlocked the first door and stood aside for him to enter. About twenty girls, ranging in age from around seven to around fifteen, almost leaped to their feet. Most had been sitting behind a bewildering variety of prewar sewing machines; the others had also been working on textiles in one way or another. An older girl had been sitting and facing the rest, an exercise book open in front of her. The smile she gave Komarov was about as genuine as a nine-ruble note. When he reached for the exercise book, she took an involuntary step backward.

The book contained the record of each girl's work, the jobs she had done and the time it had taken.

Komarov placed it back on the desk, apologized for the interruption, and walked out onto the landing.

"The other rooms are no different," the woman told him.

"Show me."

There were three of them, huge bedrooms once, their intricate cornices all that was left of the life that the revolution had brought to an end. The girls were all doing much the same work as the ones in the first room.

"Is that it?" Komarov asked as they headed back down the staircase. He could imagine the previous owners on the lower steps, welcoming the guests in all their finery.

"There's a laundry in the basement," the woman admitted.

"Show me."

It was damp and poorly lit, the stove apparently unused. The girls stood there and blinked at him, pale bare feet on the dark stone floor. It was like something out of Dickens, Komarov thought.

"Where do they sleep?" he asked as they climbed back up the stairs.

There was a dormitory out back. It had once been a stables, and each stall was fitted with three tiers of roughly built bunk beds. The small office next door, which had presumably belonged to the estate manager, was still in use, a table and chair by the only window, a bed that must have come from the house taking up most of the room.

"Who sleeps here?" Komarov asked.

"No one. Well, not on a regular basis. The manager sometimes spends the night here when he has a lot of paper work. At least, that's what he told me," she added, seeing the expression on Komarov's face.

"How many staff are here at night?" he asked.

"Usually three or four, I think. I always go home."

"How many women?"

"None," she said, looking more anxious.

Komarov ran a hand through his greying hair. "Where does the manager live?"

"In Yauzskaya. At seventeen Mashkov Lane."

They walked back around to the front of the house, where his men were still patiently waiting. He gave the address to the nearest pair, told them to pick the man up and take him straight to the holding cells on Bolshaya Lubyanka. "I need to use your telephone," he told the woman. "In private," he added when they reached her office door.

As he waited for the exchange to connect him with the Zhenotdel offices, he wondered if there was a more appropriate organization he should be calling, but couldn't think of one. It was intelligent females he needed, and who better to supply them than the women's department?

The woman he spoke to took some persuading. "The Cheka wants to borrow two of our workers for help with interrogations?" she asked disbelievingly, in an accent that Komarov couldn't quite place.

"Not interrogating, questioning. We need to question a lot of young girls—"

"What crime have they committed?"

"None. If crimes have been committed, they are the victims. And the crimes will have been committed by men. In such circumstances, using men to question the girls seems singularly inappropriate."

"I'm sure you're right," the woman said, sounding slightly mollified. "But is there no one else? We really have no one to spare today."

"I'm open to suggestions."

The woman was silent for a moment. "Are there no women in the Chekas?" she asked.

"There are a few. But none I know of who could set these girls at ease."

"Oh, very well. I will come myself and bring a colleague if I can find one. Where arc you?"

He told her.

"But that's miles away."

"I can have a car pick you up in half an hour."

"Oh. All right. You know the address?"

"I do."

Komarov smiled as he hung up the receiver. Outside, he gave the other two the Zhenotdel address and watched their Russo-Balt head off toward the city center, trailing a cloud of exhaust in the frigid air. After giving the manager's assistant her office back, he found a seat in one of the old reception rooms and stared at the discolored shapes on the wall where paintings and mirrors had hung.

He had only an hour to wait. Hearing the car arrive, he studied the passengers through the window. There were two of them, one short and slightly stocky with medium-length blonde hair and a pretty face, the other slimmer, taller, with dark reddish hair and a pale-skinned face that didn't look Russian. Both were wearing practical clothes and Zhenotdel red scarfs around their necks.

He went outside to meet them. "I'm Yuri Komarov, deputy chairman of the M-Cheka," he said, offering his hand to each woman in turn. Up close, he recognized the taller of the two, an American comrade who'd crossed his path several years before. Which explained the accent on the phone.

The other woman introduced herself as Comrade Zenzinova. "And this is Comrade Piatakova."

"We've met before," Komarov said with a smile. He had questioned her twice in the summer of 1918. On the first occasion, it had been her relationship with the renegade Socialist Revolutionary Maria Spiridonova that had brought her to the Cheka's attention. On the second, it had been an informer's report of her contact with a foreign agent. In both instances she, like so many others back in those days, had received the benefit of any doubts. And apparently deserved them, given that three years later she was still devoting her life to a foreign revolution.

"I remember," she said. "My name was Hanley back then."

"Well, thank you for coming," Komarov said. "Now let me explain the situation. This is a home for female waifs and strays. I assume it was set up by the party, but I rather doubt there's been any political oversight. From what I've seen, it's obvious that the girls are being exploited, and that a great deal needs to be done to improve the conditions. I have no evidence of worse, but I strongly suspect it . . ."

"You think they're being interfered with sexually?" Piatakova half-asked, half-stated.

"I don't know. The manager and his cronies have had the run of the place at night, and most of the girls seem frightened to death. I'm hoping you can get at least some of them to open up."

"How many are there?" Zenzinova asked.

"About sixty, but I'm hoping you won't need to question more than a few to get an idea of what's been going on."

The two women looked at each other. "Then we'd better get started," Piatakova said in her strangely accented but otherwise perfect Russian.

All work was stopped, and the girls brought together in what had presumably once been the ballroom. Two smaller rooms on the same floor were found for interviews and the first two girls delivered to their questioners by the clearly frightened staff.

It was almost four hours later when the two Zhenotdel women found Komarov in the manager's office. They both looked devastated.

"They work every hour God gives," Comrade Piatakova told him. "Apart, that is, from a short spell in the yard once or twice a week. The rest of the time they're either working or locked up in the dormitory." She raised her green eyes and gave him a look he could have done without. "Or, as you suspected, warming the manager's bed. It's sometimes just him, sometimes a few of his friends as well. They take their pick after the girls finish their suppers."

"Are any of them pregnant?" Komarov asked, knowing it was the wrong response the moment he said it.

"Probably not," Piatakova told him. "I doubt that most of the girls have ever had a period, and given the state of their health, I don't expect the older ones are menstruating either."

"How many did you talk to?"

"I talked to four and Fanya to five."

"Well, they'll all need to be questioned eventually, but first I must find people to look after them."

"Women, I hope."

"Of course. If you think of any suitable people, or of homes you can vouch for, I'd be grateful to hear. I know Comrade Kollontai was working to set up several such places in the early months of the revolution."

"I'll ask," Piatakova said. She got to her feet. "I assume your men will drive us back to Vozdvizhenka Street."

"Of course. And thank you."

She hesitated in the doorway, obviously trying to put a thought into words. "This speaks so badly of us," she said eventually.

"I couldn't agree more," he said simply.

He listened to the car drive off. A year ago he would have had the staff taken out to the yard and shot. Everyone would have been delighted—the children seeing their abusers receive their comeuppance, his men doing what they were good at, the bureaucrats in Moscow spared all that tiresome paperwork that went with trials. But now . . .

Things were supposed to be changing. The death penalty had been abolished, in theory if not quite in practice. And if they were ever to get the revolution back on its rightful course, then wrongdoing had to be exposed, not simply punished with a bullet in the back of the neck. The manager would certainly get one, but only after everyone in Moscow knew what for.

That was the easy part, he thought. What kind of future lay in wait for these girls?

He went back to the manager's office, where the woman who'd welcomed him six hours before was weeping in a corner.

"Where are the records?" he asked her.

"What records?" she managed to ask.

"The names of the girls. Their ages. Where they came from."

"He never kept any records," she said.

Komarov sighed. Even in the bad old days, they'd tattooed numbers on orphans' knuckles. "I'll send someone out here in the morning," he told the woman. "You'll be here to show her around. And then you leave."

"But—"

"Either that or join your boss in prison."

"But I didn't touch anyone."

Komarov just looked at her.

"You people think you own the world," she said, covering her mouth when she realized she'd said it aloud.

And what a world to own, Komarov thought.

CAITLIN PIATAKOVA GLANCED AT THE clock on the wall, and saw she had only an hour before the Orgbureau appointment. The last three had flown by: since the midday arrival of the twenty-four women from Turkestan the Zhenotdel offices had been a whirlwind of color, noise, and enthusiasm. A sense of liberation was catching, Caitlin thought, and more than a little intoxicating to Muscovites, who had almost forgotten how to feel so positive. And as far as she and Fanya were concerned, the arrival of the women had certainly provided a much-needed lift of the spirits after yesterday's hours at the refuge for waifs and strays.

These women had literally left their men—their husbands, fathers, and brothers—two thousand miles behind them. And, for the moment at least, they all seemed exhilarated by the freedom that distance had given them. Days like this, Caitlin thought, were what she lived for. The long hours, the endless petty obstruction, the knowing smirks and outright insults—all that men could throw at them—days like this made it all worthwhile.

They had spent the afternoon discussing the programs and material that the Muslim women would take back with them, and the Zhenotdel workers had initially feared that their visitors might prove overoptimistic about the pace of possible change. But they needn't have worried—the latter were fully aware that changing male minds in a highly traditional Muslim culture would take time and tact. As

Rahima, one of the unofficial leaders of the women, put it: "If we look too happy, they will be suspicious."

Rahima was only eighteen, but seemed a lot older, with a fund of common sense that provided ballast for her bubbly enthusiasm. She had married at fourteen, and her husband was one of the few Uzbeks prominent in the Turkestan Communist Party. He had allowed his wife to make the trip out of political duty, but she knew only too well that he found the whole business profoundly upsetting. "I will need to work on him day and night," she said. "And his mother, who keeps pouring poison into his ears."

Caitlin glanced at the clock—it really was time to leave. She checked that the relevant notes were in her bag, told Fanya she was off, and reluctantly left all the noise and happiness behind her.

Outside on Vozdvizhenka Street, a pale sun was struggling with a cold breeze. The Orgbureau offices were about a mile away, and with no tram in sight, she decided she might as well walk. The streets were virtually empty, and as she strode along, she rehearsed the arguments she would put to the committee. The issue in question was the setting up of Zhenotdel offices in a long list of provincial cities and towns, and the properties that the organization had carefully chosen to house them. There was no obvious reason why the proposals in Caitlin's bag should prove contentious, provided that they were considered on merit. But it was far from certain that this would be the case. Her friend and boss, Alexandra Kollontai, had already annoyed the party leadership by strongly supporting the Workers' Opposition faction, and the leaders might well choose to punish her by punishing the women's organization that she headed.

It was so frustrating, Caitlin thought. She loved Kollontai like a sister—a much older one who often seemed younger—and Caitlin could hardly fault her friend for sticking to her principles. But they had achieved so much over the last three years—women delegates and apprentices at every level, propaganda work among the peasants and now the Muslims, making Russia the first country in the world to legalize abortion . . . Only yesterday evening a woman from Petrograd had told Caitlin that 90 percent of people were now eating in communal kitchens. Not eating very much, she had added with a laugh, but communally. The link between cooking and domestic slavery was finally being broken!

This was what Caitlin had stayed in Russia for; this was what kept her going when less welcome things like hunger and loneliness and unwelcome political developments gave cause for doubts and depression. If you looked for reasons to feel pessimistic, there always seemed one to be found—some murderous outrage by the Chekas, some new instance of official corruption, what was going on now up at Kronstadt. But they weren't the whole truth. Good things were happening, too. The civil war was over; Muslim women were finding a voice. And who would have thought that Cheka bosses would turn into guardian angels where orphan girls were concerned?

The question, she supposed, was, which was the rule, which the exception? Sergei seemed increasingly convinced that everything was going to hell, but she hadn't given up hope. Far from it.

She was five minutes early for the appointment, but the committee was apparently running late, and the male secretary primly told her to join the queue in the waiting room. "How long do you think it'll be?" she asked him sweetly, leaning forward to read his list. As she expected, the Zhenotdel was right at the bottom.

Swallowing her anger—why make things worse before the committee had its say?—she joined the four men in the smoke-filled anteroom. Listening to their conversation, she realized that one was there to lobby for better sports facilities in Yalta, another to enlist decorators for the party offices in his local village. After seething quietly for several minutes, she took a deep breath and set to work on editing an article for *Communist Woman* that had reached the office that morning.

It was almost three hours later that she was invited into the committee room, where five comrades were seated on the far side of a long and highly polished table. She knew three by sight, including the chair, Vyacheslav Molotov. Each man had a copy of the Zhenotdel proposals in front of him, and the first objection wasn't long in coming.

"This hall in Yaroslavl," one man began. "It's currently a soldiers' club."

"It's a public bar," she corrected him.

"Which our soldiers use. Would you deny them a place to let off steam, after all the sacrifices we ask them to make?"

"Of course not. But there are many other bars in Yaroslavl, and this one has several rooms on both floors that would make an ideal suite of offices."

"Why not just use those other rooms?"

Are you serious? she thought but didn't say. "I doubt that using the same building for two such different purposes would work," she replied. "The men might feel inhibited by the presence of working women," she added with a straight face.

"Could the women not take turns meeting in one another's kitchens?" another man interjected.

She took a deep breath. "We are setting up working offices, comrades. Might I remind you that Vladimir Ilych has urged all local parties to offer assistance in this matter." Caitlin was fairly sure he had said something along those lines, and even if he hadn't, none of the men across the table would be certain whether or not he had.

"Of course," Molotov agreed. "But we have the responsibility of ensuring that the correct assistance is being offered."

And they took that obligation seriously. They offered a litany of objections to all but a few of the proposed requisitions, and though most were eventually sanctioned, the tone of the proceedings was appallingly paternalistic.

"Comrades," she almost pleaded after more than an hour had passed, "we are on the same side. Women are vital to the future of the revolution—the party says so—and the Zhenotdel is vital to the future of our women. We're not asking for the moon, just appropriate housing for our offices and educational facilities. And we have done our research—we haven't just picked buildings we liked the look of. Give us some credit, please."

Molotov had the grace to look slightly abashed, which was just as well, because his underlings merely looked sour. "I take your point, Comrade Piatakova," he said. "And perhaps we should take the remaining suggestions as read. But I think you would agree that the committee would not be fulfilling its duty if all suggestions were simply waved through without query or challenge."

"Of course," Caitlin agreed. He sounded more like a manager than a revolutionary, she thought.

Outside on the street she took a deep breath of the fresh evening air. She felt vindicated, annoyed, and depressed in almost equal measure. Why did it have to be so hard? How many years would it take to make men like that appreciate the central truth that improving women's place in the world would also make life so much fuller for men?

It was dark, the few working streetlamps like spotlights on a citywide stage. The Muslim women were going to the theater that evening—they would probably be there by now—and she had meant to go with the party. She had already seen the play, but was curious to see what their guests would make of it. After hesitating for several moments, she decided she would simply go home. The last few hours had worn her out.

Her room was a mile and a half from the office, just south of the river and canal. A safe walk these days, even after dark, now that most of the robbers who'd plagued Moscow streets in the civil war years had been caught by the Chekas. As she strode across the Kamenny Bridge, Caitlin found herself thinking about the notorious "jumpers," footpads who had—it was said—attached springs to the soles of their feet for bouncing away from Chekist pursuit, triumphantly waving stolen fur coats in the air. Had these "jumpers" ever been caught? Had they even been real?

The room she'd lived in for the last eighteen months was at the top of an old mansion on Dmitrova Street, a few hundred yards south of the river.. It was cold in winter, but less noisy than those on the floors below, which were large enough to house families. She got on well enough with her neighbors, but her fluency in Russian could never quite make up for being born a foreigner.

Despite the cold, several of the older children were out on the stoop. "Good evening, Comrade Piatakova," they all chorused. "Your husband has returned," her neighbor's daughter Lana added, with what looked suspiciously like a leer.

"How long has he been back?" Caitlin asked automatically.

"Not long. Ten minutes, perhaps."

As she started up the stairs, Caitlin tried to sort out her feelings. She was glad he was safe, glad that he wasn't one of those taking on the Kronstadt rebels. Which didn't mean she was pleased to see him.

She told herself to be more generous. Sergei was always interesting to talk to, and having him hold her in bed was warming in more senses than one, even when being held was the only thing on offer. Of all the men she'd met in Russia, he was—or had been—the kindest and most likable.

They had met at Kollontai's wedding in early 1918 and become lovers a year or so later on one of his leaves from the Volga front. The relationship hadn't been easy at first because she couldn't be her usual honest self with him. It wasn't a straightforward case of two people falling in love—she knew only too well that Sergei was filling the emotional space that Jack had left behind. But other leaves had followed, and she'd gotten used to walking the line between playing a part and finding real satisfaction in what they actually shared. They had become what Kollontai, in one of her writings on love, called "erotic friends"; they had, almost on a whim, embarked on what many party members called "a comrades' marriage." Or so Caitlin believed. She sometimes worried that he felt more for her than she did for him, but he was never fawning. He was ruthless in argument and would never do anything just because she wanted him to.

And until the previous fall they had made each other happy enough, sharing their thoughts and their bodies, and leaving their future for a postwar discussion, always assuming the war ever ended. Then, in October 1920, his regiment had been one of the units sent to Tambov province to crush the peasant rebellion, and several months later he'd come back a different man. For one thing he was impotent; for another he would often wake up shouting or—which seemed even worse to Caitlin—weeping. By day he was either depressed or angry and, on each succeeding trip to Moscow, seemed to spend more and more time at one or other of those disreputable clubs where renegades of every stripe met to share their rage and despair. When he'd last gone back to his regiment, she'd realized with a shock that all she felt was relief.

Caitlin took a deep breath and opened the door to her room. He was standing at the gable window, looking out over the moonlit roofs, and the face he turned toward her looked boyish and terribly bleak.

"Sergei," she said, walking across and throwing her arms around his neck. "It's good to see you."

He was stiff in her arms, but slowly relaxed. "And you," he said, just about managing a smile.

"How long are you here for? Where have you come from?"

He explained that the regiment was on its way back to Tambov province, and that he and many others suspected that part of the reason was to get them as far away from Kronstadt as possible. "I don't think they trust us to go against the rebels."

"That's terrible," she said.

"What is? That we couldn't be trusted or that that's what they thought?"

She shook her head. "I don't know what to make of what's happening at Kronstadt."

"As far as I can tell, it's not complicated. The sailors are the revolution's conscience, and they say the things we fought for are in danger of being lost. Have already been lost in some cases."

"But according to *Pravda* it's not the same sailors who were there in 1917, and there are Whites involved."

Piatakov shook his head dismissively. "They're lying."

"That's a serious accusation. Are you sure?"

"Not a hundred percent. But I know these men. And even if I didn't—sometimes you just know. Sometimes the facts only add up one way. But is there any news from Kronstadt? I've been on a train for more than a day."

"None that I've heard. But I was in an Orgbureau meeting for almost that long."

That made him smile. "I'm hungry," he said. "Let's go to the cafeteria, and maybe someone will know something."

"All right."

They walked the three blocks arm in arm, Caitlin silently wondering why she found it so hard to believe that Lenin was actually lying to his own party. Was it because the truth would be too damning? Would undermine everything?

The cafeteria was still almost full, despite the lateness of the hour. They queued for their soup and bread, but Sergei was more interested in asking the other diners questions than eating his food. "They say that Trotsky has appointed Tukhachevsky to lead an attack across the ice," he said, when he finally returned to their table. "Sixty thousand men against three thousand," he added, picking up his spoon and staring stonily into space.

It occurred to Caitlin that the rebels would have been wiser to wait a few weeks until the ice surrounding their island had melted, but Sergei seemed depressed enough already. On the walk back to the house, he suddenly stopped, grabbed both her hands, and earnestly looked her in the eye. "Sometimes I think it's all over," he said, "and we should just find another country, and start again from scratch, determined not to make the same mistakes."

No, she thought, remembering Rahima and the others. It wasn't over. But she didn't want to argue with him. Not tonight.

In bed, they undressed and held each other for what seemed a long time, until he murmured, "I'm sorry," and turned his back.

June–July 1921

Quid Pro Quo

It was the middle of the morning, and hunger was doing its usual best to flatter the coming lunch, when a jangle of keys announced an official visit. "Someone to see you," the screw told McColl. "Look sharp."

Who the hell? McColl thought. His mother had been down only a week or so before, and the normal hour for visits was in the afternoon. Had something happened to her?

"Who is it?" he asked the screw as they threaded their way through the wing.

"I wasn't told. This way," he added, taking an unexpected turn.

Another door unlocked, and suddenly there was a carpet on the floor.

"In here," his escort said, showing McColl into what looked like a sitting room. A desk stood against one wall; two comfortable sofas faced each other in front of an open fireplace. The governor's reception room, he guessed.

"Sit down and don't touch anything," the warder told him, as if he were five years old.

At first McColl did as he was told, but the lure of the window was too much. Standing beside it, he could see treetops above the prison wall. Trees that had sprung into leaf since his day at the Harrow assizes.

He was still engrossed in this new outside world when the door opened behind him, and Mansfield Cumming stepped into the room.

McColl had last seen the Secret Service chief toward the end of 1918, but Cumming looked more than three years older. His former boss hadn't many years left, McColl thought, surprised by how sad that made him feel.

After shaking hands, they each sat down in the middle of a sofa. "How would you like to get out of here?" Cumming asked without preamble.

"Show me a man who wouldn't," McColl admitted, wondering what the price would be. Cumming was no one's idea of a fairy godmother.

"I have a job for you. A full pardon can be arranged if you agree to do it. Are you interested?"

More so than he would have been three months earlier, McColl thought, but that wasn't saying much. "Curious at least," he said. "But I'm sure you know that the last one left a very sour taste."

Cumming had the grace to nod his agreement. On McColl's final mission for the Service, he had been ordered to participate in a plot by Russian Whites and the French secret service to poison the crops around the Bolshevik capital and thereby starve the city's residents to death. After thwarting the scheme he hadn't wanted anything more to do with the sort of people who'd dreamed it up.

"Where and what?" he asked.

"Russia," Cumming replied, with more than a hint of apology.

McColl sighed. If there was one country on earth . . . No, that was wrong. There'd been something special about Russia and most of the Russians he'd met. It had simply been the place where he'd run out of rope. "Do you still have people there? I thought we pulled everyone out in 1918."

"We did, but only for a while. We have new agents now, all of them locals. And so do Kell's people."

McColl was surprised. "What are MI5 doing there? I thought their writ was Britain and the empire."

Cumming settled back in his seat, as if finally sure he had

McColl's interest. "Last year," he began, "after the Bolsheviks held their second international jamboree in Moscow, a school for Indian revolutionaries was set up in Turkestan. In Tashkent, to be precise. Around forty men were enrolled, and they were given weapons training along with all the usual propaganda about how brutal the British have been to India. We know who most of these men are—your old friend Bhattacharyya was one of them—and in my estimation there wasn't much cause for worry, but the government, both here and in Delhi, has been close to panic ever since that idiot Dyer ordered his troops to open fire on that demonstration in Amritsar. They'd been insisting that it was vital to cut any links between the Indian opposition and Russia, and early this year they got their chance. Having virtually destroyed the Russian economy, the Bolsheviks were so desperate for economic help that they agreed to close the Tashkent school in return for a trade deal. So far, so good, you might think," Cumming said, pausing for breath.

You might if British interests were all that concerned you, McColl thought, and of course, defending those interests was the point of Cumming's job. McColl's time in India had convinced him that British rule was, at best, a mixed blessing, and he also thought it highly likely that the collapse of the Russian economy owed as much to the Whites and their Western allies as it did to Lenin's incompetence. But then, as Caitlin had always argued, and as his own experience had finally taught him, most people couldn't see past their own nationality. Even those who tried.

"The deal was signed in March," Cumming continued, "and as far as we can tell, they've been true to their word. We had a man with the Indians in Tashkent, and he recently reported that they've all been shipped back to Moscow. There's a third jamboree scheduled for the end of June, and they've been told they'll all be attending. Which is all to the good. But the other thing he reported is not. It seems that one of Kell's people has sounded out at least one member of this group for another project, but—and here's the interesting part—without revealing that he's a British agent. We don't know why or what the project might be, and Five refuse to enlighten us. They claim that our people in Moscow can't be trusted, so neither can we. And when I pointed out that Moscow was definitely not on their patch, they claimed that their business there was all to do with India, and that they were simply trying to nip potential trouble in the bud before it actually crossed the border, so to speak. Which was credible as far as it went, but I still didn't like it.

"And then we learned two other facts about this supposedly Indian business. One was that Russians were involved. Not at the official level, or not as far as we can tell. Lenin's volte-face on trading with the West hasn't pleased all his friends, particularly as it seems part of a general backpedaling that a lot of Bolsheviks find almost treasonous. I'm told that men like those might see encouraging foreign revolutionaries as a way of shaming their own leaders.

"And finally, last but not least . . . I don't suppose you've forgotten Aidan Brady?"

"No," McColl said dryly. Aidan Brady, the Irish-American firebrand whom he'd met in 1914 at a workers' rally in Paterson, New Jersey. Who had fatally stabbed a riot cop on the following day, and had left McColl himself for dead in a Dublin dock some four months later. Who had turned up again like the worst of bad pennies on that day in Kalanchevskaya Square. No, McColl hadn't forgotten Aidan Brady. "You don't forget a man who tries to kill you twice and blows a small boy's head off in the process."

Cumming gave him a sharp look. "He was caught in Ireland a couple of months ago. In a village not far from Queenstown. He obviously felt at a loose end when the Russian Civil War ended and decided to join the war in Ireland."

"So where is he now?"

"Back in Russia."

"Why the hell wasn't he tried and hanged?"

Cumming made a face. "Because Five decided they had a use for him, I suppose."

"And it was Five that sent him back to Russia?"

"Yes."

"And you think it's likely that he's involved in this Indian business, whatever it is?"

"Why else send him to Moscow?"

"But once he's out of their reach, what's to stop Brady just disappearing? That doesn't make sense."

"No, it doesn't. None of it does. Which is why I want you to go. Because you know Brady, because you know Moscow, and because I daren't send one of my own. I've been told, in no uncertain terms, to let Five get on with whatever it is they're doing."

"And yet," McColl said, smiling for the first time.

"And yet," Cumming agreed. "This is between us. I get you out of here, and you find out what the hell's going on. I'll see what I can do about arranging some help, but basically you'll be on your own. And reporting only to me."

"Won't people wonder why you're springing me?"

"I shall say you've been granted a full pardon on account of your past services to the Crown. Which you yourself could have brought up in court, if you hadn't considered yourself bound by the Official Secrets Act."

"Sounds feasible."

"Why didn't you bring them up?" Cumming asked unexpectedly.

McColl thought about it. "It didn't feel right. Like stepping over corpses."

"Does this?"

"No, not when a bastard like Brady's involved."

"Do you need more time to think about it?"

"No, I'll go. Do you know if Caitlin Hanley's still in Moscow?"

Cumming offered a thin smile. "I had a feeling you'd ask that, so I made some inquiries. The answer is yes. She works for the Bolshevik women's organization—I forget the name. She edits their magazine, among other things. But I don't think . . ."

"No, neither do I," McColl said. "Just curiosity. That flame went out a long time ago."

"She was always your Achilles' heel," Cumming mused. "You were—how shall I put it?—one of my most reliable men until the two of you tangled yourselves in knots. I hope she was worth it."

He sounded almost mystified, which McColl didn't find surprising—Cumming wasn't the sort of man to let a woman come between him and his work. "She did save my life in Dublin during the Rising," McColl said wryly. "And probably again in Moscow."

And even if she hadn't, he thought, she had made his life worth living.

MCCOLL WAS RELEASED A WEEK later, walking out through the Wormwood Scrubs gates on a sunny mid-June afternoon. The days inside had felt appreciably longer once he knew he was getting out, and the sense of relief at finding himself on a London street was even sweeter than he'd imagined. He had half expected to find someone from the Service waiting to pick him up and was pleasantly surprised that he could simply walk off down the road. A small sum of money had been left at the gate for a meal and bus fare, but by the time he'd exhausted his joy in space and movement, he was almost at the address off Baker Street that Cumming had commandeered for McColl's temporary home.

The flat was on the second floor of a four-story house, at the end of an old Victorian mews. A Secret Service hidey-hole, McColl assumed, for the use of itinerant agents and anyone Cumming might want to keep under wraps. McColl let himself in with the key he'd been given, and found he already had company: a bespectacled young man with wavy blond hair who languidly rose from an armchair and offered his hand. "Julian Bracegirdle," he said. "I'm here to get you up and running."

He reminded McColl of several former Service colleagues—adenoidal, entitled, but reasonably benign. Indulged by nanny, damaged at school and Oxbridge, finally loosed on the world. The empire's hollow spine.

McColl told himself to rein it in and give the man a chance.

Bracegirdle wasn't a waster of words. McColl would be leaving for Russia on the following Tuesday, taking ship from Harwich to Esbjerg, a train to Copenhagen, and a second ship up the Baltic to Helsinki. The arrangements for getting him into Russia were still being made, and he would probably learn what they were only once he reached Finland. Over the next few days he would be exhaustively briefed on the situations in Russia, Central Asia, and India, and on the particulars of his mission. And no, there would not be time for him to visit his mother in Glasgow before he left, but the flat did have a telephone. He could have the rest of the day to enjoy his newfound liberty—there were five one-pound notes on the mantelpiece—and a car would come to fetch him at 8:00 A.M.

Once Bracegirdle was gone, McColl explored the flat. It didn't feel like anyone's home, but wasn't as bland as a hotel room—the motley range of knickknacks, magazines, and books left behind by previous guests were more suggestive of an Indian clubhouse. The water was thrillingly hot, a private bath the height of luxury. After soaking for almost half an hour, he rummaged through the clothes that someone had brought from the room he'd rented in Kenton and dressed for an evening on the town.

The street outside was full of restaurants, but what he really wanted was fish and chips. Directed to a place near Baker Street station, he ate from the newspaper on a nearby bench, savoring each greasy mouthful. After washing his hands in the station toilet, he stood on the concourse just watching the flow of unrestrained people, wondering what to do. Visiting his friends in the disabled soldiers group seemed like a nice idea—there were trains to Wembley down the stairs—but explaining his early release might prove problematic. There'd be time enough to see them when he came back from Russia.

He took a walk through Regent's Park instead. There were a lot of people out strolling on the long summer evening, and there was a queue for the rowboats on the lake. The hundred-day drought he'd read about in prison was evident in the parched grass and undernourished flower beds.

With the sun sinking, he found a pub and sat outside with a pint of beer and someone's discarded paper. The news, as usual, was mostly bad. There were now over two million unemployed, and a similar number currently engaged in pay disputes—the promised country fit for heroes was apparently still at the drawing-board stage. A huge race riot in Tulsa, Oklahoma, had seen hundreds of negroes—men, women, and children—murdered by a rampaging white mob. Large parts of Russia, if this clearly anti-Bolshevik paper could be believed, were stricken by famine. And the English cricket team had just lost to Australia at Lord's, despite two ninety-plus innings from Frank Woolley.

Back at the flat, it took him three attempts to reach his mother before she finally answered. He expected to hear that she'd been at one of her meetings, but she'd actually been at the cinema, enjoying the new sensation Rudolph Valentino. Her delight at hearing he was out was somewhat tempered by the fact of a quid pro quo, which he didn't try to hide. She knew better than to ask where he was going or why, merely queried how long whatever it was might take.

"I should be back in a couple of months," he said, hoping he was erring on the side of caution. "How have you been?"

"Good enough. I seem to be slowing down a bit, but I suppose that's the way of it once you get past sixty. I took some flowers to the graves today and had a word with them both."

His father and brother were buried side by side, which wouldn't have pleased the latter, but which made things easier for his mother. And as one of McColl's disabled friends had put it: "Your brother's dead, so he won't really mind."

After the call McColl went straight to bed, and slept surprisingly soundly for over nine hours. Up at seven, he had time for breakfast at a nearby café before another of Cumming's helpers picked him up. His first briefer was a specialist in Russian current affairs; over the next few days he listened to several others and memorized numerous call signs. The number of wireless sets and operators that the Service had scattered across remote Central Asia was either truly remarkable or completely bonkers, and only time would tell which.

More unusually, he also spent several hours memorizing photographs of other British agents. These included Secret Service personnel, whose pictures Cumming had on file, and agents who worked for MI5 or the Indian Department of Criminal Intelligence (DCI), whose likenesses he had acquired by means best known to himself. When it came to the plot in question, the loyalties of most men concerned were largely a matter of guesswork, but a knowledge of the faces would at least allow McColl to spot an interested party.

On the day before his departure, he had a final meeting with Cumming himself. His old boss looked better than he had in the prison governor's office, but still seemed unusually anxious about the matter in hand. They talked about cars as they always did, but McColl was out of touch, and Cumming's interest seemed more halfhearted than usual. Their parting was friendly enough, but strangely tentative, as if each feared he wouldn't see the other again.

McColl took a farewell stroll down the river. It was a beautiful sunny day, the dome of St. Paul's shining like one of Wells's flying machines, the trains chugging in and out of Cannon Street as if posing for Impressionist painters. The Pool of London was full of activity, omnibuses queuing on either side of the raised Tower Bridge. The cell at Wormwood Scrubs seemed like a distant memory.

He leaned against a balustrade and stared out across the busy river, wondering what he would do when he came back. He would be forty in a few months' time—what did he want from the rest of his life?

He didn't know, which was somewhat depressing.

Then again, he might not come back, in which case the question would have answered itself.

Red into Blue

The two men stepped aboard the tram.

"Two kopeks, citizen," the driver said sharply, as Sergei Piatakov walked straight past his window.

Piatakov spun around to face him, feeling the all-too-familiar surge of resentment.

"The city soviet has reintroduced the charge," the driver added apologetically, arching back in his seat, as if half expecting a punch.

Piatakov's companion, Aram Shahumian, rummaged in his pockets, found the appropriate coins, and dropped them in the box.

Piatakov gave the driver a last contemptuous look and walked down to the far end of the almost empty tram, putting as much distance between himself and the transaction as he could. "Is this what we've been fighting for?" he asked his companion. "To bring back the rule of money?"

The Armenian shrugged.

Piatakov wasn't done. "You remember when Zinoviev gave that speech announcing that all public transport would be free. I was proud of us that day."

"Your party was never shy when it came to making promises."

Piatakov shook his head, but not in disagreement. "On my way to meet you, I saw this shirt in a shop window. On Arbat, it was. It was creamy white with fancy buttons and a floppy collar. The sort of thing a czarist gigolo might wear. And there was a little card beside it, with a neatly printed price. And do you know what it cost? Eighty rubles! In a city where half the people are hungry, where thousands are out on strike, in a country ruled by people who say they speak for ordinary workers and peasants, there are shirts on sale for eighty rubles! A month's wages, if you're lucky!"

"You know what I think of our current rulers, Sergei. What I thought of them when we met. They haven't done anything to make me change my mind."

Piatakov sighed. There was no denying his friend's consistency. Since the two men had first spent time together, sharing a hastily excavated trench in the northern Ukraine, Aram had made no secret of his anarchist beliefs. The Armenian had happily fought alongside Bolsheviks, but had never been reticent when it came to damning what he considered their obsession with power. Piatakov had liked and trusted him right from the start, which was more than he could say for many of his fellow Bolsheviks. There were no airs, no affectations, about Shahumian; what you saw was what you always got, no matter how difficult the circumstances. "And it seems you were right all along," Piatakov said wryly.

"And how I wish I hadn't been," Shahumian murmured.

Their tram continued on up Arbat, narrowly missing a woman and her sled, with its pitiful cargo of five or six rotten potatoes. Piatakov turned to the Armenian. "At least you never felt betrayed. That's what eats at my heart."

Shahumian put a hand on Piatakov's shoulder. "I know, Sergei. But it isn't over—as long as we have breath, the fight goes on. Allegiances change, and methods. Even what we can hope to achieve in our own lifetime. But the fight will go on."

The tram turned onto Nikitsky Boulevard, heading north. At Strastnaya Square the two men got off and started walking south down Tverskaya.

"So tell me what Brady's been up to," Piatakov said. The American comrade in question had fought with them both during the civil war, albeit on different fronts. When Piatakov had first met

Brady in the early summer of 1918, he had learned that they already shared one common acquaintance, his future wife, Caitlin.

"When did you last see him?"

"At the end of last year. We ran into each other in Petrograd, had a drink, and caught up. He was on his way to Ireland, to fight in the war there. Ours was over, so he thought he'd move on. I didn't think he'd be back."

"A good comrade, would you say?" Shahumian asked, with what seemed like deliberate casualness.

"He's certainly one of a kind," Piatakov responded. He had always found it hard to think of Brady as a friend, but the man had saved his skin on more than one occasion during their months together on the Volga front. "He has a way of getting people on his side," Piatakov added. "And of getting things done. I wouldn't want him for an enemy."

Shahumian grunted. "Not much chance of that. He's as sick of the way things are going as you are. Maybe even more so."

"That would be difficult," Piatakov said sardonically.

"Ah, you were always too optimistic, my friend."

Piatakov managed a smile.

"What does Caitlin think? I take it the two of you are still together."

Piatakov offered up a wry smile. "She says I'm in a permanent sulk. But it's different for her—she has work that she believes in." He shook his head and changed the subject. "Who else have you and Brady gotten together?"

"Grazhin. You remember him?"

"Ivan Vasilyevich? Of course. He's a good man." Grazhin had been in the same unit as Piatakov and Brady on the Volga. He'd always had his nose in one of Dostoyevsky's novels, all of which he carried in his knapsack.

"He's with us," Shahumian said, "though maybe not for long."

"His lungs?" Grazhin had never really recovered from the German gas.

"Yes. The last few years—well, he should be in a sanatorium, but he swears he'll give his last breath to the revolution rather than waste it in bed."

"That sounds like Ivan. Who else?"

"Three Indians. They'll be there tonight. They're all quite young—barely into their twenties, I would guess—and very keen. No experience to speak of, but everyone has to start somewhere. They were part of the group that was being trained at the school in Tashkent—remember that? They were all brought back to Moscow when Lenin decided we had to be nice to the British. All their comrades accepted it—they think the sun shines out of Vladimir Ilych's ass—but these three are really angry. They want a crack at their own revolution."

"Sounds good. So tell me what the plan is."

"I think I'll leave that to Brady."

"Once he's decided whether or not he can trust me?" Piatakov asked, not bothering to hide his resentment.

Shahumian put a restraining hand on Piatakov's arm. "Sergei, you are still a member of the party. Your wife is a deputy chair of the Zhenotdel. I know where your heart lies, and so does Ivan. But the Indians don't, and Brady has to be sure."

Piatakov sighed. "Yes, of course you're right," he said. "My sense of trust has worn pretty thin, and I shouldn't expect any better from others." He managed another smile. "But it *is* good to see you again, Aram. I'm really glad you looked me up."

They reached the building that housed the Universalist Club. There was no sign outside, only a single door that led into a narrow corridor, and that led into a broad, high-ceilinged room. Chairs and tables occupied all the available floor space, with a refreshment counter at one end and a small stage at the other. The wall between them was covered by a futurist mural of an imaginary Russian paradise. The room was ill lit, smoky, smelly, and noisy; a ragtime tune was blaring from a gramophone.

Piatakov had been to this particular club on several occasions in the months since Kronstadt, an errant Bolshevik among the various species of left oppositionists—LSRs, futurists, anarchists, imagists. They were all anachronisms, all as doomed as any prince, duke, or count of the old regime. And if, in his soberer moments, he sometimes wondered why he came, his heart was always there with the answer—that he always felt more at home in the company of rebels.

He followed Shahumian's winding path through the tables to the far corner of the room. The habitually thin Grazhin, his face lighting up in recognition, leaped up to embrace him. "Sergei, Sergei," he almost sang, "come, sit beside me."

Aidan Brady also rose to greet Piatakov with a hug. The American looked thinner than he had the previous year, and the beard was gone, but the greenish-brown eyes were arresting as ever, at one moment full of interest and concern, at another surveying the world and its people from some remote Olympian height.

The new Cheka ban on private firearms obviously didn't worry the American; the butt of a large revolver was clearly visible inside his leather jacket.

The two Indians present each offered a hand, and introduced themselves as Durga Chatterji and Habib Shankar Nasim. Chatterji was darker skinned, thin as Grazhin, with eyes that seemed to glow in his face. The more European-looking Nasim had a pleasant smile and relaxed manner. Both wore Russian clothes.

No sooner had they all sat down again than the third Indian arrived. Muhammad Rafiq was a shorter, more compact version of Nasim, with a flop of hair that he kept pushing back from his eyes. He talked fast and nervously, flashing apologetic smiles at frequent intervals.

They ordered chestnut coffee. Nasim had news from India, the importance of which only Brady and the other Indians understood. They took turns explaining matters to the others, and Piatakov was soon lost in a welter of unfamiliar names. He didn't suppose it mattered. The rebellion that seemed to be gathering pace against the British was the important thing, and a single name seemed to dominate that, one that Piatakov had heard from his wife—Mohandas Gandhi.

The Indian comrades hated this man with a passion.

Gandhi, they said, was a Menshevik, a Kerensky, a reactionary. Oh, he might have the British on the run, but the Indian working class would never see the benefit. That would go to the English-educated

Brahmins who ran the Congress Party, who would simply replace the British as a new ruling class. The flag and the faces at the top would change, but precious little else.

And the new rulers would wear eighty-ruble shirts, Piatakov thought to himself. Were all revolutions fated to follow the same downward spiral?

At that moment the lights dimmed, and a cacophony of catcalls and clapping resounded around the room. He turned to see someone clambering, with some difficulty, onto the small stage.

It was, Grazhin told him, the notorious Sergei Esenin. The poet was wearing a black velvet smock, which threw his powdered face and wavy golden hair into even greater relief. He was more than a little drunk. Piatakov, who had read and admired some of Esenin's work but never seen him in the flesh, at first felt something akin to dislike, but soon found himself, like everyone else, in thrall to the poet's presence and voice.

Verse followed verse, an avalanche of images. Esenin took them on a tour of a world turned upside down, introduced them to men turned inside out.

> *The farmhouse is lonely without me,*
> *And my old dog is gone from the door;*
> *God sent me to die in the backstreets*
> *And I can't go home any more.*

As he turned to pick up his drink, Piatakov's eyes met Brady's, and this time he found, unguarded, a blend of outrage and hurt at the state of the world that seemed to mirror his own almost too completely. There would be no happy endings, he thought. Not with Caitlin, not for Russia or himself. Which should have upset him, but for some reason didn't.

As some trench philosopher had told him once, revolutions were like candles—you lit one and it burnt itself down. And with the stub you lit another. And another.

The idea was both sad and seductive.

India, he thought.

I'm still the same
At heart I'm still the same . . .

The lines cut through Piatakov's thoughts. He felt for a moment as if Esenin were addressing him and only him, but the poet was in his own world, eyes glazed, feet unsteady, the foggy voice making common cause with the smoke that hung in the air.

Blue world, oh blue, blue world!
Even to die in this blueness would be no pain.

The voice went on, seemingly for hours, and when the last line faded away it felt like all the poet's listeners were waking from a common dream. Esenin's spell had bound them together, and in its dissolution a feeling of intense sadness gripped Piatakov, a sense of limitless waste.

Piatakov looked at Shahumian and Grazhin, and knew what they were feeling. At heart they were still the same.

But they weren't, Piatakov thought, not really. None of them were.

Grazhin was ordering vodka for everyone.

"Let me tell you what we're planning," Brady said quietly.

SHE WAS STILL ASLEEP WHEN Piatakov got back to their room, the candle still burning on the chair beside their bed. He had told her often enough that one day she'd burn down the building and everyone in it, including herself. But here she was again, fast asleep with a guttering flame, work papers rather than sheets covering her body.

She looked as lovely as ever, he thought. He sat down, pulled off his boots, and stared at her sleeping face, remembered their first meeting in Petrograd, more than three years before. He'd been one of the sailors organizing Dybenko and Kollontai's wedding ride on the city's frozen roller coaster, and they had ended up sharing a droshky and one of the thawed-out cars. She had seemed so exotic, this foreign comrade with chestnut-brown hair and the greenest of eyes, a woman who came from so far away and yet spoke the language of their revolution, and who seemed as much in love with it as any of its makers.

He remembered the first time they'd made love, on one of his furloughs from the front, in the room she'd shared on Kalashni Lane. He could still see her face in the soft candle glow, the joyous shock of their coming together. Had he ever felt happier? He didn't think so.

So how had it all gone wrong? Was it his fault or hers, or were they just another casualty of civil war? And if it was the latter, why had they—why had he—let things they knew they couldn't control slowly push them apart?

Or had he just been imagining a future that was never on offer? Sometimes he was sure she loved him, at others certain she didn't. And on those rare occasions when he'd swallowed his pride and sought reassurance, she'd usually quoted her friend Kollontai at him, stuff about love and relationships that sounded like sense but left him as unsure as ever about how she really felt. Maybe she didn't know, or simply didn't want to.

It didn't matter anymore. He knew that even as he sat there, looking at her, loving her. It wasn't politics that had come between them; it was who they were, and how their hearts and minds had pulled them in different directions.

As if on cue, the candle gutted out.

"I'D LIKE SOME ADVICE ON what to do next," Caitlin said. She, Fanya Zenzinova, and Alexandra Kollontai were sitting in the second-floor room of the Zhenotdel offices, the one usually used for internal meetings. Everyone else had gone home, but the sun was still above the rooftops, bathing the walls in golden light. "How much do you remember?" Caitlin asked Kollontai.

"Assume nothing," Kollontai said. "I've had a lot on my plate these last few weeks," she added apologetically.

Her friend and boss was still under strain, Caitlin thought. The recently concluded International Women's Conference, which had raised everyone else's spirits at the Zhenotdel, had offered

Kollontai only a temporary respite. And here was another burden to shoulder.

"Anna Nemtseva is a young woman from Orel," Caitlin began. "She turned up here about six weeks ago to report a crime. A series of them in fact. Crimes that no one else would take seriously. Anna was one of two Zhenotdel officials who ran our office in Orel. She is married, and in April this year her husband—also a party member—was suddenly arrested for 'speculation.' Meaning he had bought something on the black market."

"Since March and the NEP, the whole of Russia has been one big market," Kollontai protested.

"Maybe Orel was still catching up," Caitlin suggested. "It doesn't matter, because whether or not he did anything illegal, nearly everyone in Russia has committed the same sort of crime over the last couple of years. They arrested Anna's husband because the local party boss—a man named Agranov—had decided he wanted to sleep with Anna. The day after the arrest, she was called in to the local party office. There was no beating about the bush—if she spent that night with the party boss, her husband would be released on the following morning. She spent the day agonizing, decided she really had no choice, and agreed on condition that her husband would never find out.

"Agranov was rough with her, but her husband was released, and she tried to put it all behind her. But then another young woman, utterly distraught, came to the Zhenotdel office with a similar story to tell. And she, in turn, knew of two others who had been through the same nightmare. So Anna reported Agranov to the local Cheka. She was reluctant to mention her own experience—she was still afraid her husband would find out—or to name the other women, for fear that might put them or their husbands in jeopardy, but she was bracing herself to come clean if she got a sympathetic hearing. She didn't. The local chairman told her the women concerned must be no better than prostitutes and that, if she persisted in defaming a party official, he would have her and her husband arrested for counterrevolutionary activity.

"She thought about it for several days, and decided she couldn't live with herself if she just kept silent. Since the Chekist had also threatened her husband, she decided she had to tell him the whole story. He was horrified, but not in the way she expected. He more or less called her a slut and forbade her from pursuing the matter."

Kollontai rolled her eyes. "For heaven's sake!"

"This story doesn't paint our male comrades in the best of lights," Caitlin noted wryly. "Anyway, Anna thought, 'The hell with him,' took the train to Moscow, and turned up at our door. After she'd told her story, and we'd checked it as best we could, I took it to the Orgbureau. The members spared me the usual litany of objections and excuses and appeals for greater clarity—Molotov even admitted to being shocked—and promised immediate action. That was five weeks ago, and absolutely nothing has been done. Agranov is still in charge of Orel."

"Where's Anna Nemtseva?" Kollontai asked.

"She's staying at the house on Povarskaya," Fanya told her. "She wants to go back to Orel and her Zhenotdel work, but of course she can't. Not while Agranov and his Cheka friends are still in control of the town."

"And she's pregnant," Caitlin added. "By either her husband or Agranov—she doesn't know which."

"Oh hell," Kollontai said with a sigh. "I'd love to think this was an exceptional case, but . . ." She shook her head. "Leave it with me for a few days. I'll try and find out why nothing's been done." She glanced across at the clock on the wall. "I have to be at another meeting," she said, getting up. "It looks like this man, Agranov, has some influential friends in Moscow. If I find out who they are, we can take things from there." She paused in the doorway. "And I'll go to Vladimir Ilych if necessary—he still listens to me on issues like this."

"But for how long?" Fanya wondered out loud once Kollontai had left. "She's going to speak for the Workers' Opposition at the World Congress."

"How do you know?"

"She told me before you arrived."

"Oh dear," Caitlin said, for want of something stronger. If the

Zhenotdel director went against Lenin's wishes, and spoke up for the Workers' Opposition in front of the foreign comrades, she would almost certainly be inviting retaliation against her own organization, and Russia's women would be the losers.

"Do you think it's worth trying to change her mind?" Fanya asked. "She sometimes listens to you."

"She listens to everyone," Caitlin said. "And then she goes her own sweet way. And she's usually right. Maybe this time as well. She sees the whole picture better than we do."

"I hope so," Fanya said, sounding far from convinced. "Because if she's wrong . . ."

"The Orgbureau will have to find a lower place than last on their daily agenda."

That at least made Fanya laugh.

Caitlin picked up her bag, checked its contents. "I'm going home. It's been a depressing day, and I want to catch Sergei before he goes out."

AN HOUR LATER SHE WAS wishing she hadn't. An innocent remark of hers had sparked an argument, and that in turn had swiftly escalated into a major row, one that encompassed not only them but also their world and everything in it.

"Oh, for God's sake," she said, as he stood there with head in both hands, as if he feared it might fly off. She could feel the tightly wound force of his anger and the precarious control she had over her own.

She tried chiding him gently: "You once said that living through that first year was more than any man could hope for."

"I was wrong," he said coldly, blue eyes brimming with the pain she could never seem to reach.

"You were right," she retorted. "We have to remember how far we've come."

"It doesn't seem so far since they've started dragging us backward. And with people like you so sold on the wonders of the New Economic Policy that you won't lift a finger to stop them."

The quivering finger aimed at her face was too much. "I'm not pretending everything is wonderful," she said icily. "If anyone's pretending, it's you. It's you who's stuck in—" She heard her own voice rising and cut it off. "This is getting us nowhere."

"Stuck in what?" he asked, as if he actually wanted to know.

"In . . . in this all or nothing mentality," she said. She knew by now that she was probably wasting her breath, but persisted regardless. "You behave like a child who throws away a toy because it's not the exact one you wanted. You either sit here and sulk, or you sit in your club and get drunk with your equally apoplectic friends and wonder where utopia went. For God's sake, Sergei, if you think we're being dragged back, then why not pull in the other direction? If people like you and your friends don't take responsibility, you can hardly complain when careerists grab all the jobs that matter."

He'd been inching toward her, and for a moment she actually thought he would hit her, something he'd never done. He didn't, but the smile he offered instead was full of contempt. "You're living in a dreamworld," he told her.

"I may be," she snapped back. "I know you are. Take a walk, Sergei; look around the city. Take a train out into the country. Everyone's exhausted. Everyone's hungry. We needed peace. And by God we needed the NEP—"

"Like a man with broken legs needs brand-new boots," he said sarcastically. "You take a walk. Every day we're giving away the things we fought for, the things our comrades died for. You're so wrapped up in your women that you can't see the truth in front of your face. Don't you realize that it will all have been for nothing? All the death, all the suffering. And you have the nerve to accuse me of shirking responsibility!" He reached for his cap, face pale with rage. "Because I won't accept your blind optimism, I have to be sulking!" he almost shouted in her face. "It's you who needs to wake up!"

The door slammed behind him, and she waited for the wash of cold indifference that she knew would follow. Each time it came a little quicker. Saving her, destroying what was left of them.

She stood there, fists clenched, for several moments, then slowly spread her fingers. The papers she'd brought home from the office were on the table. There was work to be done.

IT WAS PAST MIDNIGHT WHEN she finally put down the pen, stretched out her arms and legs, and yawned. Her eyes ached and she felt thirsty. After adding the finished report to the pile, she went to plug in the hot plate under the kettle. The socket gave its usual impersonation of a firework, just in case she'd forgotten that the building needed rewiring. Some hope. The whole of Russia needed rewiring.

She remembered Lenin saying that electrification plus the soviets equaled Communism. It would probably be a long wait.

She went across to the window and leaned out. It was gone midnight, and the heat of the day seemed at last to be dissipating. In the street below, two drunks were having a loud but good-natured argument about which breeds of dog made the tastiest stew. She wondered how drunk Sergei would be if and when he came home, and whether by then he'd be angry with her or himself.

She pulled what remained of the curtain across the window and roamed restlessly around the room, waiting for the water to boil.

The box of photographs caught her eye. She took it down and sat on the bed, then, after a moment's hesitation, opened it. Her family stared up at her. They were standing outside the church on Fifty-Eighth Street, all in their Sunday best. Almost ten years ago now—her father still looked middle-aged, and so did her Aunt Orla. Her brother Fergus had either taken the picture or had already moved to Washington at the time; her sister, Finola, still looked like a child, though she must have been almost twenty. All were smiling but her younger brother, Colm, who was doing his best to look like a stranger. Colm who had died in the Tower of London, refusing to admit he had any regrets.

She didn't miss her father, nor Fergus or Finola, much though she loved the two siblings. But she did miss Colm, and by God she missed her aunt. It was almost six months since the last letter had reached Moscow, and that had been posted two months before. She had no idea whether Orla had received the last few she'd sent. Or whether Orla was still alive. Orla was sixty-eight now, and over the last few years she'd had several bouts of serious illness.

Maybe next year things would be easier here in Moscow, and

traveling abroad wouldn't be so difficult. Surely no one would begrudge her a month away, not after all this time.

Picking the photograph up, she recognized the corner of another and pulled it out from under the pile. It was her and Jack McColl, arm in arm on the Coney Island beach, in the spring of 1914. More than seven years ago.

With an angry sigh, she closed the box. The past was the past—there was no point in trying to live there, no point in trying to bring it back. Particularly when there were no real regrets. Sadness perhaps, but she'd never caught herself longing to turn the clock back, never wished she'd taken a wholly different path.

She made the tea, placed it on the chair by the bed, and undressed. She reached for the threadbare white nightgown, then left it where it was. It was too hot.

She turned off the light and sat up in bed sipping the tea. Outside in the street, two cats were screeching, presumably at each other. Like Sergei and her, she thought, remembering their row.

Cats were probably better at knowing when to let go.

HIS OWN WORDS WERE STILL ringing in Piatakov's head when he reached the house in Serpukhovskaya where Brady and Grazhin were sharing a room. He was the last to arrive: the other six already sat in a circle, some on rickety-looking chairs, the rest squatting cross-legged on the wooden floor. He joined the latter group.

"Now we're all here," Brady began. "I'm afraid there's bad news."

"Our traveling money," Shahumian predicted.

"Right," Brady confirmed. "I met with Suvorov last night, and he told me it hadn't arrived. According to Suvorov, the courier was caught crossing the border, and Suvorov has no reason to lie. He said London has sent a replacement, who won't arrive for at least two weeks. I told him our papers will be out of date by then, and that we can't afford to wait."

"What other choice do we have?" Nasim asked, sounding more curious than anxious.

"There's always . . ." Ivan Grazhin began, before succumbing to a coughing fit. His eyes were almost popping out of his head,

Piatakov noticed. Grazhin was hoping that the dry southern climate would help his lungs, but first he had to get to it.

"We can fund ourselves," Brady said, once the coughing had abated. He looked around the circle of faces. "We all feel the same about the NEP and the return of the profiteers—well, here's our chance to teach the bastards a parting lesson, and find a better use for their ill-gotten gains."

"We steal it," Grazhin rasped.

"If property is theft, it can hardly be stolen," Brady retorted with a grin. "But we could insist on a loan from the state."

"Which organ of the state were you thinking of approaching?" Shahumian asked drily.

"I'm open to suggestions. My own is a city tram depot, the one on Shabolovka Street. Paper money is useless, and the depots handle only coinage."

"I like it," Grazhin wheezed.

"I am not as sure," Rafiq said. He looked most unhappy. "Perhaps you"—he indicated the Europeans—"could do this successfully, but we Indians will be recognized so easily. How will we get out of Moscow?"

Brady waved a hand. "If we do the robbery in masks, then no one will be recognized."

"How well are the depots guarded?" Piatakov asked, wondering how much homework Brady had done already.

"One Chekist, that's all," Brady told them. "But there is a slight problem. The last trams stop early, between seven and eight, because of the electricity shortage. The money is counted immediately and then sent across the city to headquarters straight after that. Which means we must do it in daylight."

"In daylight," Rafiq echoed. "That does not sound good." He looked this way and that for support.

He didn't get any. "If that's when the money is there, then that's when we have to do it," Chatterji said coldly. "Anyone gets in our way, we kill them. It is our country, our revolution, that is at stake," he lectured Rafiq. "These things cannot be achieved without risk."

"But failure in Moscow will not bring success in Delhi," Rafiq protested.

"Then we must be sure not to fail," Nasim said. "Durga is right. We must take this gamble."

And it would certainly be one, Piatakov thought. They were almost bound to run into a Cheka or militia patrol—it was hard to go out on the street and not trip over one. He watched Brady's face as the Indians continued to argue. Did the American know what he was doing? Were Aram and Ivan, he himself—were they all so in love with the prospect of action that due caution was being abandoned?

Perhaps. But better that than the opposite crime of waiting and waiting for a perfect moment that never came. He remembered a phrase of Caitlin's—in for a kopek, in for a ruble.

"What do you think, Sergei?" Aram was asking.

Piatakov smiled to himself. "Why not?" he said.

"HOLD THE LINE A MOMENT," Fanya was saying as Caitlin entered the office. "It's the M-Cheka," she told Caitlin, covering the mouth-piece with a palm. "They say they've already telephoned once, and someone gave them your name. It's about Rahima. Her husband's kicking up a stink in Tashkent, and the Cheka down there have gotten in touch with their comrades up here."

"Where are Rahima and Laziza?" Caitlin asked Fanya, crossing the room.

"They went to the textile factory with Vera."

Caitlin took the phone. "This is Comrade Piatakova," she said. "How can I help you?" As she listened to the male voice at the other end, she relived Rahima's sudden reappearance the week before, this time in tandem with her younger sister. With all the news she had to impart about events in Turkestan, Rahima had let slip only several days later that she'd left Tashkent in defiance of her hus-band's orders. He had told her that he was still regretting her first trip to Moscow and that there was no chance at all of a second.

"She's not here at the moment," Caitlin told the M-Cheka voice. "No, she's quite safe. You can tell her husband so." She reached for a pile of homemade cigarettes and lit one, grimacing as she inhaled. "What do you expect us to do?" she asked angrily. "Send her back on the next train with instructions to be a dutiful wife? This is not . . . Yes . . . very well, I'll talk to him. Yes, I'll hold the line."

She stubbed out the cigarette. "Deputy Chairman Komarov wants to talk to me," she told Fanya. "Remember him from that orphans' home?"

"He seemed almost human for a Cheka boss."

Caitlin grunted. "Ah, Comrade Komarov," she said into the phone. "Yes, of course I remember you." She listened. "Tomorrow morning? Very well . . . No, I'm happy to come to your office—it'll make a change from my own. Fourteen Bolshaya Lubyanka. Ten o'clock. I'll be there."

"It'll make a change from your own," Fanya echoed once Caitlin had replaced the earpiece. "So would walking into a tiger's cage."

Caitlin smiled. "He suggested we talk through the problem."

"Fine, but why did you agree to go there?"

"God knows. Because I didn't want him here. Because I didn't want him thinking I was scared to. I'm not, you know," she added.

"I know you're not. Sometimes I wish you were."

"You may be right. But as Cheka bosses go—and I admit I haven't met that many—Komarov seems pretty reasonable. And now I come to think of it, if Kollontai draws a blank, we might take Anna's story to him. He owes us a favor."

NEXT MORNING CAITLIN WALKED FROM the Zhenotdel offices to Bolshaya Lubyanka, refusing to let her anxieties about the impending interview spoil her mood. It was another beautiful day, the sun shining out of a cloudless sky. Next to the Vladimir Gate, a new billboard had been erected, and a giant poster in three sections was being pasted up. ALL UNITED IN A SINGLE FRONT the first two read, and Caitlin paused to see the third one unrolled, taking guesses at what it would say. AGAINST LICE was unexpected, but unfortunately all too apt.

At the M-Cheka offices, she was shown into Komarov's empty room and asked to wait by a polite young Chekist. She declined the chair, preferring to stand by the open window overlooking the empty courtyard.

Komarov arrived a few minutes later. His hair was a greyer than it had been in March; his eyes, as she remembered, seemed to have a life of their own.

"I'm sorry to have kept you waiting, comrade," he said formally. After gesturing her into a chair, he took his own seat behind the desk and offered her a cigarette.

"I've only been here a few minutes," she said, matching his courtesy and accepting the proffered match. His cigarettes were no better made than hers.

She watched him sort through a stack of papers and saw that the hand that held the pile was trembling.

He found the file, a red folder with the Vecheka stamp on the cover.

"Comrade," she began, "I really don't understand why the M-Cheka has chosen to interfere in Zhenotdel business."

He looked up. "No? What would you say the business of the Chekas was?"

"The Chekas were set up to defend the revolution from counterrevolution. You're not suggesting that Rahima Niyazi is a counterrevolutionary, are you?"

"Of course not."

"Then . . ."

"Comrade," Komarov said quietly, "you're not as naïve as that. Sadridin Niyazi is one of the few—one of the very few—non-Russian Bolsheviks in Turkestan. We cannot afford to alienate him."

"What sort of Bolshevik treats his wife like chattel?"

"An Uzbek one, I suppose," Komarov said mildly. "But that is beside the point."

That made Caitlin angry. "It is exactly the point so far as the Zhenotdel is concerned, comrade."

Komarov sighed. "If we lose control of Turkestan," he said calmly, "the Zhenotdel will be powerless to do anything for the women who live there. You must know that. There has to be some willingness to compromise."

She shook her head. "I don't object to compromise, comrade. When it is necessary. Are you seriously telling me that the rebels in Turkestan have any chance of success?"

"I don't know. Perhaps."

"Perhaps?"

"The Basmachi are not a spent force. Not completely at any rate. And anything that weakens our position in Tashkent will give them hope." He placed both hands palm down on his desk. "She has to go back, comrade. But . . . I don't wish to be unreasonable. You must have . . . How can I put this without causing offence? You must have taught her what she needs to know by now. And surely Turkestan is the best place to put that teaching into practice, back home, among her own people?" His hand wasn't trembling anymore.

"I think the Zhenotdel is probably the best judge of that," she said tartly. "You may well be right. But there's more to it than that. Her husband treats her like a slave. That's usual in his culture—I don't blame him for it, but the Zhenotdel cannot be seen to condone such behavior. We can't—won't—simply tell her to go when he calls." She took another cigarette from his pile, and let him light it for her. "And doesn't this worry you, comrade? If we make a habit of indulging such conduct just because we find the perpetrator useful . . . well, where does it end? We have to draw the line somewhere."

He looked at her thoughtfully. "I don't know. I distrust lines. I try to deal with each case as it comes."

"So where would you draw one in this case?"

His smile was rather sheepish for a Chekist's, she thought.

"All right," he said. "I won't insist on her going back at once. But I hope you'll persuade her that she should return soon. If not to her husband, at least to Tashkent."

"She doesn't want to leave him."

"Then why . . ."

Caitlin smiled. "Rahima Niyazi may be only eighteen, but she's an extraordinary woman. She loves her husband, and she's sure he'll be proud of her—eventually—when he realizes that it's much more rewarding being married to a free, independent woman than to a slave. I hope she's right. He damn well *should* be proud of her.

It takes a hell of a lot more guts to be a revolutionary Uzbek woman in Turkestan than a revolutionary Uzbek man." She crushed out the cigarette and stood, feeling more than a little pleased with herself. "I will discuss the matter with Rahima and her sister at the earliest opportunity, comrade. I will let you know what we decide."

One for the Zhenotdel, she thought, shaking his hand and heading for the door.

A Foreign Agent

In the dawn twilight the hut by the forest's edge looked like a setting for "Hansel and Gretel." Inside it three Finns were sitting around a greasy oil lamp, apparently waiting for the world to end. They had greeted McColl and his guide, Miliutin, with politeness but little warmth; offered the two of them glasses of tea; and answered the Russian's questions with a succession of shrugs. The mysteries of the world beyond the hut, their faces seemed to say, were hardly worth unraveling.

As he waited outside for Miliutin to reappear, McColl wondered whether they might be right.

The Russian came through the door, a tall, thin man with a bushy beard and unruly black hair. Thick, badly chapped lips and sharp black eyes were visible within the foliage. It was not a physiognomy to inspire trust, McColl thought.

But the man had brought McColl safely across the border, and fifteen miles into Lenin's domain.

"This way," the Russian grunted.

They walked down between ramshackle huts to the railway tracks, where a rickety wooden shelter was posing as a station. As yet there was no one else about. Only one thin spire of smoke disturbed the serenity of forest, lake, and sky.

Miliutin settled himself on the ground, his back against the shelter wall. He was not the most talkative of traveling companions, having hardly spoken twenty words since their first meeting in Vyborg.

McColl broke his last piece of Swedish chocolate in two and offered half to the Russian. "What did you do before the revolution?" he asked.

The Russian stretched a leg, then suddenly laughed. "I dreamed of the day," he said. "You do not understand? I am an anarchist. It was our revolution, too, in the beginning. Now . . ." He shrugged. "They are all the same: czarists, capitalists, Bolshevists—a few people telling everyone else what to do. That is what a state is, my friend." He wiped chocolate from his lips with the back of a hand, then sucked the latter clean. "It's rather amusing, don't you think, that now I make my living like this? Without states there would be no frontiers or people who needed to cross them without being seen." He took a swig from his water bottle. "But no more. I will tell you—this is my last trip. With your English pounds, I can leave this wretched place. There may be nowhere a man can be free, but there are places where summer is long and you don't have to dress like a bear in the winter."

This was more than McColl had bargained for, but he was spared the need to respond by the sound of their train approaching, and the sudden appearance of several more would-be travelers, most of whom eyed his guide will ill-concealed distrust.

The train consisted of a wheezy engine and four mostly empty carriages, all of which seemed far too grand for a dead-end branch line serving small forest villages and lumber camps. Miliutin led McColl to a compartment full of polished wood in the rear carriage, and stood leaning out of the window until the train began to move. Then, with a grunt of satisfaction, he sat back beneath the sepia photograph of Lake Baikal that McColl had been idly perusing.

"At first I could hardly stop laughing," the Russian said, as if their conversation had not been interrupted. "Those dainty little aristocrats begging me—me!—to spirit them away from the Bolshevik monsters. I felt like telling them: 'Believe me, children, you have far more in common with them than you do with me. They find the masses as troublesome as you did.' But what would have been the point? You know what all ruling classes have in common? Luck and utter stupidity. All these aristocrats—they know nothing about anything. In Vyborg these days, you can have a countess for a few kopeks, which sounds like fun, but they don't even fuck that well. Outside a ballroom they haven't a clue how anything works. I almost felt sorry for some of them." He paused to pick something from between his teeth. "But not for long," he said, flicking the offending scrap away. "I lost too many comrades in the Peter and Paul Fortress while they were marking dance cards."

"They're not dancing anymore," McColl murmured.

"I suppose you find that sad," Miliutin sneered.

"Not particularly," McColl said mildly. "I doubt I'll be attending any balls on this visit."

The Russian laughed. "I suppose you're here to sell Lenin life insurance." He laid himself out across the seats, feet at the corridor end. "But what do I care?" He pulled his cap down over his eyes. "The trip should take about three hours," he muttered. "I'm going to get some sleep."

That seemed like a good idea, but McColl's brain refused to shut down. His Russian companion was soon snoring with irritating gusto, so he took himself into the corridor and watched the trees go by. The train stopped every few miles, but few got on or off at the small village halts.

He felt like a cup of strong coffee. He felt like a cigarette, though he hadn't smoked since landing in prison. On his last trip into Russia, three years before, he'd felt traces of the old excitement, that adrenalin rush that went with pitting your wits and strength against whatever the enemy put in your way. That was what had induced him to join the Service—he hadn't believed all the claptrap about King and Country since South Africa, and any residual illusions had been shredded by Caitlin and the war. But now there was no excitement either, just nerves and a grim determination. He might be working for Cumming again, but not for the Service and not for the fucking British Empire.

The trees gave way to a lake, the lake to a lot more trees.

He opened the lavatory door more out of restlessness than need and was astonished by the spotless luxury that greeted his eyes. There were even fresh towels on the rail.

He examined his unshaven face in the mirror. "Good morning, Anatoly Joseyevich," he told his reflection. The grubby white blouse, the black leather breeches, the old leather cap with the fur brim—they all looked exactly right. As they should have—each had come from a warehouse packed with secondhand émigré clothing in Vyborg.

The train was jerking itself to a halt. Several voices became audible through the frosted window, indicating a larger-than-usual station. McColl waited for the train to clear the platform before flushing the toilet, remembering the day almost thirty years before when his father had pointed out a steaming pile of shit between the rails in Fort William station. "Most people are pigs" had been the observation.

You couldn't buy memories like that, McColl thought sourly as he yanked the chain.

The rush of cascading water faded to reveal the thump of booted feet in the corridor.

McColl gripped the door handle and waited, ears straining for danger signals.

A shout turned into a high-pitched gurgle.

McColl launched himself into the corridor, and straight into someone who was scrambling out of his compartment. The collision knocked him backward into the vestibule, the other man on top of him.

For a second they looked at each other. The Russian was young, hardly more than a boy, and his eyes were wide with panic. He struggled to rise, to extricate himself, but the bandolier across his shoulder snagged on McColl's arm, jolting the young man back and jerking free the cap with its gleaming red star.

McColl brought up a knee, eliciting a heartfelt groan, and then threw a fist into the boy's throat. The young Chekist arched back on his knees, as if he'd just discovered which way Mecca was.

McColl glanced around in search of Miliutin, and the boy was on him again, the two of them clinched like drunken sailors in the swaying, rattling vestibule. McColl tried the knee again, following it with an intended pile driver to the stomach, which somehow caught the shoulder. The Chekist fell back across the handle of the outside door, opening it. He opened his mouth to yell, but his throat refused to obey. Then he just seemed to drop away, like someone who'd been horsing around on top of a wall.

McColl's first reaction was to whirl around in search of witnesses, but there was none: Had the noise of the train drowned out the sound of their tussle? He leaned out of the open door and looked back: his otherwise prone assailant was flapping an arm in the air, as if keen to point out he'd survived the fall.

"Is he dead?" Miliutin asked over McColl's shoulder.

"I doubt it," he answered, pulling his head back in.

"A pity," Miliutin murmured.

In their compartment the other Chekist had died holding the stomach that Miliutin's knife had ripped open. A case of us or them, McColl told himself—capture would have ended with a bullet. It didn't make him feel any better, but then, feeling good wasn't something that went with the job. Or shouldn't be, he thought, remembering times when it had.

Miliutin was folding the corpse in two. "Let's get this one overboard," he said.

After they'd bundled it out through the door and done their best to wipe away the blood, Miliutin laid himself out on the seat again as if happy to sleep through the rest of the journey.

McColl was astonished that no one had come to investigate. Admittedly they were in the last carriage, but they weren't alone on the train—had nobody seen the Chekists ejected, or heard the dying one's scream?

"They may have," Miliutin said when McColl asked the question. "But they won't know who screamed, and I doubt they got a look at the men we threw out. Where the Chekas are concerned, most people opt for discretion. Just being a witness can get you shot." He closed his eyes again. "I don't think we'll have any trouble."

He was right.

Two hours later they were staring across the silver-blue Neva at the cupolas of Smolny Convent glinting in the morning sun. If there had been a welcoming deputation at the Okhta station, they had managed to avoid it, getting out on the wrong side and cutting through the surprisingly busy goods yard.

On the towpath below, a succession of women were filling buckets from the river and carrying them back up the steps. "The Bolsheviks can't even keep their city supplied with water," Miliutin noted contemptuously. "This is where we part company," he added. "You know where you are?"

McColl nodded. Across the road a pyramid pile of wooden wheels was reaching for the sky. It could have been rubbish, might have been constructivist art. You never knew in Bolshevik Russia.

Miliutin put a hand on McColl's shoulder. "One piece of free advice: don't hang around here any longer than you need to—the Cheka look after their own."

McColl watched Miliutin walk away along the embankment, then started across the Okhtinsky Bridge, feeling the cool gusts of air wafting up from the water below. He felt calmer than expected, which wouldn't have pleased his old Service instructors. If your heart wasn't racing, it probably meant you'd missed something crucial.

A narrow street led through to the wider Suvorovskiy Prospect, where a banner announced that CHILDREN ARE THE FLOWERS OF OUR LIFE. So why had Lenin never had any? McColl wondered, as he turned south toward Nevsky Prospect. Many of the shop fronts and office premises were still boarded up, and the road itself was empty save for an occasional clanking tram, but the pavements were crowded with hurrying people, and there seemed less tension in the faces than there had been three years before.

The fashions hadn't changed. The women were still dressed in the full-length skirts fashionable at the time of the revolution; those men not in uniform were attired in either worn-looking suits or the traditional Russian summer wear of linen blouse, loose trousers, and high, soft boots.

Halfway down the avenue, he noticed an open basement café. On the counter several loaves and a large slab of evil-looking lard provided the choice of fare; a price list was propped up beside the bubbling samovar. McColl helped himself to the bread, took a strong-looking brew from the woman serving, and handed her the requisite number of kopeks. She gathered them up in her apron and flicked a few beads across the abacus.

He found a poorly lit corner seat, wolfed down the bread, and sipped at the scalding tea. The only other customer was an elderly man busy chewing sunflower seeds. After shelling each one in his mouth, he used his tongue to maneuver the husks onto his lower lip, where they sat in a quivering line.

McColl tore his gaze from the spectacle and went through his options again. He had originally planned to spend at least one night in Petrograd, thinking it better to arrive in Moscow with some idea of Russian conditions. But that was too risky now—the Chekist he'd inadvertently thrown from the train was akin to a spluttering fuse. He had to keep moving.

First he needed to change his clothes. A description of his current attire would no doubt soon be circulating, and in any case his travel permit was for a metallurgist.

He gulped down the last of his tea, got up, and left the café. Farther down the avenue he came across a street leading off to the left, and then an alley that ran behind a row of disused stables. A door sagging off its hinges offered a way into one of them, which looked like it hadn't been used for months. Sunbeams were lancing through gaps in the walls, and putting an eye to one crack McColl found himself watching a group of boys being drilled by a broad-chested sailor. Their formation was somewhat ragged, but everyone looked very earnest and determined to get it right.

McColl took off the blouse and leather breeches, put on a threadbare suit, and rethreaded the belt that contained his emergency supply of silver coins. A few minutes later he was back on the avenue, breeches and blouse packed away in the suitcase, a metallurgist en route to a conference in the capital.

Reaching Nevsky Prospect, he skirted Vosstaniya Square and

entered the ornate grandeur of the old Nikolayev Station. In the concourse a horde of people were milling to and fro, many of them in uniform, and around the walls a regiment of peasants sat or lay with their belongings, watching the activity with the familiar air of blank detachment. The heat was oppressive, the smell of human sweat heavy on the air.

McColl joined the scrum in the ticket hall and watched the line of harassed clerks as they examined credentials and issued tickets and permits. As far as he could see, the permits looked identical in style to his own. When his turn came, he stepped forward, resisting a ludicrous desire to turn and run, and passed across permit and papers. Without even a cursory look, the clerk used one finger to type out a ticket on an old American machine.

"When's the next train?" McColl asked.

The clerk's expression suggested he might as well have asked for a fortune-telling. "Perhaps today," the clerk said shortly. "Next."

McColl took a long look at the concourse, and tried to decide what to do. There were plenty of Chekists in evidence, and joining the waiting throng seemed like asking for trouble, but he couldn't just come back later if he had no idea when to come. He would have to trust his papers and try to be invisible. Over there, he thought, spying a corner that already seemed crowded, in the shadow of the eastern wall.

It was a long day, and McColl moved with the shadow as it circled the concourse, until darkness finally fell. Two trains were announced one after the other soon after ten, but the first didn't leave until just before midnight, a serpentine, twenty-one carriage monster hauled by three huge locomotives. Each coach was packed to the ceiling, making movement to a probably mythical restaurant car impossible, the transfer of bread from pocket to mouth merely difficult. Once on its way the train stopped with depressing frequency, though no one ever seemed to get off, and only the most determined had a ghost's chance of getting on. There was much drunken singing and much vociferous debate, mostly about politics. Sleep, McColl decided, would not be possible.

He was woken by a hand shaking his shoulder and immediately

feared the worst. Then he saw the other hand, holding in front of his eyes a card that identified the bearer as a member of the Young Communist League. Both the eyes and the card belonged to a boy of around eleven. It was Fedya, he thought for a second. Fedya returned in a dream.

"For the famine victims, citizen," the boy said, gesturing toward the collection box that his companion, a girl of about the same age, was holding out.

McColl groped for some coins and dropped them into the box. The girl smiled at him, lighting large dark eyes in a pale, emaciated face. As the two children clambered their way out of the compartment, McColl noticed that both had bare feet.

"*Rossiya,*" he murmured to himself. Russia. A time and place like no other, as someone had told him three years before. Through the window the trunks of the silver birches glowed in the morning twilight.

YURI KOMAROV ALWAYS WALKED TO the office, even though it was more than three miles from his room. Other men of similar rank—not that there were many—often used the official cars, but Komarov had never felt comfortable with privilege. He knew such self-denial made others feel guilty and himself unpopular, but people's approval had never been high on his list of priorities.

He walked down Bolshaya Lubyanka, past the criminal investigation office where he'd worked during the hectic weeks of the revolution, past the headquarters of the statewide Vecheka where its Chairman Felix Dzerzhinsky was probably still agonizing over some trivial problem that he should have left to a subordinate, and turned in through the doors of number 14. This impressive building, once home to Moscow's governor and later used as offices by the Moscow Fire Insurance Company, now housed the headquarters of the M-Cheka. Dzerzhinsky was nominally in charge of this department as well, but left its running to Komarov.

After passing through the large anteroom, he walked down a corridor, through another large office, and up a short flight of steps to his own smaller sanctum. A window looked out across the inner courtyard, where several prisoners were being given their morning exercise. The room itself conveyed an impression of bareness, despite containing four chairs, a desk, and two tall filing cabinets. The white-painted walls were yellow and pecling.

Komarov hung his jacket on the back of his chair, sat down, and rolled up his shirt sleeves. His beautifully carved wooden in-tray—left behind by its previous owners, the czar's secret police—was only half-full. He leafed through its contents: letters from relatives pleading for clemency, the latest reports on the currency-trading ring, amended schedules for supervising the movement of the International delegates.

Things were getting better, he thought; six months ago the paper pile had reached toward the ceiling. He opened a drawer and checked his agenda. The meeting to discuss the abolition of the death penalty had been scheduled for the next Thursday. It was partly a sop to the foreign comrades now swarming around Moscow, but also more than that. Many in the Chekas—like himself, like Vecheka boss Felix Dzerzhinsky—had seen enough killing to last them several lifetimes.

The weather helped, he thought, standing by the window and admiring the clarity of the blue sky. Hope was harder to come by in winter.

A soft rap on the door, and his assistant came in with a glass of tea.

"Thank you, Sasha," Komarov said as the young Lett set the glass on his desk.

The telephone rang. Picking up the earpiece, Komarov heard a crackling noise, as if someone were crumbling toast at the other end of the line.

"Yuri Vladimirovich," a familiar voice said, cutting through.

It was Pyotr Baranov, his counterpart in Petrograd. Not one of life's instinctive policemen, which, given his nautical background, wasn't a great surprise. "Yes, Pyotr Vasilyevich," Komarov said.

"Yuri Vladimirovich, we have two imperialist agents on the loose."

Only two? Komarov thought but didn't say. If Baranov had a sense of humor, he had always hidden it well.

"Yesterday morning they attacked two of my men. On the train from up near the Finnish border. Killed one of them, threw the other off the train. He had to walk ten miles with a broken ankle!"

Baranov sounded more offended than distressed, so Komarov refrained from offering sympathy. "So they could be in Moscow by now?"

"This is why I called you. Two trains left here yesterday evening. I don't know if they've reached you yet."

"Descriptions?"

"Both dark, average height, bearded, rough clothes."

"Is that all?" Komarov said, writing it down. These days half the men in Moscow looked like that.

"My man was too busy fighting for his life to draw pictures! He didn't get a good look at either of them."

"I understand . . ."

"We are still searching for them here, but if they're headed your way . . ."

"Yes, thank you. If we find them, I'll let you know."

"And I will do the same."

"Thank you, Pyotr Vasilyevich," Komarov said, and hung up the phone. "Sasha!" he called out.

The young man appeared in the doorway. "Yes, comrade."

Komarov passed him the description. "Phone this through to our office at the Petrograd station. One or both of these men may have left Petrograd yesterday evening, in which case they should be arriving today. Or have done so already."

Sasha disappeared.

Komarov sat back in his chair and stared at the pattern of stains on the ceiling. Two foreign agents. Like a couple of fleas on a bear, he thought. Hardly worth the bother, even with decent descriptions. As it was . . .

He pulled the appeals for clemency in front of him and studied the one on top of the pile. A woman in Tula explained how her son had fought in the Moscow uprising, how he . . . Komarov put the letter down. It was amazing how so many people thought their actions in 1917 granted them exemption for life. It was like claiming that being a good child gave you carte blanche as an adult.

He saw his hand begin to flutter.

Why did he read them?

"Comrade," Sasha said from the door. "Two trains arrived from Petrograd in the last hour, and the next one isn't expected until this evening."

"Right. Thank you." That was that. If the foreign agents had been aboard either train, they wouldn't have hung around waiting for taxis. Whatever it was they'd come to do, they'd have to be caught in the act.

ALEXANDRA KOLLONTAI HAD ACQUIRED A second room at the Hotel National since Caitlin's last visit. Secretaries were working on either side of a round table in the old one, Kollontai dictating a letter in the new addition. The Zhenotdel director raised a hand in welcome, and then a single finger to say she'd be only a minute. Some hope, Caitlin thought, moving a pile of papers off the one available seat. She knew from long experience how elastic a Kollontai minute could be.

This one wasn't much more than five. "So I thought we could eat downstairs, then go for a walk," Kollontai suggested once her typist had left. "It should be cooler by then."

"I'd like that," Caitlin said. Over the last three years, she and Fanya had become quite close, but Kollontai was still the only woman in Russia with whom Caitlin felt able to share her emotional life.

The canteen downstairs was smoky and loud, the food its usual pedestrian self. Several party leaders were tucking in to meals at the heavy oak tables—Bukharin and a group of his young disciples, Radek with one of the German comrades, Cheka boss Felix Dzerzhinsky sitting alone. Molotov even gave Caitlin a nod as she walked past his table. The presence of such men was reassuring. These days many like Sergei were eager to damn the Bolshevik elite, but living in luxury was one vice they hadn't succumbed to. The men below them were another matter, but they could still be brought to heel provided the leaders stayed true.

Caitlin found the looks that followed Kollontai a great deal more worrying. Three years ago these would have been mostly admiring, on occasion almost worshipful. Now they were wary, uncertain, on some faces downright hostile. These men didn't see Kollontai's support for the Workers' Opposition as a valid difference of opinion; they saw it as betrayal.

Kollontai seemed oblivious. "Let's walk around the Kremlin," she suggested once they had eaten.

Outside it was still pretty hot. "How are you these days?" Kollontai asked as they walked up the slope toward Red Square. "How are you and Sergei?"

Caitlin grimaced. "You remember your notion of 'erotic friendship?'" she asked. "Well, we're not having sex, and we're not very friendly."

Kollontai laughed and apologized for doing so.

"I don't know what happened," Caitlin said. "It seemed to work, and then it didn't. I know he saw and did things in the Antonov rebellion that he hasn't come to terms with—he still wakes up screaming or crying or both. I tried talking to him when he came back the first time, but it didn't help. And then there was Kronstadt and the NEP, and that sense of betrayal that a lot of the comrades felt. And the pain and the grief all turned to anger. Like a knot in his stomach he can't untie. He just seethes. Sometimes it makes a bizarre sort of sense, but at others it feels like he's gone a little crazy. Not all the time—he can be his old sweet self for a while, but then he slips back. I don't know what to do with him."

"Let him go?" Kollontai suggested as the two of them swerved to avoid a group of foreign comrades, most of them posing for pictures in front of St. Basil's.

"I sometimes think I should," Caitlin said. "But then I feel I'd be letting him down. He's like an angry child, and who would let one of those loose on his own?" As she'd done with her brother Colm.

Kollontai shook her head. "You're not his mother. And he would hate you thinking him that helpless."

"I know. But enough of my troubles. How are you?"

"Physically? Better than I was a few months ago. My heart's too weak for the life I live—that's all there is to it—but a few weeks in bed always seems to put me right."

"And emotionally?"

"Not so good. Dybenko and I—well, we're finished and both of us know it, even though we sometimes pretend that we aren't. We had wonderful times, and I have no regrets whatsoever. The man I truly miss is my son. Misha is still buried in his studies in Petrograd. I doubt if he even knows there is a Workers' Opposition."

"So how's your political health?" Caitlin asked pointedly.

"I like it!" Kollontai said, clapping her hands. "The three types of health—physical, emotional, and political. You should write a pamphlet!"

"You haven't answered the question," Caitlin reminded her. The river was in front of them—away to the left was the towpath where she'd told Jack about the czar's execution. Three long years ago.

"Probably because I don't much like the answer," Kollontai said, glancing up at the Kremlin wall to her right. "They see us as a direct threat," she said. "And they should because we speak for those who they always claimed were the ones who mattered. Ours was a workers' revolution. It only makes sense as a workers' revolution. It can only blossom as a workers' revolution."

Caitlin considered her response. "When it comes to things like this," she said, "I trust your judgment more than I trust my own. But in this case that doesn't mean much because I can't seem to work out what I think. So what I and most of the women at the office do is just get on with our work. But of course we all know that this other stuff matters because your standing in the party will influence the way the party sees the Zhenotdel."

"I know that," Kollontai said. "Of course I do. And yes, my support for the Workers' Opposition will hurt the Zhenotdel, at least in the short run. But would the Zhenotdel be better off if I resigned? If Klavia took over as director, for example? It might—I don't think Vladimir Ilych would be so petty as to punish an organization because I once led it. Not once he'd calmed down. But—and I may be fooling myself—I don't think my remaining leader is the biggest threat to the Zhenotdel."

"So what is?" Caitlin prompted when Kollontai fell silent.

Her friend let a few more moments pass before responding. "Ever since the civil war ended, we've been in retreat. Oh, I know we've had victories—the abortion law, the apprenticeships, the unveilings the other week—but they're all things that don't cost money and don't inconvenience men. In the factories and on the farms—in the real economy—the old patterns are reasserting themselves. Returning soldiers are pushing women out of jobs and wanting them back in the kitchen and bedroom. The Orgbureau is less willing to accommodate us now than it was a year ago, and it was damn near impossible to get them to do it then. Things I thought we'd settled for good, we're having to fight for all over again. We're regressing, in more ways than one."

Caitlin was slightly shocked. "I don't think I've ever heard you sound so . . . pessimistic."

"I don't mean to. What I'm saying is—if the system isn't working for us, then that's what we have to change. If the party doesn't respond to the current disillusion, if it doesn't turn to the sort of ideas and policies that the Workers' Opposition is espousing, then the Zhenotdel will inevitably be among the casualties. A government that needs closed doors to survive will never look kindly on an organization that delights in flinging them open."

Caitlin was silent for several moments, torn between Kollontai's vision and the unwelcome sense that it wasn't achievable.

"I know it's not easy," Kollontai said, anticipating objections. "In order to survive, we Bolsheviks have done some terrible things. We have let ourselves down more often than we would have liked. Everyone knows that. But most people—and most of our leaders—realize that now we must do better, must hold ourselves to a higher standard, if we want to save our revolution. If we don't, then heaven help Russia."

"We fight each battle as it comes," Caitlin said, more to herself than her friend.

"Every last one. Which is why I'm so reluctant to resign. And which reminds me: I haven't forgotten Anna Nemtseva. A friend of a friend who knows Orel—I think his mother still lives there—has more or less confirmed what Anna told you. I know there wasn't much doubt, but I don't want any surprises when I eventually take the matter up with the Orgbureau. And I've also spoken to a couple of comrades who knew Agranov before the war. He was a bureaucrat for the old regime back then, and he only joined the party in 1918, so his rise has been quite spectacular. Suspiciously so, I'd say. A little more digging, and I think we'll find a way to bring him down."

Kollontai sounded so much like her old self that Caitlin couldn't help but smile. "Do you know a Chekist named Komarov?" she asked.

"Not well," Kollontai said. "The M-Cheka, yes? In his early forties, stern looking, old-school."

"Fanya and I worked with him in March on rehousing a group of orphan girls. He seemed quietly outraged by what had been done to them, and he might feel the same about Anna and the others. If so, and if he has any influence with Dzerzhinsky . . ."

"The Cheka usually look after their own," Kollontai said, "but who knows? There are exceptions, and he might be one of them. I'll bear him in mind."

They parted with hugs at the National entrance, and Caitlin walked slowly home, pondering Kollontai's words and hoping that just this once her friend had read the situation wrongly. She was almost home when she passed an open window and saw two people dancing in what seemed an empty room. They were probably in their fifties, and the only music was in their heads. As if to hear it better, both had closed their eyes, and the expressions on their faces were ones of utter bliss.

THERE WAS A DINGY CAFÉ almost directly opposite the house where Arkady Ruzhkov was supposed to have a room. This was fortunate, because McColl had been nursing his glass of tea for over an hour, and lingering that long out in the street would have been asking for trouble. As it was, the crone behind the counter was eyeing him with what looked like increasing suspicion.

"You are sure my friend didn't come by earlier?" he asked.

"No one asked for anyone."

"Well, I'll give him another half an hour."

"Suit yourself."

McColl went back to his vigil. He'd always had good visual recall, if not a true photographic memory, and Ruzhkov's picture was clear in his mind. So was the man's story, which had been part of the briefing.

The Russian had come to England as an exile after the 1905 upheaval and had married another exile, a young Polish girl. They'd had three children and were, as far as Ruzhkov was concerned, a happy and contented couple. Then, one day late in 1917, he'd returned to his Shoreditch tailor's shop and found his young wife enjoying herself on the cutting table with another Russian. In a frenzy of anger, he'd picked up his tailor's shears and stabbed them both to death.

The French would have called it a crime of passion and probably been sympathetic; in England he was promised a hanging, until some bright spark in Special Branch mentioned him to the Secret Service. Cumming's people had offered him a choice: the rope or a five-year stint in His Majesty's Service back home in Russia while England looked after his children. He had, not surprisingly, plumped for the second option. Since his return three years earlier in the company of genuine political exiles, Ruzhkov had risen through the ranks of clerks who served the Moscow Cheka.

Cumming had protected Ruzhkov well. He had returned late in 1918, and had thus been spared the carnage of agents that had followed the Cheka's unmasking of the famous Lockhart Plot. Since then, Cumming had kept his "steadiest man" well away from gung ho colleagues like Sidney Reilly. Indeed, so precious was Ruzhkov considered that he'd been contacted on only a handful of occasions, in situations of minimum risk.

Until now, McColl thought, anxiously watching the time. The half hour was nearly up when his contact finally appeared, a small, wiry man with the face from the photograph. The blonde on his arm was taller than he was, with sunken eyes and prominent cheekbones. The two of them walked through the open door of the three-story building, and half a minute later a light came on in the middle floor.

McColl crossed the street, climbed the stairs, and knocked on the appropriate door.

The woman answered. Up close, her face seemed terribly gaunt.

"Comrade Ruzhkov?" he asked.

Ruzhkov appeared behind her shoulder, his round-lensed spectacles glinting beneath the shock of black hair. "What is it?" he asked sharply.

"I've come with a message from Brother Ivan," McColl said. "It's private," he added, offering the woman an apologetic look.

"Yes, Tamara, go for a walk," Ruzhkov said brusquely. She glared at him, and seemed about to object, but then brushed past McColl and headed down the stairs.

"You shouldn't have come here," Ruzhkov said reproachfully the moment McColl was inside.

"I had no choice." He told the Russian what he needed.

Ruzhkov shook his head slowly to and fro, as if he were trying to nudge his brain back into its cranial slot. "Perhaps," he said. "I will see. You must go. Two days from now at the Sukharevka Market—the music section. At noon."

McColl nodded and turned toward the door.

"Are you Russian?" Ruzhkov asked.

"No, British."

"Your Russian is excellent. My children, are they well?"

"They're all fine."

"Good, wonderful. Tomorrow you must tell me more."

McColl went down the stairs. Tamara was standing in the hall, one foot on the ground, the other against the wall, smoking a cigarette. She returned his nod with a contemptuous glance and headed for the stairs. He wondered if Ruzhkov had mentioned killing the wife in England.

Outside the light was beginning to fade, which had to be good news. The Chekist on the train might have a memory for faces, but any likeness conveyed by phone could be only the roughest of sketches. Even if Miliutin talked, McColl was surely safe for a couple of days. He would keep the beard for thirty-six hours and shave it off when he had the new papers.

NO HANDS ROUGHLY SHOOK MCCOLL awake during the night, and when he woke of his own accord, the sun was streaming in through the dormitory's high windows. Some of the twenty-odd occupants of the other bunk beds had already departed; some were still snoring with annoying gusto.

McColl lay there for a while, wondering what to do with the day and night that lay ahead. He wasn't due to meet Ruzhkov again until the following day, and until that time he was stuck with the identity papers he'd been given in Vyborg. But no one else knew the name that was on them, not even Miliutin. It would, he decided, be safer to stay another night than switch dormitories—two addresses would double the risk. And it was Sunday, which even in atheist Russia was a day of relative rest. Chekists should be thinner on the ground.

He would leave his suitcase there and spend the day out, preferably in crowded places. There was precious little chance of running into any Russian Muscovites who knew him from earlier visits, and all the English undercover men were gone. There was only Caitlin, who would probably see through the beard. Running into her would be disastrous, but also extremely unlikely, given the city's million or more residents.

His mind made up, he went for a cold-water wash. After putting his clothes back on, he asked the babushka at the door for directions to the nearest communal canteen and was nodded down the street. There was a queue at the door, but it moved quite quickly, and a brief perusal of his papers ensured the provision of a free but decidedly basic breakfast. After begging and drinking a second glass of tea, he walked back out onto a sunlit Rozhdestvenka Street. Moscow was his for the taking.

It proved a mixed day. For reasons that McColl didn't want to fathom, he felt drawn to the antiques shop on Bolshaya Nikitskaya that he and Fedya had shared for several days in the summer of 1918. It wasn't far away, he told himself, and he had to walk somewhere.

In the event, the shop was gone, replaced by what looked like a private café. He resisted the urge to look inside, standing instead on the opposite pavement, more or less where Caitlin had stood when she'd waited to warn him that the Cheka was hot on his trail. It was the last time he'd seen her.

And the next day Brady had tried to shoot him, but had succeeded only in killing Fedya. At least the boy had died instantly, which had to be some consolation.

Enough, McColl told himself, forcing his feet into motion. It was done. Fcdya was dead and Caitlin was gone. Had been for almost three years.

He walked down toward the Alexandrov Gardens, around the Historical Museum, and into Red Square. The huge space was relatively crowded and seemed, as it always did to McColl, like something lying in wait. He carried on down to the river, and wandered along the towpath, passing the spot where Caitlin had told him the czar had been murdered.

It took him about an hour to reach open country, and after a fifteen-minute rest in the shade of a riverside willow, he walked back the way he had come, the domes and spires of the Kremlin gradually filling the skyline ahead. A tram ride brought him to Sokolniki Park, which he remembered from earlier visits and which was now full of families enjoying the sunshine and sampling the many and varied entertainments. Fortune-tellers were out in force, and seemed to be intent on outdoing one another's optimistic forecasts. Jugglers, musicians, and photographers competed for attention and kopeks; an old man in a thick winter overcoat played Tchaikovsky melodies on his flute without breaking a sweat in the ninety-degree heat.

In late afternoon McColl used the distant Sukharev Tower to guide him back to the ring road, and the stretch of it that housed the Sukharevka Market, his meeting place for the following day. Having reminded himself of the lay of the land, he was wondering what to do next when he noticed a cinema just down the street. The place was filthy but crowded, and McColl found himself wedged between a boy of about thirteen and a woman

who smelled of onions. The propaganda short that opened proceedings provoked neither cheers nor jeers; the wartime Charlie
Chaplins that followed almost brought the house down. Halfway
through the second film, laughing so hard it actually hurt, McColl
knew he was close to hysteria. Normal life, it seemed, was something he still had to work at.

A Few Lines of Pushkin

Komarov got out from behind his desk and walked across to the open window. Prisoners were shuffling in the courtyard below, ravens circling in the blue sky above. As he was watching the latter, he heard Sasha clear his throat in the doorway.

"There was another call from Comrade Baranov, comrade. I told him you were in a meeting."

"What did he want?"

"They've arrested one of the foreign agents. A man called Miliutin."

Komarov laughed. "Not a very foreign name."

"No. A Russian. He was discovered in bed with two prostitutes," Sasha said in a thoroughly disapproving tone.

"Spending the money he was paid to bring the foreigner across the border," Komarov guessed.

"Yes, and he was only too eager to tell Baranov's people all about the man. An Englishman. And he was on his way to Moscow. Here's the description," he said, handing over a sheet of paper.

"But he doesn't know what this Englishman intends to do when he gets here?" Komarov asked, just to be sure.

"Baranov says he doesn't."

"Okay. Get Borin, Yezhov, whoever else is free," Komarov told him.

By the time Komarov had read the description, there were four Chekists gathered in front of his desk.

"We're looking for an Englishman," Komarov announced. "About five feet nine inches tall. Dark hair, beard, and mustache, brown eyes. He's wearing either a shabby dark grey suit or a White blouse and leather breeches. His Russian is near-perfect. His papers are in the name of Anatoly Joseyevich Mazin, metallurgist, from Monchegorsk. Or at least, one set are. He may have others. And he's armed." Komarov paused. "Right. Divide up the city among you. Start with the dormitories; then move on to the hotels. If you draw a blank with both, liaise with the Vecheka about known White sympathizers, both their own and any real ones they've left out as bait to catch their comrades. Understood? Then go."

Their boots tramped down the stairs and through the outer office.

Komarov looked at the new information again. This was better. This one they should find.

He leaned back in his chair, again thinking about Piatakova. Another foreigner, but one, as far as he could tell, who'd devoted her life to Russia and its revolution. She had irritated him—he couldn't deny it—but over the last few months, he'd had a bellyful of party idealists so busy rearranging the world that they didn't notice who was keeping it safe for them. That wasn't surprising, but finding her desirable had been—it was a long time since he'd thought of a woman in that way. Those lovely green eyes and waves of chestnut-brown hair. That fluid way of walking—all graceful limbs and head held high—which reminded him of his wife. It had been almost two years since Mariya had died, and lately he sometimes found it difficult to picture her face without the help of a photograph. At other times she was right there in front of him, almost as real as she had been in life. Only much more accusing.

A FLOCK OF RAVENS WHEELED across the corridor of pale blue sky above the Rozhdestvenky Convent, graceful, black, and silent. McColl wondered if they were the same birds he'd seen arrowing down the river the previous afternoon, the same flock that had drawn wide circles in the air above the Kremlin cathedrals that morning. If so, they seemed to be following him around.

He smiled at the thought. Considering the inherent dangers of his situation, McColl was feeling pretty good. He'd found Ruzhkov, and was, he hoped, on his way to collect a new set of papers from the Russian. He had slept surprisingly well in the visitor's dormitory on Kuznetsky Most.

He heard the Sukharevka Market before he saw it, a swelling babble of chatter and shouts that evoked memories of his times in India. Turning a corner, he saw the ragged lines of stalls occupying the wide center of the boulevard on both sides of the Sukharev Tower.

He walked down the first lane, which mostly featured peasant women sitting on rickety chairs, holding on their laps makeshift trays bearing large pats of butter, irregular scraps of sugar, or berries of various hues. One woman was carefully counting out wild strawberries to exchange for a chartreuse silk handkerchief; another was examining a coral necklace through a pince-nez with all the concentration of a Hatton Garden jeweler.

The next lane was mostly eggs and books. McColl stopped to look at the latter, which were almost exclusively romantic novels, and opened one at random. *Would she feel the same pang in her breast every time the count came to visit her husband?*

Probably, McColl thought.

"A complete set of Verbitskaya's stories—only one ruble," the woman behind the table called after him. "For next winter—they burn beautifully."

He could see the gramophone section at the end of the fourth lane, table upon table holding dozens of machines and hundreds of records. There was no sign of Ruzhkov, no sign either of more genuine Chekists.

He looked through the records, a bewildering mixture of classics, comic opera, and popular airs. There was even some of the new American jazz music. The showstopper was a recording of "Over the Sea to Skye" by the Massed Pipes of the Glasgow Cooperative. Noting his interest, the stall holder insisted on playing it, offering

McColl a seat while he wound up the gramophone and lowered the needle. Then, through a dense crackle, the sound of pipes swirled up into the Moscow air, causing heads to turn from all directions.

"What is it?" the stall holder asked. "Indian music?"

McColl shrugged. "Sounds like rats being strangled," he said.

The Russian thought this hugely amusing, and decided to play the record again. There was still no sign of Ruzhkov. McColl walked over to where a samovar was steaming, paid a few kopeks for two glasses of tea, and settled down to wait on a convenient pile of wrought-iron gates. The bagpipes droned on.

"Why don't you stand up and shout that you're a British spy?" Ruzhkov hissed in his ear.

McColl grinned, which only infuriated the Russian more. He almost slapped the folded copy of *Pravda* onto the gates between them.

"They're searching the city for you," Ruzhkov whispered angrily. "They know what name you're using. They're checking the dormitories at this very moment."

McColl's heart missed half a beat. "Then I won't go back to mine," he replied, a lot more calmly than he felt. "Have you managed things?"

"Yes." The Russian sounded almost sorry that he had. "You've been very lucky. The Indians actually asked for an Urdu translator last week. They all speak English—some of them don't even speak Urdu—but they decided they didn't want translation in the language of their oppressors." Ruzhkov snorted in merriment, then remembered he was supposed to be angry. "You weren't exaggerating when you said you could speak Urdu?"

"No."

"Well, that's something. Are you going to tell me what this is all about?"

"London needs to know if the Bolsheviks are keeping to the terms of the trade treaty, the ones to do with India. Whether they've actually abandoned their attempts at subversion."

"They have," Ruzhkov said indignantly. "All the Indians were brought back from Tashkent months ago. And London knows that," he added suspiciously. "There's something more, isn't there?"

McColl shook his head. "Not as far as I know," he lied.

Ruzhkov shrugged his disbelief. "Your new papers are inside the *Pravda*," he said coldly. "Now, tell me about my children. My son will be ten this August."

McColl repeated what the briefers had told him, that the children were all doing splendidly and happy as one could expect, given their father's absence. He could see the doubt in Ruzhkov's eyes, along with the faintest of hopes that it might be true.

McColl wanted to be moving. "Where are the Indians staying?"

"The Hotel Lux, of course. All the foreign delegates are staying there. You may have to shout a bit to get yourself a room, but they know who you are: the papers were sent over this morning." He drank the last of his tea and wistfully examined the bottom of the glass. "Ten years old," he muttered to himself.

After they'd discussed future meetings and contingencies, McColl walked back to the city center by a different route. It was the hottest part of the day, and a group of Red Army soldiers shouldering a coffin draped in a huge red flag were sweating copiously as they passed him in the opposite direction.

The number of visible Chekists seemed higher than it had been a few hours before, but was that only because he now knew that some at least were looking for him? He felt like a fly who'd mistaken a windowpane for the sky. Sitting there listening to the Massed Pipes had been unbelievably stupid.

A workers' canteen just off Petrovsky Boulevard offered a temporary haven. Behind the cover of the newspaper, he examined his new papers, and discovered that he was now Nikolai Matveyevich Davydov of Gogol Street, Tashkent. The accompanying permit authorized him to travel from Tashkent to Moscow on the given date; it was stamped for an arrival the previous day. Enclosed within the permit was a party card, which stated that he had been a member since March 1918.

Ruzhkov had excelled himself. All McColl needed was a shave, and he'd noticed a couple of barbers on Kuznetsky Most. He left the canteen, trying to appear neither casual nor hurried. No one gave him so much as a glance.

IT WAS MIDAFTERNOON WHEN KOMAROV returned from a meeting at Vecheka headquarters. Yezhov was waiting in the outer office, feet up and half-asleep.

"Well?" Komarov barked.

Yezhov sat up rapidly. "We've found where he's staying. The dormitory on Kuznetsky Most. His suitcase is there. Borin and Trepakov are waiting for him to come back."

Komarov sat down. "What's in the suitcase?"

"Some old leather trousers and a shirt."

"He's wearing the suit. Get back over there. I don't want any slipups."

MCCOLL WALKED UP TVERSKAYA TO the Hotel Lux. The long, four-story stone building had recently been painted, presumably to impress the foreign delegates. The main effect, however, was to make the surrounding buildings look twice as dilapidated. One of two militiamen guarding the main entrance gave McColl's papers a cursory examination and waved him through.

The lobby was empty of people, empty of furniture, lined with posters and blown-up photographs celebrating the Third Congress of the Communist International. A solitary clerk sat behind a reception counter long enough to accommodate twenty. McColl waited in vain for his presence to be acknowledged.

"I am appointed to the Indian delegation as a translator and interpreter," he said eventually, gently pushing his papers across the counter.

The man called for a colleague without looking up and continued sorting registration cards into neat piles.

McColl realized that he was nervously stroking his newly shaven chin, and ceased doing so. A second reception clerk emerged, one more eager to please. McColl explained the situation and was informed that the Indian delegation was on a river cruise, along with the Chinese comrades. They would be back in time for supper. And when it came to his own accommodation, the comrade had arrived at an auspicious moment. News had just reached the hotel of an arrest at the Persian border—that country's delegate had been seized by his own authorities and sent back to Tehran for questioning, thus freeing up his room. It was even on the same corridor as those occupied by the Indians. Room 453.

Pushing his luck, McColl asked for a list of the Indian comrades.

One would be typed out for him. It would be ready in an hour or so.

Feeling slightly less apprehensive, he went up to his room and lay down on the bed to await the Indians' return.

THE CRACK IN THE BOARDED-UP window offered Piatakov and Brady a perfect view of the Shabolovka Street depot, and of the tram now clanking its way through the open gates, tires squealing with resentment at the tightness of the curve. As it disappeared behind the houses that fronted the main shed, a man emerged from the depot-office doorway, strode across the cobbles, and noisily swung the gates shut.

The American checked his fob. "Half past seven," he announced. "Let's go."

He led the way down the staircase, taking care to step over the gaps where treads had been stolen for fuel.

Behind him, Piatakov felt as tense as he ever had going into battle, and far less certain he had right on his side. Accepting that any meaningful opposition required violence was one thing; finding himself face-to-face with old comrades over the barrel of a gun would be something else.

"I'll check the street," the American said, pulling back the front door and squeezing out past the corrugated iron flap that someone had nailed across the opening. Piatakov watched from the shadows, conscious of his own thumping heart and the nervous exhalations of his five companions.

Shahumian belched softly beside him. "Goddamn carrot tea," he murmured.

The Indians flashed anxious smiles.

Brady reappeared. "Okay," he said.

A horse-drawn cart was moving away down the street, but nothing was coming toward them. The sky had barely begun to darken, the daytime heat was showing no sign of dissipating, and Piatakov could feel the sweat running down his back. In the distance, the sinking sun was drawing flashes of golden light from the distant domes of the Kremlin churches.

They reached the gates, Shahumian peeling off as planned to take his position at the crossroads to the left. The others slipped into the empty yard. Leaving Grazhin and Nasim to stand guard by the entrance, Brady, Piatakov, Chatterji, and Rafiq walked along the inlaid tracks toward the depot offices.

They stopped by the side of the open door, deep in the building's shadow, and took out the masks that Brady had devised. These were more like cloth bags than traditional masks, with rough holes cut for the eyes and mouth. He had taken the idea from his homeland, where some crazy gang of negro haters, whose name Piatakov had already forgotten, used such hoods to hide their faces.

As he pulled his on, Piatakov could hear the murmur of conversation coming from an upstairs room. And the welcome clink of coins.

And someone coming down the stairs, walking toward the doorway.

The footsteps stopped, giving way to the sound of furniture scraping the floor.

Brady and Piatakov went through the doors together. In the corridor beyond, a man in a leather jacket was bent in the act of seating himself at a table, holding a glass of steaming tea.

"Who the hell—"

"No noise," Brady said quietly, showing the Chekist his Colt revolver, "or yours will be a lasting silence." The man gulped and put down the glass, slopping tea across the table. "You two stay here with our new friend," Brady told the Indians.

Piatakov followed the American up the stairs, into a room full of people counting coins into piles. One by one they became aware of the two masked men just inside the doorway, and of the guns they were holding.

"Good evening, comrades," Brady said in a soft, insolent tone, leaning back against the doorjamb.

Piatakov could picture the expression behind the mask. The man had read too many penny dreadfuls, watched too many cowboy films.

"This is what they used to call an armed robbery in the bad old bourgeois days," the American was telling the captive audience in his heavily accented Russian. "Don't do anything heroic, and no one needs to die." He paused. "And I can promise any true Bolshevik among you that the money we take will be used in the service of the revolution."

Someone giggled, probably involuntarily.

"You," Brady went on, picking out the nearest clerk and indicating a heap of canvas bags, "fill up four of those."

The man in question started toppling piles of coins off the edges of tables and into the open bags, his nervousness making him clumsy. The other eight clerks—Piatakov had counted them—sat staring at him and Brady. Judging by the noise, more coins were ending up on the floor than in the bags.

"You," the American snapped at one of the watchers, "help him."

There was a pounding on the stairs; Rafiq's head appeared, dark eyes flashing through the slitted cloth bag. "Militia patrol, coming down the street."

"Shit." Brady thought for a moment. "Tell—"

A window behind him shattered, the shot reverberating through the room. A clerk at the far end of the room was just standing there, dumbly holding the pistol, not even attempting a second shot. Brady's Colt boomed, and the man seemed to jump backward, spurting blood from his chest.

They could hear running feet outside in the tram yard.

Brady was striding down to where the spread-eagled clerk had collapsed against the wall. "You two, take the bags," he told Piatakov and Rafiq, picking up the offending pistol and thrusting it under his belt. He walked back to the top of the stairs. "If I were you," he told the assembly, "I'd think about how good life can be and just sit there quietly until this is over."

As the three of them reached the foot of the stairs, another two shots were fired outside. Chatterji was by the doorway, looking out;

behind him, the Chekist was slumped in the chair, his blouse a sea of blood, his throat slit open from ear to ear.

"Why did you kill him?" Piatakov asked furiously.

"What else could I do?" the Indian snapped back.

"You could—"

"Later," Brady interrupted harshly.

He was right. Piatakov put down the heavy bags and took a look outside. On opposite sides of the tramlines, Shahumian and Nasim were retreating across the yard, guns in hand. As Piatakov watched, the Armenian took cover behind a stationary tram, the Indian in a convenient doorway. Figures were moving behind the distant gates.

"How many, Aram?" Brady shouted.

"At least ten," the Armenian yelled back. "Ivan's looking for another exit," he added.

As if on cue, Grazhin appeared around the corner of the building. "There's a way out through the factory next door," he said breathlessly.

"Go," Brady told Piatakov, Grazhin, Chatterji, and Rafiq, who now had a bag of coins each. "We'll be right behind you."

The yard beyond the office was edged by a man-high brick wall. A grindstone offered a convenient leg up, but as Piatakov put his head above the parapet, a shout from above and behind him was followed by the sound of a vehicle driving into the yard ahead.

He dropped back down. "More militia," he told Grazhin.

They retraced their steps, feeling the weight of the coins, meeting Brady on the way. Ahead of them a bullet pinged off the metal flank of a tram.

"Maybe there's a way out on the other side of the shed," Grazhin suggested between coughs.

"I'll take a look," Brady said, pulling the bag off his head, making his hair stand up. "Can't see a goddamn thing with it on," he muttered, before taking off across the yard and disappearing into the glass-roofed tram shed.

They could hear militia behind them now, on the far side of the factory wall. Piatakov waited until a head appeared; then he fired off two shots. The head's disappearance was presumably instinctive, as he'd aimed deliberately high. It wasn't so long ago he'd been fighting the Whites alongside men like these.

He turned in time to see Grazhin, following in Brady's footsteps, caught by fire from the militia beyond the gates. As his comrade stumbled and fell, the heavy bag dropped from his hand, spilling its harvest of shiny coins between the tramlines.

Nasim's gun barked in reply, followed by Chatterji's and Piatakov's own. Grazhin, cursing loudly, hobbled on into the shed, holding his thigh.

Brady emerged from the tram shed, and signaled that he'd found a way out. He helped Grazhin deeper into the shed, and then joined Shahumian in offering covering fire for those on the wrong side of the open yard.

Piatakov made it across, slamming into a tram with rather more force than he wanted to. Chatterji was right behind him.

Rafiq tripped on a rail, went down, and then scurried on without his share of the spoils. Coming up behind him, Nasim stooped to retrieve the bag, but was instantly hit by a fusillade of fire. Flung backward across the tramlines, he came to rest with his handsome face staring lifelessly up at the sky.

When Shahumian instinctively moved toward the body, another volley sent him scurrying back, clutching his left shoulder.

Piatakov stared at the dead Indian. A blue world.

A bullet exploded a tram windshield above their heads. The militiamen from the factory were over the wall.

"Move!" Brady shouted, leading them at a run down the line of trams in the wake of the struggling Grazhin. The door at the rear of the shed was open.

Beyond it was another walled yard. In the corner a long-disused gate led into a narrow strip of waste ground between factory and houses. At its end they could see someone strolling past on Shabolovka Street. Behind them the sounds of pursuit grew louder.

They went down the passage at a run, slowing to a halt where it ran into the street. For a short moment only the stroller was visible, approaching the crossroads; then two militiamen came rushing around the corner, almost knocking him over. As Brady's gun boomed, dropping one and sending the other flying for cover, a shot from down the passage spun Rafiq against the wall.

Piatakov returned fire, pinning the pursuers down, then followed the others across the street and into the alley opposite. Rafiq had taken a bullet high in the chest; his face was the color of pastry. Shahumian was bleeding profusely, but swore it was only a flesh wound. Chatterji was now carrying both the remaining bags of coins, Grazhin leaning against a wall, holding his mask over his thigh wound and breathing heavily. Brady was reloading the Colt. "Keep moving," he said. "I'll keep the bastards' heads down."

"No," Grazhin wheezed.

Piatakov hesitated.

"I can't run," Grazhin told him and Brady. "Leave this to me." A smile flickered across his cadaverous face. "I've had enough," he added laconically.

Brady looked at him, nodded almost absentmindedly, and turned away, pulling Piatakov after him. At the end of the alley, as they caught up with Aram, Rafiq, and Chatterji, Grazhin's army pistol sounded twice in quick succession.

They all pocketed or belted their guns, crossed the deserted street in front of them, and took a turn to the north. Ahead of them the half-built Shukhov wireless tower was starkly silhouetted against the yellow evening sky. More shots echoed, sounding much farther away.

"We should split up," Brady said.

PIATAKOV EASED SHAHUMIAN'S BLOODY SHIRT up over his head, balled it up, and told the Armenian to hold it against his wound. As he placed a pan of water on the faintly glowing ring, Piatakov realized how angry he was feeling, with Brady, with the others, with himself. What had they all been thinking?

He told himself to calm down. What was that phrase of Caitlin's—crying over spilled milk. He smiled to himself—when had they last seen milk?

On the other side of the room, Shahumian was flexing his shoulder.

"How does it feel?" Piatakov asked, carrying the candle across to get a better look at the wound. "It doesn't seem serious."

"It isn't. I'll be fine in a couple of days."

"Assuming we haven't been caught," Piatakov said bitterly. "I should have spoken up. I knew it was a huge gamble, and I said nothing. Now Ivan Vasilyevich is dead; Nasim is dead; you and Rafiq are both wounded. I should have said something. Chatterji . . . I mean . . . why did he do it? Why not just knock the man out? And Brady . . . sometimes he seems like a madman. He was having the time of his life out there!"

"He was," Shahumian agreed. "But that's what makes him such a fighter. Isn't that water ready yet?"

It was barely warm but would probably take a week to boil. Piatakov carried the pan across to his friend.

"I know what you mean, though," Shahumian went on. "He really loves it. He was like that in Ukraine. And maybe you wouldn't want him to marry your sister, but if you're in real trouble . . ."

"And when he's the one who got you into it?"

"He wasn't. We all agreed, remember?" The Armenian winced as Piatakov cleaned the wound. "And don't mourn for Ivan Vasilyevich," he said a few moments later. "He was dying anyway—we all knew he was. And he made his death count."

Piatakov was winding the improvised bandage around the Armenian's waist. "I know, but . . ."

"This is not going to be easy, Sergei," Shahumian interjected. "It will probably be the end of us. But if it is . . . Sergei, I lost my Anna, and I lost my children, and we're losing the revolution they died for. I'm quite willing to give up my own life, but it sure as hell is going to cost someone." He got to his feet, stood there testing his strength. "A blaze of glory, my friend," he added softly. "If going down is all we can do, then we'll do it in a blaze of glory."

CAITLIN PUT THE MAGAZINE PROOFS away in a drawer, stretched her arms above her head, and decided that was enough for the day. She'd been at work for over twelve hours, and all her colleagues had long since gone home. Rahima and her sister, who slept on a mattress in one of the upstairs rooms, were out at a Dutch comrade's birthday party, but Fanya had made sure they had a key.

At least Caitlin was spared the walk home. She had a meeting at the Serpukhovskaya office early the next day, and Fanya had pointed out that she might as well take the department car home for the night and save herself a trip across the river in the morning.

It had been a good couple of days, she thought, as she gathered her things together, turned out the lights, and took the key from the hook in the antechamber. An up-and-down week, but one that had ended well. Since Caitlin's sobering talk with Kollontai, Sergei had seemed almost his old self, as if he'd overheard the conversation and was trying to do better. They'd even had sex the previous night. Drunken sex admittedly, and not very good sex at that, but it was something. A new start perhaps.

And things had gone well at work. There'd been no fresh news from Kollontai on the business in Orel, but the Orgbureau was proving more willing than usual to accept the department's requests, and the latest recruitment figures were up all over the country.

She let herself out the back door, and into the yard that housed the Renault CG. After checking the petrol, she took a deep breath and turned the engine over, praying it would burst into life.

It did. After carefully maneuvering the car down the narrow alley that ran beside their building, she emerged into Vozdvizhenka Street and drove up the mostly empty thoroughfare, passing a posse of workers who were busy hanging banners in celebration of international solidarity. The wheel of the open-top car felt good in her hands, the cool night breeze fresh on her face. For all the things that were getting worse, she thought, there were others that were getting better. Earlier that day, as she and Fanya had been eating their lunch in the park near their office, they'd heard the strains of a distant orchestra. They'd looked at each other and burst out laughing with pleasure. Perhaps the sound of Mozart floating through the streets was all the justification the NEP needed.

She remembered something her American friend and comrade Jack Reed had once said—that in normal times, only one in a thousand people were actively engaged in politics. In a revolutionary period, fifty times as many people were involved, a leap in numbers huge enough to create the impression, particularly in the minds of those involved, of a whole society on the move. But the impression was misleading, because fifty out of a thousand was still only one in twenty. And 95 percent of the population was still busy doing things they thought more important, like eating and sleeping and making love.

Caitlin missed Reed, and his penchant for speaking his mind to any and every audience. She wondered what he would have made of Kronstadt and the NEP. Kollontai had used the occasion of his funeral to reaffirm Reed's belief that the revolution was nothing if it wasn't a selfless endeavor, and Caitlin had never been prouder of her Russian friend than she was on that day.

But eight months on they were where they were. She could only hang on to what she knew was true. She had to do her job, had to trust herself. The Zhenotdel was making a difference—she was sure of it. And if the time ever came when she thought otherwise, then that would be the moment to do something else.

She left the car outside their building and hurried upstairs, hoping that Sergei would still be at home.

Their room was in darkness, and the electric light failed to go on. Either the power was off, or their wiring had finally succumbed, either to age or the rats.

She found one of their precious candle stubs, lit it, and stood for a moment enjoying the dance of shadows on the wall. Then her eyes caught sight of their bucket, not in its usual place.

On the floor beside it was something white. She walked over for a closer look. It was a shirt she didn't recognize, and it was covered in something dark and sticky.

Blood.

McCOLL MOPPED UP THE LAST morsels of buckwheat porridge with a chunk of black bread and contemplated the bowl of rather sorry-looking apples that adorned the center of the table. The Filippov Café on the hotel's ground floor was filled with the babble of foreign tongues, but the Indian comrades were nowhere to be seen. It looked as if the cruise had lasted longer than expected.

Picking out the least-bruised apple in the bowl, he poured himself another cup of tea and kept a watchful eye on the entrance doors. The mix of nationalities was certainly impressive—whatever you thought of the Bolsheviks, their revolution clearly had global appeal. Some of the people on view had come an awfully long way.

But not the Indians, he reminded himself. They'd been in Moscow ever since the closure of the school in Tashkent. More to the point, he couldn't be certain that one or more of them wouldn't recognize him from his time in Calcutta six years before. When he and Cumming had gone through the list of names, none had rung a bell, but the risk was there. And if anyone showed any sign of recognition, he could think of only one appropriate response. He would simply have to make for the door and the street and hope he could outrun any pursuit.

This wasn't a comforting prospect, and as the minutes dragged by, he found himself almost expecting such an outcome.

The room was nearly empty when they finally arrived, all dressed in European clothes, all looking tired out. Scanning the Indians' faces as they lined up to get their supper, McColl was more than a little relieved to see none he recognized.

Only twelve of the fifteen were there. And Cumming's man, Muhammad Rafiq, was one of the missing three.

When McColl introduced himself, the reception was almost overly warm. A translator was what they'd been praying for, not of course that one actually prayed anymore. Each Indian insisted on shaking his hand, and if any man had the slightest recollection of seeing McColl's face before, he should have been on the stage. McColl wouldn't have to run for it. Or at least not yet.

McColl took his time sipping his tea while they ate their suppers, and eventually asked about the discrepancy between his list of fifteen and the twelve men present. The other three, he was told, had not been on the cruise. No one knew why they'd been absent, but the fact that both Habib Shankar Nasim and Muhammad Rafiq had found themselves Russian girlfriends might have been significant.

As for Durga Chatterji—he was, one Indian suggested, not the most reliable of comrades.

PIATAKOV PUT THE BOOK BACK where he'd found it, tucked half under Brady's mattress. The text was in English, which Piatakov couldn't understand, but there were plenty of drawings to look at, almost all of them depicting famous gunfights of the American West. When they'd served together in Ukraine, Brady had been fond of telling western stories over the evening campfire, and was always saying that his one regret was being born thirty years too late.

Two hours had passed since the depot robbery. Piatakov didn't know how they'd all made it back to Brady's room without running into the Cheka again, but somehow they had. Not all of them, he corrected himself. Ivan Grazhin would never pick another title from the pile of dog-eared Dostoyevsky novels by his bed, and Habib Ahmed Nasim would never see India again.

Chatterji didn't seem that upset at the loss of his comrade, offering only a few stiff words extolling his glorious sacrifice. His other Indian companion had even less to say: the barely conscious Rafiq was laid out on Grazhin's bed, white-faced and quietly wheezing. He seemed likely to die with or without any medical help, and Brady had decided that seeking some out posed too great a risk to the rest of them.

He had gone back out once everyone was there. The prearranged meeting with Suvorov was now more urgent: they had planned to take southbound trains the next morning, traveling in pairs they'd drawn by lot, but that was no longer feasible—the stations would be swarming with Chekists. Suvorov might be able to help, though Brady had expressed his doubts. Even if the other man had the contacts, he wouldn't have time to make use of them.

Now they heard the returning American's heavy tread on the stairs.

"The Chekas are fucking everywhere," was the first thing Brady said, but his eyes went straight to Rafiq. "How is he?"

"No better," Shahumian told him.

"Good," Brady said. He looked around at the shocked faces. "Suvorov just informed me that Rafiq's a British agent."

Piatakov was confused. "But so is Suvorov!" he exclaimed.

"They work for different organizations, and Rafiq's people knew nothing about our plans," Brady said. "Still don't, according to Suvorov's bosses in London because Rafiq hasn't filed a report since he joined us. But Rafiq's people in London have sent someone out to contact him. Whether or not the man's arrived, Suvorov doesn't know."

They were all looking at the stricken Indian.

"So what do we do with him?" Shahumian asked.

"Let him die," Brady said simply.

"And if he doesn't before we leave?" Shahumian asked.

"He will."

There was a short silence. "Did Suvorov have anything useful to offer?" Shahumian asked.

"No, we're on our own as far as getting out of Moscow's concerned."

"Then what should we do? Wait for morning or get going now?" Piatakov asked.

Brady didn't hesitate. "Now," he said. "We're only five minutes away from the Paveletsky yards—that's why we took this room in the first place—and a freight train's our safest way out of the city. Two would be better, with some time in between. The militia must have noticed that Nasim's an Indian, so Durga should be on the first. He and Aram should leave right away."

Shahumian nodded. "And where do we meet?"

"Samarkand," Brady decided after only a moment's thought. "You can get there by train from the Caucasus or Samara, and the Cheka garrison there will be much smaller than the one in Tashkent. There's a square with madrasahs on three sides called the Registan—I was reading about it the other day. Whoever's there first, just keep turning up at noon until the others arrive. It's in the native town, not the Russian one."

"Which should we stay in?" Piatakov wondered out loud.

Brady shrugged. "We'll be more noticeable in the native town but easier to find in the Russian. We'll have to play it by ear."

"And how long do we wait?" Chatterji asked.

"For as long as you have to. The journey could take a week, but a month's more likely. And take all the coins you can easily carry."

Once they had done so, Shahumian went to embrace Piatakov. "One last adventure," he murmured with a smile. "I'll see you in Samarkand."

"You will," Piatakov said, hoping it was true. From the window he and Brady watched the twosome walk away along the empty street. There didn't seem to be any motor vehicles in the vicinity, and the distant chuff of a locomotive was reassuring.

Piatakov had wanted to travel with Aram, but the lots they'd drawn had decided otherwise, and leaving later with Brady at least offered one consolation—he could say good-bye to Caitlin.

"I'll be back in an hour," he promised after telling the American where he was going.

"You're crazy," Brady said.

"Probably."

"Is any woman worth it?" Brady asked half-jokingly.

Piatakov stopped by the door, looked back. "Yes," he said simply.

CAITLIN KNEW IT HADN'T BEEN one of Sergei's shirts. But had it been his blood? Had he been hurt, or had he hurt someone else? The only good answer was neither, and that seemed unlikely.

North of the river again, she piloted the Zhenotdel Renault through Moscow's dark and sparsely populated streets. On the door of an empty shop, someone had painted a huge bird in flight, a small biplane with German markings dangling from its claws. Farther down the same street, outside an abandoned hotel, a revolving door lay on its side like a giant's abandoned spinning top. Here and there a working lamp illuminated a boarded shop front or a group of smoking militiamen; on one corner a huge poster demanding electrification of the countryside loomed across the stripped carcass of a horse.

As she drove past the New Theater on Bolshaya Dmitrovka the giant flower stalls constructed by the futurists seemed like strange growths swaying on the floor of a dark ocean.

She felt close to hysteria, as if all the weeks and months of her struggle with Sergei had engulfed her in one moment.

An errant child, that was what he was. She was angry with him. Frightened for him.

She had to bring him home.

After driving down Kamergersky Street, she turned onto Tverskaya and pulled up outside the Universalist Club. At the entrance she hesitated for a moment, wondering whether to remove the enamel star from her blouse front. Why? she asked herself. To hell with them.

She took a deep breath and walked into the building, down the narrow corridor, and into the main clubroom. Smoke, noise, and the smell of male bodies assailed her. The handful of women all looked like prostitutes, and the men who noticed Caitlin's arrival were wondering whether she was one herself, if their head-to-toe appraisals were any indication. She didn't see a soul she recognized.

She stood there, disgusted by the atmosphere. The tinkling jazz music, the smell of marijuana—it reminded her of the seedier clubs she'd visited in prewar New York. But they'd also been home to a wild kind of joy, and here the air seemed thick with the opposite, a lovingly cocooned sense of hopelessness. Was this what Moscow's free spirits had come to?

She wanted to shout at them all, the way she'd shouted at Sergei.

A young man, obviously drunk, was leering at her. She turned to the next table, where two men were playing chess with homemade pieces, and asked them if they knew Sergei. They looked at her warily, shook their heads in unison, and bent back over their board.

"Are you looking for Piatakov?" a voice asked.

It was the drunk, teetering right behind her. She stepped back a pace. "Do you know where he is?"

"Why do you want to know?" he asked conspiratorially.

"Shut up, Belov!" someone shouted.

Belov tried winking with both eyes at once. "Has our party pretty boy got you pregnant, sweetheart?"

She'd smacked him across the face before she knew what she was doing.

He looked at her, astonishment turning to rage, then lifted a hand.

She hit him with her fist the way Colm had taught her all those years ago, right on the nose.

He collapsed backward, into a sudden silence.

"I'm looking for Sergei Piatakov!" she shouted, massaging her knuckles with the other hand. "I'm his wife."

Heads turned away. She stood there, wishing she could hit them all.

"Come and sit down," said another voice behind her, this one soft and sober.

She turned to find a middle-aged man with intelligent eyes in a battered face. He pushed out a chair.

She ignored it. "Have you seen him?"

"Not this evening. But he does come in most nights." He paused. "Though I don't think he was in yesterday either."

"What about his friends?"

"Not them either."

"Why are you telling me this?" she asked. She had the absurd feeling that he was betraying Sergei.

"You asked."

His face was somehow familiar. "Have we met before?" she asked.

He smiled ruefully. "A long time ago. At one of Volodarsky's gatherings."

She remembered the evening, the crowded room—Volodarsky had never been short of friends. "Thank you," she said. "If Sergei comes in later, could you tell him I'm looking for him?"

"I will."

"Thank you," she said again. Turning to leave, she saw the drunk trying, without much success, to get himself upright. Resisting the temptation to kick his arm out from under him, she walked back out to the street.

There she stood for a moment, the last of her anger peeling away in the night air, revealing only a numbing sense of loss.

She climbed wearily into the car and sat behind the wheel wondering what to do, where to go.

The office, she decided. She could cope there. She could always cope there.

Ten minutes later she was back in the familiar room. After lighting the candle on her desk, she took a chair to the open window and sat there wondering why the tears wouldn't come.

She heard movement behind her and looked around. Rahima was standing in the doorway in a cotton shift, watching her. "Madame Piatakova?" she asked tentatively.

"Comrade Piatakova," Caitlin said automatically.

"Yes, I am sorry . . ."

"It's nothing. Go back to sleep, Rahima."

But the girl had joined her at the window. "You are sad," she said, as if surprised to find such a commonplace emotion afflicting someone so exalted. Rahima held out her arms, and suddenly Caitlin felt herself enclosed, sobbing, the tears running down her cheeks and onto the girl's bare shoulders.

IT WASN'T A LONG WALK, but the frequent need to huddle in doorways made it seem so. As Brady had said, the Cheka was out in force, cars, lorries, and foot patrols combing the city for him and his companions.

Like Caitlin two hours earlier, Piatakov found their room in darkness. He lit their candle, noticed the bucket, the shirt. "Hell," he muttered.

After pouring away the bloody water and stuffing the rolled-up shirt in his trouser pocket, he sat wearily down on the bed.

The familiar room reached out for him on her behalf, but he knew there was no going back. Not now, not after Grazhin had given his life for their traveling money. And Aram was right. You couldn't always choose who your comrades were. As long as they were committed, and Brady was certainly that. Even Chatterji, in his own way. Maybe the Indian had just panicked—it was easy to do. He and Aram would keep things . . . What was the word he was looking for? Decent? His laugh sounded eerie in the candlelit room. After the last few years?

He got up and walked around. Where the hell was she? He wanted to part as friends, to wish her well, to know she understood.

The last six months had been hell, but the two years before that had often been wonderful, and he wanted her to know that the one hadn't wiped out the other. The good times had been something to cherish and, despite all else, still were. He remembered a stroll in the snow-covered forest outside Petrograd when their paths had crossed again in that city and several walks in the summer woods around Moscow. She had always been impressed by his knowledge of the natural world, his ability to name the trees and birds and flowers that crossed their path. She was a city girl, she said—all she knew about nature, she had learned in a park near her home. Prospect Park, he seemed to remember.

They'd sometimes gone boating on the Moscow River with her friend Fanya and Fanya's boyfriend, who had shared Piatakov's own taste in poetry but whose name he couldn't remember.

In the early days, he and Caitlin had read each other poetry lying in bed in their candlelit room. They both admired the new revolutionary poets, but the ones they loved, and could quote verbatim, were from further back—Pushkin for him, a woman named Sara Teasdale for her.

They had talked about their families—something he'd never done with anyone else—and their respective passions for teaching and journalism. All the men he'd known, starting with his father, had scoffed—gently or otherwise—at the thought of finding one's vocation in a room full of children.

And then there was the lovemaking, which had seemed so glorious at first, but had turned into something difficult, loaded down with emotions he couldn't begin to understand or control. Once you'd watched enough human bodies ripped asunder, it was hard to see them as a way of expressing love.

But they had. In the early days, they had.

He grabbed a pencil and one of the Zhenotdel flyers from her desk. How did you say good-bye to the love of your life?

The words wouldn't come, but looking up, he spied his own battered volume of Pushkin's verse. Leafing through, he found the poem he wanted and left the book open at the page in question.

She would understand.

As he descended the stairs to the street, he softly spoke the first few lines out loud:

> I loved you—and maybe love
> still smolders in my heart;
> but let my love not trouble
> you or cause you any hurt.

AS MIDNIGHT APPROACHED MCCOLL WAS having trouble staying awake. But he needed to establish contact with Muhammad Rafiq, and the later he knocked on Rafiq's door, the better his chances of finding the Indian home, and doing so unobserved. So he paced his room for another thirty minutes, until the traffic in the corridor had more or less withered away, and only then put his head around the door.

There was no one in sight.

He tiptoed down the threadbare carpet, seeking out room 467, which his list said belonged to Rafiq and Nasim. If both men were there, or only Nasim, McColl would say he'd come to introduce himself and try to catch Rafiq on his own the next day.

A strip of light under the door suggested there was someone home, and its sudden disappearance confirmed as much.

McColl rapped softly on the door.

There was no response. He briefly wondered whether he might have imagined the light—some sort of reflection perhaps . . .

Then he heard the faintest of sounds on the other side of the door.

Not wanting to knock any louder, he tried the doorknob instead, and rather to his surprise, the door swung open with a loud creak. The room beyond, now dimly lit from the corridor, was unexpectedly empty. Suspiciously so, McColl realized, just as someone else's breath almost tickled his ear.

McColl threw himself forward, shoving the door as he did so. Something swished past his head, and the room fell back into darkness.

"Rafiq!" McColl whispered loudly as he struggled to his feet. "Akbar," he added more softly, using the Indian's code name.

The response was an attack. Something flailed through the air and crashed into McColl's left shoulder, sending spasms of pain through his upper arm. He threw a punch into the darkness and felt it connect, but the something hit him again, on almost the same spot, and he went down.

A black shape loomed over him. McColl lunged forward, grappling for a hold, and they both fell across a bed, before tumbling onto the floor beyond. A foot dug into his stomach, pushing him into a wall, and suddenly a hand was at his throat, a shadow rising and falling against the ceiling. He squirmed aside, trying to knee his assailant in the balls, but managed only to lever him sideways.

McColl rolled free across the bed and back down onto the floor. As the other man came around the end of the bed, McColl threw out both legs, aiming at the shins. The man stumbled, tried and failed to keep his balance, and fell through the curtains, striking the frame of the half-open window with a soft, sharp crack.

It was a sound that McColl had heard only once before, and guiltily remembered ever since: playing for the school football team, he had wildly thrown himself into a tackle, and badly broken another boy's leg.

With the curtains now divided, he could see the prone body arched across the sill. Was the man dead or merely unconscious?

Still breathing heavily from all the exertion, McColl grabbed hold of the feet, pulled his attacker back into the room, and drew the curtains. Grabbing a sheet from a bed, McColl rolled it up and laid it across the foot of the door before turning on the light.

His assailant had been a short, powerful-looking man with thinning blond hair and a wide, typically Russian face. His head was now at an unnatural angle; the crack had been his neck. McColl turned him over to get a better look at his face, and received another shock. The last place he'd seen these features was on a photograph in Cumming's office. The man's name was Pitirim Suvorov, and he was one of Five's men in Moscow.

What had he been doing in Rafiq's room?

And had he known whom he was attacking?

McColl could ponder such questions later. He went to the door and put an ear against it. He couldn't hear movement or voices, and if no one had turned up by now, it seemed unlikely that they would. If his struggle with Suvorov had been overheard—and it beggared belief that it hadn't—then the listeners had decided it wasn't their business. Which, McColl decided, wasn't that surprising—the foreign delegates in the surrounding rooms would consider any investigation the prerogative of their hosts.

Repressing a keen desire to get out while the going was good, he embarked on a search of the room.

A jacket hung on the back of the door yielded some Kerensky notes, a few kopek coins, and an unopened packet of Russian cigarettes. On the small table between the beds, there were piles of Congress literature and three books, all in English: Dickens's *Bleak House*, a compendium of Gokhale's speeches, and H. G. Wells's *Kipps*. McColl flicked through the pages in search of handwritten notes, but there were none.

The only suitcase was Rafiq's—his name was stenciled inside the lid, along with a Lahore address. Inside it McColl found a pair of opera glasses, a small wooden Ganesha, and a crumpled map of Tashkent. The rest was clothes. There was nothing to suggest that Rafiq wasn't the foreign comrade the Russians thought he was.

McColl put the map in his pocket, thinking it might help bolster his cover, and turned his attention back to the dead man. If neither Rafiq nor Nasim returned that night, a housemaid would probably find the body next morning—the Bolsheviks, as far as he knew, still employed such people. Later, of course, would be better: the longer the corpse stayed undetected, the longer the Cheka would take to identify its owner.

So what should he do? Removing the corpse from the room would cut the connection between Rafiq and Suvorov, and help to muddy the waters, but where could McColl move it to? A bedding cupboard? The out-of-order lift?

And why take the risk? Dragging a corpse down hotel corridors was the sort of behavior that got you noticed.

The only thing he could do was hide it in the room, which meant under one of the beds. He dragged it between the two, then rolled it under the one that stood against two walls and bent the legs away from the open end. It was now invisible to anyone standing, which was probably the best he could hope for.

Standing once more with his ear to the door, he could hear nothing stirring outside. A quick silent prayer to whatever God looked after spies, and he was quietly stepping out of the room and into a gratifyingly empty passage.

A few seconds later, back in his room, he found himself starting to shake.

RAFIQ WAS DEAD WHEN PIATAKOV got back to Brady's room.

"I didn't think he'd make it," Brady said as he finished packing his bag.

"Are we just going to leave him there on the bed?" Piatakov asked. Was he imagining it, or had both pillows been under Rafiq's head when he left?

"Why not?" Brady replied.

Piatakov grunted his agreement and asked himself whether it mattered if Brady had hastened the Indian's death. Not a lot, he decided. Spies and traitors knew the price of failure.

"Those coins on the table are yours," Brady told him.

Piatakov tipped most of them into his shoulder bag, saving just a few for his pockets. With their small denominations, they wouldn't last long—a half-decent fortune-teller might see further robberies in their future. If they had one.

But the walk to the yard was less fraught than he expected, the silence of the postcurfew streets offering plentiful warning of Cheka or militia patrols, either motorized or on foot. As they passed a billboard bearing the slogan LET THOSE WHO ARE NOT FOR US LEAVE RUSSIA, Brady murmured, "We're trying."

An hour after leaving the house, Piatakov was sitting in a boxcar doorway, his legs dangling over the side, as the train threaded its way out of the vast Paveletsky yards. Brady was already asleep inside.

Another departure, Piatakov thought, another moment like the one in 1916, when he'd known in his heart there was no going back.

After that leave-taking, there'd been several months when he'd doubted the choice and his reasons for making it. His father, who'd pressed Sergei in vain to join the service after his older son was lost at sea, had died only a few weeks before, and Piatakov sometimes feared he had joined up when he did mostly to spite the old man.

They certainly hadn't gotten on in those last few years. As a child Piatakov had worshipped this large overbearing man, who appeared out of nowhere with his tales of other worlds, but he had gradually come to know his father for who and what he was. Or perhaps not gradually—something fundamental had changed after he listened in on one particular conversation between his parents. He couldn't remember what it was about, but he knew that his mother had been right and his father wrong, and that her way of seeing the world was the one he instinctively shared. His father had the practical intelligence, but he'd barged his way through life, seeing little and closing doors behind him. His mother had been too generous for her own good, but the world had been a better place for her presence.

Piatakov had been about fourteen when he'd overheard that exchange, the age at which boys usually swap their affections in the other direction. But then, he'd always been a misfit, like the man now snoring behind him.

His mother hadn't wanted him to go—which was hardly surprising given that she'd already lost a husband and son to the Baltic's icy waters—but she hadn't tried to stop him. The reason he'd given her—that someone who aspired to teach literature and history had to know more of the world than the town he was born in—was one she had understood.

In the event he hadn't seen much of the world in a geographical sense, but he had seen one world give birth to another. And not just seen: like many of the fleet's junior officers, he had sided with the men and helped make it happen.

He had still been walking on air when he'd finally found the time to visit home, only to discover that he'd left it too late. A sudden illness had taken his mother, and Olesya's parents had whisked their daughter out of Russia, beyond the reach of godless Bolsheviks like himself. If she'd ever written expressing regret, he'd not received the letter.

After donating the family house to the local soviet, he had headed back to Petrograd. It was only a few weeks later, at the sailor-leader Dybenko's wedding to Alexandra Kollontai, that he'd first laid eyes on Caitlin, and only a few months after that that he'd left Moscow on a similar train to this one, heading south and east to fight for Trotsky's newly formed Red Army on the banks of the Volga.

Now here he was again, watching the last moonlit roofs of the city recede, this time with Lenin and Trotsky's Cheka on his trail, and the city soviet's money weighing down his breeches.

There was sadness and bitterness, a sense of ill fate lodged in his heart. And yet, still, for the first time in months, he also felt at one with himself. He had climbed off the fence at last. The die had been cast.

For better or worse, he was a revolutionary.

And revolutionaries made revolutions.

Real Police Work

It had been light for about an hour, but most of the depot still lay in shadow. This was the best part of the day, Komarov thought, as he followed the official down the tramlines: a few hours of merciful freshness between a sweat-inducing night and a broiling day.

"This is where the Indian died," the official said, stopping in front of him.

The body had long since been taken away, but the blood it had shed remained visible. A few coins glinted in the running gap beside the rails, presumably dropped when the man went down.

There was nothing else to see. A strange place for an Indian to die, Komarov thought, as a tram clanked out through the distant gates. He was annoyed by how long it had taken the militia to report the robbery, but supposed he should be grateful they had done so at all—at least someone at the local HQ had realized that an Indian dying violently in the middle of an International congress was likely to have political ramifications. "The foreign comrades are here to be impressed, not perish in anarchist robberies," was the way Dzerzhinsky had put it.

Had there been only one Indian? All the robbers had been masked, but some depot staffers had noticed that two at least had unusually dark-skinned hands. Against this, two other men had been heard speaking Russian, including the one who seemed to be in charge. The latter's accent had sounded strange to all the people questioned, but not in "an Asian sort of way."

India, of course, was a British possession. Could the agent they were hunting have anything to do with this? Komarov wondered. It seemed unlikely—the man had only just arrived in Moscow.

If the witnesses were to be believed—and there seemed no reason they shouldn't be—the man with the funny accent had boasted that "any true Bolshevik" would approve their plans for the stolen money. Which hardly suggested British involvement. It was much more likely that the men concerned were renegades of one sort or another—perhaps a bunch of anarchists as Dzerzhinsky had suggested, perhaps a splinter group of Socialist Revolutionaries. There was no shortage of men with a grievance.

There was no foreign power behind this. And no organization with any prospect of widespread support. This was just another bunch of dissidents who'd grown bored with the problems of putting ideals into practice, men who thought compromise equaled betrayal. They'd be planning some sort of desperate action, something to show the world just how right they were.

Komarov's new assistant emerged from the building where the witnesses were still being questioned. His name was Pavel Maslov, and he'd been seconded from the Vecheka on account of the possible foreign ramifications of the investigation. A young fair haired Ukrainian with a childlike face, he seemed efficient enough, but hadn't yet shown signs of anything more.

"We're finished," he reported.

"Nothing to help with identifications?"

"No."

And he wasn't verbose, Komarov thought, adding to the mental appraisal. "Then we'll visit the morgue," he said.

The expression on Maslov's face asked why, but he didn't voice the question.

It was a short ride in the Russo-Balt. The pavements were thronged with people heading for work, and Komarov watched the eyes turn away from the Cheka car, pretending they hadn't seen it.

He wondered if Maslov noticed and what he felt if he did. Angry? Pleased? The sadness that Komarov himself felt?

The morgue was attached to the Pavlovski Hospital, a place he knew only too well—it was there that his wife had spent her final weeks. The main chamber was artificially cooled, and the stench of putrefaction seemed fainter than usual. The four corpses, still fully clothed, were laid out on marble slabs.

Komarov looked at the Indian first, a slim young man not much older than twenty, with sleek black hair and a rather handsome face. Two bullets had entered his chest, leaving egg-shaped brown stains on the thin white shirt. The eyes were still open and looked strangely excited.

The Russian on the next slab was familiar. His name was Ivan Grazhin, and if Komarov remembered correctly, he had been a well-known voice in the soldiers' soviets, both before and after the first revolution. The man didn't look like he'd prospered since, but the eyes were serene for those of someone who'd fired a gun through the roof of his mouth.

And then there were the real victims: one with his throat slit from ear to ear, looking as if he were wearing a blood-colored bib; another with a look of surprise on his face and a coin-sized hole above the heart. Several witnesses had said that the handgun was the largest they'd ever seen.

"Have the relatives been informed?" Komarov asked Maslov.

"I don't know."

"Call the militia and ask. If they haven't done it, then ask them to do so."

Maslov hurried off in search of a telephone. After one last look at the grisly tableau, Komarov walked back outside, where the air was noticeably warmer than it had been only ten minutes earlier.

Entering the hospital, he inquired after the wounded militiaman and was directed upstairs to one of the wards. The man had died in the last few minutes. "They couldn't stop the bleeding," a nurse told Komarov.

Five men dead, he thought, standing by the bed. And for what?

Through the window he saw a woman walking toward an

automobile, and realized it was her. She must have been visiting someone, he decided. Or maybe the Zhenotdel had business at the hospital. As she went to wind the starting handle, a soldier hurried to offer his help and seemed somewhat put out when she firmly refused.

Komarov's smile was his first of the day.

After watching her car drive away, he went down to his own, where Maslov was patiently waiting.

"There's been another killing," the young man said. "At the Hotel Lux."

"An Indian?" Komarov asked.

"A Russian. But he was found under a bed in one of the Indians' rooms."

Which had to be more than a coincidence, Komarov thought. He looked at his watch. Dzerzhinsky had asked him not to pull the Indian delegates out of the conference before the day's business was concluded unless he considered it absolutely necessary. He decided he did. He would wait for the morning session to finish, but no longer.

McCOLL SPENT THE MORNING AT his new job, translating speeches for the Indian delegation among the splendors of the Kremlin's old imperial throne room. The first speaker was Lenin, who devoted two hours to a reasoned defense of the NEP, standing between the large gilded columns and beneath a huge sheet of scarlet velvet emblazoned with a golden hammer and sickle. His speech was matter-of-fact, like a kindly uncle's address to a gathering of favorite nephews, and compelling in its simplicity. The Bolshevik leader's preeminence was easy to understand.

Translating from Russian to Urdu was a touch on the tricky side, particularly where Marxist terminology was concerned, but McColl just about kept pace, and shamelessly précised the more difficult passages. The Indians hung on his every word, and several took copious notes.

After his presentation, Lenin sat himself down on the steps leading up to the platform, notepad in hand, and offered occasional asides that made everyone laugh. McColl's translations were eagerly anticipated and usually greeted by a joyful clapping of hands.

As they all filed out at the session's end, McColl saw the posse of leather-clad Chekists waiting at the exit and, for several dreadful seconds, thought they were waiting for him.

They were, but only for his services as an interpreter. The whole Indian delegation was needed back at the Hotel Lux.

There were no protests, only a slight air of bewilderment, as McColl and the twelve Indians were walked to their destination. At the hotel they were shown into a large, luxuriously furnished room on the ground floor; the smoking room in czarist days, McColl guessed. A tall, greying man in a suit was standing with his back to them, gazing out of the window. He turned to reveal a long face, steel-grey eyes above an aquiline nose.

His name was Komarov, and unless there were two men of that name high in the Moscow Cheka, this was the man that Ruzhkov had mentioned as being in charge of the hunt for McColl. Which made his heart beat a little faster.

After introducing himself as the deputy chairman of the Moscow Cheka, Komarov asked everyone to sit down, then described the tram depot robbery and Nasim's subsequent death. He made it clear that those assembled were not, in any way, being held responsible for the actions of their comrade Nasim, but he was sure that they would realize the need for questions. One or more of them might be able to throw some light on the motivation of their dead comrade, give some clue, however small, that would help with the apprehension of his fellow robbers.

McColl interpreted all this into Urdu, absorbing the information as he did so. He'd heard snatches of conversations about a big robbery over breakfast that morning, but there'd been no reason to connect this news with Cumming's plotters.

Komarov's first question was the obvious one—were there any Indian comrades missing?

There were. Neither Durga Chatterji nor Muhammad Rafiq had been seen since early the day before, and according to the former's roommate, Chatterji hadn't slept in his bed. Rafiq had shared with Nasim, so no one could say whether he had slept in his or not.

Komarov then dropped another bombshell—the body of an unidentified Russian had been discovered in Rafiq and Nasim's room. After each Indian had been separately questioned, Komarov went on, Comrade Maslov would escort him down to the basement for a viewing of the corpse, in the hope that one of them knew whose it was.

McColl and the first Indian were taken into the adjoining room, and the interrogations began. Komarov showed no signs of impatience as the questions and answers were carefully translated, and no sign either that he had any reason to suspect the translator, but the twin imperatives of doing a decent job and making sure that his mask stayed firmly in place took all of McColl's concentration.

Komarov asked each man for his opinions of the dead Nasim and the missing Rafiq and Chatterji. One by one they all said much the same—that all had seemed fully committed to the struggle against imperialism. The notion that the threesome might have been working for the British was politely but firmly dismissed; indeed, if any political wrongheadedness could be attributed to them, it would be of the opposite type. All three men had expressed their anger at the recent closing of the Tashkent school for Indian revolutionaries.

Their social lives had given cause for concern. Both Nasim and Rafiq had been seeing Russian women—not, of course, that there was anything wrong with Russian women, but . . . Nasim's girlfriend was a teacher at the Toilers of the East University, one Anna Kimayeva. Rafiq's was a girl he'd met on the train to Moscow, Marusya Dzharova, the daughter of a railway union official from Tashkent.

When the last Indian had been interviewed, McColl was left alone with Komarov. The Russian hadn't taken any notes, but McColl suspected he remembered every word. His questioning, though diplomatic, had been thorough and forensic. McColl had no previous experience of Cheka bosses at work, but this wasn't how he'd imagined one. He realized he was sweating copiously, but it *was* atrociously humid.

Maslov returned from the basement. "None of them admitted to seeing the man before," he reported.

Komarov grunted and turned to McColl. "Are you also staying in this hotel?" he asked.

"Yes, comrade."

"Did you notice anything suspicious in the way any of them answered my questions?"

"No, comrade."

"And you haven't overheard anything relevant in the last few days?"

"I only arrived from Tashkent yesterday."

"Ah." Komarov stood. "Well, keep your ears open from now on. And as I may have need of your services again today, stay with the delegation, either at the conference or here at the hotel. Understood?"

It wasn't a request. "Yes, comrade."

Trudging back to the Kremlin for what remained of the afternoon session, McColl felt relief at escaping the Cheka's embrace but not much wiser as to what was going on. As he and the Indians passed through the Kremlin gate, he tried to take stock of what he did and didn't know. Had Suvorov known who he was? If he had, then who had told him? What had he been doing in Rafiq and Nasim's room several hours after Nasim had been killed in the robbery? And where the hell was Rafiq?

It looked as if all three Indians had been recruited by Brady on Five's behalf. But had Brady known that Rafiq was already working for Cumming? There seemed little doubt that all four had taken part in the robbery, along with sundry others. Why? For money, presumably. Money to pay their way south, if Cumming was right. If they weren't still lying low in Moscow, they were probably on their way.

Should he head that way himself or stay and follow the investigation? Keeping close to Komarov felt like a daunting proposition, but seemed to offer more than a headless-chicken rush to India. And if it was personal safety he wanted, he should have stayed in the London prison.

He did have another—safer, he hoped—lead to follow up: Suvorov's Moscow address, which Cumming had given him in London, "for emergency use only." Not tonight—he had no intention of defying Komarov's instruction to stay put. But tomorrow should be fine. The Cheka had nothing to go on when it came to identifying Suvorov, so searching the Five agent's room should still be a relatively risk-free endeavor.

KOMAROV WALKED OUT TO HIS car. "Any news of the Englishman?" he asked the waiting Yezhov.

"None. He hasn't come back to the dormitory."

Komarov took a deep breath of the early evening air. "Start going through the others again. And the hotels."

He and Maslov climbed into the Russo-Balt's rear seat, and the driver set off for headquarters. As the city center streets rolled by, Komarov went through what he suspected. The robbery itself was unimportant; what mattered were the future plans of the men involved. This wasn't just another mindless outrage; it was, he was sure, a threat that needed taking seriously. But why did he feel that? It wasn't as if the revolution's survival was at stake.

Maybe its soul was.

He gazed down at his hands, which were steady as a rock. Real police work suited him.

At the M-Cheka offices he barked out rapid-fire orders to a clutch of subordinates: bring in Kimayeva; seek out photographs of Chatterji and Rafiq, bring back the tram-depot witnesses to see if any recognized the body from the Hotel Lux.

The subordinates scattered.

Komarov sat in his inner sanctum, awaiting their findings. Maslov was the first to return. "We have no photographs of Rafiq or Chatterji," he reported. "They probably don't have passports, but if they do, we haven't found them. And there are no other records: the International Executive asked the commissariat not to ask for photographs. They were worried the foreign delegates might interpret the request as a lack of trust."

Komarov smiled wryly. "Kimayeva?"

"Borin's on his way."

He appeared a few minutes later with the woman. She was about thirty, blonde, fairly attractive in a sharp-faced way. As Komarov questioned her, anger gave way to evasion, then finally to tears. Komarov sent Maslov out on a pretext and patiently extracted a confession that she'd been sleeping with Nasim. If her husband found out, he would kill her, she said. And the affair was over anyway: she hadn't seen Nasim for more than a week. He'd said he was too busy, but the bastard had been lying—a friend had seen him drinking in the Universalist Club four or five nights ago. Not with a woman; it was true. With a group of men.

Komarov sent her home, issued Maslov with new instructions, and told Sasha to bring him some tea. Above his head the electric fan whirred erratically, doing little more than stirring the torpid air.

Maslov returned after twenty minutes or so, bearing a large stack of reports. "We had four men in the Universalist," he said, "submitting nightly reports."

It was Maslov who found what they wanted half an hour later. Three Indians had been drinking in the Universalist on the fifteenth. With four other men. They'd been talking about conditions in India and about the relocation of a military school from Tashkent to Moscow. They'd been expressing disapproval of party policy.

"Was it our three Indians?" Komarov interrupted.

"It doesn't say."

"And the other four?"

Maslov read on. "Two well-known anarchists—Aram Shahumian and Ivan Grazhin—"

"Grazhin was the one in the morgue," Komarov said. "The one who shot himself in the street."

"The others were an American comrade, Aidan Brady, and"—Maslov looked shocked—"a party member, Sergei Piatakov."

Komarov looked up sharply. He remembered Brady from 1918, when the man had turned up at the M-Cheka office to report that his fellow American Caitlin Hanley—the woman who had later married Sergei Piatakov—was in touch with a British agent who had once been her lover.

Her taste in partners seemed somewhat at odds with her politics, but she wasn't alone in that. "Get their files," he told Maslov.

While his subordinate was doing his bidding, Komarov walked around the desk and read the report himself. On the same evening, another group of anarchists had been discussing the creation of a new language in which letters would be replaced by numbers, and the report's compiler was clearly unsure whether this was politically acceptable.

Komarov snorted his disbelief.

He returned to his chair. Piatakov, Piatakova. Seeing her at the hospital. What had she been doing there?

He could think of one possibility.

Maslov returned empty-handed. "There are no criminal files on Piatakov or Brady. There were files on Grazhin and Shahumian, but they were destroyed in the fire last year—the one the anarchists were suspected of starting."

"Piatakov will have a party file," Komarov said. "I ran into his wife a few months ago," he added; "she works for the Zhenotdel. She's on the executive committee. Get her address from them."

Maslov was gone for only a couple of minutes. "One forty-two Bolshaya Dmitrova," he reported.

"Take a car," Komarov told him. "And a couple of men just in case. Bring in whoever's there. Him, her, whomever."

THE ZHENOTDEL MEETING IN SERPUKHOVSKAYA had gone on for almost eight hours, and it was virtually dark by the time Caitlin reached home. As she'd feared and expected, no light was showing in their upstairs windows, but there was a Russo-Balt parked outside the building's entrance, and she was barely out of the Renault when two Chekists appeared to block her path.

"You will come with us," one of them said.

She sighed. "I've had a long day, comrade. Can't this wait till the morning?"

"Comrade Komarov wants to see you now."

She thought about making a scene, but what would be the point? She allowed herself to be hustled into their car, and sat in simmering silence as the Cheka driver bullied his way through the still-busy evening streets. The last time she'd taken a ride like this—in far-off

Yekaterinburg—her next ten days had been spent in a cell. What did Komarov want with her? She allowed herself a moment's hope that the summons concerned Rahima, but knew she was clutching at straws. This was about Sergei. The shirt drenched in blood.

When she was finally ushered into Komarov's office, he was on the telephone. Glancing up, he gave his caller a few instructions before putting the instrument down. "Please take a seat, comrade," he said. "I apologize for the abrupt summons, but this is an urgent matter, as I'm sure Comrade Maslov informed you."

"Comrade Maslov didn't even introduce himself," she said stonily. The young man was hovering at Komarov's shoulder, like a butler at a dinner party.

"Oh. Then I must also apologize on his behalf," Komarov said without even looking at his young subordinate.

She nodded.

"We're looking for your husband," Komarov said without more ado.

"Why?" she asked, managing to keep the tremor out of her voice.

"We need to ask him some questions."

She looked at him, remembering the trembling hand. Tonight it was still. Tonight he was working. "I don't know where he is," she said flatly. "Why do you need to question him?"

"That is not your concern," Maslov interjected.

"He's my husband," she snapped back. For better or for worse, she thought. That hadn't been part of the Soviet ceremony.

"When did you last see him, comrade?" he asked.

She thought back a moment; the last few days seemed all rolled into one. "Yesterday morning," she said. "He was still asleep when I left for work."

"What were you doing at the hospital this morning?" Komarov asked.

She looked up quickly. "How . . . We really do have spies everywhere, don't we?"

"I appreciate the 'we,' comrade, but as it happens I saw you there myself. I was visiting a militiaman who'd been shot in the tram depot robbery."

"That's what this is all about, isn't it?"

"That's part of it. You haven't answered—"

"I found a shirt covered in blood when I got home last night. I thought there must have been an accident, so . . ."

"You went to the hospital. But not until this morning."

"I went looking for him, and I ended up sleeping at the office."

"Why? Surely your husband would have come back to your room."

"I . . . I don't know. I was upset, and strange as it seems, I feel more at home at work." Komarov's face told her that struck a chord.

"But was that all?" he asked. "Did you hear about the robbery while you were out looking for him?"

"No. I didn't hear anything until this morning. A comrade who came to work early had heard about it."

"And then you guessed that your husband was involved," Komarov suggested, stroking his chin.

"You didn't report these suspicions, comrade," Maslov interjected.

She gave him a withering look, said nothing.

"That was understandable in the circumstances," Komarov said. "But now that you actually know he's committed a serious crime, I expect your full cooperation. Have you heard from him since?"

"No," she said.

"He left no goodbye message?"

"No," she repeated. The verse she'd found on the bed that morning when she dropped in to change her clothes was not a message she wanted to share with the Cheka.

"Did he ever mention any future plans?"

She shook her head. "No. He was—is—angry about the way things have been going, but if he had any particular course of action in mind he never talked to me about it."

"Did he ever speak about India?"

"India?" What mad scheme had Sergei gotten himself involved in? She remembered arriving home a week or so earlier to find him and Aram Shahumian poring over a map of the world. "No, never," she said. "Comrade Komarov, I think I have the right to know exactly what my husband has done."

He leaned back in his chair. "Yesterday evening seven men held up the tram depot on Shabolovka Street. A clerk, a Chekist and a militiaman were killed, along with two of the criminals. The five who escaped have been identified as Aidan Brady, Aram Shahumian, your husband, and two Indian comrades who are here for the congress. Last night a man was murdered in the Hotel Lux. He was a Russian, but the room he was found in belonged to one of the missing Indians and one who was killed in the robbery. I suspect that the two events are connected but haven't as yet been able to establish the connection."

She felt as though she'd been hit in the stomach.

"I believe you know some of these men . . ." Komarov said.

"I have met Aram several times—he's a Red Army comrade of Sergei's, and a friend. As you know, Aidan Brady and I have a long history—he and my brother were both involved in an Irish plot against the British right at the start of the war. I came through Siberia with Brady in 1918—we just happened to meet in Vladivostok—and I saw him a few times after that. He and Sergei met independently, and they've remained friends."

"But not you?"

"No. I haven't spoken to him since he shot that boy in Kalanchevskaya Square. The incident we talked about three years ago."

"As I recall, the boy's death was an accident."

"In my experience, those sort of accidents tend to happen around Brady." Until now she had always been on the same side as her fellow American, but she couldn't remember ever liking him. Even at their first meeting all those years ago, when Brady was still basking in the role of a workers' crusader, there'd been something not quite right about the man. Something missing.

"And did your husband ever introduce you to any Indian comrades?" Komarov asked.

"No. Never."

Komarov leaned forward, his elbows on the desk, his chin resting on his interlinked hands. "You said your husband is angry at the way things are going. Why is that? The people he's involved with—most of them are anarchists, so their resentment is understandable. But your husband is still a member of our party."

"He is a Bolshevik," she said simply. A picture of the Universalist clientele crossed her mind, denying the words.

"So are you, Comrade Piatakova, but there are obviously differences of opinion between you."

"We had—have—different views on who and what we should be fighting."

"And who do *you* think the enemy is?" Maslov asked.

She didn't bother to answer. Where had they gone? Oh, Sergei.

"Answer the question," Maslov insisted.

"Bureaucrats, careerists, and Neanderthal males," she said coldly, staring straight at him. "Is that all?" she asked, turning back to Komarov.

"Almost." He asked her for a description of Aram Shahumian, and then, almost apologetically, for one of her husband. She gave him only the barest of bones, but Komarov made no complaint. "If you hear from him, please inform me," he said formally. "Your husband has an exemplary record," he added, "both with the fleet and the army. And I would like to think a tribunal would take that into account."

Caitlin gave him an incredulous look.

"I heard a joke the other day," he said unexpectedly. "Not a particularly funny one. The essence of it was that we Bolsheviks consider ourselves magicians but we've really only mastered the first half of one particular trick. We've managed to saw the person in half but not put him back together again. Well, that's what we have to do—put Russia back together again. You and your husband are not the only people fighting for beliefs, comrade."

Several responses came to mind, but none seemed very grown-up. "I assume we're done," she said, getting to her feet.

"For the moment, yes."

Turning on her heel, she strode back across the outer office, down the grey corridors, and out into the moonlit city, where people who didn't have fugitive partners were happily going about their lives.

The Only Good Indian

"We got a bunch of contradictory sightings at the railway stations," Ruzhkov said. "Someone who looked like the American at the Kazan Station, people who might have been Indians at the Kursk Station and the Kiev Station. Nothing definite. They found Dzharova's father, but he'd put her on the train to Tashkent three days before. He knew about her Indian lover—that's why he sent her home. Caught them at it apparently."

Ruzhkov's face clouded over for an instant. Remembering catching his wife, McColl guessed.

"What really enraged him," the Russian went on, "was the man's color—it seems the party's policy on racial tolerance hasn't taken hold in Turkestan." Ruzhkov looked up, as if expecting sympathy for this ideological setback. "Anyway," he continued, "they put a call through to the Samara Cheka with instructions to hold the girl for questioning when the train arrives there. Which might be today, might be in a week's time—the railways are in chaos." He snorted with apparent amusement. "Would you believe that five whole trains have been lost since the New Year? They've completely disappeared. Vanished off the face of the earth."

Thirty-six hours had passed since McColl's first encounter with Komarov, and he was beginning to feel a little more sanguine about his chances of staying free. An optimist might have considered his situation—an unsuspected spy close to the heart of an official investigation into the very matter that had brought him to Russia—close to ideal, but as far as McColl was concerned, that would be overstating the case, and he was determined not to let down his guard. Nerves were good for you, as his school PE teacher used to say, teaching his charges how to dive into an icy loch through the stunningly simple expedient of making them walk the plank.

Wending their way through the galleries of the newly reopened history museum, McColl and Ruzhkov were entering one that housed a Mongol tent or yurt. A selection of yak-tail banners, bows, and quivers hung from the walls; displays of whistling arrows filled several glass-topped cabinets, complete with typed explanations of how the Mongols had used them in battle for transmitting tactical orders.

"Fascinating," Ruzhkov said, leaning in so close to the glass that his breath formed a circle of steam.

"So they're just waiting around?" McColl asked hopefully.

Ruzhkov straightened, holding his back. "Oh no. Deputy Chairman Komarov is not the idle sort. He has no other life, so neither do his men. When there's something big on—and there almost always is—all of them work every hour God gives. And unlike most of them, he's a real stickler for the rules. His wife died of hunger two winters ago because he wouldn't bend them to get her an extra ration. At least, that's the story, and it wouldn't surprise me. That kind of dedication is frightening."

Absurdly so, McColl thought. "So what have they been doing, then?" he asked.

"There are three things Komarov wants to know," Ruzhkov said, ticking them off on his fingers. "Who the Russian was, where the American and his friends were living, and what it's all about. He grilled all our men who were undercover at the Universalist, but they weren't very helpful. All the turncoats talked about was India and some new Menshevik named Gandhi. Have you heard of him?"

"I have," McColl said. He had actually met the man twice, once over twenty years before when Gandhi and another Indian medical orderly had carried him down on a stretcher from the Spion Kop plateau, the second time in 1915 when he'd stopped to visit Gandhi's ashram in Ahmedabad on his way home from Calcutta. But this didn't seem the time for reminiscing.

"Well, the men in this group went on and on about him. And they don't like him one bit. The Indians in particular."

"Why not?" McColl asked.

Ruzhkov shrugged. "Because he's a Menshevik, I suppose. You know what they were like—they talked a good revolution, but they didn't really want much to change." Ruzhkov rubbed his eyes. "But I wouldn't rely too much on any of this. The men we had there were not the brightest."

"We" was now the Cheka—Ruzhkov had trouble with personal pronouns. "So that was all—India and Gandhi?"

"That was all."

They were now perusing an intricate re-creation of a battle—the one fought beside the Kalka River in 1223, according to the inscription. The model river itself was full of finely crafted corpses and patches of red staining. "The Mongols never shed the blood of princes," Ruzhkov said. "So they rolled the Prince of Kiev in a carpet and suffocated him." He giggled.

India and Gandhi, McColl was thinking. What were these men planning?

"Last night our men raided the Universalist," Ruzhkov was saying. "Took about fifty people in. They're still interrogating them," Ruzhkov said. "They've found out the American lived in Serpukhovskaya, but no one seems to know exactly where. They're making street inquiries as well."

"They haven't discovered anything about the Russian who died at the Lux?"

"Not a thing. He could have come from the moon."

"And the others in the group?"

"They know who they are. An Armenian named Aram Shahumian and a Russian named Sergei Piatakov. Both served with Brady in the Red Army back in 1918."

"What else can you tell me about Komarov?"

"He's a really big wheel, very close to Dzerzhinsky. Komarov was a policeman before he joined the Bolshevik underground, and it's said that the two of them met in Yauzskaya police station when Dzerzhinsky was brought in under arrest. Komarov's father was a minor clerk in some ministry, nothing grand. His wife died a year or so ago, and they never had any children. They say only Dzerzhinsky and Yakov Peters have signed more death warrants, but Dzerzhinsky and Komarov have been trying to persuade the party leadership to abolish the death penalty again. Maybe they both have writer's cramp. Maybe . . . It's a madhouse, you know, an absolute madhouse. Do you know what I had to arrange yesterday? There's some idiot wandering around the city at night painting white flowers on doors, and we can't catch him. So my boss decided we should get a painter of our own, and have him go around and overpaint them in red. If that isn't crazy, what is?"

SHE WAS ALONE AND HARD at work when he entered the office, and so absorbed that she became aware of his presence only when a shadow loomed across the desk. She looked up, felt a lump in her throat.

"No, we haven't found him," Komarov said, searching for somewhere to sit. He chose the edge of Fanya's desk, perching there like a vulture, she thought. Since their last meeting she'd asked several comrades about him, but only one had met him, more than seven years earlier, at a clandestine meeting in 1914 of the Bolshevik underground network in Moscow. According to the witness, Komarov hadn't said much, but those that did had often looked his way, as if seeking his approval.

He had a way of making Caitlin feel out of her depth, which both intrigued and annoyed her. "What do you want then?" she asked briskly. "I'm very busy this morning."

"This won't take long. Have you remembered anything since we spoke that might help us locate your husband?"

"No."

"Would you tell me if you had?"

The question threw her for a moment, partly because it seemed absurdly playful, partly because she wasn't sure of her answer. "Of course," she said, with only the faintest hint of sarcasm.

He smiled and changed tack. "Would you say your husband was a believer in permanent revolution, comrade?"

She considered. "We're all waiting for new revolutions to help make ours more secure," she said primly.

"Some of us are getting used to the idea that we shall have to survive on our own," Komarov responded dryly, "but that is not what I meant. There are some comrades, respected comrades, who argue that we can only avoid going into reverse by running faster and faster."

"What a strange image," she said, finally putting down her pen. "Did you come here for an ideological discussion, comrade?"

"Not really. Enlightenment perhaps." He kneaded his jaw with his thumb and forefinger. "I like to understand the crimes I investigate. And why they are committed."

"To help you catch the criminals?"

"In part. But I also just like things explained. Though as someone reminded me recently, to explain is not to excuse."

"Could there be any excuse for what Sergei and his friends have done?" she asked. "You told me that five men had died already, three of them innocent. And heaven knows how many more will if Aidan Brady's the one in charge."

"Our Russia's knee-deep in dead men," he said.

"Does that make any difference?"

He looked at the floor for several moments. "I really don't know," he said. "It shouldn't, but it has to. Groups of Bolsheviks committed crimes like this in the years before the revolution and probably for much the same reason—a need of funds to further their political ends. And though we said we regretted any loss of life, we saluted the deed and welcomed the money and half-believed that no one who got in our way could be completely innocent. These men—your husband and the others—I assume they feel the same. And, if by some miracle they overthrow the party and set up their own government, the crime they committed the other day won't just be excused—it'll become a glorious chapter in their new revolution's history."

"But they won't succeed," Caitlin said.

"No, they won't. But losing doesn't make them wrong, merely on the wrong side of the law."

"Your law."

"The party's law, comrade. Someone has to decide what is permitted and what is not," he said matter-of-factly, easing himself off the desk, "and for us it can only be the party."

The telephone rang. It was for him. She walked across to the window, looked out on the sunlit street, listened to him repeat an address in Serpukhovskaya.

"We've found the room where your husband's comrades were living," he told her. "And the five are now six. An Indian," he added quickly, obviously noticing her alarm. "I am sorry. I will inform you myself if your husband is found."

Before or after having him shot? she wondered, as the click of Komarov's heels faded on the stairs.

THE HOUSE IN SERPUKHOVSKAYA WAS an old one, and the single bourgeois family who'd occupied it before the revolution had given way to ten or more families living in single or paired rooms. The children playing in the stairwell fell silent as the Cheka men climbed, then burst back into noisy life the moment they reached the room at the top. Komarov could smell the corpse from outside the door; the Indian was laid out on one of three old mattresses.

This face was locked in terror.

"Take him to the morgue," Komarov told two of his subordinates after taking a long look. He went to the window for a gulp of fresh air and stood there for a moment, enjoying the view across the rooftops, before turning to examine the room.

There was a three-legged table and a homemade brick stove, its ramshackle pipe chimney disappearing through a rough-hewn gap in the roof. A rusty typewriter sat on a cupboard that had lost all its drawers. Taken for fuel, Komarov assumed, like the missing floorboards in the corner; over the last three winters Moscow rooms had been turned into stage sets by the hunger for wood. On one raid earlier that year, they'd found a room with three armchairs, each positioned over a neatly cut hole in the floor.

He stirred the ashes in the stove—nothing. He lifted each mattress, and under the third found a scrunched-up piece of paper bearing the words *Gone to Library.* The American, Komarov decided. There was something about the large scrawl that suggested a foreigner.

"Nothing," Maslov muttered.

"On the contrary," Komarov said, passing him the piece of paper.

"How does that help us?"

"Think," Komarov suggested.

Maslov thought. "If we find the library, we might get a better description," he said sceptically.

Komarov sighed. "If we find the library, we might find out what they're planning."

Maslov looked at him blankly.

"If you were planning to cause some trouble, in a place that you didn't know well, you would probably do some research."

SEVERAL MILES TO THE NORTH, McColl heaved himself up and over a brick wall. What had been a garden was now a jungle, and as he waited for his eyes to adjust to the darkness, he could hear the animal population taking evasive action. Which was all to the good. Those quadrupeds that had survived the last few winters in Moscow would have sharp reflexes and even sharper teeth.

The back door of the house sprung open at a touch. He stepped inside, heard the scamper of more tiny feet, and carefully worked his way toward the front, where a faint yellow light shone through the glassless window above the boarded entrance.

The front room was similarly lit and empty but for a large framed painting of a white country house, which hung drunkenly askew on the wall to his left. Most of the floorboards had been cut from the floor, leaving what looked like a series of runs for the rats.

The back room was completely dark, so he decided to risk a match.

The flare revealed a hundred square feet of functioning civilization: a bed, a chair, a table bearing books, an oil lamp, and a crust of bread. There was a threadbare carpet on the floor and heavy curtains pulled across the window.

McColl lit the lamp and started to search.

It took about twenty minutes—a notebook and papers were

stashed beneath a loose floorboard. He doused the lamp and left the same way he'd arrived, dropping into the darkened alley behind the row of houses and emerging back onto Bogoslovski Street. Thirty minutes later he was back in his room at the Hotel Lux, the door wedged shut, his find spread across the bed. Suvorov had possessed seven sets of false identity papers.

The notebook contained a series of messages, coded on the left-hand pages, decoded on the right. The last of these was longer than most. McColl read it through twice, then sat staring into space, stroking his lower lip with his little finger. It was more than a little unnerving to see the order for his own elimination written out in black and white, particularly when the writer was supposedly on the same side.

Not that he had a side anymore, but the bastards at Five didn't know that.

McColl had been surprised and vaguely amused by Cumming's original request to check on a Five operation in Russia. What sort of idiots spent their time and energy on supposed enemy soil plotting against their own compatriots? It had seemed absurd, still did. He'd agreed to come only because of Brady's involvement.

And because it got him out of Wormwood Scrubs.

So. What was Five planning? It had to be something unusually important—or unusually sordid—for Kell's people to declare open season on the Service. Or to even consider using someone like Brady.

But what?

He went back to the earlier messages in the notebook. Most of the recent ones concerned an operation styled "Good Indian."

He remembered Ruzhkov reporting that Brady's Indian comrades were not enamored of Gandhi. Could that be what they and Five had in common?

What was that phrase that the US general had coined? That the only good Indian was a dead one?

KOMAROV HAD IMAGINED THAT THERE were about ten libraries still functioning in the city; there turned out to be more than fifty. Since the spring they had been rising phoenix-like from the

ashes of the civil war, their book stocks preserved with a fanaticism
that Dzerzhinsky would struggle to match. Maslov, of course, found
only irritation in the unexpected scope of the search, but Komarov,
staring out of his office window at the fierce summer rain sweeping
across the courtyard, felt rather pleased; on any list of civilization's
prerequisites, he thought, public libraries would come higher than
most. It was a sign that the revolution could be normalized, that the
best of the past would still have a place in the new society.

It took his men slightly over thirty-six hours to track down Brady's
library.

Both women on duty that afternoon remembered the American comrade, and yes, he had been consulting books on India
and Central Asia: accounts of journeys, of the Russian conquest of
Turkestan; historical and political studies of the British Empire in
India; even some ancient histories of the general area. He'd always
been most courteous.

"They're headed for India then," Maslov said as the car carried
them back to the M-Cheka offices. It was still raining, but with none
of the morning's vigor.

"Apparently," Komarov muttered.

"Then our job is over. It's just a matter of alerting Tashkent and
the Frontier Cheka."

Komarov wondered if Maslov had any idea how long the relevant
frontier was. "Perhaps," he said mildly.

A message was waiting on his desk: the train carrying Marusya
Dzharova had finally reached Samara. The two men went up to
the wireless telephone room and waited patiently while the operator connected them with the Volga city. Once established, the line
was remarkably clear: Vitaly Kozorov, the chairman of the Samara
Cheka, sounded as if he might be in the building next door.

"She's not a hundred percent sure, but she thinks they're all
headed for Tashkent," he told them. He went over exactly what the
woman had said.

"Thank you, comrade," Komarov said. "Hold on to her until you
hear from me, will you?"

"That seems to clinch it," Maslov said with evident satisfaction.

Komarov wasn't listening. He had just put two and two together—the interpreter turning up from Tashkent, conveniently speaking both Urdu and English, just as the foreign agent had disappeared. Tall and dark and wearing a shabby suit.

The man had shaved off his beard.

It might conceivably be a coincidence, but that didn't seem likely and wouldn't be hard to check. Once Maslov was gone, Komarov summoned Sasha. "Get onto Tashkent," Komarov told him, "and find out if they've heard of Nikolai Davydov. He claims to be a party member. And Sasha," he added as the young man headed for the door, "keep this between the two of us."

Alone again, Komarov walked across to his window and stared out at the empty yard. The people involved in this affair seemed connected in so many ways. Brady and Piatakov's wife had known each other before she met Piatakov, but had obviously fallen out years before—it was Brady who had come to the Cheka in 1918 to report her being in touch with a known English agent.

Could that have been Davydov? There was no reason to think so. Three years had passed, and according to Piatakova—whose loyalty to the revolution seemed beyond question—her former lover had already quit the British Secret Service when she saw him back then. The alternative version—that she had been a spy for all that time—seemed preposterous. But he supposed it was possible.

Whoever Davydov was, unless Komarov was much mistaken, the man was involved in this business in some way or another. As for the renegades, they were on their way to India, a bunch of crazed Quixotes intent on torching English windmills.

He would get permission from Dzerzhinsky to go after them and—assuming Davydov wasn't who he said he was—take both him and Piatakova along for the ride, one as his interpreter, the other as the only person who could, in the absence of any photographs, identify Piatakov and Shahumian. And he would watch them both like a hawk for any telltale signs of a common purpose.

THE CLERK REPLACED THE DESK telephone and swung open the bookcase, allowing Komarov into the short secret passage that led through to Felix Dzerzhinsky's office. The Vecheka chairman was sitting behind his huge desk, looking, as usual, as if he'd been working for days on end. The eyes glittered; the cheeks were flushed; his gesture of welcome seemed stiff with fatigue.

"Success?" he asked expectantly.

"Up to a point," Komarov said, taking the opposite seat. He ran through the history of the investigation, concluding with the news from Samara.

"Yuri Vladimirovich, you've been enjoying yourself," Dzerzhinsky said with mock disapproval.

"I'm afraid I have."

"How effective are these men, do you think?" Dzerzhinsky asked after a pause.

"Very, I should say. Though they did make a mess of the depot robbery."

"Bad luck, perhaps," Dzerzhinsky suggested. "But they seem like enemies we could well do without." He tapped his pen on the desk. "Enemies," he repeated, as if he was testing the concept's viability. "I'm not at all sure the commission in Tashkent will be able to stop them. Yakov Peters doesn't have the manpower, and without photographs . . ."

"I agree."

"We could just let them go," Dzerzhinsky mused, leaning back in his chair. "A group of seasoned revolutionaries, some of whom fought with great distinction against the Whites, now carrying the banner of world revolution south into India . . . I could write the eulogy myself. *And* they'd be out of our hair."

Komarov smiled. "All true," he agreed. "But they're also renegades and murderers."

"And they wouldn't be out of our hair," Dzerzhinsky went on morosely. "They'll do something in India, probably something dramatic enough to get the English screaming mad. Then we'll either have to disown them, and look like liars or imbeciles, or say nothing at all, and look like we're breaking the treaty. Bad propaganda either way." He stared gloomily at the ceiling, then looked at Komarov. "I'm just rehearsing Zinoviev's arguments for him. If that was all, I'd let them go, and to hell with the English. But it isn't, is it?"

"We can't afford renegades anymore," Komarov said.

"Exactly. While our survival was in doubt, the Chekas had to act as an instrument of victory. But now that we've won, our only possible justification is to serve as an instrument of justice. And we must be seen to be so. I want these men caught."

Komarov nodded.

"You must go after them, in person. They have a few days' start, but that means nothing with the state the railways are in. And, as I remember it, traveling with false papers tends to slow a man down." He smiled at the memory. "Take Maslov and however many men you think you need."

"I'd like to take Piatakova."

Dzerzhinsky looked surprised, then vaguely amused.

"She has some influence over her husband, and she can recognize two of the other men involved. We have no pictures of them," Komarov added in explanation. "But she won't be willing, and she has powerful friends."

Dzerzhinsky offered up one of his famous sardonic smiles. "Not as powerful as mine," he said, standing and shaking Komarov's hand.

The latter could still see the smile as he walked back through the building; like a Soviet version of the Cheshire cat's, it seemed to hang in the corridors of the Vecheka headquarters, a comment on all it surveyed. Komarov felt sorry for its owner and knew that he was also feeling sorry for himself. "A time to kill, a time to heal," he murmured. Or all the killing would have been for nothing. He felt his right hand twitch and put it in his pocket. Why did the body take the mind so literally?

As he walked back down Bolshaya Lubyanka to the M-Cheka building he recalled the occasion two New Years ago when Dzerzhinsky had drunk far too much at a Kremlin celebration, buttonholed several party leaders, and insisted on being shot for spilling so much blood. The luminaries in question had been patronizing, embarrassed, angry, anything in fact but understanding. Komarov had been furious with them and all the other fools who thought that signing death warrants entailed no emotional cost. He still was.

Maslov was a convenient scapegoat. "Kazan Station," Komarov barked at the young Ukrainian. "Arrange for an extra coach on the next Tashkent train. If it's leaving today, then tell them to hold it. But don't use the telephone. Sort it out at the station, and there'll be less chance of a foul-up. And get hold of that interpreter with the Indian delegation—tell him he's coming with us and should be ready at a moment's notice. We need an interpreter and someone who knows Tashkent," he explained, noticing Maslov's look of confusion. "And this man's both. I'm off to the Zhenotdel."

The stroll to Vozdvizhenka Street proved enjoyable, the interview less so.

"You must be joking," Caitlin Piatakova said when he told her what was required.

"This is not a comic situation, comrade," Komarov said. They were alone in one of the upstairs rooms, but he guessed that some of her colleagues had their ears pressed to the walls.

"You expect me to travel to Turkestan, at a moment's notice . . . It can take a month to get there and back. I have work to do, Comrade Komarov. Party work. Important work. No, I will not 'accompany' you."

Komarov ran a hand through his hair. He would have preferred voluntary cooperation. "Does it not concern you, Comrade Piatakova, that your husband is doing his best to create difficulties for our party?"

"Of course it does," she said coldly. "But I am not his keeper. The Zhenotdel," she added caustically, "is not an organization for keeping husbands to the party line."

"The Zhenotdel," he said quietly, "is doing a great deal of work in Turkestan. Oh yes," he said, acknowledging her look of surprise, "we do notice the odd development here and there whenever we have time off from persecuting poets. For example, at your conference two weeks ago, several women from Turkestan walked onto the platform and tore off their veils for the audience. There was an argument on your executive committee as to whether this constituted genuine agitprop or was merely a cheap theatrical gesture. You supported the former proposition. There is also much anxiety at the moment as to whether Kollontai's involvement with the Workers' Opposition is damaging the Zhenotdel."

"And is it?" she asked. "Damaging—"

"Of course it is. Even in our party most people find it difficult to separate the cause and the person."

"Are you trying to frighten me, comrade?" she asked.

"No, I am not. I am trying to show you that the Chekas are not full of fools who have nothing better to do than find ways of wasting your time. This is an important matter, comrade. If your presence were not necessary, I would not be here." And how true was that? he wondered, even as he said it.

She looked far from mollified. "If I accept that—and I suppose I must—what you've just told me about the problems the Zhenotdel faces makes it all the more crucial that I remain in Moscow."

Komarov was beginning to wish he'd sent Maslov to collect her. "Perhaps," he said, "but this is not a request. Like any member of the party, you are subject to party discipline. I understand your reluctance, and I sympathize with your position, but you must come with us. And if for any reason this business keeps us away for more than a couple of weeks, there must be Zhenotdel work to do in Turkestan."

She gave him a furious look and slowly shook her head, but offered no further protest. She would, he thought, be angry for quite some time.

KOMAROV HAD BEEN BACK IN his office for a few minutes when Sasha appeared in the doorway, a bemused expression on his face.

"Tashkent knows nothing of an interpreter named Nikolai Davydov. Or of any local party member with that name. The only Davydov in their records is a retired soldier who grows fruit just outside the city. He's almost sixty and has no children."

Komarov nodded. "Don't mention this to anyone else."

"No, comrade." Sasha turned to leave, but his curiosity wouldn't let him. "So who is the Davydov here in Moscow?"

"A good question."

"You're not going to have him arrested?"

"Not for the moment. I think he'll be more useful free."

ONCE KOMAROV HAD LEFT, CAITLIN sat there fuming for several minutes, then went to tell Fanya what had happened.

"We guessed," her friend said. "We couldn't hear everything he said, but we didn't really need to. Are you going to ask Kollontai to use her influence?"

"I'm not sure she has that much at the moment," Caitlin said. "And what she has she should probably save for a better cause." She gave Fanya a rueful smile. "I always wanted to see Turkestan, and now it seems I shall."

"As part of a Cheka hunting party," Fanya noted.

"I know, but that was the reason I stopped arguing with him. If they do catch Sergei, I might be able to help him if I'm there. Not that he'll thank me."

"When are you leaving?"

"Whenever the Cheka and the railways decide. Which could be an hour from now, so I'd better go home and pack some clothes."

MCCOLL WAS DOZING ON HIS bed when the thunderous knock on the door woke him with a heart-sinking start. Fearing the worst, he opened the door and had his fears confirmed. Two hard-faced young Chekists pushed him back into the room, their pistols gleaming in polished holsters. It was the imperial throne room all over again, only this time it was him they had come for.

"Get your things," one Chekist said curtly. "You're coming with us," he added superfluously.

One glance told McColl that questions, let alone protests, would fall on the deafest of ears. But as he obeyed their single instruction, he also found hope in the thought that captured spies were probably not invited to pack for a future.

All he had with him were a change of clothes and a couple of books, and once these were in the suitcase, the Chekists hustled him downstairs and out. The looks he received from fellow guests—sympathetic and sternly judgmental in almost equal parts—were hardly reassuring.

A car was waiting at the hotel entrance, a young and unfamiliar driver behind the wheel, an unsmiling Maslov sitting beside him. The two Chekists who'd collected him from his room loaded McColl into the rear seat and smartly stepped back. They obviously knew the driver, whose breakneck departure took no account of the lake created by that morning's torrential rain and succeeded in drenching several less prescient passersby. Curses fading in its wake, the Russo-Balt headed up Tverskaya Street.

"Where are we going?" McColl asked, trying to sound like a man among comrades.

"You've been reassigned," Maslov told him. "The deputy chairman has urgent business in Tashkent, and he's asked for you as his interpreter."

"Asked" was probably not the right word, McColl thought, but he still felt a whole lot better than he had five minutes earlier. Tashkent might prove a problem, but there was no obvious reason for Komarov to check his bona fides when they got there, and he knew the city well enough from the months he'd spent there on Secret Service business in the summer and autumn of 1916. "What about the Indian delegation?" he asked Maslov, thinking a query would be expected.

Maslov didn't bother to answer.

McColl leaned back in the seat and let his body relax. It had turned into yet another beautiful day. The golden cupolas hung like decorations in the clear blue sky; the pastel buildings were brightly reflected in the puddles that had gathered in the hollows of unrepaired pavements and streets. The long line of tree stumps down the center of the boulevard reminded McColl of how lovely the city had been before the usual sources of fuel ran out.

On Kamergersky Street a crowd spilling out of an old church caused the Cheka driver to snort with derision and mumble something insulting. Most of the worshippers stopped on the steps as the car drove by; like a cat on a wall watching a dog pass below, they were not so much anxious as ready to be so.

"Mother wants to know how long you'll be gone," the driver said, revealing himself as Maslov's brother.

"Tell her I've no idea," Maslov said.

"You don't sound very keen on this trip."

Maslov grunted. "I don't even know why we're going. As far as I can see, it's a job for our men in Tashkent."

"It's just you and Komarov going?"

"And our interpreter here. And the wife."

"Komarov's?"

Maslov laughed. "No, Piatakov's. The American woman who works for the Zhenotdel. She knows Brady too."

In the back seat, McColl's heart skipped several beats.

"Why are you taking her along?" the brother asked.

"Who knows? I sometimes think Komarov fancies her."

"A looker, is she?"

"I suppose so. I don't imagine she'd be much fun."

McColl was only half-listening by this time. There might be other American women working for the Zhenotdel, but surely none with a connection to Aidan Brady. Caitlin Hanley, the young American journalist he'd met in China at the end of 1913. The woman he'd fallen in love with and then betrayed by agreeing to investigate her Irish republican family. Who'd given him the second chance he hardly deserved, then whisked the rug from under his feet by putting her politics first and choosing to stay in Lenin's Russia.

It had to be her. And she was married.

And why not? he asked himself, trying to ignore the sense of emptiness the news provoked. Three years had passed. Lots of time to meet other men, to fall in love, to plan a life together. Why shouldn't she be married?

More to the point, he told herself, he and she were about to renew their fractured acquaintance.

How ridiculous was that? A week in Moscow praying that he wouldn't run into her, and here they were, booked on to the very same train, for a journey that would certainly last several days, and maybe even weeks.

Which was not his most pressing problem. Her initial reaction might be the death of him, if Komarov or Maslov was there to witness it. She'd be as shocked as he was now, but without the time to rehearse a response.

She might of course choose to give him away, and he wasn't sure he'd blame her if she did. The last time they'd met he'd told her he was quitting the Service, and the only conclusion she could feasibly draw from his undercover reappearance was that he'd either had a change of heart or been telling bare-faced lies.

If she did give him up on the spot, there'd be nothing he could do about it, but—fool that he might well be—he still found it hard to believe that she would. Giving him away accidentally seemed the more likely outcome.

What could he do to prevent it?

The car was approaching Kalanchevskaya Square, the home to three of Moscow's stations. It was almost empty, unlike the day three years before when Brady had shot and killed Fedya, and McColl had managed to lose his pursuers in the milling crowd. The memory still made his blood run cold, but he forced his mind back to the present—getting himself caught or killed wouldn't bring back the boy.

As they pulled up outside the Kazan Station entrance, McColl looked for her and Komarov, but neither was there. On the platform, then. If he and Caitlin came face-to-face with witnesses present, McColl just had to hope she was willing and able to conceal the shock. If fate was kind and that didn't happen, he would have to find some way of announcing his presence in private.

The concourse was crowded, the Tashkent train at the farthest platform. "The three red cars at the front," a Chekist at the gate told Maslov, pointing him down a long line of dark green coaches. High on the wall beyond the train, a series of futuristic posters announced the delights of the Moscow Circus.

The rear coaches were crowded with Red Army soldiers— around a battalion's worth, McColl reckoned. Ahead of these were two flat trucks bearing mounted machine guns surrounded by sandbags. Five or six coaches for ordinary civilians followed, then a third flat truck, two box vans, an antique-looking dining car in faded green and gold, and finally, reaching beyond the end of the platform, the promised red carriages. Outside the first a suited man with a neat brown beard was smoking with a leather-coated Chekist, and in one of the windows behind him, a woman was stretching up to place a suitcase on a rack, emphasizing the trimness of her figure.

It wasn't Caitlin.

Komarov was standing alone by the door of the second vermillion coach, checking his watch and looking impatient. There was no familiar face in the windows behind him.

Was the Cheka boss waiting for her? McColl certainly hoped so. After Komarov had acknowledged him with a nod and told him that his was the end compartment, he manfully resisted the temptation to turn and look back down the platform.

Stepping up into the vestibule, he walked cautiously on past the attendant's cubicle and into a long and unpopulated saloon full of upholstered chairs and highly polished tables. There was a stove in one corner, a well-stocked bookcase along one partition wall. The Cheka apparently traveled in style.

He walked on through to the front carriage, which contained half a dozen compartments, each with a seat-cum-berth, collapsible table, and basin. His luck was in, McColl realized, closing the door. He could hide himself away until he knew which compartment she was in.

Which of course proved easier said than done—he had to stand with one ear pressed against the door for more than half an hour before he heard footsteps in the corridor outside. And then the voice, the faintest of American accents edging the excellent Russian as she thanked whoever it was who had carried her luggage.

Feelings welled up inside him, feelings he couldn't deal with now.

He opened his compartment door and cautiously leaned his head out into the empty corridor. The third door along was closed, all the others open.

A step across to the window told him Komarov and Maslov were still on the platform. Should he go and see her now, and hope that the two Chekists would still be there when he reemerged? Or should he wait and hope for some safer moment? It occurred to him that Komarov might want to introduce them to each other.

Now would be better, but he would have to be quick, and there was so much to explain. A note, he thought. He would write one and push it under her door.

It took him five minutes to work out what he needed to say and how best to say it. The corridor was still empty, the Chekists still on the platform. McColl walked quietly to her door, squatted to slip the note under, and then had second thoughts. He told himself he had to be sure she was in there, that no one else would read the message. And he wanted to see her.

He rapped on the door with one hand, and pushed down on the handle with the other, hoping she hadn't locked it. She hadn't.

"What—" she began, then realized it was him. "Jack!" she said, her initial look of utter surprise giving way to a gamut of other emotions, anger foremost among them.

"I want you to read this," he said quickly, offering her the note. "Before you do anything drastic," he added.

"But—"

"I'll talk to you later," he promised, backing out through the door and pulling it shut. A few seconds later he was in his own compartment hoping he wouldn't hear her leaving hers. Several agonizing minutes passed in silence, which presumably meant she was reading the note. Several more went by, leaving him pretty sure that she wasn't about to betray him. Not without giving him time to explain.

He laid himself out on the long seat, hands behind his head, listening to the bustle of activity outside. She looked different, he thought. The girl had gone, at least for the moment. The green eyes and chestnut hair both seemed duller, her complexion even paler than he remembered it. Living as a Bolshevik these last three years hadn't done much for her physical health.

But there was that feeling again, glowing inside him against all reason.

He knew what he should do. He should slip off the train while it was still in the station, somehow get back to Petrograd, and get himself over the Finnish border as quickly as he could. He hadn't completed the mission, but once he'd reported all he knew and guessed, Cumming should find it easy enough to intercept Brady and his renegade partners.

So what was stopping him? The prospect of sharing a long train journey with an enemy who was smarter than he was? Not to mention the love of his life, whom he'd barely gotten over, and who he'd just discovered was married to someone else.

He'd be facing a firing squad or a rebroken heart. Quite possibly both.

Look on the bright side, he told himself. He hadn't died in the war like Mac; he hadn't succumbed to the flu like his brother. He was already living on borrowed time.

She might have broken his heart three years ago, but the damned thing was just about mended, and probably needed retesting. She might be married now, but the fact that her husband was one of the men they were hunting suggested the marriage had seen better days.

And then there was Fedya and Brady. Reason enough, he'd thought, when agreeing to the job. It still was.

A last adventure, he thought, and if he survived, he would try something different. He was almost forty, but these days that wasn't so old. He would do something with the years he often felt he didn't deserve, those years that Jed and Fedya would never get to live. Something grounded in kindness rather than cruelty. Something that wasn't a game played by boys in adult bodies.

Outside a whistle shrieked, and a few moments later the train staggered into motion. He moved himself next to the window and, for the next fifteen minutes, watched Moscow's bedraggled suburbs slide past. Soon they were steaming past scattered farmsteads and gentle birch-covered hills, the occasional dacha set beside a dull brown stream, an old manorial house clinging to a lee slope, surrounded by tall, waving trees. Of people the land seemed curiously empty—already the train seemed headed into a void, into that vastness where the Mongol arrows had whistled, south and east toward desert wastes and cerulean domes.

Sorochinsk

It had been light for over an hour, and the other occupants of the carriage seemed to be sleeping. Caitlin had already visited the kitchen three cars down, and sweet-talked the cook into bringing meals to her compartment. She would still have to leave her sanctum when nature called, but not for anything else.

She picked up the note and read it again. *"Dear Caitlin,"* it began, *"I know that finding we're both on this train will be a shock. It certainly was for me. And I'm sure that your first assumption—an understandable one considering our past—was that I'm here on some anti-Bolshevik mission. This is not the case. I'm here in Russia as a personal favor to my old boss. It's all about Indians plotting something in India and has nothing to do with the Bolshevik government. In fact, as far as I can tell, your government has as much interest in foiling this plot as I do. If we can meet casually—on the platform at one of the stops might be best—I will explain the whole business and try to answer any questions you might have. After that—after we've officially met, so to speak—then we should be able to share the odd cup of tea without raising any suspicions. Love, Jack."*

She put the letter down again. She should tear it up, she thought. Throw the pieces out of the window.

She believed him. Or would it be more accurate to say that she didn't think he was telling deliberate lies? The last time he'd appeared like a jack-in-the-box he'd said much the same, only to later admit that he'd been fooling himself. Was he doing that again?

He was right about one thing—it had been a shock. Her life at the moment felt like a stream of unwelcome surprises: Sergei caught up in robbery and worse, the Zhenotdel under threat, Komarov virtually kidnapping her. And now Jack McColl appearing out of the blue, Jack who she'd thought was safely locked in the past.

Russia might be getting a breathing space, but her own life was being turned every which way.

"If it's drowning you're after, don't torment yourself with shallow waters." Where had that come from? It was something Aunt Orla had been fond of saying many, many years ago, when Caitlin was a child.

A brave heart, her aunt had called her the last time she'd been home. And maybe sometimes she was. But not at this moment. Her first instinct now was to hide herself away, to keep herself locked in the cabin until they reached wherever it was they were going. She had brought along a suitcase full of work, so why not make use of the time?

She opened the case, took a long look at the contents, and clicked the clasps shut once more. For the moment at least, it felt like news from a foreign country, one whose language she could barely speak.

The hours passed slowly, and she kept dozing off, often waking with a start when the train jerked into motion. It seemed to be stopping at every settlement it came to and spending more time stationary than moving. At several of the stops, she caught glimpses of McColl through the gap between her curtains, usually alone but sometimes talking with other passengers. There was something different about him, but she couldn't put her finger on exactly what it was. There was sadness there; he carried himself as if something were pressing down on his shoulders. Maybe he always had, but it wasn't how she remembered him.

He was doubtless waiting for her to come and join him, but she wasn't ready to engage with him again, not over this or anything else. And the thought of seeing him day after day—sharing "the odd cup of tea," for God's sake—was more than her not-so-brave heart could cope with.

Nor had she any desire to socialize with Komarov or his wretched assistant. They might be on the same side, they might all agree that Brady and Sergei should pay for their crimes, but relishing the hunt wasn't something she could share. Caitlin was afraid that she'd be standing over her husband's corpse before all this ended, and however far apart they'd grown, that would never feel right.

Just see it through, she told herself. And then get back to your job.

McCOLL TOOK A SIP FROM his tumbler of vodka, stared at his reflection in the glass, and realized that the train had stopped yet again. He walked out to the vestibule and pushed his head through the open window in search of an explanation. There was none to see: beyond the orange glow thrown out by the engine fires there was nothing but darkness, no station, no signal, no dwellings.

It had been a long and frustrating day. Earlier that evening one of the drivers had told him that the train had traveled only eighty miles since leaving Moscow almost thirty hours before. Since then, it had probably managed another five. A walker setting off when they had would be quite a way ahead.

He'd seen no sign of Caitlin. At every one of the all-too-frequent stops, he'd strode up and down the platform hoping she would join him, but all to no avail. The good news was that she hadn't betrayed him—if she had, he'd be in irons. The bad news was that seeing her after all this time had upset him more than he'd expected, awakening thoughts and feelings he'd hoped were dead and buried.

Things would be better, more real, he thought, once a past was not the only thing they had in common. But that could only happen if she came out to talk.

He heard footsteps behind him and knew they weren't hers.

It was Komarov, bearing a bottle and chess set. "Do you play?" the Russian asked.

"Badly," McColl replied. Playing chess with the Cheka didn't seem like the wisest of moves.

"Then we're well matched," Komarov said, ignoring McColl's lack of enthusiasm. He sat himself down in the opposite chair, smoothed out a checkered square of cloth, and began extracting wooden pieces from the lacquered box.

McColl felt bound to acquiesce. He hadn't played chess for years. His uncle had taught him originally, on winter evenings in the parlor of the Polmadie house, and he had made his first friends at Oxford through the chess club, one of the few university institutions that hadn't seemed to require a blood certificate as qualification for membership. Most of those friends had been Jews, fellow outcasts at that shrine of good breeding.

Komarov was holding out his fists. McColl picked white and began. As he moved his pawn forward, the train lurched into motion again.

At first they played mostly in silence. McColl was pleased to find that the Russian took the game no more seriously than he did, simply enjoying the mental exercise. He offered grunts of appreciation when McColl made a good move and self-deprecating laughs when it was obvious he himself had made a bad one. He won nevertheless, and offered a rematch. McColl was about to decline when he realized that he was actually enjoying himself. And that more than five minutes had passed since he'd thought about Caitlin.

While setting up the pieces for the next game, the Russian casually slipped in a question. How had McColl come to learn a language like Urdu when so few people spoke it in his native Turkestan?

"More than you might think," McColl answered calmly, though his heart seemed to be beating a trifle faster. "My father had a large cotton plantation," he went on, "and his manager was from the Punjab. In India. My mother was ill a great deal, and this man's wife was like a cross between a nanny and a governess to me. I learned a lot of Urdu from her, and when I went to school in Tashkent, I found I had a knack for languages. So I carried on with the Urdu as well as learning Uzbek and a little Farsi."

"I see," Komarov said, raising his eyes after placing the final pawn.

He seemed satisfied with the explanation, and McColl could see no reason why he shouldn't be.

"My first move, I believe."

"It is."

McColl was wondering how wise it would be to inquire after Komarov's past when the Russian introduced it himself, albeit from a curious angle.

"Have you heard of Sherlock Holmes?" Komarov asked.

"I don't think so," McColl said after studying the board for several nerve-steadying seconds.

"He is an English detective. Not a real one, a storybook character. An amateur detective, I should say, not connected with the English police, Scotland Yard. There are many stories, though I believe the author stopped writing them some years ago. If so, a great pity. They are all in Russian translations—you should read them." He stopped to consider his next move, then brought out his queen's bishop. "I first read them in, oh, about 1906, when I was a young policeman in Moscow." He looked up. "And though I shouldn't say so, they probably influenced me more than Marx."

McColl showed appropriate surprise. Was the Russian a little drunk?

"The stories," Komarov continued, "taught me that detection was both an art and a science. Which made me want to be a detective. They also helped my political education, though of course the author had no such intention. You see, Sherlock Holmes is a classic bourgeois creation—a razor-sharp mind for solving problems, a blind eye to the social context in which such problems are bound to arise. And the contradictions revealed by that basic split are wonderfully illuminating. Holmes's brilliance makes him heroic, and his obtuseness makes him a safe hero for the English bourgeoisie." Komarov leaned back in his chair and gulped down what remained in his glass.

"I shall try to read these stories, comrade," McColl said tactfully. He was trying to square this Komarov with the one that Ruzhkov had described.

"This will be a long journey. I am Yuri Vladimirovich."

"Nikolai Matveyevich," McColl responded.

"Well, Nikolai Matveycvich, it's your move."

ON THE SECOND MORNING, SHE realized she would have to meet him. The train, as her man from the kitchen informed her, had still not reached Ryazan and, at its current rate of progress, was unlikely to reach Tashkent in less than a month. If she stayed that long in her compartment, she'd probably go mad.

And, she had to admit, she wanted to hear what he had to say. Whatever he was doing in Russia, it obviously had something to do with Brady, and therefore also with Sergei. Not to mention her own forced exile from Moscow and work. She wanted to know what it was all about.

The first opportunity arose about half an hour later, but Komarov and Maslov were both standing close to their carriage, so she decided to wait for another. The moment the train stopped again, she was out on the platform and putting distance between herself and the three red cars. After joining the queue at the samovar, she looked back to see if Jack was there, and was pleased to see him striding toward her. There was no sign of Komarov or Maslov.

He insisted on shaking hands, as if they were just introducing themselves. "Let's walk," he suggested in Russian, gesturing toward the distant rear of the train. "How are you?" he asked, as if they were friends who'd been out of touch for a while.

"I'm ready for the promised explanation," she said coldly. Seeing him again up close was arousing all sorts of thoughts and emotions.

"Okay," he agreed. "But it would be better if you didn't look so angry with me. Komarov might wonder how his humble interpreter has managed to annoy you so much after such a brief acquaintance."

"Is that what you are, his interpreter?"

"I was interpreting for the Indian delegation at the Comintern conference when it all blew up."

"All what?"

"The robbery at the tram depot in which three of the Indians were involved. Along with Aidan Brady."

"He's the leader in all this, isn't he?" she asked, wondering why

McColl hadn't mentioned Sergei. He had to know that they were married.

"I think so."

"And what are they planning?" she asked, glancing down the platform to make sure there was no one in earshot.

"The murder of Mohandas Gandhi."

"What?" What madness had Sergei gotten himself into?

"They think he's a Menshevik, holding back the real revolution."

"Oh, give me strength." But the idea had a ghastly plausibility. Given how Sergei and his friends saw the world these days, it probably seemed like perfect sense to them. Another thought crossed her mind. "But then what brought you here? Why would your boss give a fig about Gandhi? Wouldn't the British government be glad to see him gone?"

"I'm sure they would, but I don't think they'd condone his assassination. It's a small group of men in one section of British intelligence that's behind all this. Not my section, and not my boss. He wants to know exactly who's involved. Who hired Brady to put the team together in the first place and who'll be helping them once they reach India."

"Helping them how?" she asked, finding it all a bit hard to believe. Reaching the end of the train, they stood there for a moment, staring down the receding track. The way back to Moscow, she thought, wishing she could take it.

"With money," Jack was saying. "And probably guns when the time comes. A suitable hideout, information. Whatever they need."

"All right. But why in heaven's name would Brady get involved with the British in the first place?"

"He was caught in Ireland, and that was their price for letting him go."

"He's using you."

"I quit the Service three years ago."

She wanted to trust him. "Okay, he's using your former colleagues."

"And they him. And as far as I'm concerned, they deserve each other. If it wasn't for Gandhi . . ."

"You always did admire him," she said, reducing McColl to silence. Referencing their mutual past was obviously not a good idea. "So why did you let yourself be press-ganged?" she asked.

He shrugged. "What better way to stay on their trail? If Komarov catches up with them, I can leave them to Soviet justice. If they get across the border, I'll find a way to follow."

"You know that one of the men is my husband?" she asked, aware she was trying to provoke a reaction but not knowing which sort she wanted.

"I do," he said calmly.

They walked several yards in silence.

"So why did Komarov bring you along?" McColl asked.

"Because they have no photographs, and he knows I can identify Sergei, Brady and Aram Shahumian. Because I might be able to persuade Sergei to give himself up. Or just because he can." Looking up, she saw that the man in question was walking toward them.

"I'm glad that you two have met," Komarov said in greeting, an almost genial smile on his face.

AFTER HIS TALK WITH CAITLIN, McColl went back to his compartment and tried to lose himself in a Turgenev novel he had borrowed from the saloon. But he found it impossible to concentrate—his unconscious mind was much more interested in endlessly replaying the conversation he'd just had out on the platform.

There was a lot she hadn't told him. She'd implied that her presence on the train was far from voluntary, and the questions she'd asked him suggested a lack of knowledge when it came to her husband's intentions. Indeed, when McColl had told her that Gandhi was the likely target, she had seemed surprised. Not to mention disapproving. She hadn't actually criticized her husband, but then why would she? It occurred to him that she and Sergei might have agreed to let each other follow their own paths and consciences for a while, just as McColl and she had done in 1916.

And then there was Brady. She must have introduced the American to her husband, which presumably meant that she was still in touch with the bastard after his killing of Fedya. Then again, she might not know that Brady had shot him.

Too many questions, he thought. Not to mention too many memories.

The train continued on its stop-start way. He got off whenever he could, to give his body exercise and his mind something different to ponder. Most of the soldiers he talked to were young and seemed strangely sullen considering they'd just won a war—there was none of the enthusiasm that he'd witnessed among Bolshevik supporters three years earlier. The cotton experts he met in one samovar queue were a very different matter. These two stocky Russians heading south on government business oozed good cheer and optimism—after fifteen minutes in their company, McColl felt positively exhausted.

There was no further sign of Caitlin, though, either on the sun-baked platforms or later in the dining car, where Komarov again brought out his chess set.

As before, McColl found it easier to accept than refuse the invitation to play, but merely being in Komarov's company demanded as much concentration as playing the game. The Russian was easy to talk to, too easy, and McColl felt the need to measure each thought before allowing it into the open.

They had just finished the first game when another man appeared, the one with the neat beard that McColl had seen by the train in Kazan Station. The newcomer shook hands with Komarov and took a seat at the adjoining table. "One of your praetorians?" he asked, indicating McColl.

Komarov smiled and introduced them. Ivan Arbatov, as McColl knew from his London briefing, was one of the last Menshevik leaders still at liberty in Lenin's Russia. Or had been. McColl remembered the Chekist escort at Kazan Station.

"Where are we sending you, Ivan Ivanovich?" Komarov asked as he reset the pieces, confirming McColl's suspicion.

"Verny. Or whatever it's called this month—your party's penchant for name changing is becoming almost obsessive."

"It's called Alma-Ata now," Komarov told him.

"Whatever. Nothing but apples to eat, they tell me. I loathe apples." Arbatov stirred his tea morosely, then smiled. "But don't let me interrupt your game. We can talk at some other time. At this rate," he added, staring out into the darkness, "we shall be spending several years in each other's company."

Komarov had finished resetting the pieces.

"It's a great relief, you know," Arbatov went on conversationally, "being ejected from the political arena. Suddenly I can say exactly what I think again, without worrying about whether that will be the phrase or the sentence that finally gets me into trouble. A relief," he repeated. "I hold no grudge against you, Yuri Vladimirovich. I want you to know that. Now I really will leave you to your game." He gave them each a farewell nod and left the carriage.

"Old fool," muttered Maslov, who'd been standing in the vestibule doorway for the last few minutes.

"Perhaps," Komarov said, "but that old fool was a comrade of Lenin's when you were still a mother's dream."

"Why is he being exiled?" McColl asked. He had found the Russians' conversation both bizarre and touching in its old-world civility.

"The usual," Komarov said, holding out his hands for McColl to choose a color.

Two hours later he had lost three games in a row and was about to plead exhaustion when the train clattered over a succession of points and began to slow down alongside another line of lighted carriages.

"Samara?" Maslov asked hopefully, looking up from his book.

Komarov was trying to see out, his hands cupped around his eyes. "No. The old fool was right—we'll be on this train for years."

It squealed to a halt, and the three of them climbed down to find themselves in a multitrack yard. Looking under their train and the one alongside it, McColl could see at least half a dozen others. He remembered Ruzhkov's remark about trains disappearing into thin air.

Komarov and Maslov were already walking past their train's locomotives, and McColl strode after them. A couple of hundred yards beyond the lines of stabled trains, the lights of a small station were burning; to left and right, on the slopes of the shallow cutting, hundreds of shadowy figures moved among myriad campfires, the sum of their murmuring voices sounding almost sepulchral. The whole scene, in fact, felt strangely biblical.

They walked on to the station, Ruzayevka Junction, as a large nameboard proudly proclaimed. An old woman was sitting on the platform, deftly spitting chewed sunflower seeds out onto the tracks.

Behind the station more fires illuminated a palisaded area no larger than a tennis court, into which were crammed several hundred prisoners. They appeared to be mostly peasants and mostly men, though there were a few young boys to be seen. Red Army soldiers surrounded the staked fencing, talking among themselves, the ends of their cigarettes occasionally flaring in the gloom.

At the door of the station building, a soldier barred their way, then examined Komarov's credentials with a thoroughness which exasperated Maslov. Eventually they were allowed inside, where the Cheka officer in charge provided suitable recompense with a display of unmitigated awe. His news was less inspiring. A bridge up ahead was down—maybe blown up, maybe simply collapsed—and for the moment no trains could continue on to Samara. There was no other route worth considering. But the engineers were working on repairing it. It would take them twelve hours, perhaps twenty-four.

Komarov asked who the prisoners were.

"Antonovists."

Komarov nodded. "Keep me informed," he said, and turned to leave. As they walked back alongside the tracks to their train, McColl found himself imagining that medieval armies occupied the slopes on either side and that dawn would see them launch their attacks across the shining rails.

THE FIRST TIME CAITLIN HEARD the sound it eluded recognition, but the second time, half-awake, she could not be deceived. It was gunfire.

She dressed quickly, exited the carriage, and walked briskly down the corridor between two trains in the direction the sound had come from. It was still early morning, the sun not yet visible over the hills ahead, and for a moment, as she stepped out into open space and saw the slopes covered with bodies, she thought she'd walked into a massacre. But then she saw heads raised among the smoldering fires, and realized that they, too, had been woken by the noise.

Another fusillade shattered the morning.

She walked on up a track, toward the source of the noise. After passing a goods warehouse that had lost its roof, she suddenly came upon it: a line of people backed onto the edge of a loading platform, facing a group of soldiers around a machine gun. Behind and below the former, a pile of bodies covered the rails.

She heard a shout, then the loud, incredibly loud, clatter of the gun, saw most of the line topple backward onto the corpses below. One man had fallen into a squat and swayed there on the brink before finally toppling over.

She couldn't move. She realized her mouth was open and managed, with great effort, to pull it shut. She felt like running back to the train and asking Komarov to intervene. But she knew what he would say; she could even see the look on his face as he said it: This is a war, and there are always casualties; rebellions must be stamped out. This is the real revolution, the one you read about in *Pravda*, sitting at your Zhenotdel desk. Real people, real atrocities; they burn party cadres alive, then slice them up and feed them to hogs. And this is how we avenge them—this is what "suppressing banditry" looks like when it's happening in front of your eyes.

This was Sergei's world. This was the war he had found himself in, the one that had let loose his demons and shut down the young man she'd known. In that moment she felt her heart go out to him, wherever he was, whatever mad scheme he might be pursuing.

Another group was being led forward. She wanted to walk away, to lower her eyes, but if standing and watching was the only way she could share in the responsibility, then stand and watch she would.

Sensing other eyes, she turned to find Komarov's. He was leaning against the wall of the roofless warehouse gazing straight at her. He quickly looked away, and neither spoke, but she instinctively felt that his heart's response to these killings was no different from hers, and that all their obvious differences paled into insignificance as long as this burden of barely supportable sorrow bound them together.

The machine gun opened up again, dispensing death and bouncing echoes down the valley.

IT TURNED INTO A LONG, hot day. Caitlin spent it shut away in her compartment, mostly lying down, listening to the sounds of the outside world drifting in through the open window. There were no more volleys of gunfire, only the distant murmur of the camps on the slopes, the occasional couple walking by outside, children playing hide-and-seek under the stabled trains. A bee searched her compartment for pollen and left disappointed. She tried to do some work, but the article she was trying to edit now seemed depressingly theoretical.

Her state of mind frightened her. Away from Moscow, away from the office, she felt alarmingly adrift, all her usual points of reference either gone or revealed in a completely different light. What had happened? Well, Sergei had deserted her, Komarov had virtually kidnapped her, and Jack had dropped himself back in her life like an unexploded emotional bomb.

She reminded herself that nothing really had changed. Okay, she was on a train, heading out to God knew where for God knew how long. But her desk would still be there when she returned. The Sergei she'd married had been gone for months, Komarov couldn't hold her hostage indefinitely, and unexploded bombs could damn well stay that way. She would get her life back.

But was it the life she wanted? Things looked different stuck on a train in the middle of nowhere with only your own thoughts for company. The job, the office, the missionary zeal—they started to feel like a life to be chosen rather than taken for granted. Take that thought further, and other jobs, other offices, became possible. Russia had stolen her heart, but it wasn't where her family was, and it wasn't the only place she could make herself useful. She didn't think she could ever abandon Kollontai and the Zhenotdel, but the way things were going she might not get the choice. Politics and loneliness were already fraying the edges of the life she had lived these last few years; sometimes she felt like a pond pierced by a stone, rippling away from her center.

Eventually she slept, and darkness had fallen when she woke up feeling cold and very alone. She needed to talk to someone—anyone. It had been almost three days since she had shared a normal conversation.

She washed her face and brushed her hair, practiced a smile in the mirror. There, she could still do it.

There were three men in the saloon—Jack and Komarov playing chess and a young Red Army officer whom she hadn't met. When the latter stood and offered the seat beside him, she thankfully accepted—sitting with her back to the other two felt like an ideal arrangement.

The officer introduced himself as Semyon Krasilnikov and told her he was on his way to take up a post in Orenburg. Rather than attempt to explain her own presence on the train, Caitlin simply said that she was a Zhenotdel official with business in Turkestan— mentioning she worked for the women's department deterred most men from probing further.

Krasilnikov proved an exception. Once they'd exchanged the usual traveler pleasantries—the excessive heat and all-too-frequent delays, the dreadful food and unyielding beds—he actually asked her to tell him more about her work. "How did the Zhenotdel come into being?" he wanted to know.

"That's a long story," she protested.

"We don't seem short of time," he said reasonably.

He even looked interested as she skimmed through the history of Russian feminism and the Zhenotdel's eventual establishment. And he asked intelligent questions. Wasn't there a danger of prioritizing gender over class? Were there enough men in the party who really supported the Zhenotdel's aims, and were most of them offering little more than lip service when a conflict of interests arose?

It was impossible to generalize, she told him, knowing she'd done so herself on more than one occasion. Some conflicts of interest were more acute than others; some made comrades more open to compromise.

Krasilnikov thought that the Zhenotdel would have its work cut out in Turkestan.

Yes, she told him, but the rewards had already been spectacular. As she recounted the story of Rahima's impromptu journey to Moscow, Caitlin suddenly realized how animated she had become—days of self-doubt were making her overcompensate.

SITTING A FEW FEET AWAY, McColl was having trouble keeping his mind on the game. He had actually started this one quite well, forcing Komarov onto the defensive for once, but since Caitlin's arrival McColl's hard-won advantage had slowly slipped away. He suspected that Komarov had noticed but hoped that the Cheka boss had put his failing concentration down to nothing more suspicious than an attractive woman's presence.

The Caitlin he'd talked to on the platform—he might have been able to shut that voice out. But this Caitlin, this woman with so much passion, was the one he'd fallen in love with, and a game of chess just couldn't compete.

"Checkmate, I think," Komarov murmured just as she got up to leave the car. Her face was flushed, McColl noticed, as she nodded farewell to him and Komarov. Flushed and full of life.

As she disappeared through one gangway door, the exile-bound Menshevik came in through the other, carrying an unopened bottle of vodka. Seeing that their game had ended, he invited them and the young officer to share its contents. Receiving their agreement, he asked the attendant for glasses and sat back to examine them all with an expression half-owl and half-bear.

The vodka was rough but strong, and McColl took care not to drink too fast or too much. The conversation, which from the outset was mostly between Arbatov and Komarov, soon became a dialogue pure and simple, with McColl and Krasilnikov no more than spectators.

"From whom do you get your mandate?" Arbatov challenged Komarov.

"From history," he retorted drily.

Arbatov grinned. "Once perhaps, but what if history changes its mind? Would you give up your power then? But then how would you know that history had forsaken you when you no longer listen to what it's telling you?"

Komarov smiled at the table. "No party, no individual, can keep itself in power against the will of history."

"Not forever, no. But for an hour, a year, a decade? What if you can hold power for that long? The peasants are against you now; the bourgeoisie always has been. And after Kronstadt it seems that most workers have lost their faith in you. My presence here on this train proves that at least half of Russia's socialists have turned against you. A handful of incorruptibles in charge of a million careerists—it doesn't sound like a recipe for socialism, does it? It sounds like a way of holding on to power."

A succinct analysis, McColl thought. He wondered how Komarov would counter it.

"We do not hold this power for our own gratification," the Cheka boss said, sounding defensive.

"Not yet. Oh, I know that you are sincere, Yuri Vladimirovich, but sincerity is an overvalued attribute. I'm sure the Spanish Inquisition was staffed by sincere men. And gratification comes in many forms. Power for its own sake, for one."

"Which corrupts those who hold it? Of course it does. But impotence corrupts just as surely as power, Ivan Ivanovich." Komarov smiled again. "And absolute impotence—perhaps that corrupts absolutely. Those who had nothing—no wealth, no power, no education, no hope—they must learn how to use the power we now hold in their name. You don't learn kindness and cooperation from capitalism, and if we want a kinder, more cooperative world, these things must be taught. By the party. Who else is there?"

Arbatov looked incredulous. "Do you really believe that a handful of incorruptibles can hold such power in trust? You can't even stem the tide you have already unleashed."

"We can only try," Komarov said, and McColl could feel the quiet desperation behind those four simple words.

"And where will our Russia be when you fail?"

"Where it is now?" Komarov rejoined. "Where we are is where we are. We can't turn the clock back four years and start again from scratch."

RETURNING TO HER COMPARTMENT AFTER the conversation with the young officer, Caitlin sat staring out at the moonlit hills. He had reminded her of someone, and it took her several moments to realize it was Sergei. The old Sergei, the one she had met and shared so much with in their fleeting times together.

It was good for her to remember that Sergei, she thought. Especially now, as part of the pack chasing the one he'd become.

For all the holding back she'd done, her affection for him had been real. If there hadn't been the passion she'd felt for Jack, there had been liking, and there had been desire. The sex had always been good with the old Sergei. There had been an innocence about him that was truly touching; he had taken such joy in giving pleasure to her that she could hardly feel otherwise.

What had become of that man? He was in there somewhere, trapped in his desperate successor, occasionally breaking out to leave Pushkin verses on pillows. She missed that man. That friend.

THE TRAIN LEFT RUZAYEVKA JUNCTION late the following afternoon and, for the rest of the day and night, meandered at not much better than walking pace through wooded hill country. Troops were frequently in evidence, milling at the small stations, camped in farmyards and fields, but only one burning building, glimpsed at the distant end of a valley, suggested that the Antonov rebellion was still alive.

In midmorning their train reached Batraki, where an armored cousin simmered on the adjacent track. With the latter leading, they left in tandem, emerging from the uplands to drum their way across the iron bridge which spanned the mile-wide Volga. With the hills receding on the western horizon, a straight run across flat farming country brought them back alongside the river in the outskirts of

Samara. The sky was rapidly darkening, and as the train pulled into the city station, rain began falling in sheets.

Komarov and Maslov went in search of the Transport Cheka office, fighting their way through would-be passengers huddled in the shelter of the platform canopy. A report on Brady was waiting for them.

Komarov half-sat on the edge of the table to read it through. *"Information gathered from Vecheka files and American comrade Michael Kelly, now teaching at Petrograd State University,"* the cable began. *"Aidan Brady, age around forty. Originally from Boston, Massachusetts, USA. Union activist (American Industrial Workers of the World union) in years before war, served short prison terms in Oregon, Illinois, and New Jersey for related activities. Also active in Irish republican politics, in both USA and Ireland. Broke with IWW in early 1918 over leadership's refusal to sanction armed resistance. Arrived in Russia soon after. Served with Red Army on Volga front that summer and later transferred to Samara Cheka. In Ukraine 1919–20, position and duties unknown due to loss of records. Left Russia toward the end of 1920, with the stated intent of fighting for the republicans in Ireland's War of Independence. Return to Russia unrecorded but probably in May of this year. Entered politics as a socialist and has subsequently shifted his position further to the left, with links to anarchist and utopian communist groups. During civil war proved intelligent, courageous, and popular with fellow soldiers. Carries an American revolver, which he usually wears tucked into the back of his belt. Family circumstances unknown. No record of marriage in Russia."*

Komarov sighed and passed the cable to Maslov. Lots of facts, but nothing that really helped. The Brady described sounded decidedly forthright, but Komarov's own abiding impression, gathered at their only previous meeting three years before, had been of a man held well inside himself, forever calculating, with more than a hint of slyness. He might have misread Brady, but Komarov doubted it. The biography in the cable sounded more like agitprop than real life.

When you boiled it down, a solitary truth remained—the man was a classic renegade.

Komarov turned to the local Chekist who was hovering anxiously by his side. "When did the last train leave for Tashkent, and when will it arrive?" Komarov asked.

The man scurried off to find out, returning five minutes later. "It left six days ago and should arrive sometime in the next three."

Komarov thought for a moment. "Chances are they know someone there," he muttered.

"Other anarchists?" Maslov suggested.

"You may be right, Pavel Tarasovich," Komarov said as thunder rolled in the distance. He turned to the local man. "I want to send a message to the Tashkent Cheka."

Returning to the train some twenty minutes later, Komarov noticed that the man he still thought of as Davydov was farther up the platform, chatting with the locomotive crew. During the first few days of their journey, Komarov had not seen anything in the man's or Piatakova's behavior to suggest a previous relationship, but if they had known each other for years, they would both be doing their best to disguise that fact. They certainly seemed to be enjoying each other's company, but that was hardly suspicious in itself. He himself had thrown them together, and traveling in the Cheka section of the train didn't invite interaction with other passengers.

IT WAS BARELY MORNING WHEN McColl climbed from his bed, the dim dawn light filtering through the shutters on the window. He rolled them aside and leaned his head out. They were still ascending the Samara valley, the line twisting to follow the river, the locomotives straining at the incline. The hills that rose to the south were wrapped in amber light.

He went out into the corridor to watch the eastern sky lighten, the crest of the hills slowly sharpening as the sun rose up behind them. And as the light grew, he became aware of movement and color by the side of the tracks. People. Some walking, some lying prone. And the latter were clearly not sleeping—they'd succumbed to exhaustion, hunger, or both.

The fact that some parts of Russia were suffering serious food shortages had been mentioned in the Moscow press, but the extent of the shortages had been left rather vague. Well, here they were, McColl thought, and it looked very much like a famine.

The sun climbed over the hilltops, flooding the valley with yellow light, laying bare the horror. Corpses were strewn on both sides of the line, young and old, male and female, each with its cloud of hungry flies. Those people still moving, stumbling northward, showed little interest in the train that was rumbling past them or the bodies that littered their passage. Each emaciated face seemed set in the same mold of utter resignation.

In the sky above, black shapes hovered, flapping their wings in anticipation.

McColl stood at the window, arms outstretched, unable to turn his eyes away. He asked himself why they weren't stopping to help, but already knew the answer: the food they had on board would feed only a few for less than a day, and hold up the train without making any real difference.

How had famine blighted a land rich as this one? Was this a consequence of the revolution, of turning everything upside down, of the bitter war between party and peasants? But then what did that matter to these figures below, trudging northward in sheer desperation?

He suddenly became aware that the young officer Krasilnikov was standing at another window only a few feet away, absorbed by the same sights as he was. And that the officer was silently weeping, tears coursing down either cheek.

ON THE OTHER SIDE OF the train, Komarov watched as the mural of pain unrolled. He had known there was a famine in the Volga region, and here it was. An emotional response would be self-indulgent and of no help to anyone but himself. The NEP would right the situation in the months to come; these poor people were simply paying one retrospective price of the civil war. The leadership in Moscow was already doing all that could be done.

The prospect of eating made him feel sick, which was all the more reason to set an example. He finished dressing and headed for the dining car, two trembling hands concealed in his pockets.

ALL DAY THE TRAIN CHUGGED up the valley; all day the hungry and starving trailed past, the number of those in motion steadily dropping in favor of those who were not. Small stations were gatherings of despair, their villages eerily empty save for the carrion birds expectantly strutting the streets.

Late that afternoon the train rattled into a station high in the hills—Sorochinsk was the name on the board. With her cabin door open, Caitlin could see that hundreds of people were camped on both sides of the tracks. Most were sitting or lying and probably lacked the energy needed to stand. In the eyes now surveying the train, she saw a range of emotions that stretched from pure indifference to manic hope.

Even before the train juddered to a final halt, soldiers from the troop car were jumping down to line up beside it, their rifles pointing outward, their faces locked in nervous immobility. As if in response, some members of the crowd rose slowly to their feet, some swaying with the effort of staying upright. A few began shuffling toward the train, and then stopped as they realized that most of their fellows were not.

"Where have they all come from?" Caitlin heard herself ask out loud. Neither Jack nor Krasilnikov, standing at the windows on either side of hers, offered a reply. And why should they? she thought. What was there to say?

They'd spent a whole day traveling through these people's graveyard, and she couldn't remember ever feeling more helpless. At first it had brought back the weeks of waiting for her brother's execution in the Tower of London, but as the hours had passed, the sheer scale of what they were witnessing had defied comparison.

The train had not stopped to offer help, only to take on the water needed to carry it free of this nightmare. Caitlin's coach was standing halfway between the station house and the water tower, where bodies had been stacked inside the girder supports. She could smell the putrefaction from her window and was not surprised to see the fireman holding his nose with one hand as he unclipped the hose with the other.

A small child, perhaps six or seven years old, was sitting, staring dully into space, not twenty feet away against a low wall. As Caitlin stared at her, the girl looked up, caught her eye, and smiled shyly, as if she had just been asked for a dance.

The incongruity tied a knot in Caitlin's stomach.

The crowd had begun inching forward, as if barely perceptible advances would deny the soldiers an excuse to open fire. But the gap was obviously closing, and the fireman was still disconnecting his hose when someone fired the first shot.

The crowd let out its anger in one enormous roar and launched a hail of stones at the troops and the train they were guarding. Yells of pain mingled with the sound of shattering glass, but the clod of earth that struck Caitlin's window merely bounced off, leaving only a starburst of yellow fragments.

The locomotive whistle screeched, as if to sound a retreat. The crowd was advancing in earnest now, the soldiers leaping back aboard, expecting the train to move. It didn't. Caitlin could hear someone on the roof shouting at the crowd, promising a relief train. The crowd believed it no more than she did, and the man was cut off in midsentence, presumably by a well-directed stone. As people began hammering on the side of the train, a machine gun opened up farther down the platform.

The whistle screeched again, but still the train refused to move. Looking to the right, Caitlin could see people swarming around the engines, and guessed that others were blocking the tracks. If that was the case, then the driver had had enough. For several seconds the train gave a good impression of straining at the bit, before suddenly bursting into motion, viciously spurting steam, and leaving agonized screams in its wake. Their carriage seemed almost to stumble as the wheels encountered something solid, which Caitlin could only hope was a brick or a stone.

Her last image of Sorochinsk was of a young boy, thin enough to squeeze through iron railings, standing by the track. After watching him wave the train good-bye, she lowered her head and closed her eyes.

LATER THAT EVENING, THE WHOLE party ended up in the curtained-off saloon. Mostly, McColl suspected, because guilt was more bearable shared.

Arbatov wanted to twist the knife. "You were warned," he said, addressing Komarov directly but allowing an accusing gaze to sweep across them all. "There was no rain last summer and precious little snow in winter, and you kept on taking whatever you could."

"The cities needed food," Komarov protested, but McColl could tell that his heart wasn't in it.

"The cities weren't *starving*," Arbatov went on, "but you decided that the workers had more right to the food that the peasants had grown than the peasants did themselves. You even took most of their seed corn! And when your own agricultural scientists produced a report outlining the mistakes you had made, you refused to publish it. Your government just sat on its hands and hoped for a miracle, which needless to say never came."

McColl expected an argument from Komarov—if not fresh facts, an insistence that everyone makes mistakes. None was forthcoming.

Red Cossacks

Sergei Piatakov turned on his heel to better take in the vastness of earth and heaven. To north and west, the desert of the last few days faded into the distance, where a low line of sand hills merged into the blue-grey sky. Away to the south, above their receding train, a line of mountains loomed out of the heat haze. A half mile or so to the east, across an arid riverbed, the small town of Saryagash seemed sunk in torpor.

"Come on," Brady said, picking up his battered suitcase. "Time to start our new career."

The accompanying grin belonged on an explorer's face, Piatakov thought. Or maybe a conqueror's. Brady was more Cortés than Columbus—he wouldn't be satisfied with looking around and reporting back.

The two of them walked across the tracks and started down the dirt road, making the most of the shade provided by the acacias that lined the route. It was incredibly hot—a hundred degrees at least, Piatakov guessed—but the air was so dry that he didn't feel that uncomfortable.

He remembered thinking that seeing the world would make him a better teacher, but backward Turkestan hadn't been high on his list of places to visit. He had always wanted to see America, and he and Caitlin had vowed to go there together once the revolution was safely entrenched. He would meet her family in New York and then perhaps travel west to see the Grand Canyon and the great meteorite crater and the geyser in Yellowstone Park—all those wonders of the world that had gripped his imagination as a child.

Well, he doubted he'd ever see them now.

Brady already had, of course, and been characteristically unimpressed. "A deep trench, a big hole, and a tall fountain," had been his verdict, when Piatakov had mentioned his ambition to see them.

"What day is it?" the American asked, interrupting Piatakov's reverie.

"Saturday."

"That's what I thought. Twelve days to travel two thousand miles." He took out his fob and checked the time. "It looks like a ghost town," he said, gazing ahead at the empty-looking Saryagash. "Maybe they're all having siestas. With heat like this, they'd need to."

Piatakov didn't bother to reply. He understood the American's slightly hysterical mood: twelve days on a crowded train, and this much light and space was enough to make anyone feel light-headed. And after only a few hundred yards, they were probably both beginning to feel the heat. The sun seemed to press down on Piatakov's cap like a steam iron.

"Uzbeks," Brady said as they saw their first people—a series of men laid out on mattresses in the shade of trees and buildings. "The Russian colonists down here call all the urban Muslims Sarts, but there are lots of different groups. You can tell them by their hats. See that guy over there?" He pointed out an old man sitting in an open doorway, wearing what looked like a long white nightshirt and a peakless embroidered cap. "That sort of hat means an Uzbek."

Piatakov grunted. He sometimes felt that Brady should have been a librarian, albeit one who took no prisoners.

They came to a crossroads where the road from the station met a wide, tree-lined avenue that boasted a number of imposing buildings. Two Uzbeks were walking toward them, toting battered kerosene cans from which they sprinkled water across the sandy street. Their bare feet were blanched by the dust.

The Russian Imperial Bank seemed permanently closed, its double-eagle plaque hanging loose on the wall by the boarded doors. Three small boys were sitting on its veranda, watching the strangers with interest.

"There," Piatakov said, pointing out another building fifty yards farther on, where a large red flag hung above an open door, low enough to serve as an entrance curtain.

Inside they found a large office, shutters closed against the sun. Two desks bore typewriters; several shelves sagged under piles of papers. The large map of Turkestan that hung on one wall looked as though someone had thrown a bottle of ink at it.

A chain of troika bells hung beside the door. Brady shook it, conjuring a mental picture of falling snow.

A bleary-eyed man emerged from the back of the building. He was a Russian, somewhere between youth and middle age, with a complexion that suggested more than a few years in Turkestan. He greeted them cordially, said his name was Ulionshin and that he was the local party secretary.

Brady passed over two of the identity papers that Aram Shahumian had forged in Moscow. Ulionshin took a pair of wire-rimmed spectacles from a drawer and examined the papers carefully. "So, Comrade Travkin," he said, addressing Brady, "you and Comrade Semionov here have come to report on the state of our roads in Turkestan." He offered a wry smile. "It will be a short report, I'm afraid. One word would suffice for most of them and not a word you use when ladies are present. But accurate. The camels have been dropping it for several thousand years. Still, what can I do to help you?"

"Somewhere to sleep tonight and a ride into Tashkent tomorrow morning, if that's possible," Brady said.

"Transport by road, you mean?"

"It's the only way to see what improvements are necessary."

"Of course, of course. But we have no motor transport, I'm sorry to say. There was an automobile," he explained almost wistfully, "but the Tashkent Cheka decided they needed it more than we did. And of course they were correct, but . . ." He shrugged. "I can have you taken by *taranta*."

"*Taranta?*"

"I'm sorry. Living here for so long, one forgets. A *taranta* is a four-wheel carriage, quite comfortable, and Tashkent is only thirty versts away. Three hours at the most."

"That sounds very acceptable," Brady said.

"Good. As for a place to sleep, I shall be honored to share my roof; you will find nowhere cooler in Saryagash. And of course you must eat with us."

It was a pleasant evening. Ulionshin's wife was a lovely, almond-eyed Uzbek, and his equally beautiful daughters had a plethora of questions about the wider world, which Brady was happy to answer. The food was the best they'd eaten for several months: thick unleavened bread, which Ulionshin called *lepioshka*, and chunks of lamb on skewers grilled over a slow-burning fire, all washed down with raisin-sweetened, bloodred apple tea. Afterward, stretched out on his back in their allotted corner of the roof, Piatakov stared up at the starriest sky he had ever seen.

He lay awake for a long time, feeling the past gnawing at the edges of his contentment. This was his new life, freely chosen. Why was it so hard to cast the old one aside?

THEY LEFT SARYAGASH SOON AFTER first light, sitting side by side on the taranta's rear seat. The driver, a young Uzbek named Mirumar, spoke not a word of Russian but refused to be inhibited by this handicap. Whenever he had a moment free from shouting at the horses, he would explain passing scenes of interest with extravagant gestures, streams of incomprehensible words, and what he no doubt thought was a winning smile.

The journey was slow but mentally relaxing, despite Mirumar's exuberance and the endless jolting of the ironclad wheels on the badly rutted road. They sat mostly in silence, aware of the heat's slowly tightening grip, listening to the heavy breathing of the two ponies, watching the mountains rise in the distance. Only once did they encounter other travelers: a convoy of camels escorted by nomad horsemen, who treated them to an array of lordly stares.

"Kyrgyz," Brady suggested, a word that unleashed a long stream of obvious invective from their driver.

As they neared the foothills of the mountains, the transition from desert to greenery was abrupt. Silence gave way to birdsong, the harsh yellow glare to a patchwork of colors less fierce on the eye. They joined the road from Chimkent, which proved just as rutted as the one from Saryagash, but which wound prettily through thinly wooded slopes and across the occasional dried-up stream. It passed through several villages, each a single street of clay dwellings surrounded by fields full of working women, each boasting a *chaikhana* or two full of lolling men, glasses of green tea and ornate hookahs only an arm's reach away.

Piatakov didn't have to wonder what Caitlin would have thought.

The sun was approaching its zenith when they drove across a wide riverbed and stopped beside a guard post on the northeastern edge of Tashkent. Two Uzbeks in Red Army uniform noted the red stars in their caps and examined the proffered papers only with reluctance, before returning to their seats in the shade. Mirumar urged the ponies forward once more, down a narrow, unpaved street hemmed in by a wall of clay houses.

Ulionshin had explained the city's layout to them: a Sart town of around a hundred and sixty thousand Uzbek natives and a Russian town of a hundred and twenty thousand colonists, side by side on either bank of the Sarla River. Coming from Saryagash they would arrive in the Sart town first, but Mirumar knew the route through to the Russian quarter.

Brady had other ideas. He leaned forward and tapped the boy on the shoulder. *"Chaikhana,"* Brady said, adding a drinking mime for good measure.

A few moments later they pulled up outside a large and prosperous looking teahouse and, after disentangling their cramped limbs and luggage from the taranta, sent Mirumar on his way with a

precious ruble. Brady surveyed the coins still left in his hand somewhat ruefully. "Rogdayev had better cough up," he said.

They found an empty mattress and sat with legs stretched out,
their backs to the side of the building. The adjoining square
contained at least twenty empty market stalls, and the wall of dun-
colored single-story buildings that enclosed it was broken only
by the streets running in and out. Above the roofs the dome of a
mosque gleamed fitfully in the sun. Most of the mosaic tiling had
fallen away, and red poppies were climbing up the dome from roots
in the supporting stonework.

"You've never been out of Russia before, have you, Sergei?" Brady
observed.

"No."

"I think we should stay in the Russian town," Brady decided, surveying the other, mostly sleeping, customers.

"We'd certainly be conspicuous here," Piatakov agreed.

Brady sighed. "Yes. But isn't it fascinating?"

"It is."

"I wonder how religious these people really are," Brady mused.
"That mosque doesn't look very well cared for. You remember Dza-
gin, on the train? He told me about a notice he'd seen in a small
town near here; it said something like: the service today is being
given by a communist priest, so members of the party are allowed
to attend!"

Brady laughed out loud, drawing stares and one or two disapproving murmurs. "He had another story about a Chinese dentist,
a traveling dentist, who used to work here in the old town. He told
all his patients that toothache was caused by maggots in their teeth,
and he'd poke around with a pair of chopsticks in their mouths,
bring out the offending maggot, and stomp on it. Then he'd give
them a pill and pocket his fee. Of course, the maggot was in a hollow chopstick, and the pill was opium, so the tooth would never get
better. But no one seemed to mind. He came back year after year
and did a roaring trade. He just had the knack of getting people to
believe in him."

Like you, Piatakov thought but didn't say.

Brady gulped down the last of his tea. "Come on. Let's go and find some lodgings."

They walked on in the direction that seemed most likely, threading narrow streets and small squares until they suddenly emerged beside a wide boulevard, just as an overcrowded electric tram squealed past. The shock of this sudden encounter with modernity was exacerbated by the tram's occupants, nearly all Uzbeks, the men in white robes and turbans or caps, the women veiled from head to foot.

A hundred yards farther on they found a tram stop leaning drunkenly into the road, bearing information in Russian.

Another tram duly arrived, every bit as full as its predecessor. They found themselves each gripping the rear veranda rail with one hand, their bags with the other, as the tram rolled down the boulevard and crossed a large square boasting two large mosques and the statue of a Russian on horseback. A long bridge over a wide, dry riverbed led into the Russian town, where the buildings were much more substantial. Most were painted in traditional pastel colors, and many had red flags hanging from poles or flying from the roof. The faces on the pavement were mostly European.

They clambered off the tram, and Brady examined the map Ulionshin had drawn for them.

Ten minutes later they were knocking on the door of a mansion in Gogol Street. An attractive middle-aged Russian woman let them in, examined their papers, and copied out the details. "For the Cheka," she explained, as if they'd just arrived from Mars. Then she showed them up to a first-floor room, the contents of which were half a dozen rolled carpets, a table with one leg missing, and a precarious tower of books.

"The bourgeois family who lived here smashed all their furniture before they fled," the woman said matter-of-factly. "And they tore out all the wiring, so there's only cotton oil for light." She indicated the twists of cotton wool on the table, lying beside a saucer of oil. "Unless you have some candles?" she asked hopefully.

"I'm afraid not," Piatakov told her. "Thank you."

"We do have water again," the woman said. "At the end of the hall. Supper is at nine."

Piatakov shut the door behind her and joined Brady at the window. A young Russian girl was cycling past on the road below, pieces of blue ribbon streaming out from her bonnet. The sound of running water drifted up from the irrigation stream which ran between the road and the parched grass beyond. In the distance, half-hidden by a line of palms, a string of camels was sauntering along.

Moscow seemed far away. In more ways than one.

MCCOLL STARED OUT THROUGH HIS compartment window, something he had been doing for much of the previous twenty-four hours. The train was stabled a few hundred yards south of Orenburg station, close to where a dirt road from the east crossed the tracks and entered the town.

The view from the window rarely stopped shifting. A steady stream of carts trundled into the town, emerging from behind a derelict warehouse like one of those endless strips of bunting magicians drew out of their sleeves. Each was driven by a peasant with an anxious expression; each carried a high pile of decrepit-looking furniture, upon which a varying number of children precariously perched. And there was often a scrawny mongrel chasing its tail down among the trundling wheels, as if survival itself wasn't hard enough.

And then there were the soldiers. Hundreds, maybe thousands, of them. Columns marched into town and columns marched out, none of them showing much in the way of enthusiasm. There were solitary soldiers, groups small and large, all milling wherever space allowed, picking up rifles and putting them down, passing around cigarettes, pissing against anything that rose out of the ground.

It reminded McColl of the Boer War. Take away the distant onion domes, and Orenburg could be any small town in the western Cape, dry and dusty, full of purposeless motion, and reeking of troop disaffection. Each time a new column appeared on the track he half expected a dolorous chorus of "Goodbye, Dolly Gray."

He had wanted to explore the town, but the passengers had all been warned—effectively ordered—not to leave the safety of the train. The only exceptions were Komarov, Maslov, and Caitlin, who'd ridden off in a droshky flanked by a mounted military escort, the Chekists intent on collecting and sending messages from their local office, Caitlin the same from hers. McColl had no idea how she'd persuaded Komarov to take her along, but perhaps the Cheka boss was offering some small compensation for dragging her all this way from Moscow. Perhaps.

There'd been no audible gunfire since their departure several hours earlier, but McColl was relieved to see their droshky appear in the distance. Soon the three of them were picking their way across the weed-infested tracks, Caitlin looking none too pleased, Komarov and Maslov chatting behind her. The two Chekists were getting on better, McColl thought; they seemed to have settled into an uncle-nephew relationship during the journey, and there was less of the abrasiveness that McColl remembered from Moscow.

Once they'd all climbed aboard, and Caitlin had disappeared in the direction of her compartment, McColl asked Komarov if he had any news. McColl meant about the train, and was more than a little surprised when the Russian delved in his pocket for a crumpled telegraph form and told him to see for himself.

McColl smoothed it out. *Fugitives left train at Saryagash. Likely now Tashkent. Search underway.* He wondered if Caitlin knew. "It's a big enough town to hide in," he said in response to Komarov's questioning look, forbearing to add that he himself had successfully done so in 1916. "Any news of when we leave?"

Komarov snorted. "God only knows."

"I'll go and ask the drivers," McColl volunteered, glad to have something to do.

He walked up the train and found that a third locomotive had joined the original pair. A driver was sitting in the cab of the new arrival, patiently splitting sesame seeds and inserting the kernels into his bushy mustache. McColl swung himself up onto the footplate. "Any sign of movement?" he asked.

The driver laughed. "Someday soon," he said. "We're waiting for a train coming this way to clear the next section. Then, maybe, we'll be on our way."

"Why three engines?" McColl asked, seating himself on the fireman's put-up. The train had been shortened in Samara.

"Because there's a fair chance that two of them will fail in the middle of nowhere." The driver grinned. "Come to that, there's a fair chance they all will."

The tender was full of what looked like broken furniture. "What about fuel?" McColl asked.

"You are an innocent. Once we're out in the desert, we collect it as we go. The engine burns saxaul roots, and when the supply runs low, everyone volunteers to get out and cut some more. It takes hours, but it could be worse. In Tashkent they've converted two locos to burn dried fish from the Aral Sea. They burn great, but the stink!"

McColl could imagine. He wished he could tell the Russian about the porter on Glenfinnan Station who'd decided to check a fish van door, inadvertently pulled it open, and buried himself in an avalanche of herring. Euan McColl had never tired of that story, but then other people's misfortunes had always made the man laugh.

THE TRAIN THEY WERE AWAITING arrived the following morning. It was the "Red Cossack," an Agitation-Instruction train, a long line of bright red cars covered in huge yellow flowers and exhortatory slogans: WOMEN, LEARN TO READ AND WRITE! FROM DARKNESS TO LIGHT, FROM BATTLE TO BOOKS, FROM SADNESS TO JOY! Caitlin watched it pull in as she ate breakfast in her compartment, and found herself seeing it through the eyes of those farther up the line. In a day or so, this gaily colored messenger of hope would be rattling through the legions of the dying, a circus for those whose thoughts went no further than bread.

Minutes later her own train was on the move, clanking across the bridge that spanned the Ural River. This, as Maslov had told them yesterday, was the boundary between Europe and Asia, but as time went by, the view through Caitlin's window showed no sign of changing—just steppe and more steppe, nothing but straw-colored grass as far as the eye could see.

PIATAKOV SPENT MOST OF THE morning by their hotel room window, enjoying the sunlight and trying to imagine how things must have been in prerevolution days. A typical colonial society, he thought, ludicrous gentility masking all the usual brutality. All the mansions taking turns holding balls, all swishing gowns and string quartets while the native servants were treated like slaves.

Brady had gone out early, intent on discovering Rogdayev's home address. Piatakov was not particularly looking forward to seeing their old anarchist comrade again. He and Brady had fought alongside Rogdayev in 1918, had shared many hardships and arguments with him, but Piatakov had never really liked him.

Why not? In those days Rogdayev had been the pure anarchist, forever mocking Piatakov's faith in the party. Now Rogdayev was the party's propaganda chief in Turkestan, and Piatakov wondered how the man would cope when confronted with his past. He understood the political arguments for Rogdayev's change of course—had heard them often enough from ex-anarchists in Moscow—but doubted that political arguments had influenced the man very much. Perhaps he was being unfair, and Rogdayev had actually had a real epiphany. But when it came to politics, the mind needed help from the heart, and Piatakov wasn't sure that Rogdayev had one.

It was early in the afternoon when Brady returned, mopping his brow.

"We'll be gone tomorrow," he announced. "I got his address from a charming young typist in the Cheka office. We can renew our acquaintance this evening."

CAITLIN WAS HALF-DOZING IN ONE of the saloon car armchairs when she suddenly realized that Komarov had joined her.

"May I?" he asked, indicating the chair closest to hers.

"Of course," she said, wondering what excuse she could make to leave in a couple of minutes.

He sat down. "Given how long you've known the man, I thought I should ask you about Aidan Brady."

She felt surprised and slightly alarmed. "What do you want to know?"

Komarov leaned back in the armchair and interlinked his hands, looking for all the world like a cop ready to question a suspect. "Where did you first meet?"

"In a town called Paterson—it's in New Jersey, an hour on the train from New York City. There was a famous strike there in 1913 and a rally the following year to show the bosses we wouldn't accept any reneging on their promises. I met him at the rally. He was an IWW man at the time—that's the Industrial Workers of the World union—"

"The Wobblies," Komarov said, pronouncing the English word with a capital *V*. "Quite a few of them came here as volunteers in 1918. Brady among them."

"I traveled across Siberia with him," she offered, hoping to make their discussion more of a two-way street. "We arrived in Vladivostok within a few days of each other, and we were both heading for Moscow. But I expect you know all this." What, she wondered, was he really after?

"You traveled together as far as Yekaterinburg," he noted. "Then he went on while you—"

"I got myself arrested for trying to catch a glimpse of the czar through his prison windows," she said wryly. "Not my finest hour."

He ignored that. "But you ran into Brady again in Moscow."

"He came to see me at the house where I was living then. But how could you know that?" she asked, allowing a little indignation to enter her voice.

"He told me," Komarov said simply. "After he reported seeing you with a known English spy, I asked to see him in person, and he told me then. You never asked me who informed on you that summer, so I assumed you knew it was him."

"I guessed."

"But Brady *was* telling the truth—you admitted as much."

"I did," she agreed, wondering, with another frisson of panic, where all this might be going. His tone was matter-of-fact, but it was taking all she had not to betray her growing anxiety. "He wanted help finding a home for an orphan boy he'd rescued," she said, trying not to sound like a supplicant.

"So you said at the time. And I believed you."

"And the last three years have proved you right," she retorted.

"I never regretted it," he said, leaving the impression that he might still do so at some point in the future. "But getting back to Brady—have you seen him at all in the last three years?"

"Once, I think." She hesitated. "He and Sergei met on the Volga front that summer and discovered they both knew me. After Sergei and I became . . . well, he turned up with Brady on one of their leaves, and I told Sergei never again."

"Because you knew he'd informed on you?"

"It was more than that. People die around Aidan Brady, and I'm not talking about other soldiers. He was partly responsible for my brother's death in England. I know he knifed a policeman in Paterson, and he probably shot two in England. I'd bet money it was him who shot the boy in Kalanchevskaya Square, and now he's murdering men during robberies. Wherever he goes, people die, and he always gets to walk away." She looked Komarov straight in the eye. "I know the revolution needed killers like him to win the civil war, but it'll all have been for nothing if we don't find a way of taking their guns away."

Something flickered in his eyes and was gone. "I agree," he said shortly. "And the English spy—did you ever see him again?"

"He went back to England, as far as I know." Her heart was suddenly racing, but at least to her, her voice seemed commendably calm.

"I always wanted to go there," Komarov said unexpectedly.

"To see Marx's grave?" she asked with a smile, just about managing to ride the wave of relief.

He smiled. "I've had enough of graves. I was thinking more of the white cliffs of Dover and Holmes's flat on Baker Street. Maybe a tour of Scotland Yard."

"I don't think they do tours," she said. This interrogation was apparently over, but she doubted it would prove the last.

AS HE AND BRADY WALKED across the poorly lit town, Piatakov sifted through his memories of the man they were about to see. One stood out. They'd just retaken a village close to the Volga, where half the men were still lying dead in the streets, and most of the women looked like they wanted revenge on any available man for what the White soldiers had done to them. When Piatakov and Rogdayev had come across a young girl cowering in a barn, they had taken her to the nearest dwelling that was issuing smoke and, after shouting a warning, had cautiously walked in through the open front door. The woman they found inside had simply screamed abuse at them, and Rogdayev had screamed right back, whereupon the girl had bolted like a hare in the direction of the river. Their unit had stayed in the village for over a week, but they had never seen the girl again.

Rogdayev lived on Samarkandskaya Street, close to the border between the old and Russian towns. He opened the door himself and, after what seemed a moment's hesitation, hugged his visitors and led them upstairs to a large, high-ceilinged room with several armchairs and a Persian rug. An open balcony overlooked the street and dried-up river.

The propaganda chief was a big man, almost as big as Brady, with a round face and short, pointed beard. His eyes were almost black and, as Piatakov now remembered, rarely showed any real warmth.

Rogdayev asked them where they were staying and then asked after Aram Shahumian, whom he'd known even longer than they had. He was certainly eager to talk about the past, and the slew of nostalgic anecdotes that followed began to seem suspicious. Why hadn't Rogdayev asked what they were doing in Tashkent? Piatakov wondered. It was a strange omission, unless he already knew. Piatakov wondered if Brady had noticed and guessed that he probably had—the American didn't miss much. At that moment he was reminding their host of an action two summers before, a skirmish in a Ukrainian hamlet in which Rogdayev had been badly wounded and carried to safety by Aram. Reminding him of what they'd shared, Piatakov supposed, or suggesting the guilt that would follow betrayal. It was the wrong tactic, he thought. Rogdayev was one of those people who never let beliefs and personal interests stray that far apart.

He was certainly playing the genial host, pouring generous slugs of vodka and laughing too loud at Brady's jokes. "You're very quiet," he told Piatakov. "Missing your lovely wife, I expect?" He didn't wait for an answer. "I must make a telephone call," he added abruptly, rising to his feet and walking across to the wall-mounted receiver.

Piatakov stiffened and saw Brady do the same, but neither of them moved. Rogdayev was still beaming at them, waiting for the connection. "At last," he said, and gave the operator a number. "Pour yourselves another," he told his two guests. "Alexander Ivanovich?" he said into the mouthpiece. "The booklets have arrived. Yes, today. Can you collect them at the station first thing in the morning? Fine. Good night."

It sounded innocent enough, Piatakov thought, but in case it wasn't, the appeal to their old comrade's sense of loyalty would have to be quickly made.

Rogdayev was giving nothing away. "Stalin's tract on the nationality problem," he explained, reseating himself. "A strangely idealistic document, considering its source. But the Uzbeks here will be reassured, and that's the main thing. You've heard of the Basmachi, I suppose? They're mostly just brigands in the pay of the Turks, but they have to be defeated, and until they are we need to keep our Muslims happy." He poured himself another measure and pushed the bottle toward them. "And now you must tell me what you're doing in Tashkent."

Brady hastened to do so, without going into specifics or mentioning the rendezvous in Samarkand. "We're not challenging the party," he said diplomatically. "We accept that there are limits to what can be achieved in the present circumstances, and we don't want to criticize anyone, like yourself, who chooses to work within those limits. Each to his own—that's fine. But we want to move on and do what we do best. And no matter what it says—or feels compelled to say—the party needs help from outside. It needs more revolutions."

Rogdayev listened without interrupting, occasionally shaking his head. "I was afraid it would be something like this," he said when Brady had finished. "I believe you are wrong; I have to say that. The old days are gone, comrades—we cannot fight forever. Why do you think I threw in my lot with the party—simply because I am an opportunist? Well, perhaps a little"—a self-deprecating smile—"but that wasn't what made up my mind. Lenin is not infallible, his subordinates even less so, but do you know of any better leaders for this country of ours? We have won, and we must make the best of our victory. You seem—forgive me, but we are old comrades, and I will be frank—you seem to be simply running away the moment things get difficult. Like knights who move heaven and earth to free a damsel in distress, then leave her locked in the tower because she has a few pimples on her face. Pimples can be treated once the damsel is free."

"And what if her face is truly ugly?" Brady asked softly.

"Then perhaps we are talking about a different damsel." Rogdayev looked into his glass. "You will do what you think is right. You do not need my blessing."

"No, but we do need your help," Brady said. "Travel money."

Rogdayev laughed, but Piatakov heard no humor in the sound. "And you think I have rubles to spare? We fought together, and as I remember it, we never received a single day's pay for the privilege."

"We don't want *your* money, Vladimir Sergeievich. Moscow must fund your work here, and a few hundred rubles won't be missed. What better propaganda could Lenin ask for than another revolution in Asia?"

Rogdayev paused before answering, and in that space of silence, all three men heard the approaching car. The gun that appeared in his hand must have been hidden under his cushion. "I am sorry," he said without much conviction.

"But your loyalty is now to the party," Piatakov sneered.

"There was a time when you didn't find that reprehensible," Rogdayev retorted.

"We must never forget Vedenskoye," Brady said quietly.

"What are you talking about?" Rogdayev asked.

Piatakov's mind went blank for a moment, but then he remembered. The maneuver Brady had taught him three years before, which he claimed had been invented out west by two notorious outlaw brothers. And which had actually saved them only a few weeks later, in that tiny village not far from the Volga. Vedenskoye.

Back then, in the summer of 1918, a White officer had been holding the gun, an arrogant little bastard who couldn't have been much more than twenty.

Piatakov leaned forward to put his glass on the table, then suddenly threw himself backward, upturning the chair and falling behind it.

A shot crashed out. Piatakov scrambled to his feet to find Rogdayev slumped back, a large bloody hole under his left eye. Brady was pushing the Colt back into the waistband of his shirt, a businesslike look on his face.

"This way," the American said, walking out onto the balcony. "It's not a long drop."

"No," Piatakov said. He could hear feet on the street outside, orders being shouted.

"What then?"

"They'd be right behind us. We have to take their car."

Brady grinned. "Good idea."

There were feet on the stairs. Brady and Piatakov positioned themselves on either side of the door and listened as the men outside decided to knock it down. They came in with a rush, almost tumbling over one another.

"The Keystone Chekas," Brady said mockingly. "Drop the guns, comrades. That's good. Now, how many more are there with the car?"

The three men pursed their lips with unanimous obstinacy.

Brady stepped forward and put a bullet through the center of one man's foot. After looking more surprised than hurt, the victim slumped to the floor with a whimper.

Brady pointed the gun at another man's knee. "How many?"

"One."

"I'll get him," Piatakov said, grabbing the cap from the fallen Chekist's head and placing it on his own. He ran down the stairs and walked calmly across to the car, aware of people down the street ducking back into their houses. They were presumably thanking God that the Cheka hadn't come for them.

"Trouble?" a bored voice asked from the car.

"Only for you," Piatakov said, pointing Rogdayev's pistol at the man's head. "We're going upstairs."

In Rogdayev's room Brady was holding a gun on the prisoners with one hand and trying to unravel the carpet with the other. "It's all there is," he said. "You watch them."

It took the American ten minutes to prize out enough twine to tie all four men up. "Tomorrow they'll be thanking us for not shooting them," he said cheerfully, before ripping the telephone off the wall. "Let's go."

Piatakov took one last look at the dead Rogdayev and followed Brady down the stairs. "I'll drive," Piatakov insisted. The only previous occasion on which he'd seen the American behind a wheel, Piatakov had been astonished by the man's timidity, which was so at odds with his usual behavior. "Which way?"

"Our lodgings," Brady said.

"Is there anything there we need?"

"Probably not, but there's something I want to leave behind. A little misdirection."

It was only a five-minute drive through virtually empty streets. While Brady went up to their room, Piatakov checked the petrol tank before climbing back in behind the wheel. He remembered how shocked he'd been to discover that Caitlin could drive, and how angry that surprise had made her. The phrase "swallowing gender-based assumptions" stuck in his mind.

Brady came out looking pleased with himself, carrying both their bags. After dropping them in the back, he took his seat in the front and pulled out their dog-eared map.

"So we're heading south," Piatakov said, just to be sure.

"Yeah. Look for a sign to Khodjend."

"How far is that?"

"About a hundred miles."

Piatakov started the car. The streets were even emptier now, just one lone walker in the city center, swaying to a rhythm that only he could hear. There were no signs to speak off, but the moon was up, and the dark line of mountains occasionally visible off to the left meant he was heading in the right direction.

They had no trouble at the guard post on the city's southern boundary; the guards saluted them through, knowing a Cheka vehicle when they saw one. After that there was only the moonlit highway, rough but surprisingly wide, the odd copse of trees a dark blotch on the star-filled sky.

Brady lit one of his foul-smelling cigarettes. "I feel like Butch Cassidy," he said.

"Who?" Piatakov asked, glad that the windows were open.

"He was the leader of an outlaw gang. Back in the States. A successful one, for a while. And when it looked like he was going to get caught, he and his partner went off to South America. Started all over again."

"Just like us," Piatakov thought aloud. "What happened to them?"

The American laughed. "Don't ask."

Arbatov's Chasm

Through that day and the next, the train made steady progress across a land growing slowly whiter, barer, less hospitable. On the third morning, they all woke to find the grass was gone; to the south the Aral Sea was reflecting the sun like a vast silver plate left out in the sand.

McColl had considered leaving the train at Orenburg, slipping into the town in the early hours and losing himself in the general confusion. He hadn't thought Komarov would delay the train to search for a lost interpreter and was as confident as he could be of eventually finding his way out of Russia. He knew where Brady and Co. were going, and was almost certain of what they intended to do when they got there—all that remained was getting the word back to Cumming.

So why had he stayed on the train? He had convinced himself that the nearer they got to Persia, the better his chances of reaching friendly soil. And he had started to wonder whether Cumming had the wherewithal to find and stop a group of renegades that was probably under the protection of both Five and Delhi's DCI. Or indeed, whether he'd want to as much as McColl did. Gandhi and his fellow stretcher-bearer hadn't carried Cumming down from Spion Kop, and it hadn't been

Cumming's foster child that Brady had murdered in Kalanchevs-kaya Square.

And then of course there was her. The woman he thought he'd seen the last of.

She might still love her husband, as she certainly did her work. But there was no point in kidding himself—he loved her as much as ever.

IN THE DAYS THAT FOLLOWED their departure from Orenburg, Caitlin couldn't shake the feeling that someone out there was testing her resolve. Sergei's departure, the carrion pile at Ruzayevka Junction, the roar of hunger at Sorochinsk . . . each accompanied by a cold voice intoning: "See, this is another price to pay. Are you willing to pay this one? If so, we'll move right on to the next."

The latest blow had been the news she'd received in Orenburg. Anna Nemtseva, the Zhenotdel worker from Orel for whom she and Kollontai had been seeking justice, had risked going back for a family emergency and been found two days later floating in the Oka River. The local Cheka had explained her death as accident or suicide and put down the gaping head wound to her striking a bridge as she jumped or fell.

Caitlin remembered Anna's arrival at the Zhenotdel's door that spring. Even after what the young woman had already been through, she'd been so full of hope for the future.

Had it been misplaced? Had Caitlin's own? As she'd also discovered that day, the Orenburg Zhenotdel's three delegates were at the end of their collective tether. Having been vilified, mocked, and obstructed at every turn by their male so-called comrades, the women concerned seemed perilously close to quitting in disgust. In the hour they'd spent together, Caitlin had done her best to provide fresh heart, but couldn't pretend she'd convinced either them or herself.

Sometimes she couldn't help feeling that it was all going wrong. Not the way Sergei thought it was—she didn't believe that the party was deliberately betraying its own ideals. It had more to do with the size of the original task, now swollen further by the depredations of the last few years. People had had enough of chaos, and their instinct was to hunker down, to defend what they had against the threat of the new.

"If we just keep opening doors," Kollontai had once told her, "sooner or later women—and men—will choose to walk through them."

Perhaps. But these days there seemed to be more doors closing than swinging open, and that augured badly for the Zhenotdel. If the revolution regressed, if democracy withered and the bureaucrats ruled, all those institutions—the party, the soviets, the unions— which conceived and realized progressive ideas would eventually turn into hollow shells, mere parodies of what they had promised. And the Zhenotdel's future would be no different. In Russia at least, the women's struggle was only one part of the revolution, and like all the other parts, it had no chance of succeeding alone.

Which was all too depressing. She turned her mind to her other immediate problem, who was probably playing chess with the Grand Inquisitor.

It was weird dealing with the false Jack, who seemed to be making up his false history as he went along. In the saloon on the previous day, he had recounted an abortive attempt to learn the piano, waxed lyrical about the color of some far-off hills, and advised them all to taste the melons in Tashkent. He had never mentioned the former in their real life together, nor taken much notice of the landscape. She wondered if he'd even been to Tashkent, let alone acquired a taste for its melons.

Every now and then, she'd had glimpses of the Jack she remembered: a facial expression, a way of holding himself, a swiftly dimmed look of the eyes. This Jack was more disturbing than the false one, mostly because this was the one she had loved. Like no other, indeed. She remembered once telling him that only the world ending could tear them apart, and then the old world had duly obliged. Or so she and millions of others had thought.

Was there any hope for them? In spite of their being part of the hunt for her husband. In spite of the fact that they were probably still on different sides. And those were just the hindrances she knew about. He might have a wife by now, and *his* marriage might have a future—he hadn't said anything, but why would he?

If she did want him back, there was no guarantee he'd want her. She didn't think she'd take him back if he'd treated her the way she'd treated him.

Why was she even thinking about this? Because she still loved him? Because despite everything, he was still unfinished business as far as her heart was concerned?

There were so many reasons not to fall in love again or give him any sign that she was doing so. She might admit to herself that she wanted him, but acting on the thought was something else entirely.

And there was still Sergei to think of. She had loved him once, though not in the way she'd loved Jack.

She often regretted letting him know that. If she'd been more willing to play a part, he might have stayed on the rails and not gone rushing off to pastures new with a killer like Aidan Brady.

No, she told herself, Kollontai's voice in her ear. The man had made his choice, and it looked as though both he and she would have to suffer the consequences.

KOMAROV WATCHED PIATAKOVA AND THE Englishman share a stroll up the platform at Aralsk, politely forcing a passage through the throng of peasant saleswomen. The wares on offer—fish and bread, cakes and pastries, even the odd duck and goose—were certainly impressive and a stark reminder of how badly the war had affected distribution. Russia had enough food—the party just had to find a way of getting it where it was needed.

Maslov was walking toward him, holding a piece of paper and smiling. In his loose shirt and army breeches, he looked like a young, off-duty cadet, the sort who would have taken a young girl rowing on the Moscow River before the war.

"A message from Chairman Peters," Maslov said, passing it over.

Komarov sat down on the carriage steps and read it. The renegades *had* known another anarchist in Tashkent. A man named Rogdayev, whom they'd robbed and killed. After which they'd taken off in a stolen Cheka car.

He sighed and swished a fly away from his face. It was beginning to look like he and Dzerzhinsky had erred on the side of optimism when it came to catching these men.

Piatakova and the Englishman were on their way back down the platform, laughing at something or other. He knew he should have pressed her harder about the agent she had admitted meeting in 1918, but had known in that moment that he was more than a little afraid of what he might find out. If a comrade with her record of service and devotion to the revolution turned out to be a traitor, there wouldn't be many left to trust.

PIATAKOV AND BRADY ARRIVED IN Samarkand late in the afternoon. The last lap of their three-day journey had been spent in the back of a peasant's cart, in the company of several hundred ripening melons. Dropped off in the heart of the old town, they just stood where they were for several moments, feeling hot and sticky, wondering where to go. Aram had forged them spare sets of papers, but the Russian town would be on full alert, with every available Chekist checking and double-checking each and every new face. This time staying in the old town made more sense.

This was easier to decide than arrange, but unsolicited help was soon at hand. The two men were sitting in a *chaikhana*, drinking tea and staring at the huge, half-ruined mosque that towered above them, when an old man came up and addressed them in heavily accented Russian. "It's called the Bibi-Khanym," he said, "after Tamerlane's favorite wife."

Brady offered him a seat.

The old man told them he was German by birth. A mercenary in the army of Czar Alexander III, he had remained in Turkestan after the Russian conquest of Transcaspia had been completed in 1881. He might have been a soldier by trade, he said, but he was a painter by inclination, and the Central Asian light . . . well, he had never known anything like it. He had lived in Samarkand for over thirty years, painting the old town and selling the finished canvases to visitors and Russian colonists. Or had until recently. Now, with the revolution, the market had more or less dried up;

no one wanted the past on their walls anymore, not even a past as ancient and unthreatening as Samarkand's. But there were still a few people with taste. "I am on my way to a customer now," he said, patting the battered leather case by his side. "Would you like to see?"

"Of course," Piatakov said.

The unwrapped canvas showed a long line of deep blue domes climbing a yellow-brown hill, set against a pale blue sky. The style reminded Piatakov of some German paintings he'd seen at an exhibition in Petrograd before the revolution, all bold colors and minimal lines. Expressionists, the artists had called themselves. He hadn't known quite how to take them, but this . . . it had a simplicity that told no lies. "It's beautiful," he said.

The old German gave them an ironic smile but seemed pleased nevertheless. "The place is called the Shah-i-Zinda," he said. "And it *is* very beautiful. About a mile over there," he added, nodding toward the east. "And you?" he asked, rewrapping the canvas. "What are you doing with your brief time here on earth?"

Brady and Piatakov exchanged glances. "We are having a little trouble with the authorities," Brady admitted with a smile. "We need somewhere to stay in the old town."

The old man didn't raise an eyebrow. "Any enemy of theirs is a friend of mine," he said brightly, and gave them directions to a place where they should find a room. "Mention my name," he said as he left, "Bertolt."

The hostel proved easy to find, a caravansary set back from the crossroads at the old town's eastern gateway; they had actually passed it on their way in. The lower floor was a *chaikhana*, above and behind which a long building with half a dozen rooms had been dug into the hillside. The proprietor, a morose-looking Uzbek, grunted on hearing the German's name but took their money and asked no questions.

The room was on a corner, with unglazed windows facing north and east. Looking through the former, Piatakov saw a summer mosque on a flattened ridge, its colonnaded prayer canopy flanked by ornate minarets. Beside and slightly below it, there was a sprawling one-story compound, containing both inner and outer courtyards. Because of the hostel's elevation, he had a view of the inner sanctum, albeit one interrupted by trees.

Joining him at the window, Brady took a look with his collapsible telescope and let out a soft whistle. He passed the instrument to Piatakov, who soon espied the reason. The courtyard was full of young women, all unveiled.

"A harem?" Brady said, as if he couldn't quite believe it.

"Or a lot of daughters," Piatakov responded drily. He was examining the view through the other window, where the line of blue domes from Bertolt's painting tumbled down their grave-strewn hillside.

"Where there's a harem, there'll be money," Brady mused out loud. "We'll soon be down to our last few kopeks again."

"Let's wait until the others arrive before we let the Cheka know we're here," Piatakov suggested mildly as he watched a huge black bird touch gracefully down on the crown of a dome.

PIATAKOV SLEPT BADLY AND WOKE up scratching a new crop of bites. The darkness was only just breaking, the town still quiet. Through the window a distant line of low hills was silhouetted against the faint glow of the coming dawn.

He left the room quietly and climbed the steps to the flat roof, where a young boy was curled up in sleep. Samarkand was spread out around him, a vista of flat yellow-brown houses interspersed with the occasional dome. Away to the west, a clutch of minarets guarded three large buildings, which themselves formed three sides of a square. The Registan, he thought, remembering the engravings Brady had shown him in the Moscow library. Their rendezvous point. He wondered if Aram was already here.

The line of hills grew darker, the sky yellower; then the first sliver of the rising sun flashed in a distant cleft. A cock crowed in response, and the sleeping boy sat up abruptly, rubbing his eyes. Noticing he had company, the boy said something in his own language, and when Piatakov simply shrugged in reply, he almost leapt to his feet and left, bare feet slapping on the earthen steps.

Piatakov took a last look around, then followed him down. Brady was awake and sitting at the window with his telescope.

"Movement," he reported, handing the instrument over.

All Piatakov saw was a woman hurrying across the inner court-yard, carrying a basin of water.

"Look to the right," Brady said, "where the road climbs level with the front gates. There's an alley there. It must go around the back; it can't go anywhere else."

"There's also a dog," Piatakov told him. It was a large wolflike creature, lying against a wooden outhouse.

"I know. But he won't be a problem."

"This one may be the exception," Piatakov suggested. But he knew that wasn't likely—the American had a way with dogs that verged on the miraculous.

"I doubt it," Brady said, in a tone that precluded even the possibility. He pulled on a shirt, announced he was hungry, and left the room. Ten minutes later he was back with a tray bearing bowls of yogurt, two small omelets, bread, and a jug of tea. There were even four large chunks of sugar.

They ate and drank with relish, then sat for several minutes in contented silence before Brady went back to the window to reexamine the view. "Tamerlane never lost a battle," he said after lowering the telescope. "I can't remember any other great general who could say that. Lee, Hannibal, Napoleon—they all lost the last one. Tamerlane won them all. He conquered Mesopotamia, Turkey, Russia, India. He was on his way to China when he died. And this was his capital," he added, raising the telescope once more. "It was about twice the size it is now. All the other cities he took, he killed every last person and made a mound of their skulls."

"A real sweetheart," Piatakov murmured.

Brady smiled. "Now we make enormous graveyards. Endless fields of crosses. The bourgeois way."

"That's progress," Piatakov said wryly. This was a typical conversation between them, he thought. Knowing and bitter. They were so tangled up in history that the present was beginning to feel unreal.

THE TRAIN JOURNEYED ON ACROSS the desert steppe. A returning traveler told McColl that in spring this stretch was a carpet of flowers, unsurpassed in loveliness, but now the land was parched and mostly bare. Not that there was uniformity: swathes of yellow-brown earth would dissolve into sand or disappear beneath drifts of snow-white salt; flat horizons would break into rounded hills or jagged escarpments; occasionally the line would veer close to the Syr Darya, the Jaxartes of ancient times, a river as brown as the land it traversed. Two or three times a day they would pass caravans of a hundred camels and more, shepherded along by tribesmen in wide skin hats, who would rein in their mounts and watch the train steam by through hooded eyes.

Small settlements were dotted along the line, each with its handful of scrawny trees and mosaic of mud houses, its cavorting children and impassive white-robed men. In the small town of Termen Tyube, they saw their first mosque, its clay dome barely rising above the roofs, a skittish mule tethered beside the arched doorway.

They were now into the thirteenth day of the journey and less than five hundred miles from Tashkent, but with the driest stretch still to come. Since Aralsk, drums of water and bricks of dried camel dung had been loaded onto the tenders at each stop, but when the settlements disappeared, there was only the desert to water and feed the engines. Every few hours parties of soldiers would trek out toward a smudge of green that the observer had spotted from his carriage-roof vantage point, some carrying axes for cutting through the saxaul roots, others rolling iron drums across the cracked earth to replenish the water supply. McColl joined the first party, his appetite for exercise overcoming his fear of the heat, and wished he hadn't. Neither in Egypt nor in India had he ever experienced such a blazing sun.

With dusk approaching, the train brought them close to a large oasis. Here it stopped for several hours, partly to take on a full load of water, partly to allow its passengers and crew the luxury of a long warm bath. Save for the unhappy shift of troops left to guard the train, everyone trailed a quarter mile out across the desert, reminding McColl of a charabanc party searching for the sea at low tide. One woman's bright pink parasol completed the picture.

Once water had been taken for drinking and the engine, everyone waded in. McColl had wondered what level of propriety the mixing of the sexes would produce, but apparently no one else had thought the issue worth considering, and as far as he could tell, the few naked women received no more attention from the men than they would have done in a doctor's surgery. It made him feel slightly ashamed of his own interest in Caitlin's slim frame, which was every bit as desirable as he remembered it.

He lay back in the shallow water and studied the empty sky. With the light now fading in earnest, stars were beginning to appear, and he found himself remembering nights on the deck of the ship that had taken him out to South Africa and the astronomy-loving sergeant who'd taught him the constellations. It seemed so long ago, yet here they all were, blinking back into view, insisting that nothing had changed.

Caitlin was a Leo, he thought, searching in vain for that group of stars. Komarov's news from Tashkent—that after murdering an old comrade, Brady and her husband had managed to escape—had clearly upset her, but she now seemed increasingly resigned to their trip proving longer than expected.

McColl wasn't about to complain. He was in no hurry to leave her again.

AN HOUR OR SO LATER Caitlin and McColl were both in the saloon when the train clanked wearily to yet another halt. She put her face to the window, shielding her eyes against the reflected light. "Let's go outside for a minute," she suggested.

They climbed down and walked a few yards from the train. The desert stretched darkly away, the receding curves of the dunes like an ocean of sleeping giants. In the sky above, the Milky Way floated like a jeweled veil.

All down the train, people were getting out to stretch their legs. She considered putting her arm through his but decided it wasn't a good idea.

"Tell me about your husband," he said, denting her sense of well-being.

"What would like to know?" she asked, more brusquely than she intended.

"How did you meet?"

"I met him first at Kollontai's wedding, at the beginning of 1918. But we didn't . . . didn't become lovers until the spring of 1919, a long time after you and I . . . And we didn't see much of each other—I was in Moscow, and he spent most of his time away at the front."

"Why did you get married?"

"He wanted to. I was never sure why, and I don't think he was either."

"I see."

No you don't, she thought. "It was part of the war," she said, feeling she owed him some sort of explanation. "Most people called them 'comrades' marriages'; Kollontai's phrase was 'erotic friendships.' People who liked each other sharing a bed, without thinking too far into the future."

"Ah."

"What about you? Have you married again?"

"No." He hesitated. "I was with someone for a while. It sort of started by accident and lasted a few months."

She was surprised that hearing this hurt and more than a little disappointed in herself. "So what else have you been doing with yourself?" she asked lightly.

"Repairing automobiles. Converting some for disabled veterans. And I've just spent a few months in prison."

"What for?"

"Knocking a policeman over."

"That doesn't sound like you."

"It's a long story. Next time we have an hour to spare . . ."

"How's your mother?"

"Flourishing, despite everything."

"I was sorry to hear about Jed," she said. Jack's brother had been dead for almost three years, which seemed a long time to delay her condolences. She dragged herself back to the present and asked him what he thought of Komarov's chances of catching Brady and Sergei.

"Not bad, I'd say. I don't know about your husband or the Armenian, but Brady and the Indians should stick out like sore thumbs in Turkestan, and there must be a lot of Cheka offices between Tashkent and the border."

"Yes," she agreed. She no longer knew whether Sergei's capture would relieve or dismay her.

"I suppose you'll be returning to Moscow the moment this is over," McColl said.

"Of course," she replied automatically.

MCCOLL ADVANCED HIS SECOND PAWN and took a large sip of vodka. Caitlin had retired for the night, and Arbatov had recently discovered that one of the women traveling alone was also bound for Verny. Maslov was probably polishing buttons or boots.

"Do you have any brothers or sisters?" Komarov asked.

"No, none," McColl replied, instantly on guard.

"I had a brother," the Russian said. "He was older than me, three years older. He joined the navy in 1900, and we celebrated his commission and the centenary with a single party." He smiled wryly. "Which felt ironic even then."

"What did?"

"Oh, all that stuff about the new century: the fresh start, the new man, peace between nations. All of it. And there we were happily assuming that the military offered the brightest of futures."

"What happened to your brother?" McColl asked two moves later.

"Vassily went down with his ship at Tsushima. I was twenty then, and my father expected me to follow my brother's example. But I refused. Not for political reasons or none that I'd consciously worked out. As you no doubt remember, when the Japanese War ended the military's prestige was lower than ever. I was a student at the time, a law student in Moscow, and the last thing I wanted to do was fight for the czar. People used to assume that all law students were reactionaries, but in most cases the reverse was true, and for good reason. It's only in countries like England and America that lawyers make money, because there the law has an empire of its own, independent from the state. We had no such expectations, and most of us were constitutionalists, dreaming of parliaments and bourgeois democracy."

He paused to bring out a knight. "Fortunately I failed my law exams. There was too much to learn, and I had too many other interests—politics, women, playing cards. Rural property law couldn't compete. So, I became a policeman. A friend of my father's secured me a post at the Moscow Investigation Department, and rather to my surprise, I found myself loving the work. There was something different every day, and it was always interesting."

"Then how . . . ?"

Komarov poured them each another couple of inches. "How did I get from there to the deputy chairmanship of the M-Cheka? Well, I'd always been politically minded—my mother once told me how enraged I'd been as a four year old when we found ourselves watching a column of men in chains on their way into exile. In my first year as an investigator, I was just a problem solver, and quite a good one, if I say so myself. But if that's all a city policeman does, he ends up holding his nose. There are no men better placed to understand a society than those that police it and no men more wary of radical change because they know they'll be in the front line when the bombs and bullets start flying. Which is one of the reasons policemen drink a lot," he added, tipping back the glass of vodka.

"I was made the liaison officer for the Investigation Department's dealings with the Okhrana," Komarov continued, "which meant doing the investigative legwork on political cases whenever the Okhrana was overstretched. Which was most of the time after 1905. And I met quite a few of our current leaders over the years, sitting across a table from them in some Moscow station-house basement. It was usually an illuminating experience. Not always—the bourgeoisie has never completely cornered the market in morons—but usually. Most of them were better educated than my law professors, let alone me. I started reading socialist theory so that I could counter their arguments." Komarov laughed. "I still don't understand half of it, but I don't suppose it matters. Arbatov understands everything perfectly—he could quote you the footnotes in all three volumes of *Capital*—and look what good it's done him! That was always the trouble with the Mensheviks: they actually believed in a blueprint, a revolution in orderly stages. When reality proved resistant and Lenin had to tear up their precious plan, they all felt personally insulted. They still do.

"Anyway, one night I was working late at the office, and this Okhrana agent walked in through my door. I'd met the man several times and thought him a reactionary bore, so my first thought was that they'd searched my apartment and found some of the forbidden literature that I always had lying around. But no. He said he and his friends had been watching me for some time and asked if I'd consider working for the Bolsheviks. He, it turned out, had been one for years.

"I was astonished, but I didn't think twice, which was extremely stupid of me. He could have been an agent provocateur, and I should have checked him out first. But I was lucky—he was genuine.

"That was in September 1908, just before the Bosnian Crisis erupted. I went home to my wife, bursting to tell her, but she'd already gone to bed. I sat there looking at her sleeping face, and suddenly realized that I couldn't ever let her know. She was one of those people who never learn how to dissemble—her face always gave her away. When she discovered, after October, that we were on the winning side, she could hardly believe it." Komarov sighed. "But she died the next year," he said eventually. "What about you, Nikolai Matveyevich? Are you married?"

"Separated," McColl said, as he rushed to rebuild his mental defenses. Komarov's reminiscences were usually engaging enough to make you forget all other concerns, and McColl sometimes wondered if that was the aim.

"That is sad." The Russian emptied the second bottle they'd gone through that night into their glasses, and for a moment McColl thought he was about to receive his first dose of Russian sentimentality from a political policeman. He should have known better; Komarov was as practical drunk as he was sober. "Marriage may be a bourgeois institution," he said, only slightly slurring his consonants, "but I liked it. Remember what Vladimir Ilych said: you have to learn bourgeois manners before you can move on to proletarian graces. I don't think we're ready for free love, no matter what Kollontai thinks."

"I don't think Comrade Piatakova would disagree with you," McColl said, rather intemperately.

Komarov smiled ruefully. "No," he said, "but she is one of our best." He rose a trifle unsteadily. "I shall wish you good night."

McColl sat by himself for a few minutes, sipping the last of his vodka. He had, despite himself, come to like and respect Yuri Komarov, but letting that color his judgment would be extremely unwise. He suspected that Moscow's prisons were full of people who had found the man a good listener.

Walking back to his compartment, he stopped on the coach veranda to savor the cool night air, then impulsively clambered up the iron ladder and onto the swaying roof. The moon was higher and brighter now, suffusing the desert with a pale silver glow. In all directions the featureless landscape stretched out to the flat horizon, and McColl had the fleeting impression that the train was stock-still on moving tracks, throwing fiery sparks into the night but actually going nowhere.

CAITLIN WAS UP EARLY NEXT morning and found herself sharing the saloon with a talkative Arbatov. The Menshevik's suitcase was beside his chair.

"I'll be leaving the train soon," he explained. "Aruis is the railhead for Chimkent and Verny, and I'm told we should be there soon after eight. I can't say I'm looking forward to the road journey, but at least it'll be a change."

"Do you know anyone in Verny?" she asked him.

"Not a soul. But making new friends is always good, and I expect some old ones will be joining me soon."

"You really think it's all over, don't you?" she asked, surprised at the resentment she heard in her own voice.

He didn't take offense. "In the sense you mean—probably yes." He sat back in his seat, looking very much the professor. "Think what Lenin promised us in 1917." He ticked them off on his fingers: "A free press, a multiparty democracy within the framework of the soviets, a state run by the workers and policed by a workers' militia, an end to the death penalty. And what do we actually have? A gagged press, a one-party state run by that party's leaders and policed by its own militia, executions by the thousand. There have been some achievements—of course there have—but most of them are fragile. Take your Zhenotdel and what it's tried to do for Russia's women. Changes like those make sense to you and me, but the timing's all wrong. It's simple really. We're too late for capitalism and too early for socialism, and our Russia has fallen into the chasm between them. One that I fear will grow deeper and darker."

She wanted to argue with him, but the fears he was expressing were ones she felt herself. "I hope you're wrong," she said, for want of anything better.

"Oh, so do I, but I'm usually right about things like that. And I do believe this is my stop," he added as the train began to slow and another cluster of pale brown dwellings slid into view.

Caitlin wished him a good journey and watched through the window as he and Komarov exchanged jovial good-byes. As a less convivial-looking Chekist led Arbatov off toward a waiting line of horse-drawn carts, the train jerked back into motion.

Tashkent, as Maslov informed her a few minutes later, was only four hours away.

For Tonight's Sake

The booking hall at Tashkent station was wide, airy, and far from crowded. Komarov sat on his upturned suitcase, feeling impatient. He had sent Maslov off in search of transport, but the rest of the party were standing in a group awaiting salvation, metaphorically clinging to one another like any bunch of strangers in a strange land. Even the cotton experts were reluctant to leave and were busy blaming each other for the fact that there was no one there to meet them.

Maslov returned with the air of someone whose mission had been accomplished. "Our car is here," he announced, "and there are native troikas on their way from the hotel to collect the others."

"You go with them," Komarov said. "Yakov Peters is an old colleague," he added in explanation. Which was something of an understatement—for several months in 1918, the two of them had virtually run the Moscow Cheka in tandem.

Maslov hid any disappointment well. "It's the Tzakho Hotel," he said.

"Right." Komarov nodded farewell to the party and walked out to the forecourt. The sky was a bleached blue; the pastel-colored buildings on the far side of the park shimmered in the heat. A short, dark-haired Russian was standing by a dust-begrimed Fiat, holding the rear door open.

"I'm not royalty," Komarov told him, letting himself into the front.

The road into town was wide and flanked by artificial streams that flashed in the sunlight. At first there was little in the way of traffic, but when, after half a mile or so, they turned onto an even wider thoroughfare, he felt he was entering another, busier continent. Long strings of heavily laden camels vied with mule- and horse-drawn carts; dust and the flat smell of animal dung both hung in the air. Yet the buildings were still European, and tramlines shone in the earthen highway.

They veered around a large park, full of office workers taking their lunch in the shade of spreading trees, and entered a narrower street. This, Komarov guessed, was the oldest part of the Russian town. Ahead of them a pair of parked cars indicated the position of Cheka headquarters, while away to his right, a slim, incredibly graceful minaret rose above the square Russian mansions, like a flower climbing out of a tomb.

The Cheka building had clearly been a ballet school in a previous incarnation: in the hall off the vestibule, now filled with typists and desks, exercise bars still clung to the walls. Yakov Peters's office was on the first floor, a spacious room with a view of gardens and not much furniture: a camp bed, several native rugs, and a wide polished desk encircled by upright chairs. Three of the walls were hung with tapestries; the fourth had a large map of Turkestan and a framed portrait of Lenin.

Two ceiling fans were noisily whirring, but it was still incredibly hot.

Peters came out from behind the desk to embrace Komarov. The two men had never socialized much, but they'd done much the same job for the last three years and dealt with the same inner demons.

"Something to eat, something to drink?" Peters asked. He was wearing an open-necked shirt, baggy trousers, and sandals. A cigarette smoldered on the edge of an ashtray.

"Tea," Komarov said, remembering that the Lett was a teetotaler. Peters's complexion had been coarsened by the local sun, but Turkestan's Cheka plenipotentiary looked in much better shape overall than he had on the occasion of their last meeting, eighteen months before. The haunted eyes were gone. "You're looking well," Komarov said, feeling almost envious. "This place must agree with you."

Peters nodded. "Things are more clear-cut here; that's for sure. I don't keep bumping into old friends in the interrogation room."

"Why is Vladimir Ilych up on the wall?" Komarov wanted to know. Lenin was notoriously averse to that sort of idolatry.

"That was put up before my time. I was told there used to be one of the czar," Peters explained, "and that when it was taken down people used to stare at the patch on the wall. So someone decided to replace it."

"A new father figure."

"Exactly. People down here seem to want one."

The tea arrived, two steaming glasses and a bowl of lemon slices.

"It's a long journey from Moscow," Peters said, condemning one cigarette and lighting another. "And I still don't know why you needed to make it," he added with a smile.

"Ah."

"I have my suspicions, of course."

It was Komarov's turn to smile. "Which are?"

"Felix Edmundovich is trying to tangle himself up in laws again. 'Please, Vladimir Ilych,'" Peters said in a fair imitation of Dzerzhinsky's breathless voice, "'let me capture a real murderer or two.'"

Komarov laughed. "Something along those lines. But it's more than that. These really are dangerous men."

"And hard to catch. Ignore my cynicism, Yuri Vladimirovich."

"You haven't caught them, then?"

"No." Peters didn't sound that apologetic. "We had some bad luck. The two of them left the train at Saryagash—you know that— and they must have come into Tashkent by road. Unfortunately, the train they abandoned broke down ten miles short of here, and we only got to check and question the passengers on the following afternoon. By which time they must have passed through the guard posts. We started a city search at once, but . . . well, you have to understand the situation here: I don't have many men, and half of those I have are worse than useless. This is not Petrograd. The party and Cheka are almost a hundred percent European, but Europeans are less than half the population. The other ninety percent, well, they don't fight us in the cities the way the bandits, the Basmachi, fight us in the countryside, but few lift a finger to help us. They're waiting to see if the next wind blows us away."

He grimaced. "And then there's our side. I've got the usual quota of zealots who want to revolutionize Turkestan overnight—shut the bazaars, free the women, shoot the Muslim priests—and the usual quota of timeservers who don't want to revolutionize anything in case we all end up being roasted on some tribal spit out in the desert. And as if that wasn't enough, I've had three Zhenotdel women murdered in the villages in the last fortnight and the local delegates ringing me every ten minutes. First they won't have anything to do with the brutal Cheka; now they're demanding that we shoot the Muslim men in batches!"

Komarov smiled. "I've brought one with me," he said, and went on to explain Piatakova's presence.

"She's the American, yes? I met her several times in Petrograd after the revolution—she took a letter to my family in London. And I saw her again in Moscow, during the LSR uprising. She never struck me as a man-hater."

"I don't think she is. But she's certainly committed. Anyway . . ."

"Yes, where was I?"

"Shooting men in batches. What about the other two, the Indian and the Armenian? Any news of them?"

"None. But getting back to Piatakov and the American: the first we heard of their arrival was a telephone call from Vladimir Rogdayev. I'd spoken to him after getting your wire—he was the only ex-anarchist we knew of down here—and it turned out he did know Piatakov and Brady. We agreed that they might try and contact him, but he thought it was pointless to keep him under surveillance—that it would just scare them off. At the time I thought he was right, so we arranged a coded telephone message instead.

"Unfortunately, I was out dealing with the murder of the third

Zhenotdel woman when the call came, and it was taken by a man named Dubrovsky. Not the cleverest of men. And not the most mobile these days," he added as an afterthought. "Dubrovsky took three men to Rogdayev's apartment at around ten in the evening. And that was the last time anyone gave them a thought until the next morning, when one of my abler assistants realized they hadn't come back.

"We found them there, all tied up. Rogdayev was dead, shot in the head, and Dubrovsky had been shot in the foot trying to disarm them, or so he said. The car was gone, and we later discovered that it passed through the Salarsky Bridge guard post at four minutes past eleven." Peters sighed. "The idiots were so busy recording the exact time that they neglected to check the men's papers."

"That probably saved their lives," Komarov murmured.

"A small consolation," was Peters's rejoinder. He lit another cigarette; the smoke curled away out through the window. "We found the lodging house where they'd stayed the night before—as party members—road inspectors, would you believe! Their stuff was still there, including a map on which a route was marked out, south from here to Khodjend, then east to Andijan and over the border to Kashgar."

Komarov smiled.

"Exactly. It felt like a deliberate deception, even before we discovered that they'd returned to their room *after* killing Rogdayev. Some nerve, though, hanging around like that. Most people would have headed straight for the hills."

"Oh, they have nerve, all right. Which direction is that bridge you mentioned?"

"South. So maybe a bluff within a bluff." Peters got up trailing ash and walked across to the map. "These are the possibilities," he said, and went on to outline the various permutations of road, rail, and river travel.

"You've done your homework," Komarov concluded.

Peters took a bow. "We provincial policemen do our best," he said mockingly. "And," he added more seriously, resuming his chair, "I want them caught. The alternative sticks in my throat." He rummaged around in a desk drawer and pulled out a crumpled telegraph message.

It was from Dzerzhinsky and, for him, unusually terse. "If necessary, alert British," Komarov read aloud. "I don't like it either," he said, passing the message back, "though," he added thoughtfully, "I think the British know more about this business than we do. By the way, I have one of their agents in my party."

Peters looked astonished, then burst out laughing. "I assume he doesn't know you know."

"No. Nor does my assistant." He explained about Maslov. "He's better than I expected, but he can't control his face. As for the Englishman, I'm hoping he'll help me untangle this mess, without of course knowing that that's what he's doing. And as a bonus, he should lead us to all the agents they have down here. So we must put some men on him immediately—the best you can spare. He's not a fool."

NO ONE SEEMED TO BE paying him any attention, but Piatakov kept to the shadows as he walked south along Tashkent Street. The previous day they had decided that only one of them should attend the Registan on each appointed day and had drawn cards to see who would go first. Piatakov had "won," much to Brady's annoyance—their enforced seclusion was denying him Tamerlane's city and all its wonders.

There were many people on the street and much activity. Piatakov walked past richly carpeted *chaikhanas* full of gossiping men, and eating houses with large open windows, through which he could see, hear, and smell large chunks of lamb sizzling on skewers above the glowing charcoal braziers. Farther on, stall after stall was selling rice, then melons, then sheets of silk in an amazing variety of patterns and colors. In the square where they'd met Bertolt, several camels were tied up outside the *chaikhana*, presumably waiting for their owners to finish their teas. On several stalls Piatakov noticed a mélange of objects from distant Russia, presumably loot from the long-fled local bourgeoisie.

Above this tumult the soaring broken arch of the Bibi-Khanym seemed almost contemptuously otherworldly. According to Bertolt it had started crumbling as soon as it was completed; like Tamerlane's empire its initial conception had simply been too ambitious. "Still, even vanity is awesome on such a scale," the German had remarked.

A little farther down the street, Piatakov found himself passing a school. Through a line of open windows, he could see rows of children sitting on wooden benches and hear the teacher addressing them in what was presumably Uzbek. The pupils looked more attentive than his had sometimes been, but that had always been one of the challenges that made the job so rewarding.

He remembered the conversation he'd had with Caitlin after his first tour of duty in Tambov province. He'd done enough, she'd said with her usual bluntness—why not go back to teaching?

He'd scoffed at the idea. How could she talk about *teaching* when there was so much that needed *doing*?

Because that was what *she* did, had been her answer. That was what the Zhenotdel did. She and her comrades taught women to want and ask for more and men that their lives would also be fuller if women received it. The new society wouldn't just spring into existence because the faces changed at the top. People had to learn—had to be *taught*—how to live in a different way.

At the time he'd said, "Yes, but," but maybe she'd been right. It hardly mattered now. That ship had sailed.

Piatakov walked on, through a section of moneylenders, their rates chalked on boards beneath open windows. The crowd was thinner now, and he began to feel conspicuous. The towering Registan was visible above the roofs about half a mile ahead, and he decided to risk losing himself in the back streets. These were mostly empty and considerably cleaner than their counterparts in Tashkent. And though the Registan soon disappeared from view, he trusted his sense of direction. "So much iron in the brain," had been Caitlin's expression, one she had learned from her favorite aunt.

A church bell was tolling noon in the Russian town as he approached the Registan. The three huge madrasahs—they looked just like mosques to Piatakov but were, according to Brady, religious schools rather than simple places of worship—occupied three sides of a square, the fourth side being open. The two structures facing each other were similar, each with two flat-topped minarets flanking an oblong façade that contained a giant pointed arch. The third structure, sitting between them, was lower and wider, its façade flanked by two storys of small arched openings, like a Muslim version of the Colosseum.

The buildings were far from ruins, but they weren't in good repair. Myriad pieces of blue, green, and golden mosaic had fallen away, leaving patches of the yellow-brown walls exposed. Like the Bibi-Khanym, these ancient structures were a sight to behold, yet seemed almost incidental when compared to the world at their feet, where another cacophonous market sprawled. The open space was about four hundred feet square, and all but its rim was sunk some six feet below the level of the madrasahs. Steps descended from each main entrance into the jumble of stalls.

Piatakov's approach had taken him between two of the madrasahs, and he found himself looking out over the market, exposed to any searching eyes. He quickly walked across to the steps in front of the central building and took a seat halfway down them, level with the heads of the milling shoppers. If Aram was there, he would see him.

But there were no European faces in sight. Piatakov wiped his brow on his sleeve and waited. It was already five minutes past the appointed hour. How long should he wait? Another five minutes? Ten?

And then he saw the familiar wiry figure, walking slowly down the central aisle, patiently scanning those to left and right. There was no sign of Chatterji.

Piatakov was in the act of rising when two armed Russians brushed roughly past him as they descended the steps. Chekists! He looked around for others, but couldn't see any.

There was nothing else for it. He stood and waved his arms, hoping to get Shahumian's attention. A few more paces, and the Armenian suddenly noticed him. Shahumian grinned and waved back.

Piatakov desperately gestured him sideways; the two Chekists had seen his friend and were pushing their way through the crowd toward him, guns in hand.

Aram couldn't see them. He was still smiling at Piatakov, holding his hands up inquiringly, when the two men appeared in front of him. One held a gun to his head while the other reached for his papers.

Piatakov raced down the steps and into the crowd, which, with some trepidation, was edging away from the Chekists, creating a pool of space around them and their victim. By the time Piatakov had fought his way through to the front, Aram was loudly disputing his arrest, and claiming a lasting friendship with Lenin that his captors seemed reluctant to credit.

Piatakov gripped the butt of the revolver inside his shirt. There seemed to be only two of them, but what could he do with the crowd all around them. Which way would the Chekists take his friend? Did they have a car?

Piatakov looked around to see another two Chekists hurrying down the steps. At the same moment, a gun boomed, the crowd exploded in a hundred directions, and Piatakov was knocked to the ground. Scrambling to his feet, he saw an Uzbek—no, it was Chatterji—frantically trying to draw a bead on the Chekist wrestling Aram for possession of a gun. The other Chekist was writhing on the ground, holding his groin.

Another shot and Aram crumpled, still grasping the Chekist's gun hand. Chatterji fired, and the Chekist flew backward against a stall, scattering apples.

Piatakov sped across the widening space, shouting, "It's me!" as Chatterji whirled toward him. Behind him the other Chekists had been temporarily swallowed by the retreating crowd.

Aram was dribbling blood from the mouth; there was a gaping hole in his chest. But he was conscious. "Get out of here!" he wheezed.

"But—"

"A blaze of glory, Sergei! Go!"

Piatakov turned to Chatterji, who was skipping from foot to foot like a dancer on hot coals, a manic look in his eyes. He grabbed the Indian's arm and pulled. "This way!"

He sped down one rapidly emptying aisle, then turned into another where an overturned stall had created a bottleneck. The panicking crowd did its best to part before them, but there wasn't the space to do it quickly.

"Halt!" a voice screamed out in Russian. A shot was fired, the bullet crashing into a woman just beside them. She sunk to her knees; everyone else flung themselves into the dust. Piatakov and Chatterji raced on, hurdling over prone bodies and leaping up steps as bullets gouged showers of tile from the ancient walls of the central madrasah.

They ran into the building through the nearest doorway, only to find there was no way out.

For want of anything better, Piatakov pulled the Indian into one of the arched enclosures.

The pursuing Chekists followed them in at a run, which was a serious mistake. Piatakov shot one in the legs, Chatterji one in the torso. The two of them raced back out through the doorway, and found themselves facing an audience of thousands. Piatakov had the fleeting sense of coming out onto a stage.

Away to the left, two cars were squealing to a halt in the open space fronting the square. "This way," Piatakov said, pulling the Indian along the front of the madrasah toward the gap he'd arrived through.

They sped down the dark passage between the buildings, almost knocking over a group of veiled women, dodging under a line of stationary camels straddling the street, and ran into a narrow alley. A hundred yards, two hundred, their feet splashing through the dust, their breath now loud and ragged. For one dreadful moment, it seemed like a dead end, but a concealed turning took them through a yard full of tall clay jars and out into another narrow street. This one was empty and led them to Tashkent Street just in time to watch another car roar past in the Registan's direction.

Fifteen minutes later they were at the hostel. Piatakov sat down heavily, mopping the sweat from his face.

"Where's Aram?" Brady wanted to know.

"They got him. He's probably dead by now." Piatakov explained what had happened, dragging out each word with what felt an immense effort.

"You left him," Brady summed up coldly.

Chatterji also looked at Piatakov, as if expecting a new and better explanation. What blame there was was his, Piatakov thought angrily. If the Indian hadn't started shooting . . . Piatakov looked up at the American. "He told us to. And he was right. We couldn't have moved him, and the Chekists would have had us all."

Brady took this in, standing with one hand clenched inside the other. The Indian still looked resentful.

Piatakov felt sick. First Ivan, now Aram. But what else could he have done?

"You think he was dying," Brady muttered. "What if he doesn't?"

Piatakov gave him a cold stare. "You know Aram as well as I do. You know he would never give us up."

"I know, I know. And he doesn't know where we are in any case." Brady was pacing the room like a caged animal. "And the moment it gets dark we'll be on our way." He paused at the window and stared at the sprawling Uzbek compound across the street.

"What if they find us before then?" Chatterji asked. He was still breathing heavily, his cheeks twitching. Brady glanced at the Indian, saw something he didn't like, and walked across to throw an arm around Chatterji's shoulder. He began talking in a quiet, hypnotic undertone.

On the other side of the room, Piatakov watched the Indian's body relax, the dangerous glitter fade from his eyes. Piatakov walked across to the other window and the line of blue domes. A blue, blue world. Another comrade gone.

McColl had never seen Caitlin so upset.

"They sent the last girl back in a sack," she said, in a voice that made him think of broken glass. "They'd cut off her head and her arms and legs, and they pinned a message to the sack: *This is your women's freedom.*"

A late-afternoon sunbeam lay across the white tablecloth, revealing a mosaic of ancient stains. McColl put down his glass of beer, adding another ring to the pattern.

"She was only seventeen," Caitlin continued. "Her name was Ulugai, and she wanted to teach her friends to read."

"Not a lot to ask," McColl said quietly.

"They read, they learn, they question. And then they say no," Caitlin told him.

They were sitting in the huge communal room that took up most of the party hostel's ground floor. At the time of McColl's only previous visit to Tashkent, this had been the dining room of the Hotel Tzakho, invariably packed with people eating and talking to the strains of a full orchestra. Composed mostly of Austrian prisoners of war, the orchestra had included a bewildering variety of national melodies in its repertoire. Now the room was nearly empty and almost silent, just them and three Russian men, who were chatting in desultory fashion at a table ten yards away.

"Another woman was lynched for suggesting a husband shouldn't beat his wife," Caitlin said with a sigh, as if she couldn't quite believe it.

"Komarov thinks that the Zhenotdel workers may have been too confrontational," McColl said, remembering his conversation with the Russian earlier that afternoon. "For their own safety, that is," McColl quickly added when he saw the look on Caitlin's face.

"Does he indeed?" she said sarcastically. "And what does he suggest?"

"That the killing of Zhenotdel workers should be classed as a crime against the revolution, rather than as simple murder. I know," McColl said, raising both palms, "but it does make sense, at least in the short term. Men like these put no value on their own women's lives, but if they know that the government holds your delegates in the highest regard, they might think twice about killing them. Which won't help ordinary women much in the meantime, but at least you'll be able to operate."

"Perhaps," she said, looking slightly mollified. She was wearing a long Uzbek dress that she'd bought in the market that afternoon, dark blue with a pattern of large pink and white flowers. It suited her and went well with the bright red Zhenotdel headscarf that was loosely draped around her neck.

Suddenly her face lit up. McColl turned to see two women threading their way through the tables toward them, one dark and probably Uzbek, the other blonde and probably Russian.

Caitlin was on her feet, hugging the former. "This is Rahima," she told McColl eventually. "We met in Moscow."

The Russian's name was Shurateva. "I've got two soldiers outside," she said after the introductions had been completed. "Just in case."

Caitlin turned to McColl. "It seems you're not required."

McColl didn't hesitate. "I'll come anyway," he told her. He needed to establish wireless contact with India but still hadn't decided what to tell his putative listener. Attending a Zhenotdel meeting in such a hostile environment would be interesting for him and might prove dangerous for her. The empire could wait another day.

There was a *taranta* waiting outside. On the floor between the seats, there was a film projector and a boxed reel of film. Two Red Army men, small and rather frail-looking Russians, were leaning up against the vehicle, rifles cradled in their arms.

The *taranta* creaked alarmingly as they all clambered aboard, and the axles squealed as the driver set the ponies in motion. McColl was pleasantly conscious of Caitlin's thigh against his own, but she was in animated conversation with the other two women. Soon they were crossing a dry riverbed and entering the old town, drawing stares from the local population. Shurateva shouted directions at the driver, who gave no sign of hearing her but went where she directed.

"What's the film?" McColl asked Caitlin.

"*Makul-Oi,*" Shurateva answered him. "It's the story of a Muslim girl who refuses to marry the old man her parents have promised her to."

And who wins out despite many setbacks, McColl thought but had the sense not to say. Why did propaganda always sound faintly ridiculous, even when it made such perfect sense?

The *taranta* rattled down a narrow street and crossed a square that housed a large mosque. The sky was rapidly darkening, and a large flock of birds was drawing wide circles in the air above, cawing fit to burst. McColl felt a chill run up his back, leaving a sense of unease that he couldn't begin to explain. He closed his eyes for several seconds, then opened them just in time to see a scrawny tortoiseshell cat slither under a gate.

They arrived at the meeting place. McColl and one of the soldiers carried the projector through an arched wooden doorway and into a large courtyard. Rugs covered the ground, and about thirty Uzbek women were sitting cross-legged, their veils lowered, chatting with one another. When McColl and the soldier appeared, they turned their faces away, raising the veils as they did so.

"You'll have to stay outside," Caitlin told him.

McColl nodded and withdrew, joining the two soldiers outside the main doorway. This was set back from the street, on the rim of a semicircular space. A row of small trees on either side provided daytime shade for the wooden benches that lined the compound walls. Seating himself on one, McColl examined the scene. It was a wide street for the old town and seemed unusually quiet for the time of day.

As if to confirm his suspicion, two young Uzbek men squatted down across the way, taking occasional glances in his direction.

Through the door he could hear Caitlin talking in Russian, then pausing while Shurateva translated her words into Uzbek. The two women were setting the scene for the film they were about to show.

One of the soldiers offered McColl a cigarette. He took it, feeling his hands needed something to do. Was he imagining the tension in the air? The two young Uzbeks across the street were staring straight at him.

The whir of the projector was suddenly audible through the door, and flickers of light danced on the higher walls.

McColl got up and placed his eye against one of the star-shaped holes in the wooden door. The film was flickering on the earthen courtyard wall, which had the strange effect of dragging it into the past, offering only sepia when black and white was required. But the women, once more unveiled, were drinking it in, wonder in their eyes and upturned faces. On the other side of the courtyard, Caitlin was seated on the edge of a veranda, elbows on knees, her attention switching back and forth between the film and its audience, a smile of serene contentment lighting her face.

McColl felt a surge of sadness. For what? For whom?

Back in the street, the two young men had turned into five. They stared at him, and he stared back, then ostentatiously slid his pistol out of his belt and laid it on the bench beside him. One man began whispering excitedly to the others; then all turned their heads in the same direction, looking down the street at something he couldn't yet see.

He was not in suspense for long. Another dozen men of varying ages walked into view, and the whole assemblage squatted down in a circle, like a bunch of soldiers receiving their last instructions before setting off on a mission. Which wasn't an encouraging thought.

After a few minutes, the meeting seemed to break up. They all rose to their feet, and two of the older men started across the street, walking slowly but with obvious purpose. McColl picked up his pistol as his Red Army companions reached for the rifles they'd leaned against the compound wall. When the Uzbeks were about twenty feet away, he raised his hand to halt them. "Good evening," he said cheerfully in their language. "How may I help you?"

The use of their mother tongue seemed an unexpected development. The shorter, more intelligent-looking of the two offered a respectful bow. Like his partner he was dressed in a white linen shirt, matching trousers, and embroidered cap. "We wish to speak with our wives and daughters," he said.

"The meeting will soon be over," McColl told him.

"We wish to speak most urgently."

Too bad, McColl thought. "I regret that that is not possible," he said. "This is a party meeting, a government meeting," he added, remembering Komarov's advice. "It cannot be interrupted. But it will be over in a very short time," he promised, hoping it was true. A fresh contingent was approaching up the street opposite, and some of the newcomers were carrying flaming torches, which seemed to wrench the scene back several centuries.

"It is not right," the other Uzbek was saying, revealing several gold teeth in the process. "These are our women."

McColl just looked at him. The torches, the whining husband, the ludicrous religious trimmings. He thought of Ulugai, sliced into pieces by men like these.

"It is not right," the man repeated patiently, as if McColl hadn't heard him the first time.

"There is nothing more to be said," McColl snapped, and dismissively turned his back. When he looked again, the two men had recrossed the street, but an imam had also arrived, and was intoning passages from the Koran, jabbing away with his fingers to emphasize each point. McColl stood and watched, thinking it must have been scenes like this that had greeted suspect witches in medieval England.

He considered advising Caitlin to end the meeting before matters got out of hand, but loud applause and a quick look through the star told him the film had just finished. Two women were lighting kerosene lamps and hanging them from veranda beams; Caitlin and Shurateva were taking up position where the "screen" had been. When questions were asked for, several hands shot up.

Across the street the imam's voice grew louder and shriller. McColl had no idea where the nearest telephone might be, and any kind of search would mean leaving his post. The two soldiers were looking increasingly nervous and casting frequent glances in his direction, as if willing him to conjure up the magic carpet that would whisk them back to the safety of their barracks.

McColl made up his mind. "Tell Comrade Piatakova what is happening," he was telling the nearer soldier, when a stone bounced off the man's shoulder, knocking him back a pace. Two more thudded into the wall close by. The crowd was advancing slowly across the street, all except for the imam, who was urging them on from behind, wearing the sort of facial expression that Haig might have worn at the Somme. McColl wondered if shooting the man would help. The rest might be shocked into flight. Or tear him limb from limb.

He fired into the ground ahead of the advancing feet. The effect was dramatic: the voices both inside and out broke off abruptly, leaving only the city's murmur.

Then the men started forward again.

"Inside," McColl snapped, somewhat unnecessarily: the two soldiers were already halfway through the doorway. McColl ducked in behind them, and began searching for something heavy to reinforce the door.

Caitlin was at his side. "What's going on?" she asked. The smile was still there in her eyes—it had been too bright to fade so swiftly. Behind her the seated women were all turned toward them, their faces hard to read in the dark.

"A deputation of concerned menfolk," he told her, finally noticing a useful stretch of laddering. It might do. "Is there another way in or out?"

Caitlin asked Shurateva, who asked an indomitable-looking middle-aged Uzbek woman. The sitting women all scrambled to their feet on hearing the question. "No," the Uzbek replied in Russian. She walked past McColl to the door. "Who dares to violate my house?" she shouted through it.

Angry cries responded. "Wife stealer! Daughter of Satan!"

There was a thunderous crash, the sound of splintering wood. Before McColl could move, one of the soldiers fired through the wood, eliciting a yell of pain from the other side.

Then the door fell inward, spilling men into the courtyard. The Uzbek women retreated into the farthest corner, some yelling defiance, others streaming tears.

"Stop!" Caitlin cried out in the loudest voice he had ever heard her use. She stood fifteen feet from the invaders, palms held up to ward them off, her eyes brimming with anger. And for a moment she held them, but only that. She knew no words of Uzbek, and Shurateva, joining in, lacked Caitlin's natural authority. With a thrill of horror, McColl noticed that one man was carrying a sword.

He grabbed Caitlin's arm and tried to pull her away.

"What are you doing?" she shouted.

He kept pulling, but she squirmed out of his grasp. "Don't you want to fight another day?" he yelled back.

"I can't just abandon them!"

McColl instinctively dropped his head as something swished past his ear, then turned to see something flash on the end of an upraised arm. He pulled the trigger, and the man just dropped, his sword falling behind him.

Caitlin was trying to reason with another man, who seemed far more interested in splitting her skull. McColl put a bullet in the back of one of his thighs, and the single shot turned into a volley. A machine gun was firing in the street outside.

A man fell backward through the broken door like a bloodied sack of potatoes. His Uzbek friends were spinning this way and that, uncertain what to do. McColl walked slowly backward, pulling Caitlin with him, until he could feel the wall at his back.

No one came after them. Some men pulled themselves up and over the wall, silhouetting themselves against the night sky before they disappeared. Others just threw down their makeshift weapons and stood there waiting, suddenly submissive. They edged away from the sword on the rug, as if afraid it might explode.

The outside shooting stopped, and at least a dozen armed Chekists rushed in, forcing the Uzbeks onto their knees. The man striding in behind them could only be the local Cheka boss, Yakov Peters.

Komarov followed, his eyes ceasing their search only when they finally fell upon Caitlin.

As Peters's men began taking the Uzbeks away, the wives who tried to follow were roughly prevented from doing so.

"Let them go with their husbands if they wish," Peters said, staring at Shurateva.

She met his eyes but had obviously been shaken by the events of the last few minutes.

"Why wasn't the Cheka informed of this meeting?" Peters asked her.

"We did not think it necessary," Shurateva said quietly.

"You were wrong," Peters said flatly. "It's time you accepted that the Zhenotdel cannot function in Turkestan without our protection."

No one answered him.

Out in the street ten or more bodies were spread-eagled in the dust, each with an attendant woman sobbing, keening, beating her breast.

"And with their protection it becomes meaningless," Caitlin said bitterly to no one in particular.

An interesting equation, McColl thought, on the drive to Cheka headquarters. Perhaps what Arbatov had meant by his chasm.

Peters conducted the postmortem. Watching him at work was interesting, if only for the way he defied the usual expectations: McColl saw no signs of the man's legendary ruthlessness; he seemed like an ordinary, overworked copper. Peters listened patiently to Shurateva, only occasionally interrupting with a pointed question or comment. Komarov perched on a windowsill, face impassive, saying nothing.

Rahima's husband arrived, a handsome Uzbek about ten years older than her. He was clearly frantic with worry and was overjoyed to find her safe. She held his hand as if he were a little boy who needed comforting.

Caitlin at first seemed withdrawn, pale, almost in shock, but gradually the color seeped back into her face, the light to her eyes. Eventually something Shurateva said produced the faintest of smiles—an impoverished relation of the one McColl had seen on her face while the meeting was underway.

He and she were driven back to the hotel by a taciturn Chekist. They walked up the stairs together; then, just when he thought she would disappear into her room without a word, she turned and took his hand.

"I don't want to sleep alone tonight," she said softly, "but . . ."

What was the "but"? McColl wondered as the syllable hung in the air. He tried to read her expression, then gently kissed her on the lips. "For old time's sake?" he asked.

"For tonight's sake."

She led him into her room.

They undressed in the dark, shadows to each other across the room, then lay down side by side on the mattress. McColl lifted himself on one elbow and kissed her again, his hand stroking the underside of her breast. Her arms encircled his neck and pulled them together.

WHEN DARKNESS FELL SOON AFTER eight without any sign of the Cheka, Brady convinced the others that delaying their departure until the town was asleep was the sensible thing to do. He was probably right, Piatakov knew, but the extra hours still passed with agonizing slowness.

It was just past midnight when the three men clambered out of their hostel window and dropped onto the bare hillside. All were wearing the native clothes that Brady had bought at the market the previous day.

A half-moon hung in the eastern sky, throwing off just enough light for them to quietly negotiate the steep slope down to the street. There they stopped to listen for any unwelcome sounds, but the road was empty, the silence so complete that Piatakov briefly wondered if he'd lost his hearing. The scrape of Brady's boot on a stone was reassuring.

They scurried across the street and slowly walked past the summer mosque. The minaret above glinted in the moonlight, but the compound and the alley beside it were shrouded in shadow. "Remember," Brady whispered, "no shooting, whatever happens."

They advanced along the alley in single file, the turbaned American leading, left hands keeping contact with the compound wall. The yard ahead was bathed in grey light, and as they approached it, the dog began to growl.

Brady murmured something in English, using the same tone he'd used with Chatterji that afternoon. Piatakov wondered if the Indian was noticing the parallel.

The dog continued growling but didn't bark. They could all see it now, straining at the end of its tether, waiting to wag its tail. Brady kept murmuring encouragement until he was within reach, then ruffled the back of the neck with one hand and cut the throat with the other. The dog keeled over with hardly a whimper.

The American led the way, tiptoeing along a flagstone passage and into the inner courtyard. There was light in the window of the opposite wall and the whirring sound of an electric fan. After quietly edging around the perimeter, the three of them slowly eased their eyes over the sill of the open window.

Chatterji's gasp was understandable, Piatakov thought, and fortunately masked by the sound of the fan. Inside the room a young woman was sitting astride the master of the house, the tableau lit by a host of flickering candles. He was moaning with delight as she eased to and fro. Long black hair hung down her naked back, and her small breasts shone with sweat in the yellow light. It was a highly erotic sight, Piatakov thought, until he noticed the expression on the girl's face, which was cold, indifferent, almost bored. She might have been riding a rocking horse in a nursery, and idly wondering which toy to play with next.

Another short passage led into the house, where the door to the room stood half-open. Brady pulled out his Colt and walked in.

The girl saw him at once; she stopped moving but said nothing. The man asked her something, then opened his eyes. Wider and wider.

"Be very quiet," Brady said softly, reinforcing the request with a flex of the gun. Piatakov hoped the man understood Russian.

He did. "Who are you?" he half-whispered. When the girl abruptly pulled herself free of his shrinking penis, he grabbed one of her hands in his, as if they needed each other's protection.

"I'm Ali Baba," Brady said, "and you must be one of the forty thieves."

The room was certainly luxurious: the floors thickly carpeted, the walls hung with silk tapestries. Gleaming ornaments sat on several tables.

"I sometimes wonder if our revolution was only a dream," Brady said conversationally, putting the Colt back under his belt.

"No, no." The Uzbek pushed the girl aside and sat up, pulling a robe around himself. He was about forty, Piatakov thought, and no stranger to privilege. "You don't understand," the man said indignantly. "I am a member of the city soviet."

Brady and Piatakov both burst out laughing. Chatterji was still staring at the girl, who stood to the side, watching them through expressionless eyes. "Cover yourself," the Indian told her angrily in English.

She didn't understand him. Piatakov picked up what looked like a robe and offered it to her. He also felt uncomfortable, both sexually aroused and ashamed to be so. She couldn't have been more than fourteen.

"Well, comrade," Brady said sarcastically, "the party requires another generous contribution."

"But I am a not a rich man," the Uzbek said.

Brady's look around the room was an eloquent rebuttal. "Coins," he said succinctly, holding the man's eyes.

The Uzbek had a sudden realization: "You are the men they are searching for!"

"Don't you mean 'we?'"

"Yes, of course, we."

Brady shook his head. Piatakov wondered if the Uzbek was aware of how little life he had left. Not a great loss to the party.

The man was taking an embroidered purse from the table that held most of the candles. "How much?" he asked.

"All of it, comrade."

"But . . ."

"You won't be needing it."

The man's eyes widened in understanding; his mouth opened to cry out, but the sound was choked off by the knife sliding up through the ribs and into the heart. *"Allahu akbar,"* Brady murmured, wiping the blade on a chair.

Piatakov was watching the girl, whose eyes were no longer devoid of expression. She took a quick step forward and spat in the dead man's face.

Brady eyed her with what might have been amusement, then went back to examining the contents of the purse. "Good enough," he said finally. "This should get us to Afghanistan."

"We must kill the girl, too," Chatterji interjected.

Piatakov was outraged. "No!" he almost shouted with a violence that surprised even him.

Brady gave him a hard look, then turned to the Indian. "She's his enemy," Brady said, gesturing toward the dead man on the floor, "not ours."

"But what if she runs to the Cheka the moment we're gone? We must at least take her with us," Chatterji insisted.

"That seems sensible," Brady said quietly, looking at Piatakov. "We can leave her in a village."

"Dressed like that?" Piatakov asked.

"She'll be fine," Brady said. "It's not that cold."

Piatakov took the sash from the dead man's robe and passed it to her, indicating that she should use it to tie up the one she was wearing. She smiled faintly and did as he suggested.

The three of them retraced their steps across the inner courtyard, the girl walking with them unconcernedly. No one had thought to gag her, Piatakov realized, but apparently there wasn't any need—she showed no sign of making a fuss. They stood in the yard for what seemed an eternity until Brady led out three saddled ponies, their hooves muffled with sacking.

Piatakov mounted his, and Brady hoisted the girl up in front of the Russian, muttering, "Your baby, I believe." Piatakov was acutely conscious of her perfumed hair just beneath his face and of the warmth of her body through the thin robe.

"What's your name?" he asked in Russian, not really expecting an answer.

"Haruka," she said.

The other two mounted, the Indian looking slightly uneasy, though the ponies were docile enough. They walked them down the dark alley, the dust and muffles reducing the sound of their passage to almost nothing. At the crossroads they turned southeast and continued along past the foot of the avenue of mausoleums. The moon was high now, the blue domes shining in its glow. The girl's hair shifted in the breeze.

They walked the ponies for an hour, drawing a wide circle around the southern edge of the town. When they struck the dirt track that ran westward alongside the railway, they stopped, got down, and took off the muffles. According to Brady's watch, it was almost two in the morning.

Once they had all remounted, the American started down the track, Chatterji close behind him. Piatakov held the reins loose for several moments, then put his hands on either side of the girl's narrow waist and gently lowered her to the ground. When she gave him a questioning look, he pointed her toward the town.

She turned to see what he meant, then looked back up and raised her hand to touch his leg.

He watched her walk off with a sharp sense of loss and then wheeled his pony to follow the others.

THE CLOCK IN THE LOBBY claimed it was half past midnight. Komarov paused at the foot of the stairway to yawn, then slowly began to climb, marveling at the survival of the rich carpet, heedless for the moment of the vital role it was playing in silencing his approach. Maslov was a few steps behind him.

As his eyes came level with the floor above, Komarov brought himself to a halt. At the end of the dimly lit corridor, a man was opening a door with the kind of elaborate caution that suggested it wasn't his room. After a cursory glance around, he disappeared inside.

"Wait here," Komarov whispered to Maslov. Taking his gun from its holster, Komarov advanced down the corridor on the balls of his feet.

He reached the door, which was standing slightly ajar. Inside the room it seemed dark. There was no sound.

Komarov pushed the door back slowly, and there was the man, standing over the bed in a pale wash of moonlight. A knife gleamed in his hand.

He seemed at a loss.

"Put it down," Komarov said softly.

The man's head jerked up in surprise, but his shoulders sagged when he saw the gun. He placed the knife down on the empty bed.

"Now come with me." Komarov backed into the corridor, turning so the would-be assassin would come out of the room between himself and Maslov.

The man emerged, his features clearer in the kerosene glow. He was a Russian, probably in his early twenties, with fair hair and a flat, slightly Mongoloid face. Komarov pointed him down the corridor toward Maslov. The three of them descended the stairs in silence.

"Take him into the dining room," Komarov said. He checked the room number on the register, and a smile flickered on his face.

Maslov had sat the man down. Komarov took a chair and sat astride it, his arms crossed on the backrest, facing his captive. Maslov remained standing just behind the man's right shoulder.

"What's your name?" Komarov asked.

"Aleksandr Polyansky," the man said sorrowfully. He looked as if he was about to burst into tears.

"Why did you want to kill Nikolai Davydov?"

Polyansky wrung his hands. "I . . ." His face brightened suddenly. "But he's not really Davydov. He's an English spy, an enemy of the revolution!"

"We know," Komarov said, wiping the incredulous smile off Maslov's face. "I have known since Moscow, Pavel Tasarovich," Komarov told the young Ukrainian. "I decided it would be easier for you to behave naturally if you remained in ignorance." He turned back to Polyansky. "Why did you want to kill this man? And don't pretend it had anything to do with him being an English spy."

Polyansky searched the ceiling for inspiration but found none.

"Who hired you?"

The look of defeat returned. "A man in Samarkand," he mumbled.

"His name?" Komarov persisted.

"He never told me his name. An Indian. He came to me, gave me this man's description, said that I would find him here in Tashkent. He told me the man was an English spy. But I didn't do it for the money, you understand . . . It wasn't . . ."

"What did you do it for?"

Another silence. Maslov moved behind Polyansky and placed a hand on each of his shoulders, as if about to offer a massage.

"You must tell us, citizen," Komarov said.

The words came out in a sudden rush: "Passports, English passports for my family . . . We were branded as bourgeois . . . I can get no work . . . I . . ."

"Enough. Describe the Indian."

"Just an Indian." He shrugged helplessly. "About forty, maybe. Quite small. An Indian."

So it wasn't Durga Chatterji. "Did the Indian tell you where the English passports were coming from?"

Polyansky gave him a disbelieving look. "From the English."

"Telephone for someone to come and collect him," Komarov told Maslov. The whole business made less and less sense. Komarov tried to think coherently but thought only of how tired he was. He got to his feet and started pacing up and down between the lines of tables.

There was a quarrel between Englishmen—that seemed certain. A quarrel that had something to do with the American and his renegade friends. Was it possible that one group of Englishmen opposed their endeavor—whatever it might be—while another group supported it?

Perhaps. But why would *any* group of Englishmen give support to men like Brady and Piatakov? Either Komarov was missing some obvious point, or someone else had.

Where was Davydov? Komarov suddenly wondered. The Chekists outside had reported his and Piatakova's return to the hotel, and the Englishman had not gone out again.

A probable answer came close on the heels of the question. Komarov grunted. It looked as though Davydov and Piatakova had each unwittingly saved the other's life that night, he by leading his Cheka tail to the women's meeting, she by taking him into her room. As Komarov's father used to say, good fortune had a habit of repeating herself.

He heard the car pull up outside and told Maslov to take Polyansky out.

Alone in the empty dining room, Komarov turned his thoughts to Davydov and Piatakova. If he wasn't the English agent she'd met up with in 1918, then Piatakova had made a third disastrous choice when it came to romantic attachments—two foreign agents and a renegade wouldn't do much for anyone's political reputation.

If Davydov *was* the same man, and he and she had known each other for years, they'd done a wonderful job of concealing the fact. Had they been partners all this time? Had they acted out a growing friendship on the train so that finally sharing a bed would seem quite natural? Was Caitlin Piatakova an English agent, too, or simply so besotted with love or lust that she was willing to put her own life at risk?

He couldn't believe the former. She'd been living in Russia for years, and unless he'd completely misread the woman, her work at the Zhenotdel was a labor of love. She and the revolution's leading lady were bosom friends.

And she'd married a Russian, for God's sake. A committed Bolshevik then, a leftist renegade now.

So perhaps she'd told the truth in 1918. Perhaps Davydov's reappearance had come as a total surprise.

What would Komarov have done in her shoes? He would have asked what the hell her former lover was doing in Russia and, depending on the answer, decided whether or not to give him up.

If that was what had happened, she must have been satisfied with his explanation. And if Komarov was right about her, that could mean only that Davydov's presence in Russia was all on account of the men they were chasing, and wasn't part of any fresh attempt by the British to undermine the Bolshevik government.

Was it possible, Komarov wondered, that he and Davydov were actually on the same side?

Maslov was standing in the doorway, apparently waiting for his presence to be acknowledged. "What about the Englishman?" he asked when Komarov finally looked his way. "Should we arrest him now?"

His Majesty's Wireless
in Samarkand

Caitlin was woken by the sunlight streaming through the uncovered window. His hand was resting lightly on her hip. She carefully moved it aside and got to her feet, then walked across to the window, the breeze caressing her skin. The distant mountains were wreathed in shadow; on the street below, a boy was sprinkling handfuls of water across the dusty sidewalk.

She turned her gaze to the sleeping McColl. What had she been thinking, inviting him in? And not just him—their whole damn past. And yet, and yet. She couldn't deny it—not to herself—it had been as sweet as ever. He might not have been God's gift to every woman, but there was something about him—about *them*—that made her want to weep with joy.

It had been that way from the start, she thought. A love so sweet and all consuming that it left no room for the rest of who she was.

He stirred and opened an eye. She reached for the blue dress and pulled it over her head. "I'm going to the bathroom," she mumbled, and fled.

She washed herself from head to foot and examined her face in what was left of the mirror. "What should I say?" she murmured. That she'd enjoyed it, that they should do it again sometime soon. If she was using him, that was only what men had been doing to women since time began. Which of course was no excuse.

She made a face in the mirror and walked back to the room.

He was dressed and smoking one of her cigarettes.

"Let's not say anything," she said.

"All right."

"So let's go and find some breakfast."

ONCE CAITLIN HAD LEFT FOR the local Zhenotdel office, McColl ordered more tea and lit another cigarette. Why was he smoking again? What in God's name should he do?

Making love again had been wonderful, and he told himself to cherish what had happened, not use it to build up hopes of something more. Whatever would be would be and might well depend on how long they stayed in each other's company. Sooner or later her husband would either be caught or cross the border, and she would go back to Moscow to resume her work and life.

He hoped it would be later. In the meantime, he still needed a clearer picture of what Brady and her husband were actually planning and what support they had from whom. In his last conversation with Cumming in London, they'd agreed that if, as seemed likely, the mission took McColl toward India, he should attempt to contact DCI HQ in Delhi. "If the people you speak to know nothing about Brady and Co.," Cumming had said, "then you've alerted them. If, as seems more likely, they're up to their necks in the plot, you won't have told them anything that they don't already know."

McColl finished the apple tea and pocketed the raisins in the accompanying saucer, wondering which made the world go 'round—love or bastards in Whitehall.

Outside the sun was already busy transforming the city into an oven. It was just past nine o'clock, and the temperature had to be into the eighties. He walked down Chernyaevskaya Street, keeping to the shade of the *karagach* trees, and caught a tram heading east at the bridge that linked the old and Russian towns. A familiar poster caught his eye: the Moscow Circus was about to arrive in Tashkent.

He alighted from the tram outside the Kukeldash Madrasah and walked up a wide, stall-lined street that he seemed to remember led into Iski Juva market place. It did. He ordered tea at a *chaikhana* and cooled off in the welcome shade.

There was one other European face in sight, and it belonged to a man who had been on the same tram that he had. Was he being followed? And if so, why? Why would Peters keep a watch on one of Komarov's assistants? The man's presence could have been a coincidence, but he did have a sneaky look about him.

Another white face appeared right in front of McColl. Its owner, it seemed safe to assume, was not employed by the Cheka. He was about sixty, had a prematurely wizened face surrounded by white hair and beard, and carried a bright green parrot on his left shoulder. A large canvas bag hung from the other. "You want your fortune told," he told McColl, first in German, then, with bewildering fluidity, in a succession of other languages, most of which sounded vaguely Balkan.

McColl laughed. "Why not?" he replied in Russian. "How much?"

The man looked surprised. "You are Russian?"

"Of course."

The man just shook his head.

The Cheka could use this old man, McColl thought. "How much?" he asked again.

"A Kerensky note."

It was only an opening bid, but it was far too hot for bargaining. McColl took a note from his pocket and placed it on the mattress on which he was sitting. The man unslung his bag and opened it up at the neck, then offered it to the parrot, who delved in and brought out a tiny envelope in its beak. After offering the prize to its master, the parrot turned its gimlet eyes on McColl, with a look that said: "Why do I do all the work?"

The old man passed the envelope on to McColl and scooped up the note with his other hand.

"And where do you come from?" McColl asked.

The man cackled. "I was born in Serbia, but that was a long time ago." He was slowly backing away, as if concerned that the fortune foretold in the envelope might not be to his customer's taste.

McColl watched him sidle off as he opened the envelope. On a small piece of rice paper, the words "She loves you" had been neatly printed in several languages. He smiled to himself and placed it in his pocket. "Maybe she does," he murmured. In the distance the parrot squawked, probably in derision.

The Chekist—if that was what the man was—was still calmly sipping his tea. McColl would have to lose him, without giving the appearance of doing so. Which shouldn't be too hard in the alleys of the old town, McColl thought. Without another glance in the man's direction, McColl left the *chaikhana* and headed up Takhtapul Street, steadily increasing his walking pace as he did so. One abrupt turn led into another, and a half-demolished cart offered something to hide behind. If the Chekist saw him, he could say that he'd taken the man for a footpad; if he didn't . . .

After a minute had passed, he reached the conclusion that he wasn't being followed after all.

Watching out for the man just in case, McColl retraced his steps to Takhtapul Street and continued up it until he reached the covered bazaar he remembered from 1916. After passing booths containing silk workers, coppersmiths, and carpet makers, he recognized the narrow alley alongside the large rug emporium and, after one last glance around, ducked into it. Counting off the doorways, he let himself into the fifth.

The Indian was sitting in the small courtyard, watching one of his wives energetically beating the dust out of a Bokhara rug. He leapt up in alarm when McColl abruptly appeared, but once he realized who it was, his smile was almost too effusive. "Welcome to my home once again," he said formally, offering space on the carpet. He shooed his wife into the house with a few sharp words, then quickly recalled her to order tea. "I trust you are fighting fit, Mr. Voronovsky," he said in English.

"Yes, thank you," McColl said. "But I am now Mr. Davydov. I hope you and your family are all in the best of health."

A second wife, clothed in a jade-green sari, appeared with a silver dish of sweetmeats and was swiftly followed by a third with a plate of fresh figs. The two men nibbled in silence until the tea arrived, and all the women were back inside. McColl wondered, not for the first time, why sitting cross-legged was so uncomfortable.

"It is very hot, is it not?" the Indian said politely.

"Yes, it is. This meeting must be a short one, I'm sorry to say. I need to make contact with the head office."

The Indian poured the tea unhurriedly. "I most regret," he finally said, sounding not in the least regretful, "that our wireless set has not been received. They promise machine for several months, but . . ." He shrugged. "Do you wish sugar?"

McColl found it hard to conceal his annoyance.

"However," the Indian continued, "not all is despairing. I can get a message to Delhi in three weeks."

"Thank you, but I'm afraid my need is more urgent than that." He got to his feet. "I will remind London that you're waiting for a wireless."

"That will be most exciting of you," the Indian said solemnly.

McColl let himself out and walked slowly back through the old town. What should his next move be? The wireless in Samarkand was still operational—or had been when he left England—but that was a full day's journey away. And once he'd abandoned Komarov, there'd be no coming back. He would lose touch with the Russian's pursuit and, of course, with her. Again.

As it turned out, he was given no choice in the matter. Two Chekists were waiting outside the hotel; they bundled him into the back of their car, where his suitcase was already resting. Which was probably a good sign—if this was an arrest, they wouldn't have bothered to collect his belongings.

He also recognized the street the car drove down—they'd come down it on their way from the train station.

The train was waiting in a bay platform: one locomotive and two crimson coaches. Komarov and Maslov beside it, obviously waiting for him. The fact that they'd delayed their pursuit for a mere interpreter was gratifying but also seemed slightly mysterious.

"Where now?" he asked them cheerfully.

"Samarkand," Komarov said shortly. "Get the train moving," he told Maslov.

It seemed that fate was conspiring to help him. "Have they been caught?" he asked Komarov.

"No. But one of them's been killed—we don't know which. Not an Indian."

"So it might be Piatakova's husband."

"Yes, she's distressed. As you would expect."

McColl boarded the train, wondering why Komarov hadn't asked where he'd been that morning. Then again, his fictional self was supposed to come from Tashkent, so maybe the Cheka boss had assumed he was visiting family or friends.

He rapped softly on Caitlin's compartment door and, when he got no answer, gently pushed it open. She was sitting with hands clasped between her knees, a glimmer of tears on her face.

"Can I help?" he asked.

She looked up, managed a quarter smile, and shook her head. "No. Thank you, but no. I need to be alone."

"Are you sure?"

"Yes."

He retreated into the corridor, taken aback by how upset she was and disappointed with himself for feeling that way.

In the saloon he found Komarov and Maslov. "If one man was killed, what happened to the others?" McColl asked the senior man.

"They escaped," the Russian said wryly. "And at this rate we're never going to catch them. Why the hell aren't we moving?" he asked, sticking his head through a convenient open window in search of the answer.

As if in response, the wheels jerked forward, causing Komarov to draw in his head, and spread his hands wide like a magician completing a trick. McColl couldn't help laughing; Maslov's expression suggested they'd both taken leave of their senses.

The magic soon wore off. The train kept stopping and starting at what seemed increasingly frequent intervals. McColl took up residence in the saloon, which by now felt almost like a home away from home—the smell of leather and the rattling wheels, the familiar books and companions. It took him most of the afternoon to notice what had changed; Maslov was no longer able to look him straight in the eye.

McColl got up and walked through onto the rear veranda, feeling butterflies looping the loop in his stomach. He lit a cigarette and watched the rails recede across the empty desert. What had he done to cause such a change in the way the Ukrainian looked at him? He couldn't believe that his sleeping with Caitlin would affect the young man so.

No, they knew. Perhaps there'd been more than one shadow that morning; perhaps the Indian had already been under surveillance or was himself a Cheka informer. It hardly mattered. They knew.

McColl's admiration for Komarov went up another notch. A lesser man would simply have arrested him. He also realized with a sinking heart that now he'd have to keep his distance from Caitlin. If he didn't, she might wind up in front of the same firing squad.

PIATAKOV CROUCHED DOWN BESIDE THE tracks, supporting himself with one hand on a coach buffer, calculating distances and angles. The two Chekists were leaning against the wall of the Kagan station building, talking idly to each other and smoking cigarettes. They had checked all the alighting passengers' papers when the train arrived but had shown no inclination to investigate those still on board. Presumably the search was still unfocussed: there would have been no time to get a message through before they'd cut the wires. Though that in itself, once discovered, would be suggestive enough.

A one-coach train was sitting in a bay platform some hundred yards away. Beyond it, across a wide expanse of yellow-ochre desert, Piatakov could make out Bokhara's mud walls and a line of trees that presumably followed a river. Which probably meant that the small train was headed that way. In which case, where was the one to Kerki? The only other wheeled vehicles in sight, aside from the train he'd been on, were the rusted wagons standing in the sand-blown siding.

The two Chekists were looking away, talking to someone inside the station building. Piatakov took his chance, moving out from behind the train in a crouching run. After reaching the end of the building without raising any alarm, he took a cautious look around its farther corner, and found himself eye to eye with a middle-aged Russian woman. She was sitting in a droshky, shading herself with a red parasol. An Uzbek was busily tying her luggage onto the back, stressing the efforts he was making on her behalf with a series of groans and mumbled asides.

Piatakov walked across and offered a respectful bow. "Good afternoon, madam," he said. "Would you happen to know if there's a train to Kerki?"

She stared at him for several seconds, probably wondering how a wretch in native clothes could act and talk like a civilized Russian, then decided to be generous. "I'm afraid not," she said with a gracious smile. "I have only just arrived here myself. My husband is the new consul in Bukhara," she proudly added in explanation.

"Kerki," the Uzbek said, emerging from behind the droshky, "*nyet.*" He made a throat-cutting motion to emphasize the point. "Basmachi trouble," he added with a grin, and swung himself up into the driving seat. He flicked the whip casually across the back of the pony, which turned to look at him as if expecting confirmation of these travel arrangements. The driver provided it with another flick, and the pony, apparently satisfied, set the droshky in motion. As it turned a tight circle and clattered off, the new consul's wife gave Piatakov a suitably regal wave.

There was no one else in sight. A whistle announced the departure of one of the trains. *"Nyet"* seemed clear enough, the Basmachi rebels a reasonable explanation. Piatakov walked back along the end of the station building and again put his head around the corner.

The two Chekists had disappeared, and the one-coach train was in motion, chuffing its way down the single track toward the ancient city walls. He walked swiftly across to the stationary train, stepped up onto the rear veranda, and made his way forward to the carriage they were sharing with a horde of Uzbeks. There were no empty seats and barely room to sit on the floor, but they'd managed to colonize a corner.

"No," Piatakov told the others in response to their questioning looks. "It'll have to be the boat."

AS THE TRAIN CONTINUED ITS fitful journey, Caitlin braced herself for the news that Sergei was dead. It felt such a waste, seemed so stupid, and the sorrow she half expected was already riddled with anger. In truth, she didn't know what she was feeling, only that something was tearing at her heart.

Waking in the night, she was suddenly convinced that her sleeping with Jack had rebounded on Sergei, that by betraying her husband, she'd somehow abandoned him to the ultimate fate. Which was, of course, absurd. Sergei had left her. He had chosen to follow Brady and Shahumian, and whatever he was, he wasn't a fool—he must have known what the likely end would be.

Which was no consolation at all. Had she tried hard enough to stop him? Had she been too impatient, too involved in her work? Had she loved him enough? Had she ever loved anyone enough to put them first? A brave heart was good, but maybe a kind one was better.

When the sun eventually rose on another day, she sat and watched the desert go by, thinking that she'd never felt less sure of who she was and what she wanted.

The train reached Samarkand early that afternoon. In the stone station building, a Cheka chauffeur was waiting to lead them to the shiny car parked in the forecourt. It had obviously just been washed in their honor: the ground underneath it was damp; a pile of empty kerosene cans lay scattered on the verge.

They crammed into the car, which should have been parked in the shade. The metal was too hot to touch, the interior like an oven. Caitlin shared the back seat with Maslov and Jack, feeling like she hadn't slept for days.

The drive through the Russian town took five minutes, ending outside a small house where several Uzbek militiamen were reluctantly standing to a semblance of attention. A thin, bald, and rather cadaverous Russian emerged through a doorway to greet them.

"Welcome, comrades," he said. "Chechevichkin, chairman of the

Samarkand Cheka," he introduced himself, before leading them through a detention room full of anxious faces, across a shaded inner courtyard, and into his personal office. A map and several exhortatory posters lined one white wall; on another a single framed photograph held pride of place. It showed a mass meeting in a square surrounded by mosques; the caption underneath read, THE PROCLAMATION OF THE REVOLUTION, 28TH NOVEMBER 1917, IN THE REGISTAN.

"Where is the body?" Caitlin wanted to know.

"In the next room—"

She strode past Chechevichkin and through the open doorway. A wooden coffin lay in the center of the floor, and for a moment she hesitated, fearful of whom she would find inside it. Then, with what felt like enormous effort, she moved herself forward a couple of paces.

It was Aram Shahumian, or rather his corpse, stripped to the waist, laid out on a bed of half-melted ice. Dried-brown blood caked his chest and folded arms. A handful of flies hovered hopefully over the open box, drawn by the flesh but repelled by the cold.

Caitlin let out an explosive breath. She had met the Armenian on several occasions, and while she'd considered him one of Sergei's more likable friends, she'd been wary of his chronic restlessness, the trouble he had in simply sitting still. Now his face looked almost serene, as if aware that his struggles were over. For a moment she wished it were Sergei lying there, anger and heartache gone, finally at peace.

"Have you nothing to cover him with?" she heard herself ask.

Chechevichkin looked at Komarov, who nodded. "Aram Shahumian, I presume?" he asked her quietly.

"Yes," she said softly. Next time it would be Sergei.

Chechevichkin came back with a sheet and draped it across the coffin.

"Did he ever regain consciousness?" Komarov asked him.

"Only for a short time in the car. He only said one thing." The Chekist hesitated.

"Yes?"

"Long live the revolution."

Caitlin didn't know whether to laugh or weep.

AFTER KOMAROV HAD SENT THEM both off in a droshky, McColl wasted no time in telling Caitlin his news. "He knows I'm a spy. God knows how, but I'm sure he does. I doubt he knows that you know— I don't see how he could—but then I didn't think he knew about me. We need to keep our distance from each other, in case we give him ideas."

She looked at him. "You must run."

"I will. As soon as I get the chance."

"Where will you go?" Caitlin asked.

"I'll have to head south to the border, and if Komarov doesn't catch Brady on this side, I'll do my best on the other."

She placed a hand in his. "Jack."

"Yes?"

"If you can, spare Sergei. He's not a bad man, and he's doing what he thinks is right."

And killing people who get in his way, McColl thought. As he had himself, for masters no better than Brady. "I will," he promised as their droshky drew up outside the Kommercheskaya Hotel.

Four rooms had been requisitioned, apparently at rather short notice: the previous occupants were still disputing their eviction in the lobby when Caitlin and McColl arrived. He asked the clerk for directions and was swiftly besieged by an angry mob. For a second he looked for someone to hit—it had been a stressful day. The thought must have shown on his face—the complainants went back to work on the clerk.

Their rooms were on the upper floor. Caitlin disappeared into hers without speaking, closing the door behind her. His was next door, the usual white-walled square with its soiled mattress and jug of dirty water. He folded back the shutters to reveal the boulevard. Across the way an ex-bank was boarded up behind a row of ragged trees. The soft clatter of typing drifted up from a room below.

It would be dark in an hour and easier to lose whomever Komarov would have on his tail. And that would still have to look accidental, or Komarov might decide there was no point in leaving him free.

He felt tired, incredibly tired. But there was no knowing how long they'd be in Samarkand or how long he'd be at liberty. It might be days, might be hours. He paced up and down, willing the light to fade, wondering how to do it. Nothing clever occurred to him, but then the old tricks usually worked.

He walked down to the lobby and noticed the men on either side of the door. So far, so good. He called the reception clerk over and loudly asked to be woken in three hours' time, then hurried back up the stairs. The window at the end of the corridor looked out over a small yard. He straddled the sill, then swung the other leg out, gripping whatever he could until he hung by his fingers and was able to let himself drop. The entrance to the yard gave out onto the street some thirty feet from the hotel door. He walked off briskly, glancing back every so often to check there was no pursuit.

High to his left, a large fortress gazed loftily down. Up ahead the road crossed a wooden bridge and deteriorated into a track, before burrowing into the old town's maze of alleys and narrow streets. McColl stopped on the bridge to light a cigarette and watched the meagre water trickling across the stones.

"Taxi, mister?" a young voice shouted in heavily accented Russian. McColl looked up to see a grinning Uzbek boy, about twelve years old, in the circle of light thrown by the lamp on the bridge. He was sitting in the driving seat of an old, much-repaired droshky, holding the reins of an even-older-looking mule.

"Tashkent Street," McColl told the boy as he climbed aboard the creaking contraption.

Motion seemed to suit it, and they were soon rattling along a potholed Registan Street, receiving raucous cries of encouragement from the denizens of the *chaikhanas* that spilled their light across the road. They skirted around the Registan, just three huge shapes against the sky, and entered Tashkent Street. Throwing caution to the winds, McColl asked the boy to take him to Biruni's carpet shop. The mule snorted.

They passed a large mosque with a cloven arch, and a few minutes later clattered to a halt outside Biruni's shop. Two Uzbeks were busy carrying rolls of carpet into the dimly lit interior.

When McColl handed over a Kerensky note, the boy's face dropped. "Coin," he demanded. McColl fished in his pocket and found one, restoring the habitual grin. "I wait," the boy announced.

"No," McColl insisted, handing over another coin, "no wait." He asked one of the carpet-bearers for Ali Zahid and was pointed through the door. He went in, down a short passage, and out into a yard. An Indian was sitting on a wooden bench beside an open door. "Ali Zahid?" McColl asked.

The Indian nodded warily.

"I come from your brother-in-law," McColl said.

The Indian's eyes widened fractionally, but he said nothing.

McColl sat down beside him. "He said to tell you that your new niece's name is Benazir and that your sister now has three gold teeth." This had been the standard introduction in 1916—swapping Indira for Benazir when the agent was a Hindu—and McColl was hoping it hadn't been changed.

Ali Zahid was smiling now, albeit anxiously. "What do you want?" he asked in a whisper.

"The wireless. I must talk to Delhi."

"It is far away, hidden. Perhaps tomorrow."

"No, now." Why had the man been surprised to see him? And why was he trying to put him off?

"Tomorrow no problem, sahib," the Indian said ingratiatingly.

"Tomorrow I may be in the hands of the Cheka. And they may force me to name my contact in Samarkand."

Ali Zahid seemed to digest this information quite literally, making chewing motions with his mouth as he stared at the ground. "Very good," he said at last. "Wait here." He disappeared inside, and McColl could hear him and a woman talking. A few minutes later the Indian reappeared at the door, beckoning. McColl followed him into a richly decorated room and was handed a set of Uzbek clothes.

"You must wear these," Ali Zahid said. "I will wrap your turban."

Ten minutes later they were working their way through another maze of narrow streets, the delicious mélange of cooking smells offering McColl an acute reminder of how long it had been since he'd eaten. Another few minutes and they arrived at the foot of a low cliff. Worn steps led diagonally up the face; at the top there was only the darkness of open country.

"It is not so far," Ali Zahid said encouragingly, almost disappearing from sight as he strode off down a near-invisible path. McColl's eyes slowly grew accustomed to the dark: they were making their way through a cemetery that sprawled across acres of undulating bare earth. A copse of trees loomed in front of them, and beyond it a dry riverbed. Behind them the meager lights of the town had faded completely from view.

"We are almost there," Ali Zahid said. He now seemed as eager to please as he had been to thwart.

They traversed a rock-strewn gully and emerged onto a wide shelf, beyond which the land dropped away again. The gnarled trunk of an ancient tree stood in splendid isolation.

"See here," Ali Zahid said, pointing. A low sarcophagus lay in the sandy earth; at its head two long poles bearing horsetail emblems fluttered uneasily in the breeze.

"The wireless?" McColl asked.

"No, that is a little farther. This is the grave of Daniel."

"Daniel who?"

The Indian smiled, his teeth flashing. "In your Christian book, he fought lions, I think. See these stones—they move a little each year as his body grows."

"What?" If there was one thing McColl hadn't expected that evening, it was a Bible class.

"He grows, about one half inch in every year. And that," he added, pointing at the trunk, "is the sacred tree. Its touch cures leprosy."

McColl looked at the tree, then the Indian. Which of them was crazier? "And the wireless?" he asked patiently.

"A little farther," Ali Zahid repeated. "I thought you would be interested," he added, sounding slightly indignant. "Come."

McColl followed, doing the sums in his head. By his reckoning Daniel should have been around a hundred feet long by now.

They clambered down onto the desert floor, and had been walking for only a couple of minutes when dark shapes loomed ahead—the broken walls of abandoned houses. The Indian threaded his way between them, stopped at the side of a disused well, and started removing loose bricks from the base of the wall. The hole that someone had dug in the space beneath contained a bulky package wrapped in sacking.

His Majesty's wireless in Samarkand.

McColl looked around as Ali Zahid unwrapped it. The moon would soon be rising in the east; a silver glow was already seeping above the distant hills. The night was silent save for the murmur of the town to the north. A train whistle blew, a long way off.

The Indian was fiddling with the dials, the headphones clamped against his turban. "Calling Red Fortress. This is the City of Gold calling Red Fortress. Come in, Red Fortress." He repeated it several times. McColl could imagine some Indian dashing down from the IPI communications room to tell the former public schoolboy on duty that Samarkand was sending a message. He felt a wave of disgust with the whole business. With himself.

Ali Zahid was handing him the headphones.

". . . is Red Fortress, City of Gold," a voice was saying, in exactly the accent McColl had expected.

"This is Bonnie Prince Charlie in the City of Gold," he said slowly. Bite on that one, lads, he thought maliciously.

The silence at the other end seemed to last a long time. "We've been expecting your call, Bonnie Prince Charlie," the voice said eventually.

Like hell you have, McColl thought. The moon was easing itself out of the hills, washing the plain with spectral light. It was all absurdly beautiful. "Agent Akbar is dead," he said. "The Good Indian team is headed your way."

"Understood," the voice in Delhi said.

Almost smugly, McColl thought.

"Where are they now?" the voice asked.

"Unknown. Probably still on Russian territory."

"Understood. Does the opposition know of their plans?"

Which opposition? McColl wondered. Presumably the Cheka. "In general, yes."

"Is the opposition attempting to interfere?"

"Yes."

"Understood. You must facilitate their escape from enemy territory if possible, Bonnie Prince Charlie."

"Please repeat that instruction."

"You must facilitate their escape from enemy territory—"

"Understood." Only too fucking well. "Over and out," he said coldly, losing his turban as he ripped off the headphones. He hadn't really expected anything else, but had, he realized, still felt a flicker of hope.

Not anymore.

Ali Zahid was looking at him anxiously, even fearfully. "Are there troubles to come?" he asked.

"Facilitate," McColl muttered. "You speak better English than that bunch of bastards."

The Indian's smile was doubtful.

They returned the wireless to its hiding place and walked back to the city. Boy, mule, and droshky were still waiting patiently outside the carpet shop. "You should be in bed," McColl said as he climbed aboard for the return trip. And so should I, he thought. Tiredness, hunger, and anger were congealing into a dull despondency.

He lit a cigarette as they rattled slowly up Tashkent Street, and recalled the impression that Gandhi had made on him all those years ago. And again, in 1915, when McColl had stopped to see him at the ashram outside Ahmedabad. Everything he'd learned first-hand about Gandhi, everything he'd read about him in the mostly hostile British press, told him that this was one of nature's better men, a force for good in a world so full of the opposite. A trouble-maker where trouble needed making.

But as far as the powers-that-be were concerned, the only good Indian was a dead one.

"Shashlik, mister?" The boy's face was turned to his; they were outside an eating house. Probably the boy's father's.

McColl looked at his watch. Two hours had already passed, so what difference did it make? "Yes," he said, his mouth suddenly watering at the prospect. He flicked his cigarette end into the street, and three young boys appeared out of nowhere to fight for its possession.

CAITLIN LIT ANOTHER CIGARETTE—SHE WAS smoking far too much—and accepted another inch of whatever the local liqueur was. It had a kick like a mule, as her father might have said, and the hint of apple reminded her of Arbatov, who would now be commencing his five years of exile in apple-growing Verny.

She and Komarov were sitting in the otherwise empty hotel dining room. Her lack of sleep the previous night had left her tired enough for bed, but when he had suggested a drink, she had thought it prudent to accept. With enough of whatever it was inside him, he might let something slip.

Or not. The more shots Komarov put away, the more he seemed drawn to the past. "I once worked with a man named Dvoretsky," he said. "Pyotr Dvoretsky. I was his immediate superior in the Investigation Department, and I knew him quite well. A good man, all in all. Kind to his family, always generous when the charities came to the office. No politics to speak of. The revolution didn't fill him with joy, but it didn't make him angry either. He was more bewildered than anything else, like many ordinary people.

"Then, at the end of 1918, his wife became ill. All four parents were still alive and all dependent on him. He convinced himself that he needed the extra rations, and from there it was a short step to buying coupons he knew were forged. Which made him an enemy of the revolution.

"He was caught almost immediately. And he sat there in my office, frightened of course, but not without dignity, and he said, 'What would you have done in my place?' And I had no answer for him. Or rather, no answer that would have been relevant. It didn't matter what I would have done—how could my principles as an individual determine the rightness of his actions? He'd done what he thought was right."

As Komarov paused and reached for his glass, Caitlin felt sure he could still see the man in question on the other side of his desk. "What happened to him?" she asked after several moments of silence.

"Oh, he was shot that evening. My duties as a Chekist were clear. That is the point. For a long time, I carried on interrogating prisoners like a policeman, treating them as people, because only in that way can you begin to understand their motivation. I hadn't realized that motivation was now beside the point and that I could no longer afford to treat our enemies like people. The strain was just too much. Because they had principles, too, and theirs often seemed as consistent with who they were and where the revolution had taken us as mine were with who I was. It was impossible. We could have turned the prisons into endless seminars on political philosophy. Everything seemed arbitrary. Everything but power.

"I had the power, so my truth was the one that counted. I believed in that truth; I believed I was right, and that had to be enough."

"We can never be certain," she said tentatively.

"No, but we must act as if we are. So many comrades refuse to take that responsibility. 'Power is the only truth'—that's what they say. It sounds convincing if you say it loud and often, but it's nonsense. Power may be essential, but it isn't a truth. If we want a victory that lives up to our dreams, we can't afford to forget the truth, so we simply have to suspend it. We have to split ourselves, keep the truth—in all its complexity—safe in the back of our minds, while we act as if there's only the one simple gospel and one right way to do things. And since, when we choose our one and only truth, we are also choosing to condemn those who think differently, we must take the responsibility on our own shoulders and not pretend that history is making our choices for us. That's one form of cowardice. The other is refusing to choose because all that means is that you're passing the burden of choice to someone else."

She gazed at him through the smoke from her cigarette. Was he testing her? she wondered. Did she deserve to be tested? "I understand," she said. And she thought she did. "But what if the cost is too high?"

"What do you mean?" he asked.

He wanted to hear her say it, she thought. For her sake or his?

"Take men like Arbatov and my husband," she said. "They supported and fought for the revolution, but now even people like them refuse to abide by your simple gospel. Doesn't that make you wonder whether we've narrowed the path too much, whether we're closing the door on too many people? On too many ideas?"

"That is the danger," he agreed.

"Well, how do we avert it? When I'm working at the Zhenotdel, I feel positive. There are plenty of days when it feels like one step forward, two steps back, but generally speaking, I feel that we're still breaking ground, that month by month we're still opening doors." She paused to stub out her cigarette. "But lately I've begun to feel that all this is happening in some sort of cocoon. And that when the day comes for us to break out, we'll find that the rest of the party has been moving in the opposite direction. And the rest of the party, being much stronger than us, will first set aside our work and then forbid us from spinning any more cocoons."

His grunt sounded appreciative.

"But giving up won't get us anywhere," she went on. "So we put our fears aside and go back to work. What else can we do?"

"*You* could walk away," Komarov suggested.

"Because this isn't my real home?"

"Because you seem to believe—wrongly I hope, but maybe not—that the struggle for women's rights in Russia over the next few years won't get the priority you think it deserves. Maybe somewhere else it will."

"Maybe." Was he giving her some sort of warning? Or just being honest? "But leaving would feel like failure," she said. "This is where we made the breakthrough, where the future seemed so full of hope."

"Seemed?" he said. There was more sadness than accusation in his tone.

"Sometimes I fear so," she conceded. "Sometimes I don't."

He gave her a wry smile. "I know what you mean."

PIATAKOV OPENED HIS EYES TO see Chatterji squatting by his side. "It is time to go," the Indian told him.

He half-walked, half-slid down to where Brady was gazing through his telescope. The moon was high now, the lights of Charjui on the western bank mostly extinguished. The width of this river still astonished Piatakov; the Moskva, the Neva, were streams by comparison. Above their heads the iron bridge blocked out half of the star-filled sky.

"Stealth or force?" he asked the American.

"Stealth, I hope. There have been four or five Chekists sitting around on the quay all day. There's at least one there now; someone lights a cigarette every so often. But the way I see it, with the moon over there, this bank will mask us for most of the crossing. Once we get nearer, we'll have to play it by ear." He stood. "Ready, Durga?"

They slid the boat into the water and clambered in. The hull creaked, but the bottom was bone-dry; Chatterji had stolen well.

The Indian sat in the bow, Brady in front of him at the oars. Piatakov lolled in the stern, wondering how Czar Alexander had felt on his way to meet Napoleon in the middle of the Neman River.

A slight breeze seemed to be following the water downstream. "The mighty Oxus," Brady drawled softly.

The current was stronger than it looked, but the American's shoulders were equal to it. He kept the boat close to the bridge on the downstream side, counting off the piers as he passed them in a satisfied murmur. The moon was hanging directly above the upper reaches of the river, loosing a cascade of silver toward them. Like a magic carpet, Piatakov thought.

Soon they were roughly halfway across, both shores looking distant. Piatakov aimed the telescope at the bank they were moving toward. There were several boats at the quay, but they were still too far away for him to pick out theirs.

"Fourteen," Brady muttered. "Eleven to go." He was breathing heavily now, and stopped rowing for a minute or so to flex his shoulders and massage his forearms. "Your turn, Sergei," he said, just as they heard the fast-swelling drumbeat.

A train was coming. The American cursed and took up the oars again. They had drifted more than fifty yards from the shelter of the bridge, and Piatakov could hear the rumble deepen as the approaching locomotive abandoned solid ground and ventured out onto the iron lattice. Soon he could make out the orange glow from the firebox and the pulse of smoke gathering moonlight.

They were still some way downstream from the bridge when the train passed overhead, a line of unlit cars behind the locomotive. As far as Piatakov could see, the driver was staring straight ahead and hadn't noticed the small craft below. "I don't think so," he said in answer to Brady's inquiring look.

The drumbeat faded; the American rowed on, his weariness apparently gone.

Piatakov raised the telescope again. There were several barges lined up at the quay, some piled high with cotton, others awaiting their share of the towering mounds on the quayside. And there, a couple of hundred yards downstream, was their passport to Afghanistan. The riverboat was more than a hundred feet long, with a deck barely five feet clear of the water, and what looked like a long two-story house squarely plonked amidships. The line of portholes on the upper floor suggested passenger cabins; the lack of windows below suggested space for freight. At the bow end, a small square bridge was set atop and forward of the main structure; in the stern, a large cylindrical casing covered a giant paddle wheel. Red lights glinted at either end, but there was no sign of life between them.

Ten minutes later Brady maneuvered their boat alongside the riverboat, only a few feet away from where someone had neatly stenciled "Red Turkestan." Chatterji grabbed hold of the deck edge and squeezed himself up through the railings. He stood there and listened for a second, then disappeared into the darkness, gun in hand.

Brady and Piatakov followed, leaving their skiff to drift away downstream. Like a balloon released into the sky, Piatakov thought—a sad sort of freedom. One of Aram Shahumian's favorite epigrams came to mind: a revolution was like a wild horse; it wasn't a matter of whether you'd be thrown from its back, simply of when.

Scorpions

"Act naturally," Brady said as they reached the door that led out onto the deck. The three of them had spent the night in a storeroom, and the *Red Turkestan* had been underway for over an hour, having departed Charjui soon after daybreak.

The American opened the door and stepped through. Behind him, Piatakov shielded his eyes against the sudden glare. The world outside looked like a child's painting: a shiny white boat on a bloodred river under a bright blue sky. At the river's edge, green reeds gave way to yellow-brown desert, making the most of nature's palette.

Ten yards away two men were leaning over the port rail, shouting to make themselves heard over the din of the paddle wheel. One glanced at them as they emerged, but without apparent interest. Brady led the way aft, hesitating only fractionally at the sight of three uniformed soldiers sitting around the foredeck-mounted machine gun. "A lovely morning," he shouted in Russian, and one soldier raised an arm in reply. The American turned up the stairs to the upper deck, a smile on his face.

A man and a woman were standing side by side at the bow rail, smoking cigarettes, gazing straight ahead. Leaving Chatterji to stand guard, Brady and Piatakov ascended the short flight of steps that led to the bridge. As the American stepped through the open doorway, he pulled the gun from his waistband.

There were two men inside: one, burly and fair-haired under his peaked cap, was sitting with his back to them, booted feet resting on the ledge beneath the open window; the other, short, wiry, and dark, was standing at the wheel, resting his weight on one leg.

"Crew only," the man with the cap said without bothering to turn his head.

"Have I the honor of addressing the captain?" Brady asked.

"You . . ." The intended sentence died as the eyes took in the revolver. "What the hell . . . ? What do you want?" The man seemed more surprised than frightened.

A veteran of some war or other, Piatakov thought. Who wasn't?

Brady leaned himself against a convenient wall. "We want to go to Kelif."

"Well, that's just where the ship is headed, so you can put the gun away."

Brady smiled. "You might find this hard to believe, Captain, but there are people who don't want us to get there."

The captain smiled back. "And why would that be? You don't look like fleeing nobility."

Brady's grin broadened. "See?" he said to Piatakov, who was standing with his back to the doorjamb. "I told you our disguises were perfect."

"If only we could persuade Anastasia to take off the tiara," Piatakov said, surprising himself. How long had it been since a joke had come out of his mouth?

Brady and the captain both laughed. "What's your name, Captain?" the American asked.

"Nikolayev," the captain said.

"Well, Captain Nikolayev, where do you normally stop between here and Kelif?"

"Burdalik, Kerki, and wherever we're flagged down."

"Do you need to stop? For food, fuel, anything?"

"We might need to take on more fuel."

"Which I assume means you might not. So we'll deal with that when we have to. In the meantime, we travel nonstop."

"That's what you think. This boat stops every time it finds a sandbank. I suppose you could try shooting them," he suggested with a grin.

Brady ignored him; he never seemed to register other people's sarcasm. "How many people are there on board?" he asked.

"Four crew, eleven passengers. Paying passengers, that is," he added pointedly.

"How many soldiers?"

"I've no idea. Lev?"

"Four. Three men and one officer," the helmsman said stiffly, not taking his eyes off the river.

Brady pulled himself upright. "Right. Captain, we're going to bring all the passengers and crew—all but Lev here—to the lounge. And once we've relieved them of any weapons they're carrying, Sergei here will search the cabins and storerooms. Durga will stay up here on the bridge and keep Lev company."

"So who are you really?" the captain asked, in a tone that suggested he didn't expect a serious answer.

Piatakov also waited for the joke, but for once Brady was otherwise concerned.

"Soldiers of the revolution," he said absent-mindedly. "With nothing left to lose," he added, looking the captain straight in the eye. "I used to pilot a boat like this. On the Missouri River in America. You understand? No one here is indispensable."

CAITLIN AND HARUKA SAT ON one side of the desk, Komarov and Jack on the other. They were in Chechevichkin's office, which at this hour of the morning was blissfully cool and filled with dappled light. Caitlin had noticed that the coffin was gone from the adjoining room; the Armenian must have been buried the day before.

Komarov had asked the questions, Jack translating them into Uzbek. The girl had told the story of her husband's murder—the "beast," she called him—and was now describing her journey on horseback and expressing her surprise that the Russian had let her go on the outskirts of town.

Caitlin tried to picture this man as her husband. He seemed both closer and more distant, like a part of herself she was losing contact with.

But Sergei had cut himself loose from more than her. His bitterness had been understandable, but the man who'd joined Brady on this murderous odyssey had clearly taken leave of his senses. What did he think he was doing taking terrified children for moonlit rides?

She switched her attention to McColl, watching his lips as he interpreted, remembering their lovemaking only three nights before. He would soon be gone, she supposed, in prison or over the border. And how would she feel then?

Komarov was standing, thanking Haruka for her cooperation, asking Caitlin if arrangements had been made.

"She's going back to her family," Caitlin told him. "On one condition—that they don't sell her into another marriage against her will. A condition the local Cheka will need to enforce," she added pointedly. "It's the best I could do at short notice."

Still, the girl was smiling as Maslov escorted her out to the waiting father. McColl asked Komarov if he'd be needed in the next couple of hours.

"No, but don't stray far."

"I'm going to take a look at Tamerlane's Mausoleum," he said, glancing at Caitlin.

"I could do with some exercise," she said, seeing a chance to find out why he was still around.

"Take a look behind us," he said when she asked the question, and there, a hundred yards back, two armed Chekists were sauntering in their wake. When they all reached the mausoleum, the Chekists perched on a broken-down wall while she and McColl admired yet another blue dome.

"They're sticking closer," he told her on the walk back. "I don't think Komarov wants to lose me."

Neither do I, she thought. But one way or another, she would.

KOMAROV MOVED HIS CHAIR INTO the courtyard and rummaged in his pocket for the latest cable. Sasha had been his usual thorough self, and the facts his assistant had gleaned from the few available records had refreshed his own memory of that summer's events. The name of the British agent that Aidan Brady had accused Caitlin Hanley of meeting was Jack McColl. And it had of course been Brady who'd shot the boy in Kalanchevskaya Square. Two reasons for the Englishman to hate the American, but if Davydov really was McColl, surely there had to be more to his presence in Russia than a three-year-old vendetta.

There was nothing to suggest that Piatakova had lied about her relationship with McColl, other than Komarov's own impression at the time that she'd cared about him more than most people did about long-abandoned lovers. Maybe she had, but another three years had passed since then, and no one Sasha had spoken to doubted her loyalty to the revolution. Which was, he realized, a relief.

There was more. Within hours of this McColl's escape from Moscow, two crates of crop-rotting poisons had been left on the Vecheka's doorstep on Bolshaya Lubyanka, and two White agents had been found shot in an Arkhangelskoye dacha, one dead, one severely wounded. Reading the wounded man's description of his assailant, Komarov could see nothing to rule out the Englishman now masquerading as an interpreter from Tashkent. McColl, it seemed almost certain, had foiled a plot by Russian allies of his own government to destroy the crops that fed Moscow. Which should, Komarov thought, have been the end of his official career as a spy. So whom, if anyone, was he working for now?

The question was still exercising his brain when Maslov ushered a young and uniformed Russian into the courtyard. "Tell Comrade Komarov what you just told me."

The man was a railway guard. His train had been crossing the Amu Dar'ya bridge the previous night when he had spotted a small boat in midstream. There had been three men in it.

Komarov slapped an armrest with the palm of his right hand, causing the railwayman to step back a pace. "The boat from Charjui to Kerki—when does it leave?"

"It should have left this morning, comrade. At dawn, I think. It was waiting for the spare parts we brought in from Krasnovodsk, so—"

"Check it!" Komarov snapped at Maslov. The subordinate lifted the telephone and asked the operator to get him the Charjui Cheka. The three of them waited in silence, the guard shifting uneasily from foot to foot.

"You can go," Komarov told him. "Thank you."

The man needed no second bidding.

Maslov was through at last. "Well, find out!" he shouted down the line. "They're—"

"I heard," Komarov said. He was examining the map, remembering that Peters had mentioned how slow the boat was.

"It left at dawn," Maslov confirmed, "but our men were not on board."

Komarov grunted. "Ask them when it's due to reach Kerki."

Three or four days was the answer.

"Right. Get Chechevichkin in here."

The grains of rice that clung to his beard indicated the local chairman had been eating his breakfast. "Yes, comrade?"

Komarov passed on the new information. "I must get to Kerki in three days," he added, studying the map once more.

"I don't see how—"

"That's exactly what you must do. Look, here. This road—is it passable for automobiles?"

Chechevichkin considered. "Well . . ."

"There is a garrison at Karshi, isn't there?"

"Yes, but—"

"But what?"

"Half of them are down with fever."

"Then half of them are not."

THEY DROVE OUT OF SAMARKAND soon after noon, cruising along a surprisingly smooth road toward the distant mountains. But not for long. As they left the last habitations behind, the road threw aside any need to keep up appearances, and swiftly degenerated into a jarring duet of potholes and ruts. The first tire burst after about ten miles, the second two miles farther on, making McColl understand why they'd bought eight spares for the two vehicles.

While the drivers busied themselves with the second wheel change, he walked forward along the road, which ran up a wide, dry valley before disappearing between the yellow rock walls of a gorge. Behind him the sand dunes stretched back to the distant line of green that marked the course of the Zeravshan River. Caitlin was sitting on the running board of one car staring thoughtfully into space. Komarov was pacing up and down, his grey hairs glinting in the sun beneath the edge of his cap. Maslov was arguing with the two drivers, probably about their productivity.

They had passed two camel caravans soon after leaving the city, but now seemed alone in the middle of a very large universe. Or almost. A large scorpion emerged from between two boulders not a yard from McColl's feet, its upflung tail swaying gently as it advanced. He flicked some dust with his boot and watched it scuttle back into the shadows. Like a spy, he thought sourly. Why had Komarov brought him on this last leg?

Maslov was waving everyone back to the cars, and soon they were driving on toward the next blowout. It occurred high in a mountain pass and was swiftly succeeded by another, but then either the road or their luck improved, and they motored safely down into another wide valley, the ancient town of Shahrisabz a growing splotch of green in the distance. Darkness was falling as they entered the main street, pursued by a crowd of children and watched by the curious eyes of the older inhabitants. The local party official had apparently been warned that they were coming; he suddenly appeared in front of them waving a large red flag. McColl wondered if the man intended to walk ahead of the cars all the way to Karshi.

McColl climbed out to interpret, but the Uzbek's Russian was up to the task of explaining the arrangements for their overnight stay. The drivers were sent off to find spares for the spares; the rest of them were led up onto a spacious roof where food was already being prepared. A large, black, semispherical iron bowl was sitting on a circle of bricks above a wood fire; inside it McColl could see and smell pieces of mutton, onion, carrot, and tomato sizzling in the fat—the beginnings of a pilaf. Cups of water, sliced peppers, and rice were arrayed on a tray beside the fire, ready for adding when the time was right.

He sat himself down, suddenly feeling ravenous. Komarov was talking to the party official; Maslov and Caitlin had disappeared. The street below was still full of children, many gazing up at the roof with disappointed faces, as if shortchanged on a promised entertainment. Most of the town was visible, or would have been half an hour earlier. Now only the higher slopes of the surrounding ridges were bathed in violet light, and as McColl watched, the stars grew sharper above the jagged mountains to the south.

Caitlin came out onto the roof with an Uzbek woman, having let down her hair and changed into a multicolored dress and shawl. She threw him a smile as she and their hostess sat down on the other side of the fire.

The meal was ready in about an hour, although it seemed three to McColl and his stomach. The food was delicious and, by some miracle of local requisitioning, came with a liberal supply of wine. A quintet of Uzbek musicians appeared to serenade them, three playing a stringed instrument that McColl didn't recognize, the other two beating out rhythms on tabla and tambourine. With the stars bright above, his head full of wine and music, McColl felt a rare sense of contentment spreading through his being. If he was living on borrowed time, all the more reason to enjoy it.

Every now and then, his and Caitlin's eyes would meet across the fire, and they'd been lovers long enough for him to recognize her look. He knew they shouldn't, that sleeping with him again might even prove fatal for her, so he tore himself away from the eyes and the fire, and announced that he was having an early night.

She had other ideas, catching up with him as he reached his door and putting her arms around his neck.

"This is too public," she said after a long, intention-sapping kiss.

"It's too dangerous," he told her, resisting her gentle tug on his arm.

"I know," she said. "But if making love with you makes me an enemy of the revolution, then it's not the revolution I chose to serve. Now come."

He went.

Later, as they lay in each other's arms, she ran a finger across his chest. "Sometimes I think that we're the hardest thing I've ever tried to understand."

"I know. And yet sometimes—like now—it seems so . . . self-explanatory."

She propped up her head on an arm and looked into his face. "So are you still in love with me?"

"I'm afraid I am," he answered with a lightness he didn't feel.

"I'm not," she said, laying her head back onto his shoulder.

An hour later, he left her asleep and padded silently back to his own room, hoping to maximize any thin chance of concealing their liaison. Still feeling wide awake, he went out onto the creaking balcony and watched a pair of scrawny dogs prowling the empty street.

Had he left it too late to escape? He probably had. If he took off now in one of the cars parked below, he'd either die in the desert or find the Cheka waiting in the first town he reached. And if the party ever reached Kerki, he doubted that Komarov would leave him untended again. The die seemed cast.

Perhaps it always had been. He'd left it too late to leave because this was where he wanted to be.

TWO HUNDRED MILES TO THE west, the anchored *Red Turkestan* rolled gently in the smooth current of the Amu Dar'ya. Red lights shone at either end of the superstructure, though what purpose they served was beyond Piatakov; no boat would be moving on such a treacherous river at night.

They had run aground about half a dozen times that day, and both passengers and crew had been forced to take to the shallow water and bodily heave the boat off the sandbanks. The civilian passengers had taken less kindly to this unwelcome exercise than they had to the news that their boat had been hijacked. That minor detail had been accepted with a stoicism that bordered on masochism. The boat was still headed in the right direction, so why worry about who was in control? Better to shrug and enjoy what shade you could find. It was Russia writ small.

Brady was lying close by on the deck, covered with a greatcoat he had found in one of the cabins. Piatakov had watched the American's face age as he drifted into sleep and had thought that with most people it was the other way around: he remembered Caitlin's hair spread around her pale child's face. Most people, he guessed, reverted to childhood in sleep, dragged back by dreams to a simpler world.

Did Brady revert to childhood when he was awake? Now, that was a disturbing thought—people who found life simple were always dangerous.

The American seemed to be growing more savage with each passing day. Had the civil war made him that way or merely set free what had been in there already?

Several years earlier, as they'd waited to set out on a night infiltration, Brady had told Piatakov that he'd been born in the year Krakatoa exploded and that, according to his mother, he'd rarely seen sunlight in the first three years of his life. This, he had said, at least half seriously, was probably why he loved darkness so much.

Piatakov thought about his own mother, and the picture that came to mind was her sitting in the overgrown arbor at the bottom of their jungle-like garden. She had loved its wildness, hated formal gardens—the newly fashionable topiary had been one of her few pet aversions. Nature was everything.

What would she think of what he was doing? She'd never condemned, always encouraged. "You're such a good boy."

What was good? Fighting for what you believed in? Well, people got hurt when you did that, and could hurting people be good?

He let out a sigh. Lately so many memories seemed to be claiming his attention. Why was that?

It didn't matter. There was nothing threatening about them. On the contrary, the way they tied his life together was strangely comforting.

THEY LEFT SOON AFTER DAWN, jolting their way through sparsely inhabited hills, skirting the occasional village that clung to their slopes. As the bright white sky slowly turned to blue, the land began to flatten out, and the cars could sometimes run side by side, sparing each the other's dust.

The forty-five miles to Guzar took most of the morning. It proved a very small town, perched on the rim of the desert where dried-up rivers converged in a cluster of black elms and mulberry trees. Their arrival was unheralded and provoked a range of astonished glances and gaping stares from the watching inhabitants, few if any of whom could ever have seen an automobile. The local party official was eventually hunted down in the town mosque, where he claimed he'd been doing educational work.

He arranged refreshments with alacrity and eagerly asked for news of the wider world from each man in turn. He didn't speak to Caitlin, but couldn't stop staring at this strangest of creatures, the so-called "comrade woman." Every other woman in town was draped head to toe in the usual shroud.

The road onward to Karshi followed the rapidly evaporating river out across the desert, passing through a few small villages, all with fortified towers in various stages of decay. The track had been worn smooth by several thousand years of caravan traffic, and they covered this thirty-mile stretch without mishap in a little under three hours, entering what looked like a war-damaged town late that afternoon.

The local Soviet boss was waiting outside his red-flagged residence, ready to explain. The Basmachi had attacked the town twice before the recent deployment of a garrison, blowing up several buildings and riding off with all the food and drink they could carry. As a consequence, the hospitality he could offer his eminent guests from Moscow was somewhat limited.

Komarov waved all this away impatiently and asked if everything had been arranged for their desert crossing. It had. The garrison commander would supply the details, but of course they would travel by night. Komarov asked to see the man in question immediately and advised the others to get some rest while they could.

PIATAKOV MOPPED HIS BROW WITH the front of his blouse for about the hundredth time that day. The sun seemed hotter than ever, beating down out of an ivory-colored sky, drawing agonized flashes of light from the rippling water.

They were approaching Burdalik, according to the captain, and the passengers had all been locked in their cabins. The desert had drawn back from the river over the last few miles, giving ground to reedy flats alive with wild birds and increasing stretches of culti-vated land dotted with grey-brown houses and copses of mulberry trees. Every so often a small group of women appeared in the riv-erside fields, and when one spied the boat, they would all look up, then stretch their backs in unison, as if doing physical drills.

The *Red Turkestan* was inching around a shallow bend in the river when a posse of children appeared on the nearer bank, waving and shouting and running to keep pace with the boat. Two houses came into view, larger and closer to the river than others, and between them a road sloped down to a landing stage that extended some fifty feet out into the rust-colored water. Several small boats were tethered to one side, a large, flat ferry-raft to the other. A score and more people were gathered at its end. Some seemed to be arguing with a group of soldiers.

Three of the latter clambered into one of the small boats and pushed off into the current.

Brady appeared with the firing mechanism for the machine gun, and slotted it into place with a metallic clang. Piatakov watched the soldiers rowing out toward the center of the river. The gap between the two craft steadily shrank.

They must be mad, Piatakov thought.

Brady fired a burst, shattering the still air. The soldiers stopped rowing; the crowd on the landing stage rushed pell-mell for the safety of the bank. The children stood watching, every one on tip-toe; Piatakov could physically sense their excitement.

One of the soldiers raised a rifle, and Brady fired another burst, this time much closer. An argument broke out in the small boat, and the rifle was knocked aside. At that moment a bullet whined off the metal rail only inches from Piatakov's hand.

He spun around. The young officer was taking aim with both hands, his eyes squinting against the sun, sweat pouring down his face. Piatakov dived to one side and was still reaching for his own gun when another two shots rang out in quick succession. Neither came anywhere near him.

He looked up to see the officer slide down the upper deck rail, his gun dropping onto the planking below and bouncing over the side. Chatterji walked off the bridge to examine the body and signaled that the man was dead by drawing a hand across his own throat.

The small boat was retreating toward the landing stage. Piatakov glanced across at Brady and found him staring straight ahead.

"Mountains!" the American called out, and sure enough, looming through the heat haze, a faint but enormous wall rose up to meet the southern sky.

THE PARTY LEFT KARSHI SOON after dusk. The garrison commander, with only ten fit men at his disposal, had refused to spare more than four without explicit orders from his military superiors in Tashkent. There had been no volunteers, and the chosen quartet, all local men, didn't bother to hide their lack of enthusiasm. The guide, a local Turcoman of unfathomable age, was of a more sanguine temperament. He listened to Komarov's instructions, translated in halting Turkmen by McColl, and nodded. "Two nights," he said in Russian, holding up the appropriate number of fingers for emphasis.

They left town with the disused railway, but the tracks soon diverged and were lost in the rapidly darkening night. Their ponies were all stallions, and none, McColl noticed with interest, had been castrated. They were suitably frisky.

Their road, increasingly ill defined, wound its way through the rolling terrain. Seeing them by day, McColl had taken the humpbacked shapes for dunes, but there was nothing temporary about them. It looked like some passing Medusa had turned this sandy desert to stone, leaving the impression of an ocean petrified in midstorm.

There was life, though, and in abundance. Large, ratlike creatures with long hind legs and tails darted across the moonlit slopes; tortoises in astonishing profusion crawled out of the party's path as rapidly as nature allowed. More worryingly, an immense number of fearsome-looking scorpions seemed to be lining their route like a gruesome guard of honor. McColl imagined them falling in line behind the procession, a swelling army of trembling pincers waiting to devour their prey at a site of their own choosing.

Every couple of hours a well tower would loom up against the night sky, and there, for reasons that seemed both clear and truly bizarre, they would pause to quench their thirst with water they'd carried from Karshi. The Turcoman told McColl that one well was 750 feet deep; two camels were needed to raise the bucket over the wooden pulley. McColl imagined the women weaving the seemingly endless rope, as the men delved deeper and deeper.

The tower that greeted them as the sky began to lighten was ringed by long-abandoned huts, and the guide announced that they would spend the day in the latter's shady interiors. But only, he added, once the scorpions had all been flushed out. After the soldiers had been to work and pronounced the chosen huts clear, the Turcoman still insisted on a daylong patrol of the perimeter. Otherwise, he said with a knowing grin, someone was sure to be stung in his sleep.

Komarov claimed the first watch, and the others laid themselves out on the rock-hard ground. McColl was the first relief and, after sweating his way through an hour of invigilation and beating the odd transgressor to pulp with the butt of his borrowed rifle, passed on the weapon to Maslov and went back to sleep.

PIATAKOV HEARD IT BEFORE HE saw it. He was sitting aft, half-hypnotized by the undulating reeds, when the airplane's drone seeped out of the noise of the riverboat's progress. Jerking his head around, he saw it, a biplane flying low over the water, coming downstream toward them, out of the yellow sky. He had no sooner identified it than the plane was above and past him, the clatter of its engine drowning the splash of the paddle, its shadow flashing across foredeck and bridge. Leaping to his feet, Piatakov saw it reappear, a flash of red above the ship's superstructure, gaining height as it turned a wide half circle above the desert.

Brady was hustling down the steps. "Which way did it go?"

Piatakov pointed out the dark spot, fading southward.

"Looking for us, then."

"Probably."

The American wrung his hands with what looked suspiciously like glee. "Kerki," he said. "They'll be waiting for us."

Kerki

It was still light when McColl felt a rough hand on the shoulder and opened his eyes to see Maslov pointing a Webley straight at his head. "Come outside," the young Ukrainian ordered.

McColl rose to his feet and made his way out into the early evening sunlight, where Komarov and Caitlin were waiting, the former's face expressionless, the latter's a study in torment.

"Would I be right in thinking your real name is Jack McColl?" Komarov asked.

There seemed no point in denying it. "You would."

"And do you admit to being an English agent?"

Scottish, McColl thought perversely. And serving a man rather than a country. But why waste his breath quibbling? "I do," he said.

"An imperialist spy," Maslov said smugly, as if delighted that life had so generously lived up to his expectations.

"I have some questions," Komarov said, squatting down on his haunches and idly picking up a saxaul twig.

McColl leaned back against the wall of the hut, wondering if anyone was still on scorpion watch.

"Are you willing to answer them?" Komarov asked.

"That depends on what they are." He couldn't tell from Caitlin's face whether or not Komarov had already accused her of knowing who he was.

"Of course." Komarov drew a circle in the sand with the twig. "What is your part in this business?"

"I don't have one. Not directly. My old boss in London sent me here to find out what 'this business' is."

Komarov drew another circle inside the first. "What is this man the boss of?"

McColl looked up at the rapidly darkening sky. He was more than ready to betray his King and Country, the one a pampered figurehead, the other a convenient fiction that had recently all but murdered a million of its citizens. "He's the head of the British Secret Service. Which I used to work for."

"I know of it. So why did this man send you into Russia? Why not one of his current agents?"

"Because he knew he could trust me. There is a second British intelligence agency, which is known as MI5—Five for short. Five deals with Britain and the British Empire, the Service with the rest of the world, which of course includes Russia. My boss discovered that some people in Five were mounting an operation that involved both Russia and India. He had no idea what the operation was; he didn't know whether these people had the support of their own bosses or whether they were receiving help from Service people here in Russia. He sent me to find out."

"Ah," Komarov said. "And what is your boss's name?"

"I won't tell you that."

"Who helped you get into Russia?"

"I won't tell you that either."

The Russian smiled. "Good. I was beginning to think you were too obliging to be true."

McColl stole a glance at Caitlin, but the sun was sinking behind her, and he could hardly see her face. "Yuri Vladimirovich, I will not endanger those who helped me, but I'll tell you anything else you want to know."

"Miliutin was shot," Komarov informed him.

McColl sighed. "I'm sorry to hear that. He was planning to retire," he added inconsequentially.

"Someone telephoned his whereabouts to the Petrograd Cheka. One of your people, I think. Your Five, if what you say is true. And one thing you don't know: a man with a knife broke into your room in Tashkent. A Russian named Polyansky who'd been hired by an Indian in Samarkand. Luckily for you, you weren't in your room at the time."

"I see," McColl said, noting Maslov's accusatory look at Caitlin and the stony stare she offered in return. It looked like he might have brought her down, too—if so, he doubted she'd ever forgive him, not that he'd live long enough to find out.

Komarov had other questions. "Who killed Muhammad Rafiq in Moscow?" he asked.

"I don't know. Brady, probably." He would talk to Komarov in private, McColl thought. Try to convince the Cheka boss that Caitlin's only crime had been her failure to give him away. And that she'd only agreed to keep quiet once he'd convinced her that he meant no harm to their revolution.

"And the Russian at the hotel? Was it you who killed him and stuffed him under the bed?"

"Yes, it was. His name was Suvorov, and he did his best to kill me. I thought at the time I'd surprised him in Rafiq's room, but he might have been waiting for me."

"Because you threatened the operation?"

"I can't think of any other reason. Suvorov certainly worked for Five, and it seems to be their operation."

"I understand the Indian involvement, but why Brady and the other Russians? How did they get involved?"

"Five caught Brady in Ireland and gave him a choice between hanging and working for them. I can see why he chose not to hang, but I don't understand his reasons for doing their bidding now that he's beyond their reach."

"So what exactly is this operation?" Komarov asked.

"They're going to assassinate Mohandas Gandhi. The Indian nationalist leader," McColl added, mostly for Maslov's benefit.

The sun was almost down, the desert a rapidly deepening shade of gold.

"Why?" Komarov wanted to know. "If the British want him dead, why not just arrest him and have him hanged for treason?"

McColl smiled. "That would turn him into a martyr. You don't understand the beauty of this scheme. Brady's team will be helped into India, given as many shots at Gandhi as they need, and then arrested. The hard-liners in London will have the proof they want that Russia has broken its promise to leave the empire alone. Those Indians who want to replicate your revolution will find themselves pariahs once Bolsheviks are accused of murdering the people's hero. And Gandhi will be gone. Three birds with one stone."

Komarov said nothing for several moments, and McColl could almost hear the Russian's mind clicking its way through the facts. "I can see what the English in London and Delhi have to gain," he said eventually, "and that Aidan Brady might hope to earn his freedom with such a deal, but why would men like Piatakov and Shahumian want any part of it? If Gandhi is truly a threat to your empire, why would they want to kill him?"

"That's easy. None of the Indian comrades I met in Moscow had a good word to say about Gandhi. They called him a Menshevik, a false revolutionary, someone who'd put Indians in charge of the same rotten system, not change the system itself. And the Russians that Brady has recruited sound like men who think the same way, men who fought a revolution to change more than faces and who now believe that they've been betrayed by their leaders. They can't do much about that, but they can stop it happening again in India."

"So, a simple convergence of interests as far as Brady is concerned?" Komarov asked.

"I don't believe he's really working for Five."

"Well, if they succeed in killing Gandhi, his true allegiance won't stay hidden for long. Because that's when the British will seize their scapegoats, and either he'll be one of them, or he'll mysteriously disappear."

"True."

"I don't believe it," Caitlin interjected. It was the first time she'd spoken since McColl's arrest. "Aidan Brady may be a heartless bastard, but he would never willingly work for the British government—it would destroy his sense of who he is. And Sergei's not stupid; neither was Aram for that matter. If we can guess what the British have in mind, so can they. And Brady won't shirk from taking them on—he's always had more confidence than any man's entitled to. He'll have something up his sleeve."

"I agree," McColl said. "But what?"

"Once we've caught them, we can ask," Komarov said, rising. "It's time to get moving."

McColl liked the "we," but doubted its use was deliberate. If he was going to be shot—an outcome that seemed inevitable in a strangely abstract sort of way—it would probably be in Kerki, though there also seemed a chance that he'd be taken back to Tashkent or Moscow for a suitably public trial.

As he looked to the west, the last slice of sun slipped below the horizon, pulling the night down across the desert. It wasn't a place you escaped from.

THE COLUMN OF PONIES MOVED across the stony desert at walking pace, the starlight turning everything to silver grey. When they'd set off on their night trek, and no apparent restrictions had been placed on Jack, Caitlin had expected an early conversation, but as the miles went by, it became clear he had other ideas. He was, she realized, trying to protect her.

A nice thought, but a little late in the day. Komarov hadn't said anything, but he knew. So why keep silent? She found it hard to believe he was playing with her, so perhaps he didn't know himself. Or did he still think she might prove useful when they caught up with Sergei?

He had turned a blind eye three years earlier when she'd admitted not reporting Jack's presence in Moscow—in those days comrades still forgave one another the occasional transgression. But he had also warned her that he wouldn't do so again, and these were harsher times.

Should she talk to him, try to explain? She might end up admitting things he didn't know and make it worse for herself. Or Jack.

If she was arrested, too, there wouldn't be much she could do. Asking Kollontai for help might do more harm than good—there were plenty of men who'd jump at the chance of punishing her friend by proxy. She would just have to hope for the best—deportation rather than internal exile, internal exile rather than prison or worse.

She might have been kidding herself, but such prospects still seemed unreal. Komarov hadn't said anything in front of Maslov, which might mean nothing, but certainly gave him the option of turning another blind eye and allowing her to resume her work.

And that, she supposed, was what she wanted. Or was it? When she'd been dragged away from Moscow, there'd been no doubt in her mind. Being press-ganged into a hunt for her renegade husband had been downright annoying, and she'd known the hunt itself would probably have a heartbreaking ending, but once it was over, she would soon be back at her desk on Vozdvizhenka Street.

The doubts had slowly crept in. Nemtseva's fate had shaken her, and so had her comrades' reports of cutbacks in Zhenotdel funding. The film show in Tashkent had restored some of the hopes dented by the delegate murders, but the riot and its aftermath had, for the moment at least, left those hopes hanging by a very thin thread. Were the Zhenotdel's best years coming to an end? If so, if doors were now closing instead of opening, was Moscow where she wanted to be? As a sympathetic male comrade had once told her, pushing against a badly stuck door, you might force it open; banging your head against one that was locked would probably give you a concussion.

And then there was Jack. Would she be asking these questions if he hadn't reappeared in her life? She had chosen the revolution over him, taken the once-in-a-lifetime chance it offered to do something utterly new, to make the most of herself and the world. But would she do so again, if the choice was now between him and years of frustration? If the postimperial Jack looked a better prospect than the man she'd abandoned in 1918, the revolution she'd abandoned him for seemed a poorer one in almost every respect.

She told herself that quitting Russia would not mean quitting politics, that over the next few years, the causes she wanted to fight for might do better elsewhere. That she would get to see her family, that she would finally get to live with Jack, after almost eight years of their on-off affair. That she wouldn't be giving up, that throwing in a towel was okay as long as you picked up another.

And yet. She *would* be giving up; she *would* be conceding defeat. And conceding defeat wasn't something she knew how to do.

She lifted her gaze to the star-filled heavens. As things stood, any choice she made was purely academic. Even if they allowed her to leave, why would they let Jack go? All governments believed in punishing spies they caught, and he had freely admitted he was one. Even if Komarov wanted to, he couldn't just shove Jack across the border with a flea in his ear.

No, either Jack escaped or he was done for, and he must know it, too.

Was there anything she could do?

There was no one she could go to, no heads she could bang together. What mattered was what Komarov chose to do with Jack, and whether he caught up with Sergei, and what happened if he did. All she could do was wait, and as she knew very well, patience had never been one of her virtues.

TO THE SOUTH THE LINE between mountains and stars slowly rose. The traveling party stopped to eat by another ancient well tower, and McColl listened to the soldiers debating whether Kerki was more of a dump than Karshi. As they trekked onward, he imagined he could feel Maslov's blank scrutiny, Komarov's impatience, and Caitlin's dismay, each a moving ball of emotion, rolling on across the empty wastes.

The first hint of light was showing on the eastern horizon when Komarov maneuvered his horse alongside McColl's. "The Turcoman says we're only an hour away from Kerki," the Russian said conversationally. "You didn't seem very surprised," he said, shifting subjects without shifting tone.

"I was surprised you waited so long. When did you find out?" McColl asked.

"Before we left Moscow."

McColl shook his head, then laughed. "Sherlock Holmes," he murmured to himself.

"When did you realize I knew?" Komarov asked.

"The morning we left Tashkent. Your disciple couldn't look me in the eye anymore."

"He'd never make an actor," Komarov admitted. "I think that's why you're good at what you do," he went on in the same conversational voice. "Because your disguise feels more real than who you actually are."

McColl said nothing to that, just hoped it wasn't true.

"But you're finished with all that now," Komarov said, sounding almost sad that their contest was over.

"It's your world."

"Yes it is, but that's not what I meant." Komarov was staring at him in the growing light. "I suspect that you've run out of people you can put your faith in. Either as friends or enemies."

McColl thought about that for several moments. "You may be right. But not completely, not when it comes to enemies." He paused as he guided his pony around the skeletal remains of a sheep. "I watched Aidan Brady knife an American riot cop in 1914. That summer he damn near killed me in Ireland and then murdered two cops in England. In 1918 he had another go at shooting me and shot an eleven-year-old boy instead. And my erstwhile colleagues in London, when they finally caught him, decided he'd be more use alive than dead. Instead of the hanging he so richly deserved, they gave him this job. When my old boss found out and asked me to come here, I only said yes because it was Brady."

Komarov was silent for a minute or more. "If you didn't have Brady, I suspect you would find someone else—people need to put faces to what they abhor. Years ago, before the war, when I was still a city policeman, a political prisoner asked me how many enemies I had in Brazil. None, I told him, as far as I knew. He explained to me that the Russian government, which paid my wages, had colluded with other capitalist powers to force down the world coffee price. As a result the plantation workers were earning even less of a pittance than usual, and their children were dying in droves from starvation. Now, why, this man asked me, would those children's mothers consider me anything other than an enemy?"

McColl smiled. "What did you say?"

"I said this was all very abstract, and what could I, personally, do about the world coffee price? He said: 'Join the revolution.'"

McColl looked across at the Russian. There was no kindness in his face, but neither was there any trace of evil. There were deep lines around the eyes, etched by fatigue and something more corrosive, and the eyes themselves seemed to be pushing outward, as if they were trying to escape from the memories that lay behind them. "I think I've lost my chance to do that," McColl said wryly. "Maybe you'll put in a good word for me."

"Maybe I will. There is something you could tell me—just to satisfy my curiosity, you understand. Just between us."

"Yes?"

"Did you kill two members of the Trust in Arkhangelskoye in the summer of 1918?"

McColl could remember the room, the older man calmly explaining why Moscow was a harder city to starve out than Petrograd was. "I did. They were planning to poison all the fields around Moscow, and they had the stuff to do it."

"From your people?"

"The French actually, not that it matters."

"And it was you that left the supplies of poison in the car on Bolshaya Lubyanka."

"It seemed the safest place," McColl said.

"May I ask why? Why you killed your allies and thwarted their plot, I mean."

McColl took his time to answer. "I had Caitlin to think about. And the boy I'd just brought to Moscow, the one that Brady shot.

We all want to win, to see our ideas triumph, but there are some things you can't do . . . or at least I can't."

AS THE SUN ROSE OVER the mountains, the yellow-brown desert abruptly gave way to yellow-green cultivation. They rode downhill through the welcome shade of a peach orchard, emerging onto a dusty track that ran between fields of golden grain. A mile ahead the river lay on the green swathe like a red-brown snake. On its far bank, the buff-colored houses of Kerki were spread across a line of low hills, and beyond these the desert reasserted its sway.

Another beautiful day, McColl thought. Perhaps his last, but probably not. There were many obvious questions to which Komarov would still want answers.

"So much for impassable deserts," the Russian muttered beside him.

The Amu Dar'ya, here about three hundred yards wide, posed more of a problem. The ferry-raft was berthed on the other bank, and it took three rounds from Maslov's revolver to roust out the operator. Once alerted he stared across at their party, vigorously scratched his head, and disappeared back into his house. Minutes dragged by, and Maslov's finger was tightening on the trigger once more when the ferryman emerged with what looked like three sons, arranged in descending order of height.

They pushed out from the far bank, pulling the guide ropes free of the water's surface as they did so.

The raft proved larger than it had at first appeared, easily accommodating both humans and ponies. The ferryman was clearly curious, but Komarov met his questions with discouraging grunts. The current was smooth and powerful.

Across the river they could see a wooden landing stage and, behind it, set back from the embarkation area, the ubiquitous *chaikhana.* On the latter's right, there was a long wooden building, which one of the soldiers said was the town barracks. Between the two buildings, a road led steeply up to a half-ruined fortress. Red flags fluttered on the two towers that flanked its entrance gate; staring up at the battlements, McColl caught the flash of sun on glass.

Komarov was more interested in the barracks, which looked ominously quiet. "Ask him how many soldiers are stationed here," he instructed McColl.

"About fifty," was the initial reply, "when they're here," the unfortunate caveat.

"Ask him where they are."

They were out chasing the Basmachi.

It was the first time McColl had heard Komarov swear.

The ferry was halfway across the river. As two men issued from the fortress gates and started down the hill, half a dozen soldiers appeared from behind the barracks and hurried toward the landing stage, most still arranging their dress. By the time the ferryman had pulled his craft alongside the landing stage, the soldiers had turned themselves into a ramshackle guard of honor, lining each side of the ramp and channeling the new arrivals into the welcoming arms of the officials from the fortress. One of these, to McColl's amazement, was bedecked in a full-length leather coat, the sort that even stylish Chekists usually kept for winter. The other was a woman, and a handsome one at that. She was probably in her forties, and her eyes sparkled with an intelligence that seemed lacking in her male superior.

The man in the leather coat was the chairman of the Kerki Soviet. "How many men have you got?" Komarov asked while they were still shaking hands.

"These," the chairman said, airily indicating the now-at-ease guard of honor. He was a Pathan, McColl thought, or maybe a Tajik. "You'll take tea?" the man was asking Komarov.

"Tea? Oh, yes, I suppose so."

"This way, comrade."

They were led into the *chaikhana* garden, where a line of iron bedsteads topped with mattresses gave the usual impression of an open-air hospital. The woman disappeared into the building and shouted at someone.

"We have news," the chairman announced importantly, once they had all sat down. "The *Red Turkestan* should be here sometime this afternoon."

"How do you know this?" Komarov asked, obviously surprised.

"We have an airplane. Since the message arrived from Samarkand, our pilot has flown down the river each day and kept track of their progress."

"Is the airplane armed?" Komarov asked.

"No."

"A pity. But perhaps we could use it to drop explosives."

The chairman looked uncomfortable. "I regret to say that we have run out of fuel. The pilot barely had enough for his last return flight."

Komarov buried his nose in his hands. "When are the troops due back?"

A shrug. "Who knows? The garrison commander is a fool."

"Probably not for several days," the woman said, rejoining them.

"Twelve men," Komarov muttered.

It was enough for Jesus, McColl thought flippantly. He sipped at the hot, sweet tea, staring up at the serried ranks of mud houses climbing the hill. He had the strange feeling that he was seeing Asia for the first time.

Maslov proved more oblivious to their surroundings. "What shall I do with the Englishman?" he asked Komarov, as if McColl were a piece of shopping they'd just brought home.

"There's a lockable room in the barracks," the woman said, eyeing McColl for the first time.

"That'll do," Komarov told Maslov.

As he was led away, McColl took a look downriver. There was no sign of the expected riverboat, but his ears picked up the faintest echoes of distant gunfire. It might have been hunters or the town's absent troops trading fire with a band of Basmachi. Or maybe his one indisputable enemy, only a few hours away.

PIATAKOV WATCHED THE PASSENGERS WADE ashore, still grumbling loudly. They didn't know how lucky they were. Farther upstream a battle was waiting for the *Red Turkestan*, and thanks to him they were going to miss it. Brady had considered keeping them aboard as a disincentive to artillery, but had been won over by Piatakov's counterargument that too many strangers would get in their way.

He went back to constructing a makeshift breastplate for the machine gun. Having already taken the cargo-space doors off their hinges, he lashed them to either side of the mounting to give himself some extra protection. It had already been decided that he would man the gun and that Chatterji's first responsibility was looking after captain and bridge. Brady would go wherever he was needed.

The American was full of confidence, and Piatakov was inclined to feel the same. The captain had cheerfully warned them that Kerki had a sizeable garrison and that the river there was appreciably narrower, but as long as the ship didn't run aground, it would certainly take some stopping. As Piatakov had discovered on the Volga, boarding a moving ship in the face of hostile fire was a daunting prospect for even the best-trained troops, and there wouldn't be many of those out here in the middle of nowhere.

IN KERKI THE MORNING PASSED slowly. McColl had been shut in an officer's room; it contained a bed, a cupboard, one pitted enamel bowl, and two books: *The ABC of Communism* and a volume of Pushkin's verse. The door was not locked—to Maslov's chagrin the key could not be found—and only a single soldier was presently standing guard outside, making escape to the nearby border a highly feasible proposition.

Yet here he still was. It might have been foolish—it almost certainly was—but he couldn't bring himself to hightail it over the hill at this stage of the proceedings. It would be like leaving a nickelodeon with the heroine still in the villain's grasp or walking out of Ibrox with Rangers and Celtics tied in the final minutes and a penalty kick about to be taken. He would slip away only when he knew that she was safe and that the final result was no longer in doubt.

The open window looked out across the river, and as the room grew hotter, McColl took up station beside it, enjoying the breeze that blew down from the mountains. He watched with interest as two antique muzzle-loading cannons were trundled past him and out of sight to the left. Around noon six soldiers assembled on the wooden landing stage and sat down on its edge, their feet dangling over the water.

Not long after that, his door swung open, and Komarov walked in. The Russian looked, if possible, even more exhausted than he had in the hour before they'd reached Kerki. He sat down on the bed and stifled a yawn.

"Will those guns actually fire?" McColl asked.

"I hope so." The Russian massaged his chin with his left hand. "I have another question for you. Nothing important, just to satisfy my own curiosity." He looked McColl straight in the eye. "After you lost your tail in Samarkand, why didn't you make a run for it then? It wouldn't have been difficult."

"I'm sure you know the answer to that, Yuri Vladimirovich."

"She means that much to you? You could not have stayed here, my friend, and she would not have left. Her work is here."

"Women are no better treated anywhere else," McColl said.

"Perhaps not, but she is part of this."

McColl sighed. "She was. She may be still—I don't know. I haven't asked her."

Komarov gave him a searching look and seemed satisfied with what he found. "I have a proposition for you. I have only twelve men out there, and most of them are boys."

"I will gladly join you," McColl said simply.

Komarov shook his head. "No, that would be misunderstood. I have something clse in mind."

AFTER A SHORT BUT SURPRISING talk with Komarov, Caitlin spent the rest of the morning at the Soviet offices up in the fortress, talking, or rather listening, to the woman who had greeted their party at the landing stage. Her name was Shadiva Kuliyeva, and at any other time, Caitlin would have found the woman's story as fascinating as it was inspiring. Only a year earlier Kuliyeva had been the veiled slave-wife of a local rice merchant, and now she seemed to be running the local Soviet—and the town of Kerki—in all but title.

She could certainly talk the average Russian under the table. Or perhaps it was simply the excitement of having a "comrade woman" to talk to. The flow of anecdotes and stories dried up only when Caitlin's yawns became too frequent to ignore. "You must get some sleep," Kuliyeva said, not at all offended.

"No." Caitlin slowly got to her feet, still stiff from the two nights on horseback, and took a look out of the window. The river below was empty, but the view downstream was cut off by a protruding tower, so for all she knew the riverboat might be approaching. A swift descent to the quay was tempting, but Komarov had made her promise to stay out of harm's way, for all of their sakes. "What time is it?" she asked Kuliyeva.

"Half-past twelve."

"Then they should be here soon," Caitlin said, mostly to herself.

"Is it true that your husband is one of the . . . ?" the Uzbek woman asked.

"Yes, he is," Caitlin acknowledged. And her lover was locked in the barracks. And her comrade—and that, she realized, really was how she saw him—was down by the river getting a dozen boys ready to fight three dangerous men.

Kuliyeva waited patiently.

"It's a long story," Caitlin said wearily. Down below two boats were inching out into the current. "Is there somewhere we can go with a better view?" she asked.

"Of course. The roof. Here." Kuliyeva picked up a pair of binoculars from the desk and handed them to Caitlin. "Come."

As they climbed the steps, Caitlin found herself going through all of the feasible outcomes, and realizing that every last one was freighted with sadness and grief.

KOMAROV COULD HEAR THE DISTANT churning of the paddle, but the ship itself was still hidden from sight by the bend in the river a mile or so downstream. There both banks rose into cliffs, and the paddle steamer, when it did appear, seemed dwarfed by nature, smaller than he had imagined. It was a dazzling white in the afternoon sun, pumping dark grey smoke into the clear blue sky.

The timing was almost perfect. By the time the boat reached

Komarov's position, the sun would be ideally placed to cover his intended angle of approach. Making use of this blind spot might not provide much of an edge, but it was all he had. If the riverboat slowed to its usual speed on this treacherous stretch of the river, and if the four of them rowed fast enough to catch it, then they might get aboard unseen. All the evidence pointed to there being only three renegades, and one at least would be on the bridge. The others, he hoped, would be suitably distracted by the cannons on the opposite bank and the boats up ahead in midchannel.

Komarov scrambled down the bank and into the skiff, which was screened from view by the drooping branches of a large and ancient willow. When Maslov and the two soldiers all looked up expectantly, he found himself feeling almost irritated by their touching faith in his leadership.

Three-quarters of a mile farther upstream the other two boats were inching out into the center of the river, each with its crew of three soldiers. These men had shown rather less confidence—they were quite likely lambs to the slaughter, and some of them seemed to know it. If the cannons could silence the mounted machine gun, they had a good chance of survival. If not . . .

The paddle steamer was less than half a mile away, and appeared to be moving slower than Komarov had expected. Which, if true, was excellent news.

There was no sign of passengers or crew, no movement on the outside deck—if not for the churning wheel and the steam pulsing out of the funnels, it could have been a ghost ship.

But then a steam whistle pierced the air, once, twice, like a bugler announcing a charge, and Komarov could make out a blond-haired figure on the foredeck, crouched behind the mounted machine gun. The latter's position gave it a wide field of fire, but as Komarov had hoped, the riverboat's superstructure, rising behind it, precluded it from covering his intended approach. His plan might work.

The seconds ticked by, the distance shortening—surely it had to be in range by now. "Fire, for God's sake," he heard himself mutter.

Somebody heard him. First there was a puff of yellow smoke,

then a dull boom that rolled across the water. The outflung ball splashed into the river behind the churning wheel.

The *Red Turkestan* drew level with Komarov's position. "Go," he told the others, leaning into the oars.

"HOW MANY GUNS?" PIATAKOV SHOUTED.

Brady was standing on the steps up to the bridge, examining the southern bank through the captain's telescope. "Two!" he yelled back. "And they look about a hundred years old. If only we had a Jolly Roger!"

The second cannon fired, its ball falling fifty yards short. Piatakov could see the guns now and knew they were still beyond his machine gun's range. So were the two small boats up ahead, but he aimed a short burst at them anyway, hoping they'd realize the cost of staying where they were.

There was another puff of smoke on the bank, and this time the ball crashed into the ship's superstructure with a deafening clang. Piatakov instinctively flinched, then saw that the culprit was trundling off down the deck like a bowling ball.

He and Brady grinned at each other. The enemy might as well have been throwing cabbages.

KOMAROV SWORE UNDER HIS BREATH. The cannons were next to useless—only a direct hit on the machine gun or the paddle would cause the renegades a significant problem. And God only knew what the machine gun would do to the men in the boats up ahead.

The men on the landing stage had opened fire with their rifles—he could hear the bullets pinging off the metal sides. His boat was now about a hundred yards adrift and slowly gaining. Sweat was pouring off their faces as they strained at the oars.

There was a thumping explosion on the far bank, and Komarov lifted his eyes in time to see something—or someone—heading skyward above the muzzle-loaders.

One of the guns had exploded. The Kerki Soviet would probably need a new chairman.

PIATAKOV FIRED A BURST OVER the heads of the soldiers in the two small boats, hoping that they would turn tail like their colleagues in Burdalik. A bullet whining off his improvised breastplate suggested that they intended otherwise, and he raked one boat, dropping at least one soldier and causing two others to take to the water. But when he tried to swing the barrel into line with the other boat, it wouldn't move.

"What's the matter?" Brady shouted.

"The mounting's jammed!"

"Leave it!" Brady yelled as he ran down the steps. "You take the port side," he told Piatakov, gesturing in that direction. "Anyone tries to get aboard, tell them they don't have a ticket."

As KOMAROV'S SKIFF PULLED ALONGSIDE, a well-aimed grappling hook tagged it to the moving paddle steamer. He watched as Maslov and the two soldiers clambered up and through the deck railings, then followed. There was no one else in sight. The machine gun had fallen silent; the only firing was coming from the landing stage, the bullets bouncing off the ship like blind mosquitoes. So where was the enemy?

Someone ran along the deck above them, the footfalls disappearing around the stern.

"Take the other side," he told Maslov. "You go with him," he told one of the soldiers. "Shoot on sight."

The young Ukrainian tried for a gallant smile and only narrowly failed. Komarov stood where he was for a moment, watching the two men go, aware of the sweat running down either side of his nose. He hadn't felt this frightened since his days as a trainee policeman.

"All right," he said calmly, as much to himself as to the soldier beside him. "Slowly."

They edged forward, Komarov in front, trying to keep their heads below the windows. The rifle fire from the landing stage had stopped, and all he could hear was the thunderous spinning of the paddle wheel. Then someone shouted something from a long way off, something unintelligible.

Komarov stopped abruptly, and the soldier stumbled into his

back. The engine room! They should have gone straight for that and put the boat out of action. He remembered all the times he'd thought that you couldn't make a policeman out of a soldier. It seemed the opposite was also true.

Two shots rang out on the other side of the boat, one crack, one boom. Maslov! Komarov hurried forward, looking for a way across, but all he found was a view across the open hold. Maslov was nowhere to be seen, but the soldier who'd gone with him was draped across the deck rail like a casually thrown-off coat.

"Comrade!" a mocking voice shouted behind him.

Komarov whirled, and what felt like a sledgehammer hit him in the right shoulder. He tried to lift the arm, and realized the gun was gone from his hand. The soldier's rifle clattered onto the deck.

Piatakov was standing some twenty feet away, holding his gun on both of them.

Hearing footsteps behind him, Komarov turned, hand on his shoulder. The American was walking toward him, a smile on his face.

"Deputy Chairman Komarov himself," Brady said. "We *are* honored."

Komarov stared stonily back at him. He could feel the blood coursing through his fingers.

"Start swimming," Brady snapped at the soldier, who, with one guilty glance at Komarov, vaulted the rail and disappeared into the foaming water.

"He'll make a useful hostage," Piatakov was saying.

"I don't think so," Brady said.

Komarov examined his gore-soaked hand. Stretching away behind the American, the red-brown Oxus looked for all the world like a river of blood. As the other man pulled the trigger, his late wife's face appeared in front of his eyes.

REALIZING THAT HIS GUARD HAD vanished, McColl had walked down to the landing stage. "If I fail," Komarov had told him, "then you will have your chance."

Aboard the receding riverboat, Aidan Brady and another man were standing over Komarov's body, both looking back at the town.

Then Brady reached down and dragged the corpse to the edge of the craft, before tipping it into the river with a thrust of his boot.

CAITLIN LOWERED THE BINOCULARS, LOWERED her head. Her fingernails bit into her palms.

"They are escaping," Kuliyeva said disappointedly, as if they were watching a film and the ending had proved unexpectedly sad.

"I'm going down," Caitlin told her.

"But—"

"I'm going down."

Kuliyeva stepped aside, then followed her down the stone steps and out through the crumbling gateway. In the middle of the river, a man or corpse was being dragged aboard the surviving skiff. The paddle steamer had passed from view around the next bend in the river, a hanging line of smoke offering proof of its passage.

Less than an hour had passed since Komarov had ushered her into Kuliyeva's empty office, shut the door behind them, and told her he had no doubt of her loyalty to the revolution. He had, he said, already informed Ghafurov and Kuliyeva that they should, in the event of his and Maslov's deaths, take their orders from her.

Satisfied that her English lover was interested only in thwarting his own people's plot, Komarov had further arranged that McColl would be freed to continue the pursuit, should failure on his own part make that necessary. He hoped Caitlin would offer the Englishman any assistance he needed to reach the border. Whether or not she went with him was of course up to her.

As Caitlin started down the narrow road, she caught sight of Jack on the distant jetty, staring up the river, like someone who'd just missed a boat.

September 1921

Unworthy Empire

The tonga deposited Alex Cunningham at the end of the Kudsia Road. He lifted out his suitcase, paid the preagreed amount, and assured his young driver that there was no point in waiting. The boy turned the horse in a tight half circle, and offered up the usual reproachful look before gently twitching the reins and rattling off down the road.

Cunningham took a deep breath and started walking, mindful of the hot tropical sun and the strange, sweet scents of the flourishing gardens. Hundreds of invisible birds seemed to be singing their hearts out, and the distant sound of racket on ball, interrupted by bursts of excited laughter, offered evidence of human life behind the curtains of bougainvillea.

At a cursory glance, the Indian Political Intelligence building was just another European bungalow in the Delhi cantonment, but the soldiers lurking in the trees and the wireless mast reaching up to the heavens rather gave it away. A replacement had presumably been included in the plans for the new city five miles to the south, but Cunningham doubted the setting would have the same charm.

He had no sooner shown the soldiers his papers than a tall, fair-haired young man in a shirt and slacks appeared in the doorway. "Cunningham?" the man asked with a faint Yorkshire accent.

"Morley, Nigel," he said, offering his hand. "We've been expecting you." He looked around. "You might as well leave your luggage here for the minute. We've got you a bungalow near the Ridge. Come this way."

Cunningham followed him across the marble-floored hall and into a large reception room. "Help yourself to a drink," Morley said, pointing out the decanters on the side table. "I'll see what the colonel's up to."

Cunningham poured himself a generous whiskey and looked around the room. The creamy white walls were patterned by sun and shadow, the furniture a mixture of raffia and mahogany. Not a lot had changed since his last visit in 1918.

"The colonel will see you now," Morley said from the door.

Another corridor took them through the bungalow and out onto a bougainvillea-draped veranda. Colonel Mortimer Fitzwilliam was sitting in an incongruously European chair with a polished walnut frame and burgundy velvet upholstery. His suit—the sort of limp white affair favored by tropical traveling salesmen—had rather less class.

Cunningham shook the outstretched hand and accepted the offer of a simple wooden chair. Morley remained standing.

"Glad you made it," the colonel was saying. "How was the trip up from Bombay?" he asked, with the tonelessness of one repeating an oft-used phrase.

"No worse than usual," Cunningham replied noncommittally.

The colonel smiled. "Ah, well, I expect we'll be using airplanes soon." He looked up at the sky, as if expecting one to appear at that very moment. "Ah, well," he repeated, turning back to Cunningham, "I just wanted to welcome you in person. As to your *business* here"—the tone implied distaste, but whether that came from patrician breeding or a lack of sympathy with this particular endeavor wasn't clear—"Morley here will fill you in on the current state of play."

It sounded like a dismissal, and Cunningham got to his feet.

"At any rate," the colonel said, staring at his garden, "it must be for the best that we're all working together on this one."

Cunningham presumed he meant Five, the IPI, and British India's Department of Criminal Intelligence. "Indeed," he agreed.

"You spent several years here, didn't you?" the colonel asked.

"Three in Calcutta, two here in Delhi."

"Then you know what we're up against."

"I hope so, sir."

"Good, good," the colonel said, finally signaling the end of the interview with a limpid wave of the wrist. A muttered "desperate remedies" floated after Cunningham and Morley as they reentered the bungalow.

Two short passages brought them to a small and untidy office. The walls were covered with maps, the desk with papers; a line of papier-mâché elephants sat atop a display cabinet packed with handguns that went back a century or more. Morley moved a pile of files onto the floor and offered Cunningham the newly empty chair.

It seemed hotter than it had outside, despite the fan whirring erratically overhead.

One of the maps was peppered with colored flags representing various expressions of political dissent. There seemed to be a lot of them, and more than half were red, depicting the highly serious kind. "How bad *are* things?" Cunningham asked.

Morley followed his gaze and shrugged. "Who knows? I think London's been getting a trifle complacent lately. No offence, old boy," he added with a crooked smile.

"None taken. There's no money to spare, and complacency's a damn sight cheaper than panic."

Morley was rummaging around in a desk drawer. "Right," he said, extracting a bulging folder, "I'll give you the news as we got it ourselves. Seventh August—we had the first report of a gun battle in Kerki . . ." He turned and reached an arm toward the large map behind him. "Which is here," he added, tapping with a finger. "There were Europeans involved, but we didn't find out who until"—he moved on to the next message—"the eleventh. The battle took place on the twenty-eighth of July. The local Russian authorities—led, incidentally, by some high-ranking Cheka boss from Moscow—tried to stop a riverboat heading upstream past the town. Several men were killed, including the Cheka boss. There were two Europeans on the boat, who turned out to be members of the Good Indian team. By the time we heard about all this, they were halfway across Afghanistan, on their way to Kabul."

"And McColl?"

"We had that message you know about, the one from Samarkand on"—he checked through the file—"on the twenty-fourth of July, and nothing since. According to our source in Kerki, the Cheka boss was already holding an Englishman, who might have been McColl. If so, he was probably taken to Tashkent, questioned, and shot. Which will save us the trouble."

"Was there really no way of bringing him back on board?" Cunningham asked.

"When?"

"I don't know. There must have been almost a month between his arrival in Moscow and his reaching . . . wherever you said the battle was."

"Kerki." Morley shrugged. "Maybe. But once Suvorov had taken the 'need to know' directive as literally as he did . . . well, the colonel decided we couldn't take the risk." He looked at Cunningham. "You knew McColl, right? I've talked to others who knew him in Calcutta during the war, and they all said much the same thing, that they never really thought of him as one of us."

"No, he wasn't." Cunningham couldn't say he'd ever liked the man's holier-than-thou approach when it came to dealing with Indians, but he had been annoyingly proficient.

Morley turned to another page in his file. "Brady made contact in Kabul on August nineteenth and collected all the papers he and the others needed. He was told about Gandhi's plans to visit Delhi in the third week of September." Morley looked up. "Our loin-clothed friend is planning to stir up trouble during the Prince of Wales's visit," he explained. "And Brady was pleased to hear that—he thinks the local police will be stretched to the limit while the prince is here. Oh, and we did ask him about McColl. Brady said he hadn't run into him in Russia."

Morley consulted the next cable. "August thirty-first. They didn't want to spend more than three weeks in Delhi, so they stayed a fortnight at Flashman's Hotel in Peshawar and only arrived here a couple of days ago. We've put them up at Sayid Hassan's . . ."

"Who's he?"

"Ah, since your time. He's from some tin-pot royal family or other—somewhere in Rajasthan, I think. Fortunately for us, he has some rather disgusting habits, and last year he got a little carried away with one of his little boys. We helped him out of the mess, which rather put him in our debt. He's gone off to the hills for a holiday while this business is completed." Morley grinned. "We've provided the Good Indian team with servants, a genuine one and three of our men. The real one's there to show the others how it's done. The team has been asked not to stray—we told them it's for secrecy's sake, but really it's because it makes the surveillance that much easier. If and when they try to twist things around, we'll be on them like a ton of bricks."

"If? I don't think there's any doubt that Brady will try."

"When, then."

"Desperate remedies," Cunningham murmured to himself.

"You don't sound too sure about all this."

"I'm sure enough. Whichever way it goes, they'll be dead. And with any luck, Gandhi will be, too."

"We certainly won't be sorry to see the back of him. He can't be ignored, he can't be arrested without making things worse, and he can't be killed by any obvious friend of ours without turning him into a martyr . . ."

"I know the rationale," Cunningham said dryly.

THE SHADOWS WERE LENGTHENING ON Chandni Chowk, but the offices on one side of the street were still bathed in dazzling sunlight. On the other, leaning in a derelict doorway, McColl idly wondered what the street had looked like before the bomb attack on the viceroy had prompted the authorities to cut down all the trees.

Few in the throng gave him more than a passing glance. Those who did saw a tall, dark-skinned figure with a thick mustache and beard wearing a large floppy turban, an embroidered waistcoat over a white kurta, and matching cotton trousers. In the shadows he convinced as a Pathan, and even in full daylight, most would take him for one of the half-caste unmentionables fathered by British soldiers and administrators over the previous century.

The door across the street opened, and two men emerged, one in Indian dress, the other in a smart European suit. Harkishen Sinha was the latter.

Almost a decade had passed since their paths had last crossed, here in Delhi during McColl's last visit as an automobile salesman. That meeting had not gone well. Sinha had suspected, quite rightly, that his old friend was also involved in intelligence gathering for the British government, and McColl had found the Indian's views on British rule both glib and judgmental. Their prewar years at Oxford, and the friendship they'd forged as outsiders at the shrine of English breeding, had felt like a distant memory. In the intervening years, both men had written a few stilted letters, as if reluctant to accept that their friendship was actually over.

A situation like this one, McColl thought, could hardly have been foreseen by either of them.

Their conversation over, the two Indians went their separate ways, the stranger heading west, Sinha crossing the street on a diagonal and walking south. McColl started after him, keeping a fifty-yard gap between them, and remembering a summer day almost twenty years before. They'd been sitting outside a pub by the river, and Sinha had suddenly exclaimed, in his perfect English, how *muted* everything was. "The sounds, the colors, the smells—everything. I feel like I'm wrapped in cotton wool."

His old friend turned down a twisting street that McColl remembered came out in front of the Jama Masjid mosque. But after a couple of hundred yards, the Indian turned left into what appeared to be a dead-end alley, and McColl reached the corner in time to see Sinha vanish through a gateway.

A few seconds later McColl let himself through the gate and into a pleasant courtyard, where a servant moved to intercept him.

Sinha, glancing back, saw only the costume. "What do you want?" he asked curtly in Urdu.

The servant was trying to push him back, but McColl stood his ground. "Hello, Harry," he said.

Sinha's mouth gaped open. "Jack?" he asked, as if he could scarcely believe his ears.

"In person."

"What . . . ?" Sinha noticed his servant watching with interest. "Nikat, shut the gate," he told the man abruptly. "Jack, come this way," he urged, hustling McColl through an archway, across another courtyard, and into what looked like his study. Legal briefs were neatly stacked along one wall.

"How are you, Harry?" McColl asked.

"I'm well, thank you. But . . ."

"And the children?"

"They are well . . ."

"I—"

"Jack, what is this?" Sinha almost shouted. "Why have you come to my house dressed like a Punjabi bandit? Is this some stupid trick of your political police?"

McColl put a hand on the Indian's shoulder. "No," he said calmly. "I have come for your help."

"But why this fancy dress, as you English call it?"

"Because it would be dangerous for both of us if I was seen visiting you. Even this is risky, but . . . well, I have no other choices."

"I do not understand. Who is looking for you?"

"My own people. The 'political police' you were just talking about, I suppose." It crossed his mind that using the same words to describe the Cheka and Five seemed less ludicrous than it would have a couple of months ago.

"But why?" Sinha wanted to know. "Why are your people after you? Have you stolen a polo trophy or something?"

McColl laughed. He was, he realized, really pleased to see Harry Sinha again. Whatever happened.

Sinha looked at him, then burst out laughing himself, and for a moment it felt as if the last twenty years had evaporated, and they were back in one of their college rooms, finding a shared hilarity in the farcical vagaries of Oxford life.

Could he tell his friend the whole story? McColl asked himself again. He could but he wouldn't. Or at least not yet. It wasn't just a matter of trust: Sinha would feel he had to tell others, to warn Gandhi, and who knew where that might lead? It would increase the danger to Sinha himself, and it would put both McColl's and Caitlin's freedom at risk. And, as McColl was prepared to admit to himself, it would take matters out of his hands. Somehow, deep down, absurdly or not, this had become an intensely personal business in so many different ways, between him and Brady, between Caitlin and Sergei, between her and himself.

"I can't tell you much, Harry," he said. "Only that I am not working for British intelligence anymore."

"Then whom?"

McColl smiled inwardly at his friend's perfect grammar and at the question. Who was he working for? Cumming? The dead Komarov? "Harry," he said, "I know you want self-government."

"More than that. Swaraj. Complete independence."

"Okay. I can only promise that we're on the same side and that if you knew the whole story, you would support me in what I'm doing. If I didn't believe that, I wouldn't be asking you for help."

Sinha gave him a long, hard look, sighed, and finally smiled. "I believe you," he said. "But how can I help?"

"I need to borrow a little money."

"That presents no difficulty."

"And I need somewhere to stay. In the Indian part of the city. For a week, perhaps two."

"You are welcome here."

"I have someone with me."

"Oh . . ."

"A woman. I think it would be better, in the circumstances, to say she is my wife."

"She is English?"

"American. But she has been living in Russia for the last three years."

"Russia?" Sinha exclaimed.

"As a journalist at first, and since the revolution she's been working for the Bolsheviks' women's department."

"My God," Sinha said. "How long have you known this 'wife?'"

"Eight years. It's a long story, and I hope to bore you with it later. But for the moment . . . well, the less you know, the better for you."

Sinha shook his head, but more in amusement than disbelief. "I am pleased you came to me, Jack. But I am not surprised by all this. You were always—how do you say it?—the stranger at the feast? That is why you became my friend at Oxford and why you became a spy, and it seems to me most likely that this is why you finally came to realize that your empire is not worthy of you."

"Perhaps," McColl said, remembering what someone had told him once—that old friends were always the best mirrors.

"So when will you bring your wife here?"

"This evening, if that's okay?"

"I will be waiting for you."

HALF AN HOUR LATER McCOLL ducked out of a busy street, passed through the narrow doorway of a serai, and walked across its inner courtyard. The proprietor's wife looked up from her spinning wheel and gave him an uncertain smile—Pathans were not universally popular in Delhi. He wished her a good evening in Urdu and headed up the creaking stairs.

In their room two geckos were contemplating each other on the ceiling. Caitlin was out on the balcony, dozing on the mattress. He stood and gazed down at her, the hair half hiding the face he knew so well, the white cotton robe wound tightly around the body that never failed to arouse him.

Seven weeks had passed since that day beside the river, since Komarov's death and their decision to continue the pursuit together. She was thinner now, browner, the lines of her face drawn a shade harder. He found it difficult to believe that he could ever love anyone else.

It had taken them more than a month to cross Afghanistan, eking out McColl's emergency supply of silver coins. They had sometimes journeyed alone, sometimes with caravans, once even with a traveling cinema, rarely covering more than ten miles a day, but knowing that their quarry would be moving little faster. No one hurried in Afghanistan, a land where time was kept by the rivers and mountains, where humans still recognized forces greater than themselves. It had felt like time on loan from the rest of their lives, doing what humans had always done: eating, drinking, traveling, sleeping, and making love.

Then, one night in September, they had passed between the jaws of the Khyber with a Pathan caravan and seen the plains of the Punjab laid out below, a patchwork of greens fading into the east. Two evenings later they had boarded the train in Peshawar like people stepping back into civilization's dream, with hardening faces, touches that felt merely physical, words that seemed bogged down in consonants.

Another three dawns had brought them to the Delhi station. McColl, turbaned and bearded, had walked out past a DCI man he recognized from 1915; Caitlin, tanned and veiled, had attracted even less attention. They had taken this room in a nearby serai. From its balcony they could see, in one direction, the station itself, forever smoke-signaling arrivals and departures, and in the other, looming above the ancient city, Shah Jahan's Red Fort, stone at the heart of the British Empire.

McColl's insistence that they rest for a day had less to do with physical need than his acutely felt reluctance to raise the curtain on the final act. That night, as they'd moved together in such effortless harmony, he'd had the sudden terrifying feeling that the two of them had crammed a lifetime's love into only a couple of months.

And now the curtain was going up.

Until he met her, he had always thought people in love arranged their lives around that emotional fact. But Caitlin took the opposite view, that people should decide what they wanted from life and adjust their love lives to fit. This, she said, was what men did anyway, usually at the woman's expense.

He could see her point, but . . .

He still had no idea whether or not she was going back to Russia or how he could live without her if she did.

As if in response to this thought, Caitlin opened her eyes. "Hello," she said sleepily. For a moment she looked vulnerable, but the world soon took her back. She pulled herself up into a sitting position, her back against the balcony wall, and gave him a questioning look.

"Yes," he told her. "We can stay with Harry. He's expecting us in an hour or so."

"I'll get ready."

DARKNESS HAD FALLEN BY THE time they started the short journey across the city. Caitlin still felt uncomfortable—not to mention vaguely ridiculous—wearing the veil, although after a month of doing so, she supposed she should be used to the damn thing. It wasn't just the political insult it reflected; the cloth itself felt physically restrictive, as if it stopped her from breathing properly.

"It's all in your head," McColl had told her half seriously when she first mentioned it.

She had felt like kicking him, and apparently it had shown.

"When all you can see is the eyes," he'd remarked, "it's amazing how expressive they are."

They were passing through the Queen's Gardens now, gigantic palm fronds swaying above the tonga. "This is beautiful," she murmured in Russian. As McColl had pointed out, two many Indians understood English for them to use it in public.

"Make the most of it," he replied. "You may be stuck indoors for several days."

"I know," she said tersely. He had already explained that here in Delhi women—whether Hindu or Muslim—rarely went out alone. Even veiled, she would stick out like a sore thumb. "I sometimes think," she added tartly, "that there's a man inside you that likes the idea of the woman imprisoned at home."

"You don't believe that," he said equably. "I just know how much trouble you have pretending to be someone you're not. An admirable trait in itself but not a very useful one in these circumstances."

"All right," she said grudgingly. "Tell me more about where we're going. Is it a big house? Who else lives in it?"

"It's huge. And probably home to at least twenty people once you include the servants. Both of Harry's parents died in the flu epidemic in 1919, and he's the eldest of four brothers. They all live there, and at least three of them are married with children. As head of the family, Harry's like a minor dictator—what he says goes, and no one would question his authority. Men or women." McColl gave her a sideways glance. "I hope you're not planning a full-scale agitation."

"Not immediately," she told him with a smile.

They drove past the Town Hall and into the bedlam of Chandni Chowk. On Caitlin's side of the street, a line of customers in various stages of lathering, like frames from a moving picture, were awaiting a barber's further attention. A man walked across the street in front of their tonga, holding two children with great delicacy, just a finger and thumb on each child's wrist, guiding rather than pulling. She watched as they were swallowed by the throng on the sidewalk, fascinated. Such gentleness seemed more alien than any sight or smell.

"Your friend," she asked McColl, "is he a member of the Indian National Congress?"

"Yes."

"And he is rich. A lawyer, you said. Educated at an English school?"

"Winchester."

"This National Congress party—is it an anti-imperialist party?"

"That depends on what you mean by anti-imperialist. They don't like the empire they're in."

"Mmm. And are all the leaders rich people educated in England?"

"I don't know," McColl replied. "I don't suppose there are many peasants and workers in the leadership, but most of those will be far too busy trying to keep their heads above water to attend conferences. From what I saw in Moscow, the Asian delegates at the Hotel Lux were mostly intellectuals from well-to-do families."

"I suppose so," she agreed. They had turned down a narrower street, past a row of shops whose insides glittered and shone.

"Goldsmiths," McColl explained unnecessarily. "This is the Dariba Kalan."

The name meant nothing to her. Their driver edged the tonga past a cow that was idly nosing through a pile of refuse, then continued down the narrow lane with its high walls and carved wooden doorways. Bright eyes in dark faces lifted to watch them go by, then returned to the business at hand.

McColl stopped the tonga at the end of the cul-de-sac and paid off the driver. Sinha was waiting in the outer courtyard, still dressed in the European suit, looking more than a little anxious. He was, Caitlin thought, extraordinarily handsome.

He closed the gate behind them before going through the process of a formal greeting, shaking McColl's hand and offering Caitlin a *namaskar*, hands held together as if in prayer. "Some supper is being prepared," he said. "But first let me show you your room."

He led them through the archway, and up some winding stairs to a veranda that overlooked another courtyard, in which several seats were surrounded by a circle of tropical plants. An oil lamp above one doorway suffused the space with golden light, turning it into a mysterious grotto.

"What a lovely place," Caitlin murmured.

"That is the women's courtyard," Sinha told her.

They reached the room. It was large, but the only items of furniture were a huge double bed and an old chest of drawers. A basin of water sat on the chest, and two towels had been laid out on the embroidered coverlet. Overlapping rugs in Asian styles covered the wooden floor.

"If there's anything else you want . . ." Sinha said, looking first at McColl and then at Caitlin.

"Nothing," Caitlin told him. "And thank you for taking us in." If you're ever in Brooklyn, she felt like adding, but first she had to be there herself. "I would be honored to meet your wife," she added. "Whenever it is convenient."

Sinha smiled and said he thought that would be possible on the following day.

Another thing occurred to her. "Have you any objections to my wearing Western dress while I'm here?"

"None at all," Sinha said. "As you see, I wear it myself. Caitlin . . . I'm sorry, but Jack hasn't told me your surname."

"Hanley," she said, because it required no explanation. And, she knew, because that was who she was again.

"Well, Caitlin. There are those in my country who wish to beat the English at their own game, and there are those who would rather go back to the game we played before they came. I am in the former camp," he concluded with a smile. "And much as I like my wife in a sari, I also like her in a dress." He turned to McColl. "Perhaps we could talk in the morning, before I leave for work?"

"Of course."

"Then I'll leave you to get settled in."

Soon thereafter, food arrived: an enormous tray with at least a dozen different dishes. Once they'd eaten, different servants showed them to the bathing quarters. Caitlin threw water over herself with more energy than she'd known she had, and returned to their room to find a gorgeous red-and-blue sari draped across the bed.

Having slowly but surely mastered the art of putting one on over the last few weeks, she couldn't resist the temptation.

"You look like a princess out of the *Arabian Nights*," McColl said from the doorway.

She raised her eyebrows. "You wouldn't be thinking yourself a sultan?"

"I wouldn't presume."

"Very wise," she said. "If you think of yourself as a servant, you could come over here and unwrap me."

SOME TIME LATER SHE SNUGGLED up into his shoulder, one arm draped across his stomach. "Jack," she began, "tell me again—why are we here?"

"In this house? I thought—"

"No, in Delhi. In India. I know we've talked about this," she said. "I just need to be clear." Though whether it was clarity or certainty she needed, she wasn't sure. Perhaps, in this instance, they were one and the same.

He was silent for several moments. "To stop them is the obvious answer."

"And why is that important to you?"

Another pause. "Because I like and admire Mohandas Gandhi and because saving his life seems a thing worth doing. Because I loathe the people who set this thing in motion. The sort of people who thought naming this operation after some homicidal general's remark was a clever joke." He sighed. "And, I suppose, because I feel I owe it to Cumming and Komarov," he added, thinking how appalled the two men would be to find themselves sharing a cause.

"And that's all?" she asked once he had fallen silent.

"No," he admitted. "It isn't. I want revenge—justice—for Fedya. And for all the others: that mounted cop in Paterson, the constables in Hampshire, the night watchman at the quarry. Not to mention all the people he's killed in the last three months."

"And revenge for what he did to you?"

"For trying to kill me in Dublin and Moscow? No, I don't hold a grudge over that—*I* wasn't an innocent bystander."

She twisted onto her back, eyes on the slow-moving fan. "This is all about Brady. What about Sergei?"

"I don't know him," McColl said simply. "But they all have to be stopped."

She turned to look at him, her head supported on one arm. "You don't resent him for what he meant to me?"

"Not enough to kill him. What about you? Are you only here to save him from himself?"

She ignored the flicker of anger. "I'd like to, but it's not why I'm here."

"Then why?"

"Because I want to stop them, too. I don't know about Gandhi— maybe he's what you say; maybe he's the Menshevik that Sergei thinks he is. But assassinating anyone is just plain wrong. It's the opposite of politics, a way of avoiding the necessary work, a lazy thinker's shortcut. And this particular assassination would give the revolution a bad name here in India and all over the world. It would demean us and make us think less of ourselves. Komarov was right—without the rule of law, everything else will turn to dust."

"I understand."

"Do you?"

"There has to be something better. Brady's small-fry compared to the bastards who run countries, but they both think stepping over corpses is the only way to get anywhere. Komarov stepped over them, too, but at least he noticed what was under his feet. He knew that killing should hurt the killer and that, when it didn't, no good would come of it. Which is Gandhi's philosophy in a nutshell. The world can't afford to lose him."

She moved her head back onto his shoulder, feeling a sudden surge of love. They lay there for a minute and more, the sounds of their breathing underlining the silence.

"So what's the plan?" she asked at last.

"There are things we need to know before can we make one."

"The first being where they are. We're not even sure they're in Delhi."

"No, but it's a very good bet. According to Komarov it was the only Indian city that Brady researched in the Moscow library."

"How are we going to find them?"

"I don't know yet. First I want to know who authorized the whole business. If this is some lunatic scheme thought up by a small group of mid-ranking hotheads, then all we need to do is alert their superiors. Either with the help of my old boss in London or more directly." He smiled. "I could climb in through the viceroy's bedroom window and tell him in person."

Caitlin tried to ignore the mental picture his suggestion evoked—the viceroy and his wife in matching nightcaps, spluttering indignation. "But you don't believe this is some small cabal."

"No, but I've been wrong before."

"So how do we find out?" she asked, idly stroking his belly.

"That's easy. I ask someone who'll know. At gunpoint."

"And if that person tells you it goes right to the top?"

"Then it's up to us."

Her hand came to rest. "How long do we have?"

"According to the newspaper I read today, Gandhi arrives in Delhi a week from tomorrow."

The Women's Courtyard

The morning sun was still peering through the mist above the Yamuna River as they drove south through the half-completed new city. The road, never good, rapidly deteriorated as they headed out into open country, causing Sergei Piatakov to bounce up and down on the leather-upholstered back seat.

The Ford belonged to their absentee Indian landlord, and the three of them—ostensibly two Europeans and an Indian acquaintance interested in tiger hunting—were being chauffeured to a suitable spot for testing the three modern German rifles that their British hosts had supplied.

The guns weren't the only thing they'd found waiting for them at Sayid Hassan's luxurious villa. The four servants' eagerness to please their foreign visitors had done nothing to allay Brady's suspicions, and he had instructed Piatakov and Chatterji to search their quarters while he lectured the servants on their duties. Copies of the same neatly typed instructions had been hidden under three of the mattresses.

As Aram had said more than once, if it occurs to you, it has probably also occurred to them.

In the seat beside the driver, Brady turned to ask Chatterji if he'd ever been on a tiger hunt.

"Yes, many times when I was a boy." The Indian began recounting a long anecdote, the obvious purpose of which was to distance himself from his privileged upbringing. Piatakov's attention soon wavered. He had once had a Siberian tiger in his sights but hadn't been able to pull the trigger—the animal had seemed so full of life and grace.

He allowed himself a rueful smile. After the last three years, he no longer had that problem where humans were concerned.

They motored on through several villages and stretches of semi-jungle, the day warming, dust rising in a long cloud behind them. Almost two hours after leaving the city, the car turned in through a ruined stone gateway, drove down a tree-shaded avenue, and emerged at the top of a large open space. The slope before them was littered with pieces of brick.

They all got out and walked a short distance, the servant-chauffeur carrying the three rifles, Brady their box of shells.

"Must have been a temple," the American said, stopping to pick up a lump of brick that showed traces of faded red paint. He looked up. "How about down there?" he suggested, indicating a group of strange-looking trees some two hundred yards away. "That's farther than we'll have to shoot."

The servant walked off down the slope to place the targets. He looked somewhat nervous, Piatakov thought. A premonition, perhaps.

Brady was helping Chatterji with the loading. The two of them had grown closer since the gunfight at Kerki, the American teaching the young Indian all the gun tricks he'd learned in his years as a rebel. Piatakov wasn't sure he believed even half of Brady's stories, but there was no doubting the man's love affair with the fabled American West or his proficiency with the heavy Colt revolver. The Indian seemed enthralled, and probably was. Like a child who'd found a more suitable father.

Piatakov had been fond of Brady himself in the early days, and could understand the attraction. But he and the American had been drifting apart for quite a while. They were still allies, still comrades in the way that soldiers often were, but it no longer felt like a friendship. Perhaps it never had been. Perhaps Aram had been the glue that held the two of them together. Or perhaps they'd been more like people falling in love, seduced by the thought of a fresh beginning, the prospect of a new and better life.

As with lovers, the excitement had slowly worn off.

He thought of Caitlin thousands of miles away in Moscow, banging heads together, getting her work done. He smiled, just at the moment the first shot crashed out, pulling silence down across the jungle in the wake of its echo.

AFTER SEARCHING IN VAIN FOR any Russian news, Caitlin put aside the *Eastern Mail,* which a servant had brought with breakfast. She stared at the ceiling for a minute or so, then abruptly swung herself off the bed and started pacing to and fro. It couldn't have been more than an hour since Jack had left, which meant it was only midmorning. Lunch, the next item on her sparse agenda, was still a long time ahead.

When Jack wasn't with her, the reality of her situation quickly reasserted itself. The frustration and boredom that came with enforced seclusion was bad enough without the knowledge that what followed might well be worse. When she did get to leave the house, it would probably be to see Sergei, and since she doubted that anything good would come from the meeting, that prospect was far from enticing. She didn't want anyone killed—Jack, Sergei, even Brady—but a peaceful resolution was hard to imagine.

She thought about their conversation of the night before. Jack had been honest, she thought, probably more so than she had. She still wasn't sure why she'd come all this way, or which of the reasons she'd given were half-truths and rationalizations.

It was certainly true that she felt an obligation to Sergei and, rather more surprisingly, one to Komarov as well. What she hadn't mentioned to Jack was her reluctance to leave him again.

All feelings, of course. A cold appraisal told her that Sergei and Komarov had respectively abandoned and kidnapped her and had thereby forfeited any claim to loyalty. And if her work in Moscow wasn't more important than her feelings for Jack, why had she given him up in the first place? With the Zhenotdel facing a probable crisis, getting home to the capital should have been her top priority.

She told herself things might have been different if there'd been an easy way to return, if trains had been running to Kerki, if it hadn't seemed certain that Brady and her husband would disable the *Red Turkestan*. She could have insisted that the soldiers take her back across the desert, but memories of the way some had looked at her on the outbound trip had been enough to quash that idea. Being raped, murdered, and left for the vultures hadn't seemed like much of a future. So going on with Jack had hardly been irrational.

Trouble was, she knew she'd have done it anyway.

And even more disturbing than the knowledge that she wanted to go with him was the realization that she had no burning desire to go back. Or at least not yet. She remembered telling Jack, on the day they left Kerki, that as far as each other was concerned, they would have to learn to live in the present. And for seven wonderful weeks, they'd given a good impression of doing so. But she'd known it couldn't last forever, that sooner or later the future would come banging on her door.

Did she just need a break? Her life over the last three years had been a damned sight easier than the lives of most Russians, but it had still been a great deal harder than anything she'd ever known before. Ten-hour days and six-day weeks without any breaks in a country whose economy had virtually collapsed and whose people were dying in droves. It might have been worth it—she still thought it had been—but the cost had been high. Almost everyone she knew seemed physically and emotionally drained, herself included. So why not take the long way back—leave India with Jack, visit her family in Brooklyn, and only then return to her desk in Moscow?

Or was that also self-deluding? Over the last few months, other people's doubts and worries about the state of the revolution had felt like constant companions. Sergei's sense of betrayal, Komarov's fear of where all the killing would lead them, Kollontai's pessimism, and Arbatov's gaping chasm—only four years had passed since all these people had ecstatically welcomed the revolution, and now the only thing they had in common was the sense that it was all going wrong.

The revolution had certainly lost its soft edges, its warmth and comradeship. And, she thought, its outlandishness, its impudence and cheek. It had become less Irish, more English. Lenin might look like a leprechaun, but these days he felt more like an irascible principal whose pupils had let him down.

The sound of children's voices came floating through the window, but she couldn't see anyone. They were probably in that courtyard she and McColl had been shown. Why not go down and see? Harry Sinha hadn't objected to her meeting his wife.

She dressed in her Russian clothes, which she had finally managed to wash and dry in the serai the previous day. The long skirt and linen blouse seemed modest enough, as did the leather sandals she'd been wearing since Kabul.

It took some time to find her way down to the courtyard because the house—houses, really—seemed like a labyrinth. The young voices rose and fell, coming from this direction and that, until she turned the handle on a large wooden gate and found herself the object of many astonished eyes.

One of the women—a girl, really; she couldn't have been much more than fifteen—broke the spell by walking forward, smiling, and ushering Caitlin to one of the seats. "You must be our father's guest," she said slowly in English, before unleashing a torrent of Urdu at the other women and children.

Caitlin introduced herself.

"I am Maneka," the girl said, bringing her hands together in a *namaskar*. Like all the other girls, she was wearing a white muslin shift with a colored border. Bangles carved from bone circled her forearms. "You are English?" she asked.

"American. I grew up in New York City. Have you heard of it?"

"Yes. There's a picture in one of my books—the Statue of Liberty."

"That's the place. Now can you tell me the other girls' names?"

Maneka introduced everyone in turn, starting with Katima, whom Caitlin knew was Sinha's wife, and then presumably working her way down through the family pecking order. The three adult women smiled and brought their palms together; the seven other girls giggled and did the same. The big bright eyes in the dark brown faces made them all seem astonishingly beautiful.

Katima's English was not very good, and after sharing a warm but halting conversation with Harry's wife for several minutes, Caitlin was claimed by one of the girls, who shyly asked her to come and see a pair of lizards resting on a rubbery leaf on the other side of the courtyard. Then another child demanded attention, and another, until Maneka pulled rank and asked for help with her English. By the time an hour had passed, Caitlin was feeling almost part of the family.

On those rare occasions when she had some time for reflection, she felt the gentle pull of two contradictory emotions: on the one hand, the old anger at women's position in the world—these women sequestered in their courtyard, while the men ran the world outside—and on the other, a slight hint of envy.

What was she envious of? The simple camaraderie, perhaps. And knowing your place in the world rather than having to fight for it every day. Which was no more than she should have expected— no one knew better than a Zhenotdel worker how hard it was for women to set aside those expectations learned in childhood and reinforced each day thereafter.

Watching one of the smaller girls rocking a doll to and fro in her arms, Caitlin wondered, not for the first time, whether she wanted children. Maybe later had always been the answer, but she was in her thirties now, and she didn't want age to decide the matter for her.

Something of this must have shown in her face, because Maneka's next question was on the button. "Children," the girl said tentatively, waving an arm at the ones all around them. "You have?"

"No," Caitlin said. She still could. She could turn her back on Russia, stay with Jack, hope to bear their children. Was that a life she wanted? Was that the life she wanted most?

DEEP INSIDE THE HEAVILY PERFUMED bush, McColl removed the kurta, dhoti and turban he had been wearing on top of his

European shirt and trousers. That was the trouble with the British Empire, he thought, rolling the trouser legs down—if you didn't want to stick out like a sore thumb, you had to swap outfits every time you changed social circles.

After stuffing the Indian clothes into a carpetbag, he emerged from the bush, lingering in its shadow until he was sure that the dark road was empty. Once convinced, he started walking. Ahead and to the left, the Delhi ridge was silhouetted against the stars; on either side of the rutted road, large, sprawling bungalows nestled beneath the trees.

He walked on, following the road around the base of a low, forested hill until he saw the familiar shape of the visitors' bungalow. McColl had lodged there himself in 1916 and, during his reconnaissance that afternoon, had not been wholly surprised to find someone he knew in residence. The fact that it was Alex Cunningham, whom McColl had worked and often sparred with in 1915, had been something of a bonus. The other man was bright enough, but he was also one of Five's less industrious agents.

There were no lights shining. Cunningham, McColl knew, was rather partial to a social drink, and would probably still be at the club. And, like any prudent intelligence agent, he had always insisted on the servants living out.

As McColl walked up the path, the breeze rose, stirring the branches of the tamarind trees and scenting the air with jasmine. Above the bungalow roof, a crescent moon was hanging in the eastern sky.

The front door opened to McColl's push. He went in, down the short hall, and into a large but sparsely furnished room. In the reflected moonlight, he could make out a gramophone with a huge silver trumpet perched on a tea chest. A low table bearing a brass tray with whiskey decanter and glasses stood next to a familiar armchair. Beside it, on a chest of drawers, sat a large, ornate paraffin lamp and a box of safety matches. A writing table stood against the opposite wall, flanked by two upright chairs.

McColl poured himself a whiskey and sat down to wait, the Webley within easy reach on the writing table. As his eyes became accustomed to the darkness, the room began to look more familiar, like a photograph in a developing tray. He had spent several weeks living in this bungalow, but it felt like aeons ago.

An hour or so had passed when he heard a tonga coming up the road. The rattle of hooves slowed and stopped; a barely audible spoken exchange gave way to the sound of footsteps on the front path. McColl put down his glass and picked up the gun.

Cunningham stumbled slightly as he came through the door, and his efforts to light the paraffin lamp—burning his finger on the first match—made it clear that he'd been drinking. His success with the second augured rather better for the conversation McColl hoped was at hand.

"Evening, Alex," he said softly.

The Five man spun around, almost too fast for his impaired sense of balance. There was nothing wrong with his brain, though: recognition of both man and gun was instant. An ironic smile flitted briefly across his face.

"Sit down," McColl said, indicating the armchair by the low table. He stayed where he was, in the upright chair with his back to the wall, out of sight from either window.

"Bonnie Prince Charlie in the flesh," Cunningham said distinctly. "You made it. I suppose congratulations are in order."

"Probably," McColl said dryly.

"Want another drink?" Cunningham asked.

"No thanks."

"Mind if I do?"

"Not so long as you keep a clear head. I have some questions for you."

"What makes you think I'll give you any answers?" Cunningham asked as he poured himself a generous measure.

"I may shoot you if you don't. I've got nothing to lose, as I'm sure you know."

"True." Cunningham took a sip of whiskey. "But since you've managed to get this far in one piece, why not just keep going?"

"I intend to. But first—and just between us—whose bright idea was Good Indian?"

Cunningham considered. "The idea came from here, originally. Given the Russian involvement, they thought about asking your lot for help, but came to the conclusion that Cumming wouldn't approve. Much too old-school for this sort of caper. So they came to us instead."

"And Cumming still doesn't know?" McColl asked.

"Oh, I'm afraid he does, old boy. He was still in ignorance when you set off for Moscow, but he knows all about it now. The PM insisted he be told. I hear he kicked up a bit of a fuss at first, but, well . . ."

It was McColl's turn to consider.

Cunningham put the thoughts into words for him. "Yes, even Lloyd George. So there's no last court of appeal, no one you can go to. Look," he said, easing some fake sympathy into his voice, "I can understand how you feel, but it was just bad luck that you ended up in the firing line. You know how it is. Just disappear; that's my advice. Start again somewhere. If there's one thing you learn in this job, it's how to be someone you're not, and you must know a dozen places in India where you can pick up a set of false papers." He grunted. "And you won't have any problems with the lingo, will you?"

McColl sighed. Not too dramatically, he hoped. "You may be right. But whose idea was it to use Brady, for God's sake?"

"Brady's, of course. He suggested it to us."

"What makes anyone think he can be trusted?"

"No one does, old man."

"Then why?"

"Let's just say there were no other viable candidates. The theory was—is—that they'll do it for their own ends and because they think they can fix it on us. We let them do it, then fix it on them. And we'll have the easier job. This is our country—so to speak—and there are more of us. They're under twenty-four-hour surveillance."

"I still don't like it," McColl said, realizing how easy it was to slip back into this kind of detached risk appraisal.

"Look," Cunningham said, with a gesture that suggested his last glass of whiskey was taking effect. "Aidan Brady may be a bastard of the first order, but he's brought us a bona fide Bolshevik to kill Gandhi with. What more could we ask?"

So they were in Delhi, McColl thought. "I can't believe the political situation is that bad," he said.

"Isn't. But it soon will be if we let the old scarecrow keep at us in the way he's been doing. The stakes are just too high. Can you imagine where we'd be without the empire? Just a small island on the edge of Europe. Another Ireland, for Chrissake!"

McColl sighed again, more genuinely this time. "Maybe," he said, standing and gesturing with the gun. "Come over here, will you?"

Cunningham emptied his glass and obeyed. "Turn around," McColl said when they were both invisible from outside.

"At least I won't feel . . ." Cunningham was saying as the gun butt came down on his head. He crumpled onto the carpet, and McColl left him there, faceup.

"God save the King," he murmured, as he blew out the paraffin lamp.

Outside, the moon was high in the sky. He was walking down the road, still wondering where it would be best to change his clothes, when an empty tonga materialized out of a side road.

"Where to, sahib?" the driver asked. "The club?"

"The railway station," McColl said, climbing aboard. If the IPI traced the driver, it would look like he'd followed Cunningham's advice and taken off for points unknown.

The tonga rattled along the mostly empty roads of the British quarter. A dead city, McColl thought, an alien city. He hadn't enjoyed his time here in 1916, and then he'd felt a lot less alienated from his fellow countrymen.

Komarov had been right, at least in that. There was no going back. And, despite what Cunningham had said, no running away either. One way or another, McColl was going to see this through.

They entered the Indian city by the Mori Gate, and McColl paid off the tonga driver at the northern entrance to the station. Relying on five-year-old memories, McColl bought tea in an empty room of a first-class restaurant, retired to the toilet to change back into the Pathan clothes, and walked brazenly out through the kitchen. He left the station via the southern entrance and walked through the Queen's Gardens to the still-throbbing Chandni Chowk.

The contrast to the Civil Lines was hard to ignore. Nasal songs blared out of doorways; children scampered and shouted. In the distance a clashing cymbal or a reverberating gong occasionally split the night. Lights flickered like fireflies in each twisting alley; the glow thrown by oil lamps filled most open doorways. Fathers and children ate from brass trays on the doorsteps, the mothers often standing behind them and scanning the street, as if taking the chance to get out.

Another alien world, but somehow more inviting.

At Sinha's house the servant let him in and told him the master had retired. McColl was glad—he didn't want a barrage of questions from his friend.

Caitlin was waiting anxiously in their room, and he wasted no time in telling her what he'd found out. "Right to the top. Right to the bloody top."

"As we expected," she said quietly, putting her arms around his neck. "But what about you?"

"I'm a potentially dangerous loose end. If I don't disappear myself, they'll do it for me."

"Oh, Jack, maybe you should."

"We've been through that. If I didn't owe it to others, I'd owe it to myself. And I know you feel the same."

She sighed and let him go. "I do," she agreed, walking across to the window and leaning back against the sill. "So how are we going to find them?"

He smiled for the first time that night. "I saw a sign outside a shop this afternoon."

SOON AFTER NINE ON THE following morning, McColl paused in the shadow of another doorway, this one on Ballimaran Road, a few hundred yards from its junction with Chandni Chowk. The day's heat was still building, and the light seemed preternaturally bright, turning each passing tonga's dust into a whirl of flashing specks.

Across the street, a professional letter writer was seated at his folding desk, taking dictation from the client who sat cross-legged in front of him. Ten yards to his left, a group of young boys, the oldest no more than twelve, were sparring good-naturedly in the mouth of an alley. Between these two centers of activity, a doorway opened onto a flight of stairs, and above it hung the sign that McColl had noticed the previous day: AHMED MIRZA—CONSULTING DETECTIVE. The same words appeared on the larger board that fronted the balcony above, and there was movement in the windows behind.

Glancing up and down the busy street, McColl saw no sign of fellow Europeans or Indian policemen. He waited for a gap in the procession of tongas, then sauntered across the sunlit road at a suitably Asian pace and started up the stairs.

A woman kneading dough on a wooden board was sitting on the top step, and after squeezing past her, McColl found himself facing a door bearing another notification of Ahmed Mirza's profession. He knocked, and a voice called, "Enter," in Urdu.

The room was spacious and surprisingly cool. Like most Indian rooms, it seemed half-empty to a European, but the detective's desk almost made up for the lack of other furniture—it was at least six feet long and more than half that wide.

There were two men present. The one behind the desk presumably greeted most of his clients Indian-style; shaking hands across it, as he and McColl discovered, was a serious test of balance. "I am Ahmed Mirza," the man said in English. He was in his forties, McColl guessed, but looked physically fitter than most Indians of that age. His hair was cropped quite short, unlike his mustache, which seemed in serious danger of running riot. As if in recognition of this fact, the detective began stroking it back into submission the moment he had reseated himself. His clothes were European; a lightweight white suit, white shirt, and red bow tie.

"And this is my friend and colleague Dr. Din," Mirza added, gesturing toward the other man. The doctor was older than Mirza and dressed in traditional Indian clothes. He brought his palms together and flashed a smile full of golden teeth at McColl. "You may say before this gentleman anything you say to me," Mirza added. "He is completely deaf."

McColl sat back in the upright seat. "My name is Stuart," he began spontaneously. "Charles Stuart. I assume that anything I say in this room will be treated with the utmost confidentiality." He was speaking Urdu, hoping to show the detective that he wasn't a complete beginner where India was concerned.

"Of course, Mr. Stuart," Mirza said. "I must say, your Urdu is excellent," he went on in English. "Which language would you prefer to use?"

"Your English is also excellent," McColl said.

"I was in the army for eighteen years. Subahdar-major, Sixty-Sixth Punjabi Rifles."

McColl was impressed, which was presumably the intention. "May I inquire as to why you changed careers?" he asked, thinking it a good idea to find out as much as he could about his prospective employee.

"It was time for a change," Mirza said, not at all disconcerted by the question. "And—perhaps I should not say this; I do not wish to be political—but I had risen as far as is possible for someone like myself, and it is not a good feeling to pass down orders to brave young men knowing that those orders are not sensible."

"The Sixty-Sixth were in Mesopotamia, yes?" McColl asked. They seemed to have settled on English as their lingua franca.

"Indeed so."

"Then I can sympathize with your feelings." Compared to the Mesopotamian campaign, the one on the Somme had been almost inspired.

The Indian nodded absent-mindedly, as if the memories had taken over for a moment.

"And so you became a 'consulting detective?'"

"Yes. I'm sure you recognize the phrase." He smiled brightly. "I read my first Holmes omnibus in Kut-al-Amara, during the siege, and it was the only book I had in the Turkish prison camp. Which turned out to be a good thing. But that is often the case, is it not? The darker the place, the easier it is to see the light." He stroked his mustache again. "So, to business, Mr. . . . I assume Stuart is not your real name, and I assume you're in trouble with the British authorities?"

"What makes you think so?" McColl asked, thinking he already knew the answer. What other reason would a European have for visiting an Indian private detective?

"There is a faint line around your head dividing two areas of skin, one slightly darker than the other. Since the exact curvature of this line is unique to those wearing Afghan turbans, I must assume that you have been disguising yourself as a tribesman, and since you have come to me for help, it seems unlikely that you've been dressing that way in the service of the king-emperor."

McColl smiled. "I'm impressed," he said. "But I'm afraid I have only a straightforward task for you. I want you to find some people for me."

Mirza picked up his pen and pulled a sheet of paper onto his blotting pad, looking slightly disappointed. "Very well. Who are they?"

"Three men. An American named Aidan Brady, a Russian named Sergei Piatakov, an Indian—a Bengali—named Durga Chatterji. They are probably staying somewhere together—the American and Russian almost certainly so."

"A group like that should not be hard to find in Delhi," Mirza suggested.

"They will not be making themselves obvious. They'll probably be staying in a private house and rarely, if ever, going out."

"Why is that?"

"I would rather not say."

"Ah. But you are certain they are here in Delhi?" The detective seemed more interested now.

"Yes."

"Very well. Can you give me descriptions?"

McColl did so, relying on memory for Brady, Caitlin's account for Piatakov, and the photograph that Cumming had shown him for Chatterji. Mirza wrote it all down in bright blue ink, his British-made pen scratching at the rough Indian paper.

"I very much doubt they'll be staying in the Civil Lines," McColl added. "They'll be avoiding any contact with the British authorities."

Mirza looked even more interested. "Curiouser and curiouser. But that will make my job easier," he went on. "White faces stand out anywhere else." He put his pen down.

"May I ask how you intend to proceed?" McColl asked, hoping he wasn't breaking some arcane rule of etiquette. "Speed is important, I'm afraid."

"Of course. Did you happen to notice a group of boys outside?" McColl nodded.

"They are my 'Baker Street Irregulars,'" he said with a wide smile. "Or 'Ballimaran Road Irregulars' might be more correct. They will scour the city for your friends. One day, perhaps, two days at most. If these men are still in Delhi, the boys will find them."

"Good. When they do, I want the men watched. I want to know who comes to see them, where they go, and whom they meet if they do go out. Can you manage all that?"

"Of course."

"Excellent." McColl removed a tattered wallet from his pocket. "Now, what are your fees?"

"We can settle accounts when the case is concluded."

McColl demurred. "I would feel happier if you accepted a deposit. As you can see, I'm not wearing a turban today and rather more visible than I want to be."

Mirza grinned at him. "Very well. My rates are fifteen rupees a day."

McColl counted out three ten-rupee notes from the money Sinha had loaned him. "Take this for now," he said, passing it across. "And you will need to know where I am staying," he added with only the faintest of misgivings. If he wanted Mirza to do the job, he had to trust him that much.

"I was about to ask that very thing," Mirza told him.

McColl gave him Sinha's address, which caused the detective to raise an eyebrow. He said nothing, though.

"When you leave a message, leave it for Mr. Stuart," McColl said.

"That is most clear."

McColl got up. "Thank you," he said. "I hope to hear from you soon." He turned to wish Dr. Din farewell, but this Holmes's Watson was fast asleep.

The Indian Mrs. Hudson was still vigorously kneading her dough on the staircase. Komarov would have been more than a little amused, McColl thought as he went down the stairs.

"YOU CHECKED WITH THE RAILWAY authorities?" Colonel Fitzwilliam asked Nigel Morley.

As far as Alex Cunningham could tell, the IPI chief hadn't moved since the previous day. Fitzwilliam was sitting in the same chair, wearing the same clothes, and seemed to be halfway through the same drink. His copy of the *Eastern Mail*, however, though lying in much the same position, boasted a different front page. And his mood was undoubtedly darker.

"Yes, sir," Morley replied, glancing at Cunningham for corroboration. Cunningham was more concerned with the throbbing headache that a surfeit of port and the Webley butt had left him with.

"And?" the colonel asked with exaggerated indifference.

"Nothing. Only seven Europeans bought tickets at the booking office in the last twenty-four hours, and they've all been accounted for. If he's traveling in native disguise, then no one noticed."

"They wouldn't," Cunningham said, stirring himself. "McColl spent three months in Afghanistan and Turkestan in 1916 without getting caught. He knows the languages, knows the area, knows how to blend in. He's very tanned. And there are so many different communities in Delhi that anyone looking at him twice would assume he came from one of the others. If he's gone, there won't be any traces."

"But has he?" the colonel wondered out loud. He turned his gaze from the garden to Cunningham. "Do you think he has?"

"I don't know."

"What if he hasn't?" the colonel insisted. "You talked to him. Is he likely to do anything with his knowledge? I mean, is he the sort of chap to take things personally?"

Things like your ordering his execution, Cunningham thought sourly. "Not in the way you mean," he said, thinking back over the conversation. "He seemed more curious than anything else, and there weren't any threats. But he *was* a bit of an Indian lover back in 1915; I remember how impressed he was by Bhattacharyya and Jatin Mukherjee. He always did his job, though—I have to give him that." He shrugged. "People do change."

Fitzwilliam shook his head. "Rarely in my experience. Could he stick his oar in if he wanted to?"

"He'd have to find them first."

The colonel grunted, apparently in agreement.

"There's no way he could know about Sayid Hassan's house," Morley added. "That business happened after he went back to England."

"Are we going to tell the Good Indian team?" Cunningham asked Fitzwilliam.

"Good Lord, no. What would be the point?" The colonel sighed and closed his eyes. "I'll be glad when this business is over."

Snapshots

Having set the search underway, McColl and Caitlin spent almost all of the following forty-eight hours together in their room. They reminisced and read, ate leisurely meals, and took naps in the fearsome heat, and tried not to let their fears for the next few days drown out everything else.

It was midway through the second morning when a rap on their door announced the head servant, bearing a sheet of the consulting detective's personal stationery. Mirza's message was brief and to the point: "Success. Rendezvous, Central Post Office, Noon." McColl passed it to Caitlin, who read it and took a deep breath. He could only guess how hard this was going to be for her.

"I don't suppose it would be a good idea for me to come," she said.

"No, it wouldn't," he agreed, looking at his watch. He had plenty of time to get into costume and walk to the post office.

She came across to him, and he thought she was going to give him an argument, but she simply held him close for a minute or so. "I suppose you want me to wind your turban?" she said playfully, releasing him.

"If you would be so kind."

An hour and a half or so later he was climbing aboard Mirza's tonga.

"An excellent disguise," the detective said, studying McColl's outfit with interest. Mirza was also dressed in Indian clothes—a simple white shirt and dhoti.

"You have found them?" McColl asked.

"Of course. Did I not announce 'success' in my message? We are going there now."

"How far is it?"

"A mile? Perhaps a little more. They are staying in the home of one Sayid Hassan. He is not there, but it was arranged with him before he went away. No one seems to know where he has gone, but"—Mirza looked at McColl—"perhaps he is putting distance between himself and something particularly unsavory?"

"I don't know," McColl said, somewhat disingenuously.

The tonga rattled south down Faiz Bazaar, driven by a young boy whom McColl thought he recognized from the "Ballimaran Road Irregulars." Did Mirza picture himself in a London hansom hurrying toward some leafy suburban scene of derring-do? McColl hadn't read a Holmes story since before the war, but he remembered that several had Indian roots. Monkeys and mutiny treasure, or something along those lines.

After about five minutes, the Delhi Gate loomed ahead, but rather than pass through it, the tonga took a sharp turn to the right, heading west along the inside of the still-impressive city wall. A few minutes later the boy pulled the pony to a halt beside a semiderelict flight of steps.

Three of Mirza's "irregulars" were sitting on the bottom tread.

The eldest reported to Mirza. The three men staying in Sayid Hassan's house had been out for most of the morning and had only just returned. The two white men had simply driven around the city, up Faiz Bazaar and Elgin Road, along Chandni Chowk, and back through the Lal Kuan and Sitaram Bazaars. The Bengali had left the tonga in Chandni Chowk, walked to a house in a nearby street, and rented two rooms for a week, saying he and two friends would move in on the following day.

Mirza looked inquiringly at McColl, as if expecting an explanation.

"Where is Sayid Hassan's house?" McColl asked.

"You will see it. Come." Mirza turned and led the way up the crumbling steps. "Look out for snakes," he said over his shoulder.

As they neared the top of the flight, Mirza advised that they should both keep low, and the two of them made their way half-crouched along a short stretch of passable rampart to the protruding remains of a guard tower. Here another of the detective's "irregulars" was sitting and dozing with his back to the wall, a pair of British army binoculars reposing in his lap.

Mirza gave him an affectionate cuff. "The house is straight ahead, about two hundred yards away," he told McColl. He pointed to a large gap in the brickwork and passed him the binoculars. "Don't push them too far forward, or the light will reflect on the glass."

McColl took his first look with the naked eye. Sayid Hassan's house looked like a small estate, with several buildings set within spacious grounds alongside the old Circular Road. A magnificent banyan stood on the eastern edge of the gardens, and a man was sitting in its shadow.

McColl raised the binoculars and brought the figure into focus. A white face, Slavic and handsome, slightly cadaverous. Sergei Piatakov.

Gandhi's would-be assassin. Caitlin's husband and lover. According to her, yet another victim of the war.

Weren't they all?

A pair of legs walked into view beneath the canopy of leaves. And then the familiar figure, face, and shock of hair. Aidan Brady. Laughing about something.

McColl wondered what he would have done with a decent rifle.

"That is them?" Mirza whispered in his ear.

"Oh yes," McColl said. He lowered the binoculars and edged away from the gap. "Let's go back down."

Getting down the broken steps was harder than getting up.

"You can keep watching?" McColl asked when they finally reached the bottom.

"Of course. As long as you wish it."

"It won't be for long." One way or the other, he thought, climbing back aboard the tonga. They turned back toward the city center close by the Turkman Gate, and passed through a succession of unusually lifeless bazaars. McColl was puzzled. "It's not Sunday, is it?" he asked.

"No . . . Ah." Mirza realized what was puzzling his companion. "A hartal—a shop owner's strike—has been called by Gandhi's supporters," he explained. "Many are closed. Many Hindu shops, in any case; the Muslims are not so keen."

"I see."

"Gandhi will be here himself in a few days," Mirza added.

"What's your opinion of him?" McColl asked the detective.

Mirza shrugged. "An unusual man, certainly. Half saint, half Artful Dodger. A rare combination. But I will offer you a prediction, my friend. One day India will be ruled by Indians—perhaps better, perhaps worse—and Mohandas Gandhi will probably hasten that day. But in the end his only legacy will be a faint whiff of guilt hanging over future generations. The time for spinning wheels is past."

IT WAS LATE IN THE afternoon, the shadows lengthening almost visibly, but even in the shade, the heat was still intense and, to Piatakov's taste, unpleasantly humid. He would have been cooler indoors, sitting beneath the efficiently whirring fans, but over their five-day stay, Piatakov had grown to love the views at this particular time of day. There was something quite magical about the mix of light and color: the dark palms framing the distant silver river, the towers and domes of the city slowly catching fire in the brilliant sunset. Delhi seemed to glow with inner light, as if its walls were hung with a million burnished icons.

Piatakov smiled ruefully at the image. He felt at peace with himself, more so as the day grew nearer. It was funny how people took to such situations differently: Chatterji was like a spring coiled tighter and tighter; Brady had become relaxed to the point of avuncularity. Their two reactions seemed symbiotic, as if each had taken half of the other's personality.

Piatakov could hear them now, inside the house, talking in English. If they survived the next few days, he could imagine them going off somewhere as partners. Well, good luck to them—he had no idea what he would do. He had, he realized, not even given his possible future a moment's thought. Returning home was out of the question and would remain so until true revolutionaries seized back control of the party. Which could happen only with help from abroad—a new revolutionary wave to lift their stranded Russian boat. It was why they were here in India.

That morning they'd taken a rickshaw into the city for a look at the killing ground. Driving down Chandni Chowk, he'd gone through it all in his imagination: the seething crowds, the bands playing, the people hanging from windows; the squeezing of the triggers, the cracks, the wailing panic. The two of them hurtling down a flight of steps and onto the flat roof in full view of the watching crowds. White men with guns, the snapshot of guilt.

And then with any luck they would be gone, into the British cantonment, where their faces wouldn't stand out, and they'd be no more at risk than thousands of other white men caught in the chaos of a broken empire.

Piatakov smiled to himself in the gloom. It was a wonderful plan. He slapped at and missed a mosquito on his forearm. It was time to go back in. The sun was gone, the sky rushing through the spectrum as if each color were clamoring to replace its predecessor, fearful that darkness would come before they all had time to shine.

CAITLIN SAT ON THE EDGE of the bed while McColl went over what he had seen. His portrait of Sergei alone in a garden almost made her cry, but knowing how he would misread them, she managed to keep the tears in.

"And now all we have to decide is what we intend to do," he concluded wryly.

"I've been thinking about that while you've been out," she said. "It's simple really."

He gave her a doubtful look. "Go on."

"Your government wants Gandhi dead and Sergei and Brady to take the blame. I expect they have some plan for twisting things around the other way. But your people can't afford the connection to be exposed, can they? If we can find a way to expose it, then the whole thing falls to pieces."

"Yes," he said, in a tone that suggested she'd merely stated the obvious. "The problem is how."

"All we need is a good modern camera. And to get, say, Cunningham and Brady to the same spot at the same time."

That got him thinking. "It would have to be Sergei. He's the Russian Bolshevik."

She realized he was right. "I suppose it would," she concurred reluctantly.

"But they're not going to agree to pose for a group photograph," he continued, as much to himself as to her.

"No, Jack," she said, surprised at him for being so slow. "We trick them. You ask Cunningham to meet you. And you fake a message from Cunningham to Sergei asking him to the same place."

He shook his head. "Not quite. The first part would work, but not the second. We don't know how they've agreed to communicate with each other in an emergency, and if we get it wrong, which we probably would, Brady will smell a rat." He looked at her. "The note must come from you."

"Oh . . ." She stood and went to the window, angrily brushing away an unexpected tear. "You're right," she almost whispered, still looking the other way.

"If it's too hard, we'll think of something else," he said, walking across and putting an arm around her shoulders.

She was grateful for the offer, but knew this was something she had to do. She gently untangled herself. "Once we have the photograph, what do we do with it?"

"We send a copy to Cunningham and friends, I assume. It's your plan, my love."

She made a sweeping gesture with her hand, as if brushing aside the endearment. "And Sergei and Brady? What will your people do with them once they know the plan won't work?"

"I don't know. They might send them back to Russia . . ."

"Or kill them quietly here?"

McColl shrugged. "Maybe."

"Either way it's a death sentence. I have to give him a chance, Jack. You do understand that?"

"Yes, but how?"

"I don't know." Another thought occurred to her. "And what about you? What will your people do to you?"

"Nothing good. But they have to catch us first."

She let the "us" go by. "We could say that a copy of the photograph has been sent to someone—your detective perhaps—with instructions to send it on to a newspaper if anything happens to you."

"If they call it off, then the photograph won't mean a thing," he told her. "We need to work out what our options are."

Which might have been right, but was easier said than done. "Once we've seen this through," she promised. And then she could go home. Wherever that was.

PIATAKOV WAS WOKEN, AS USUAL, by the sound of sweeping; first the soft brush inside the house, then the more rasping tone of the twig broom being used on the paths outside. On the other side of the nearby wall, sounding like faraway raucous birds swapping opinions, muezzins were calling the Muslim districts to prayer.

He climbed off the hard bed and washed himself as thoroughly as he could with the water left in the earthenware pitcher. Throwing a kurta over his head, he walked through into the kitchen, where one of the servants was already making him a glass of chai. He stirred in two chunks of sugar and carried it out to his chair in the garden.

Thick morning mist shrouded the river away to his right; the sun glowing through it was a fuzzy orange ball. The crows had begun their incessant crowing; the parakeets, as ever, seemed unsure which tree best suited their mood. On the lawn in front of their absent host's house, another servant was flailing the grass with a bamboo switch to take away the dew. According to Brady, if this wasn't done, the grass would scorch in the noonday sun.

Piatakov sipped at the tea and let his mind wander. Since their arrival in Delhi, he had spent the early morning hours like this, sitting and watching the sunrise, letting the mesh of light, sounds, and smells wash over him. It did him good, made him feel that somehow he was back in touch with something real. It might be— probably was—the equivalent of the condemned man's last meal, but that didn't seem to matter: it was enough to know he was still connected, however tenuously, to that sense of life's possibilities that had made him a revolutionary.

He had sadnesses but, in the end, no regrets.

The mist was clearing, sharpening the sun. He heard light footsteps behind him and looked around expecting to see one of the servants.

It was a youth he'd never seen before, holding what looked like a letter. Piatakov reached out to take it, expecting the usual two-way mime, but the boy was instantly on his way, breaking into a run as he disappeared behind the house.

Turning to the letter, Piatakov saw his name in Cyrillic script in her unmistakable hand. For a moment he thought he was dreaming and just sat there staring at the envelope, his mouth hanging foolishly open.

He tore it open and pulled out the folded sheet.

"Sergei," she began. No "dearest," he thought in passing, just "Sergei, I must talk to you. Meet me in the European restaurant room on Platform 1 of the central railway station at one o'clock today. Come alone. For both our sakes. Caitlin."

No kisses either.

He read the note again, still struggling to take it in. She was here, in India, in Delhi. Why? How? As the different emotions and thoughts jostled for precedence, he felt a sudden constriction in his chest from holding his breath for too long. He heard his own laughter and the hint of hysteria that bubbled within it.

"What's going on?" Brady asked from behind him. "I heard someone running."

Piatakov passed him the letter but didn't say anything. Brady looked through it, his expression moving swiftly through curiosity, amusement, concern, and anger. "Your wife?" he asked incredulously.

"Yes."

"But how did—"

"I don't know any more than you do," Piatakov said. Somehow Brady's sense of shock was exorcising his own.

"It must be Komarov," Brady decided.

"He's dead," Piatakov said flatly. "You shot him, remember?"

"I know. But he's reaching out from the grave. Or it's Peters. She must be here on your party's behalf."

"Maybe she's here for herself," Piatakov said quietly. Still trying to save him. The thought brought him joy and sadness in what seemed equal measure.

"Whatever. You can't meet her."

Piatakov looked up at the American, the shock of dark hair hanging over the angry eyes, a glimpse of the long-vanished child in the pouting mouth. "I have to," he said. He hadn't said good-bye to her in Moscow, and now he could.

"No," Brady argued. "You could risk everything." His hand reached almost absent-mindedly toward the place where he normally carried his gun, but he was still wearing his nightshirt.

Piatakov noticed but didn't care. "I won't betray you or back out, if that's what you're thinking. And since it won't affect our business here, it has nothing to do with you."

"It must affect our business here. How has she found you?"

"I don't know. Maybe the local party helped her look."

Brady shook his head.

"Who else?" Piatakov asked. "The British won't have told her."

"It stinks." Brady looked at the letter again. "Are you sure it's her handwriting?"

"Of course I am. Look, what can happen in a station restaurant room? My guess is—they think they know what we're planning to do, and she's been sent to try and change our minds. She won't. Okay?"

Piatakov got up out of the chair and looked out across the flats toward the river. "But I want to see her. And I'm going to," he insisted, before walking off toward the house, leaving Brady still staring at the letter.

COLONEL FITZWILLIAM REFOLDED THE LETTER, replaced it in the envelope, and handed it back to Cunningham. "What do you think he wants?"

"Probably money," Cunningham guessed. "To travel with," he added.

"And what will he do if he doesn't get it?" the colonel asked, helping himself to a chocolate biscuit.

"He doesn't say," Cunningham said pointedly, wondering if he and Morley would be offered biscuits. Or cups of coffee, come to that.

"But what's your best guess?" the colonel asked tetchily. "I suppose you two want coffee," he added ungraciously.

"Yes, thank you," Cunningham said. As the colonel signaled to his hovering servant, Cunningham reached for the biscuit tin, and offered it to a surprised Morley before helping himself. "It seems to me," he went on, "that McColl has very few options. The one potentially damaging thing he could do is give the story to foreign newspapers. They'd certainly be interested after the event, but the deed would be done, and we'd just have to manage the aftermath. It won't be hard to discredit McColl as a source. He was recently in prison; there's his history with the American woman who now works for Lenin. Etcetera, etcetera. Some Indians will hear the story, and some will believe it, but they'll be the ones who think the worst of us anyway."

"And at least we know the bastard's still in Delhi," Morley said hopefully.

"Which makes it all the more disgraceful that he hasn't been found yet," the colonel retorted.

"We're sure he's not staying in any half-decent hotel," Cunningham said unapologetically. "We've checked out the people we know he had contact with during the war. And we're still waiting for London to check through any Indians he might have known at Oxford or met in his time selling luxury cars. There's nothing else we can do, other than the obvious."

"Which is?" Morley asked.

"Well, we do know where he'll be"—Cunningham looked at his watch—"in two hours and forty minutes' time."

"We know where he says he's going to be," the colonel corrected him.

"What have we got to lose?" Cunningham asked.

McCOLL WAS PICKED UP OPPOSITE the Fatehpuri Mosque at a quarter past eleven.

"It is all arranged," Mirza announced as the boy driver set the tonga in motion. The detective was wearing the usual white shirt and dhoti, this time topped off with a fez-shaped red cap. "Here is the camera," he said, taking a worn leather case from the seat beside him. McColl undid the strap and took out the Leica that Mirza had offered to loan him. An Arab had stolen it from one of the Turkish army's German advisers during the war, and Mirza had bought the camera a year or so later for a fraction of its real worth. He claimed—and McColl had no reason to doubt him—that it would take the picture required.

"And the place?" McColl asked.

"All fixed," Mirza said with a smile. "You asked for"—he began ticking off fingers—"one, somewhere out in the open, which is, two, close enough for a clear shot of the faces and, three, not so close that we risk apprehension by the men concerned. And we have such a place—it is all as you wished."

"Wonderful," McColl said.

"I have been thinking about this business," Mirza went on. "These people. One from your political police and the other a Russian revolutionary—there must be a simple reason why you want them to share a photograph, but I cannot deduce what it is." He shook his head. "But I shall," he added. "I shall."

"Mr. Mirza," McColl said, "you do understand that helping in this matter could get you into trouble with the authorities. I don't—"

"Yes, yes, I understand. You told me this yesterday. Do not concern yourself. Holmes once said that it is worth committing a felony to save a soul, and I am satisfied that we are on the side of justice in this matter. The opinion of the authorities is of no interest."

McColl couldn't help smiling. "Okay," he said.

They were approaching the Queen's Road entrance to the

station. Mirza tapped the boy driver on the shoulder, and the tonga was brought to a halt. The two men alighted, and Mirza led McColl through an unmarked gate and down a passage between temporary huts. A narrow alley in a row of offices brought them out into an open-air canteen, where Mirza was greeted by several of the patrons. "Many men from my regiment got work on the railways," he told McColl in explanation.

They walked along two sides of a large shed and onto a loading platform packed with wooden crates. A line of empty freight cars, their doors flung open in expectation, blocked their view of the station.

They reached the end of the train as a locomotive approached from the east, belching grey smoke into the sky above the distant Red Fort. A minute or so later the line of packed carriages pulled into a platform three or four tracks away, wheels bouncing on the uneven rails. "Over there," Mirza shouted in McColl's ear, pointing out the signal cabin that straddled the tracks some fifty yards ahead and setting off across the shining rails like a man advancing on Turkish guns.

McColl hurried after him, remembering days as a boy risking the wrath of railway officials. This time there were no angry shouts, and soon they were climbing the stairway up to the box. The two men working among the gleaming levers greeted the detective like a long-lost uncle; their boss was in a small office at the other end. "My friend, Shah Ali Khan," Mirza said, introducing the uniformed official. "And this is our hide, as you call it," he added, swinging open a shuttered window. "There," he said, gesturing outward.

The roof of the office on the northernmost platform was mostly flat, but the small raised section containing a door promised access from below. A man on the roof would be only ten yards away, and at roughly the same level. A train passing between them would be beneath the line of sight. Only smoke could spoil the picture, and for that their luck would need to be truly out.

"Yes?" Mirza asked.

"It's perfect," McColl said.

PIATAKOV ARRIVED AT THE STATION almost half an hour early and sat for several minutes in the back of Sayid Hassan's tonga, trying to let the whirl of emotions settle. It wasn't easy. Assuming she knew what they intended to do—and her presence here surely meant that she did—he knew only too well what her objections would be. They'd had variations of the same argument over and over again during the winter and spring, and they all came down to a single judgment—whether or not their party was beyond redemption. She said it wasn't, and he said it was, and that was all there was to it. So why would she travel thousands of miles to tell him something he'd already heard a dozen times?

If she'd come out of love . . . well, that would warm his heart, but it wouldn't change his mind, and she had to know that. She who'd been fond of quoting Kollontai's dictum that passion was transient, the political struggle unending.

It was a quarter to one by the huge station clock. He climbed down, told the servant-driver to wait, and walked in through the entrance arch. The booking hall was a seething mass, the adjoining platform just as crowded and noisy. After the garden's serenity, the cacophonous racket felt like a physical battering.

At least the platforms were prominently numbered—a request for directions in Russian or schoolboy French would probably have gone unanswered. The restaurant room for Europeans was also easy to find and empty save for one middle-aged pair, presumably English, who gave him synchronous nods, as if they shared a puppeteer. He returned the gesture and chose a table as far from them as possible.

The room was surprisingly cool and quiet considering how few feet separated it from the heat and bedlam outside. He asked the hovering waiter for chai, knowing the word meant the same in Delhi as it did in Moscow.

The steaming cup arrived as the clock on the wall reached the hour. He handed the waiter the five-rupee note that Brady had provided with the air of a parent handing out pocket money, accepted the frown and small mountain of coins in exchange, and stirred in some sugar from the small brass bowl. The minute hand clicked again.

An Indian boy darted in through the doorway and handed him a note. The waiter moved to shoo the youth out again, but Piatakov held up an arm to stop him while he took in the message. "Come with this boy and wait for me," it read. The writing was hers.

He followed the boy out onto the platform and up across a foot-bridge that straddled several tracks. After taking the last steps down and walking the length of the station, they finally arrived at what looked like a storchouse. The room within boasted a stack of red flags, shelves of paraffin lamps, doors to apparently empty offices, and a stairway to the second floor. Piatakov followed the boy up two flights of stairs, emerging onto a roof just as a freight train steamed majestically past. There was no one else there. The boy said something incomprehensible and promptly disappeared.

CUNNINGHAM ARRIVED AT THE NORTH entrance soon after twelve-thirty and spent the next half hour as instructed, walking from one end of Platform 6 to the other.

It was more like an obstacle course than a path. Indians provided the obstacles, they and all the mercantile and domestic activities they'd managed to cram onto a platform thirty feet wide. It seemed to Cunningham that an Indian was incapable of traveling anywhere without taking his entire family, all its belongings, and enough hardware to cook six-course meals. Many had also brought livestock—goats, chickens, pye-dogs—and at least two sacred cows were trundling up and down Platform 6 in search of something to chew.

There were also coconut sellers, soda-water sellers, toy sellers, and sticky-sweet sellers. Toys and sweets, Cunningham thought—that was what Indians loved. Toys and sweets in the brightest imaginable colors. Children, every last one of them. The real children made faces and giggled each time he went past; the adults only wanted to.

One Indian was tugging at his sleeve. As he turned, a note was pressed into his hand by a young adolescent. *Come with this boy. Alone. McColl.*

"Lead on," Cunningham invited his guide. They crossed to the farthest platform, entered one of the railway offices, and climbed two flights of stairs to the roof. A white man was waiting for him, but it wasn't McColl. In fact the features were distinctly Slavic.

"Who are you?" Cunningham asked.

The man was looking over his shoulder. Cunningham caught the glint of reflected glass from the signal box across the tracks, the shutters closing around it like a snuffer on a candle. Someone had taken a picture of him and the Russian, which could only be bad news.

As Cunningham hurtled back down the stairs hoping to catch whoever it was, he realized his young guide had disappeared.

After reaching and crossing the platform, Cunningham jumped down between the nearest rails, and was almost run over by an idling shunter. By the time he reached the foot of the signal box steps and took a few seconds to look around, there was nothing to see. No one running. No McColl. Even the Russian had vanished.

He went up anyway, but the Indians on duty responded to his shouts with the usual infuriating smiles. The little office at the end was empty; the head signalman, he was told, had gone to lunch.

"Christ, what a mess," he murmured as he took in the view from the cameraman's window. Fitzwilliam was going to love this one.

CAITLIN SPENT THE MORNING ALONE in their room at Sinha's house, and her mood had not been improved by the reading matter. McColl had come across the Indian communist newspaper on his way back from the station the day before and thought it might contain the recent Russian news she craved. Reading through it, she told herself to be more careful in what she wished for. There was indeed a feast of news—the latest trade deals and production targets, more peasant rebellions ended, a united party still set on delivering its brave new world. The NEP was undoubtedly working, the famines apparently loosing their grip. It was all good, all true, as far it went. And yes, the revolution had been about increasing production, giving people a better material life. But that wasn't the end of the story. It had also been about building a real democracy, one unfettered by money and privilege. And, in those joyful early days, it had been about creating a new man and woman.

And there, in one small paragraph, was the news that meant something to Caitlin.

The "woman's advocate" Alexandra Kollontai, the Indian writer noted, was leaving Moscow for "six months of agitational work in Odessa." With the women's issue now "resolved," Kollontai's "separate organization" had "surely fulfilled its purpose."

Caitlin read it several times, and could find no silver lining. They were moving her friend away from the heart of power, and it felt like a small step from there to moving women away from the heart of the party's concerns.

All of which made Caitlin consider her own position. If Russian men—Bolshevik or otherwise—had absorbed all the change they were ready for, then surely it made more sense for someone like her to continue the struggle elsewhere. On the other hand, if the Zhenotdel was under serious threat, it would need the help of people like her. So wouldn't she just be running away?

Was she just looking for reasons to stay with Jack?

That thought brought her back to the present and her constant companions of worry and guilt. Each time Jack went out, she wondered if she'd see him again, and the knowledge that she'd written those notes to Sergei seemed to hang in the back of her mind like a small dark cloud.

The knock on the door broke into her thoughts, and Maneka's abrupt appearance threw them aside.

"English downstairs!" she said excitedly. "English with guns! You must get what you need and come with me."

Repressing the urge to seek clarification, Caitlin took a brief inventory of the room and decided there was nothing she couldn't live without. But as Maneka was already bundling some of Jack's clothes into their suitcase, she threw in some of her own.

As they left the room, footsteps were audible on the nearest stairs. Maneka grabbed Caitlin's wrist and set off in the other direction, down a narrower flight, through an arch, and along a corridor lined with boxes of vegetables. Two servants stepped sharply out of

Maneka's path, and offered Caitlin *namaskars* as she hurried by. She and Maneka were almost at the end of the passage when a shout rang out behind them.

Not pausing to see whose it was, Caitlin followed the girl through another door and found herself back in the women's courtyard. The children all stared at her and the suitcase as Maneka tried to explain her presence to the older women. The debate was hardly started when someone rapped on the gate that guarded the second entrance, and an angry dispute erupted beyond it. The men of the household were telling the white invaders that they weren't allowed in the women's preserve. The white invaders were demanding the key to the door.

They'll break it down, Caitlin thought. If she'd been wearing the Indian clothes, they might not have noticed her. As it was . . .

"Please," Maneka was saying, tugging again at her wrist. There was a third door half-hidden by foliage, which at first refused to open but then did so with an angry squeak. Another corridor, another gate, and they were out in an alley.

"That way," Maneka said, pointing her toward the busy-looking road at the end.

Caitlin took the girl's hand and squeezed it. "Thank you," she said as the sound of screams came over the wall to her left. The "English" had invaded the women's sanctum.

"Go," Maneka told her.

She went, hurrying down the alley with the suitcase in hand, wondering where she should go and how she and Jack would find each other again. Their old room at the serai, she decided, if she could find it.

She needn't have worried. As she inched her way out of the alley, a brown hand in a uniformed sleeve closed around her neck. When she struggled, the policeman quickly released her, but not, she soon realized, from any intention of letting her go. He was shocked at having laid hands on white skin.

While his partner recovered the suitcase she'd dropped, he harried her down the street like a sheepdog, urging her this way and that without coming too close. Several hundred interested eyes watched them pass, and some at least had the sense to look amused. An open car had been backed into Sinha's street and now stood waiting by his gate, upper body gleaming and lower half caked in dust.

Her captor's partner dropped her suitcase in the back seat and disappeared into the house, emerging a few moments later with a red-faced Englishman in civilian clothes. In their wake a posse of outraged Indian men were protesting the breaking of purdah with shaking fists and shouts of defiance.

Without looking back the Englishman flicked a hand at them, a gesture of dismissal that Nero might have practiced.

"Where's Jack McColl?" he barked at her.

"I don't know," she said.

"When did he go out?"

"He didn't. He's been staying somewhere else," she added, hoping it would help Harry.

"Where?"

"I told you, I don't know."

"I don't believe you."

"That's your privilege."

He took her upper arm in a tight grip, walked her across to the open car, and told her to get in. She did as she was told. Kicking the overgrown schoolboy might make for a few joyful seconds but probably wouldn't be wise.

MCCOLL ARRIVED AT THE END of Sinha's street at the same time as the car. He took in the scene in an instant: the pedestrians and slow-moving tongas choking the Dariba Kalan, the open car with the Indian soldiers up front, Caitlin and the IPI's Morley sitting behind them.

Morley saw him in the same instant, but his true identity clearly took longer to register. McColl had one foot on the running board and the Webley out from under his dhoti, before the other man could react.

"Don't anyone move," McColl said, holding the gun against Morley's head. "Let's go," he told Caitlin, aware of the growing space around him as the locals slowly backed off. How could he disable the car and its occupants?

"Why don't we take the car?" Caitlin suggested.

He grinned. "What a good idea. Out!" he told the two Indians. They obeyed.

"Now start walking. That way." He gestured toward the south.

With one last hopeless look at their English boss, they started trudging away.

"You won't escape," Morley said without a great deal of conviction.

"Now you," McColl ordered, stepping back to let him out. "Take out your gun, and put it on the ground," he added.

Morley did as he was told.

"Now walk." McColl picked up the gun intending to hand it to Caitlin, but she was getting in behind the wheel. "I should have guessed you'd learned to drive," he said. He climbed in beside her, once again conscious of the multitude around them.

As Caitlin drove carefully up the crowded street, the onlookers' stares grew no less incredulous. It took a few minutes for McColl to realize why: a white woman chauffeuring a native man was not a common sight in British India.

The Hardest Thing

"I never liked this damn business from the beginning," Colonel Fitzwilliam said, losing his usual linguistic precision in the stress of the
moment.

Oh yes? Cunningham thought. The plan had originated in
Delhi, if not in Fitzwilliam's brain, with his obvious approval and
encouragement. Cunningham idly wondered who, if anyone, would
garner the blame. Always assuming that anyone would ever admit a
mistake had been made.

"Too tricky by half," Fitzwilliam was muttering as he strode up
and down the room, glass of whiskey in hand. Through the window
other club members could be seen in various degrees of midafternoon wakefulness.

The colonel placed his glass on the polished sideboard, extracted
an oval Turkish cigarette from his silver case, and lit it with an English match. "You *are* certain a photograph was taken?"

"Not absolutely. But I saw something reflect the light, and what
other reason would he have had to set up such a meeting?"

The colonel stared at his whiskey. "Pity you didn't think of that
before," he said, adding a withering look for emphasis.

Cunningham returned the gaze and said nothing.

"But I suppose the damage is done. I suppose we'll be hearing soon enough what McColl has in mind. Either blackmail or the fool's picked up a bleeding heart in Russia."

"I'd guess the latter," Cunningham said.

Fitzwilliam grunted his disbelief, though whether in McColl's new organ or the concept itself, Cunningham couldn't be sure. "What about the Good Indian team?" Cunningham asked.

"Yes, I was coming to them. Did the Russian see the camera?"

"He must have."

Fitzwilliam gulped down the last of his whiskey. "Well, we weren't planning on giving them knighthoods." He thought for a minute, leaning against the sideboard, the cigarette curling blue smoke across the back of his hand. "In fact," he said finally, "our options seem extremely limited."

Cunningham nodded. "Brady won't be any great loss to humanity."

"An arrest that goes sadly awry," Fitzwilliam murmured, half to himself. He looked at his watch. "It'll be dark in three hours. You'd better take a platoon—we don't want any more slipups. And you can bury them there." He allowed himself a wintry smile. "If we ever need more on Sayid Hassan, we can dig them up again." He stubbed out the cigarette and turned for the door. "If only Gandhi had a garden," he said over his shoulder.

If only, Cunningham thought, as he picked up the club secretary's telephone. After arranging the troops for that evening, he strolled back down to the IPI bungalow. He'd been there only a few minutes when Morley returned, looking hot, disheveled, and angry.

"What happened to you?" Cunningham asked.

"That bastard McColl," Morley spluttered, wiping the back of his neck with a damp-looking handkerchief. He told the story between gulps of ice water.

"But who was the woman?" Cunningham wanted to know.

"Not a clue, old man. She didn't deny knowing McColl, but she claimed he wasn't staying there. Lying like a trooper, of course. She had a faint American accent, I think. A looker, all right. Chestnut hair, big green eyes."

"Nice tits?" Cunningham asked sarcastically.

"Sorry, I didn't have time to take measurements," Morley retorted in the same tone.

Cunningham laughed. "Okay, okay. It doesn't matter now." He explained about the setup at the station and his conversation with the colonel.

Hearing someone else's tale of woe raised Morley's spirits. "So what now?" he asked with his customary air of boyish expectancy.

"We clear up their mess. What else?" Cunningham gazed out of the window, wondering why he felt vaguely envious of McColl.

WHEN PIATAKOV GOT BACK TO the house, he found Brady waiting in the chair beneath the banyan tree. When the American heard what had happened, he burst out laughing, loudly enough to bring Chatterji out of the house.

"What is happening?" the Indian asked with an uncertain smile.

As Brady repeated the story in English, Piatakov asked himself for the umpteenth time if she really was in Delhi, if she really had betrayed him.

"The police must have engineered it," Chatterji said without stopping to think.

"No," Brady decided. "Why would they? We're not the sort of friends they'll want to publicize."

"Then who? Why would anyone do this?" the Indian asked nervously.

Brady raised a hand to quiet him, but said nothing for several moments. Then his face broke into a smile. "It doesn't matter," he said. "Look—"

"Who could have forced her to write a note like that?" Piatakov interjected in Russian. "I don't understand it. If she's a prisoner, then maybe. But whose? It doesn't make sense."

"Sergei, for Christ's sake, get a grip," Brady said coldly. "You left her and your precious party behind. What does it matter what intrigue she's gotten herself mixed up in?"

It matters because I cared about her, Piatakov thought. And still do. You could leave a lover behind, but not the heart that loved her.

"You didn't see her," Brady continued remorselessly. "You don't even know she's here."

"It was her handwriting!"

"Christ! Maybe someone had a copy from somewhere . . ."

"Who?"

"I don't know. I don't care. She's history! Forget her. Forget about whoever it was sent that note. You spend your life wondering why other people are doing what they're doing. Who cares? Now listen. Whoever was behind that camera—they've actually done us a favor. Because now the English have lost any chance of pinning it all on the Bolsheviks—not when there's a picture showing one of them hand in glove with . . ." His voice trailed off. "Fuck!" he exclaimed. "What's the time?"

Chatterji told him.

"Pack up all our stuff," Brady told them. "We're moving out now, as soon as the sun goes in."

"Why?" Piatakov asked.

"The English will know that we know. And there's only one way that they can be sure of calling the whole thing off."

The American was right, Piatakov realized.

"Durga," Brady said, "why don't you bring the servants together?"

Piatakov thought about protesting but decided against it. There was no time to find out whether one of the servants was genuine and, if so, which. The struggle was a lottery, claiming innocent and guilty alike. He remembered the woman in Samarkand, the shock on her face as she sank to her knees, blood coursing out through her fingers.

During the war Piatakov had heard several soldiers say that the more they saw of death the more careful they were with their lives. Not me, he thought. He was becoming more careless, with his own and everyone else's.

CAITLIN LEANED AGAINST THE BALCONY rail, watching the street life below. She preferred their old room at the caravansary to the one in Sinha's house—it might be dirtier, smaller, devoid of extras, but it had this window on the world. She could still feel like part of the human race.

Jack had gone off to see about the photographs, his mood a lot lighter than it had been for days. She wanted to share his confidence, to believe they had found a solution that scuppered the plot without costing Sergei his life, but she couldn't quite bring herself to believe it. Something kept nagging at the back of her mind, but she didn't know what it was.

Maybe it was nothing. She watched two girls walk by in identical chrysanthemum-colored saris, their hair oiled, their eyes surrounded by pools of dark makeup. At what age, she wondered, was freedom curtailed and purdah imposed? Were there big differences between the religious groups? She would have liked to find people to ask, but even if she hadn't been stuck there in her own peculiar purdah, her lack of the relevant linguistic skills would probably have proved a significant obstacle. She had no idea how many of the people walking by on the street below spoke English. Indeed, until the last couple of weeks, India itself had hardly featured in her consciousness.

She noticed Jack coming up the street, his turbaned head bobbing above the shorter locals. He was cradling a bag with one arm, and idly swinging a rolled-up newspaper with the other. Seeing her there on the balcony, he waved the paper and disappeared through the doorway below. A few moments later he was wrapping his arms around her waist and kissing the side of her neck.

"I bring food," he said.

She followed him into the room, where uncorked pots of rice and sauce were gently steaming on the floor. They ate with their fingers, something both had grown increasingly proficient at in the last couple of months, while McColl told her all about Mirza's friend with the darkroom and their picture taking form in his developing tray.

"It's perfect," he said. "They didn't say a word to each other, but they look like they're deep in conversation."

"That's good," she agreed.

"Mirza's sending one to Fitzwilliam, and there are a dozen copies going out to all and sundry—foreign correspondents, the nationalist groups—"

"It won't work," she said abruptly. Reaching out for the jug of water, her eyes had caught the photograph and story on the front page of the *Eastern Mail*, and suddenly it all made sense.

He looked surprised. "Why not?"

"You sent the warning to Sergei and the others?"

"Yes, we agreed—"

"I know. But it won't work." She leaned across, grabbed the newspaper, and placed it in front of him. "Look, Jack," she said, jabbing a finger at the picture.

"It's the Prince of Wales."

"I know. When does *he* arrive?"

"In a few days." He shook his head. "No . . ."

"When was the visit arranged?"

"Months ago, I expect."

"It has to be. He's the one they plan to kill, not Gandhi. They think your government will overreact and turn the whole country against it."

"They're probably right." He shifted his gaze from the picture to her. "Why did you ask whether I'd sent the warning?"

IT WAS ALMOST SEVEN WHEN Cunningham, Morley, and three carloads of infantry roared up Sayid Hassan's drive, bounced across his lawn and flower beds, and drew up in front of the house. No lights sprang on; no shouts of alarm rang out.

Cunningham elected himself to check out the house and found the four servants. Each had been strangled with a silken cord—thuggee-style. Either Chatterji had traditionalist leanings, or one of the others had gone native.

He went back outside. "Get the shovels," he told the platoon commander.

IT HAD BEEN DARK FOR over an hour when Ahmed Mirza announced his arrival with a knock on their door. McColl introduced him to Caitlin.

The detective grinned. "The woman who drives! All of Delhi is talking about you."

She smiled back. It had been a memorable few minutes.

They got down to business. "All the copies have been delivered by hand," Mirza told them. "Including the one to Kudsia Road."

"And the warning was delivered?" Caitlin asked.

"To the three men we have been watching? Yes, but not at that house. They left there . . . but I am losing the logical progression of events. When the Russian arrived back from his appointment with my camera, he told the American something, and the American just laughed. Then the Indian came out, and they all had an argument. After that they went back in and stayed in the house until it got dark. Then they all left together."

"How? Did they walk?"

"To the Delhi Gate, where they hired a tonga."

"And you know where they went?"

"Of course. To the room overlooking Chandni Chowk that the Indian rented yesterday morning. That is where the warning was delivered—one of the boys slipped it under their door." Mirza hesitated. "But there is something else I must tell you. The servants at the first house—they are all dead. Once the three men were gone, the boy in charge took a look through the windows, and he saw the bodies. I have to say, it does not feel acceptable, letting them lie there."

McColl was less surprised than Caitlin was. "Can you inform the police?" he asked Mirza. "An anonymous tip-off, perhaps."

The detective looked grateful. "I will do so. And now I await your instructions."

"You've done a wonderful job," McColl told him, "but I must take it from here." He reached for the purse he'd bought in the market. "You must tell me how much I owe you."

Mirza looked disappointed. "I am not to be present at the final conclusion?"

"I'm afraid not. It is a family matter," he added, which was true enough. "But I promise I will come and see you once everything is settled and tell you the story from beginning to end."

The Indian gave him a rueful smile. "That is good," he said. "Not good enough, as you English say, but still good. I believe thirty rupees are outstanding."

McColl handed him the requisite notes, and the two of them shook hands. After seeing the Indian out the door, he turned to find Caitlin sitting on the side of the bed, hands interlinked on top of her head, bleakness in her eyes.

"What now?" she asked.

He sat down beside her. "I think we have three options."

"Which are?"

"We could tell Fitzwilliam where they are and let him deal with them."

"Kill them, you mean?"

He decided not to sugarcoat the pill. "Probably."

"And you think that's what they deserve," she replied. It was more a statement than a question.

"If anyone does. They *have* just murdered four servants."

She gave him a despairing look. "I know."

He threw her a lifeline. "I don't want to hand them over either."

"For my sake?"

"Partly," he conceded. "But I'm also afraid that Five will find some other use for Brady."

"All right," she said, as if knowing he had a reason legitimized hers. "So what are the other two options?"

"The easiest one is just to walk away."

"And not lift a finger to save your prince?"

McColl laughed. "He's not my prince. And the thought of either of us dying to save him . . . well, it's too ridiculous for words. If I don't believe that Jed and Mac gave their lives for anything worthwhile, then why would I want to risk yours and mine?"

She was silent for several moments. "Russia will get the blame," she said. "The trade deals will collapse, and the famines will go on forever."

"And we're still guessing about the target," he added. "If it is the prince, he'll be well protected. If it's Gandhi, we're his only hope."

"And walking away never feels right."

"No," he agreed, wondering what that might mean for their future. Whatever she decided, she'd be walking away from something.

"So option three is stopping them."

"Yes. Which won't be easy."

"Sparing Sergei complicates matters, doesn't it?"

"Of course, but . . ."

"Maybe I can talk him around." She had a sudden memory of Sergei telling her how much cleverer she was than him.

"You really think that's possible?"

"I don't know. If we can get him away from the other two . . . then perhaps. But Jack, Sergei knows about you, that I had a long love affair with an Englishman. He never asked any questions—he's old-fashioned in that way—and I don't remember whether I ever told him your name. I am sure I never told him whom you worked for, but Brady probably has, and you being there will make it less likely he'll listen to me. So . . ."

"You're probably right, but I won't let you go alone."

"Sergei wouldn't hurt me."

"Maybe, but Brady or Chatterji might."

She gave him a despairing look. "Couldn't you hide behind the door or something?" she asked, only half seriously.

"It might work," he said. "If there's somewhere close by I can stay undetected, then I needn't show my face until he makes up his mind."

"That would work."

"Then that's our plan," McColl said, with as much confidence as he could muster.

She wasn't fooled. "It sounds ridiculous, doesn't it?"

"I can't think of anything better. And if by some miracle Sergei agrees, we can stick him on a train to somewhere and shop the others. If he doesn't . . ."

"Then what do we do?"

"We could disable them all. A bullet in the kneecap is very effective."

She looked shocked, but only for a moment.

"You walk again eventually," McColl said, far from sure it was true.

She looked unusually waiflike in her uncertainty. He pulled her head onto his shoulder, and they sat like that in silence for more than a minute. "I sometimes think of Sergei as a grown-up boy," she said eventually. "And in some ways he is. But he's been at war for years, and he knows how to fight."

"I guessed as much."

"And in case you don't know—what worries me most is the thought of losing you."

He held her a little tighter and wished they could stay where they were.

"So when do we go?" she asked.

"Later this evening, but I'll need to do a reconnaisance first. The more we know, the better our chances."

CUNNINGHAM FOUND THE COLONEL SITTING in his usual chair, the tip of his cigarette glowing in the darkness as he gazed out into the wind-twisted shadows of the garden. Cunningham expected a tongue-lashing, but Fitzwilliam listened to his report with a faint smile and then offered him a cigarette.

The Turkish tobacco seemed, as ever, faintly redolent of decadence.

"Any sign of McColl?" Fitzwilliam asked.

"No."

"He'll have made a run for it," Fitzwilliam said confidently. "He's thrown his spanner in the works. Why would he hang around?"

To make sure, Cunningham thought. "You're probably right," he conceded out loud. "And the Good Indian team must know we're scouring the city for them."

"You think they've made a run for it, too."

"Probably," Cunningham said carefully. "Their plan may have failed, but Brady can congratulate himself on cheating the hangman, at least for a while. If they haven't, and they do stick around for a crack at Gandhi, then we'll have some questions to answer."

"The photograph?"

"Precisely."

"Maybe it's not such a problem. You're the one in the picture, and once you're on the boat home, we can deny all knowledge of you. Or better still, find someone willing to testify that you're another Russian. It'll be a hard job proving otherwise."

Cunningham took a last drag on the cigarette and stubbed it out in an ashtray. "One other thought occurred to me."

"That the Prince of Wales might have been their target?"

"Might still be. I think we have to consider the possibility."

"I already have. Our usual security arrangements have worked well enough in the past. And I don't think it would help to confuse matters at this late hour." He turned to take another cigarette from the case on the table and lit it from the stub of the last. "Good Indian was authorized by London," he said, meeting Cunningham's eyes for the first time that evening. "They can hardly hold us responsible if anything goes wrong, can they?"

"But . . ."

"You see, I've been giving this matter a great deal of thought. If Brady and his friends do nothing, then no harm's done. And if they do make use of the guns, then we'll have the excuse we need to nail down the lid on this country."

"And the prince?" Cunningham heard himself ask.

"Oh, there's always another one waiting in line."

WAITING ON THEIR BALCONY, HALF-LOST in the street's mosaic of lamps, Caitlin was brought back to earth by the voice calling up from below and felt for one beautiful moment like someone's misplaced Juliet, a rose by any other name.

Or had she gotten that the wrong way around?

She walked down the stairs, adjusting her veil, thinking that here it was—the moment she'd been dreading.

The source of her trepidation was harder to pinpoint. Why should the prospect of seeing Sergei and his murderous friends evoke this hideous sinking sensation? Wisely or not, she felt no fear for her life, but she was afraid of something. Her sense of who she was seemed far too fragile, as if she'd spent the last few years pretending to be someone she wasn't. A broken future could be repaired; a broken past could not.

McColl helped her into the tonga and, after climbing aboard himself, gave the boy driver their destination. As they rattled down the street toward the station, the boy let loose a string of shrill exhortations to clear their passage through the knots of evening strollers.

A glance at her companion confirmed Caitlin's feeling that he was—if not quite in his element—much more at home in such situations than she was. She could see why he'd kept that job for all those years, despite a growing disenchantment with the cause it served. He loved thinking on his feet; as she'd now seen on more than one occasion, he functioned well in a crisis.

Well, he had one here.

The boy swung them around a corner and into an even busier street. Even in summer Moscow's streets would have been practically deserted at this time of night—just a handful of drunks and Cheka patrols. As they rode between lines of still-open stalls, she remembered the last time she'd gone looking for Sergei, driving past the futurist flower stalls on Bolshaya Dmitrovka.

Moscow—Russia—seemed a long way away. Fall would be almost half-done, winter already looming. So much energy spent in simply keeping warm, so little light to live by. Yet so much warmth in people's hearts, so much brightness in their eyes. A whole other world.

She found herself thinking how utterly Russian the revolution had been, how thin its subsequent claims to internationalism, no matter how sincerely meant. People like her and Brady, who came from a similar political tradition, could lend the Russians a helping hand, but what were he and she and Sergei doing here, far from any way of life they really understood? Scratching an itch until it bled?

Their tonga should have been a troika, she thought. Plowing through snow rather than dust.

She hugged herself against the sudden chill.

HER SILENCE WAS SLIGHTLY UNNERVING, but also hardly surprising. McColl hoped she was gathering focus and strength, like a last man waiting to bat, and not already saying good-bye.

The world had always divided them, he thought, as their tonga skirted the chaos of the station forecourt. In a room, a bed, there were no borders. Traveling across the Pacific, America, and Afghanistan, they had been like Lenin in his famous sealed train. But now that their lives were bound up with those all around them, the boundaries were slowly materializing, like invisible writing exposed to the sun.

In his more optimistic moments, McColl believed that things had improved, that during the years apart, their approaches to life had actually grown more similar. Their politics were certainly less incompatible, mostly because of the distance he had traveled. Her opinions had hardly changed in seven years, but then, events hadn't proved her wrong. The future he'd been hoping for had died in the Flanders mud.

She had changed, though. The questing intelligence and almost reckless determination that he'd first encountered in China were still there, but they'd been tempered by age, work, and unhappy knowledge. All the brittleness was gone, leaving her stronger and surer of herself. She had come into her own in Russia.

Was that reason enough for her to go back? Over the last few weeks, they'd discussed the situation in Russia almost daily, and sometimes she seemed to be saying it was. At others she didn't seem half so sure. Lenin's Russia was changing, she said, and people like her might soon find it hard to get anything useful done.

But she had never said that she wanted to leave that country behind. Not once. Not for political reasons and not for love of him.

As he turned to look at her, she wrapped herself up in her arms.

"Are you cold?" he asked, surprised.

"No. How much farther is it?"

"Not far."

"I just want it over. I expect you do, too."

Part of him did, though what came after might be worse.

Assuming they survived. Going up against three armed men—at least two of whom were seasoned fighters—felt like a real roll of the dice.

They were passing the Queen's Gardens, heading up toward Chandni Chowk. The town hall clock struck eleven as they turned onto the wide thoroughfare, too British a sound for such a hot night. The number of people still in motion was rapidly diminishing, the pavements filling with would-be sleepers and more than a few crying babies.

A hundred yards short of their turnoff, McColl leaned forward and tapped their driver's shoulder. "This will do."

The boy hauled back on the reins and guided them into the curb. A man on the nearby pavement raised his head in surprise, then gently laid it back on his makeshift pillow.

McColl paid off the boy and pulled Caitlin into the shadows of a shop front. "See that side street?" he said, pointing it out. "Number four is about twenty yards in. You can just see the corner of its roof from here," he added. "Take the staircase right to the top—"

"And it's the door on the left. I haven't forgotten." Farther up Chandni Chowk, the dark outline of a huge fortress was visible. "Your prince will come this way?" she asked.

"Yes." He tried to picture it. Soldiers and elephants, rajas and banners. Presumably the homeless would be moved out first.

The veil was now a neck scarf. "So this is where we part."

"Yep. But I won't be far away. You just keep them talking."

"Oh, I don't think the conversation will flag," she said drily.

"You are sure about this?"

"As sure as I can be." She gave him a farewell kiss and was halfway across the street by the time he realized she was gone.

McColl pulled his service revolver from his waistband and checked it. "Time to be myself again," he murmured, unwinding the turban and hanging the doubled-up strip around his neck.

SHE FOUND THE HOUSE WITHOUT difficulty. Her knock on the door brought an Indian, so she pointed upward. The Indian smiled, said something incomprehensible, and gestured her toward the stairs. She climbed to the top and found a door with a strip of yellow light beneath it.

She rapped on it softly, and after a few seconds, the light all but disappeared.

"Sergei, it's me," she said loudly, the words sounding strangely inadequate.

The door edged opened, and the familiar features stared out of the gloom. His face was a picture.

"Caitlin! What—"

"Get inside," Brady said, bustling past them onto the landing, clearly intent on making sure that she was alone.

She followed Sergei into the room and watched as he turned the lamp back up. Their Indian comrade was staring at her, a gun hanging loosely in his hand.

"What in God's name are you doing here, Caitlin?" Sergei wanted to know.

He sounded so distressed, as if her appearance was the worst thing he could have imagined. Which might even have been a good sign. "I—"

"First things first," Brady said, striding back in and leaving the door slightly ajar. "Durga, check the roof. And you," he said, turning to Caitlin, "will explain how you found us."

She and Jack had expected the question. "With Indian comrades' help," she said curtly. "We knew the British would want to keep you at a distance, and finding two white men in the Indian town isn't so difficult."

"What were you trying to achieve with that business at the station?" Brady asked.

"That was aimed at the British," she patiently explained. "We thought you might be playing into their hands, so we had to make sure they didn't come out on top."

Sergei looked like he might explode. "But who is this we? And what does this have to do with you?"

"I am here on behalf of the Cheka," she told him, noting in passing that this wasn't a sentence she'd ever expected to hear herself say. "The Cheka that your friend here once served," she added with a contemptuous glance at Brady. "But I know I won't change his mind. It's you I've come to plead with," she told Sergei. "The party—*your* party—the one you made the revolution with, the one you served for all those years. It opposes this. It asks you to think again."

OUT ON THE ROOF, CROUCHED in the shadow of a large tin chimney, McColl could see Chatterji in the open doorway, his gun gleaming blue in the somber light. Behind the open window off to the Indian's right, there were three people conversing in Russian: Caitlin, Brady, and a second man, who had to be her husband, Sergei.

On his reconnaissance earlier that evening, McColl had been tempted to go it alone and simply kill or disable all three men—he hadn't got around to deciding which. With surprise on his side, his chances of survival would have been much better, and there would have been no need to put her at risk. She would have been furious with him for presuming to know what was best for them both, but that he could have coped with—his problem was, he knew why she wanted to give Sergei a chance. Her husband had been responsible for several innocent deaths over the last few months, but McColl was willing to believe that Sergei was following his conscience. Just as Caitlin's brother Colm had done; Colm, whose death would always haunt McColl's relationship with her. Just as he himself had done while working for the Service. You did what you thought was right, and people died. Because you made a simple mistake, or didn't think things through, or were simply wrong to begin with. It was hard playing God without the omniscience.

He could see Fedya's face as the boy told him good-bye.

The latch clicked as Chatterji pulled the door shut. It was time to get closer.

SHE KNEW SHE WAS WASTING her breath from the look of amazement on his face.

"This is insane," Sergei said. "That you should come all this way . . . it's . . . Go home, Caitlin. Go back to your work. There is nothing for you here."

She met his eyes, knew it was true.

"You and the party disapprove of our plan," Brady said, "but you don't even know what it is."

She glanced at the American, now sitting on the edge of his chair, but still outwardly unruffled. "You're going to shoot the

English prince," she told him. She turned back to Sergei. "I remember when you had nothing but contempt for this sort of terrorism," she said. "All that killing this prince will do is give the English the excuse they need to cancel the trade treaty. And we cannot afford to be alone in the world. Russia will starve."

Sergei stared her straight in the eye, and she could feel the sadness and rage washing around inside him. "It was the party leadership that betrayed the revolution," he said, grinding out each word. "It wasn't me."

Chatterji reappeared. "Nothing," he told Brady before taking a seat at the table and placing the gun within easy reach. As far as she could see, neither Brady nor Sergei was armed.

"Women always say they have more imagination than men," Brady was saying, a self-satisfied smile on his face, "but I'm afraid you haven't bothered to apply yours. I'm sure it will be satisfying to assassinate a prince, but as you say, that on its own is hardly likely to set India ablaze."

Caitlin just looked at him.

"We are going to assassinate him, but not only him. While Durga does the honors from the roof outside, Sergei and I will be half a mile away, executing the sainted Gandhi. An Indian killing an English prince, white men killing India's favorite son. It's called a double play in baseball, as I'm sure you know." He grinned at her, relishing the moment. "And India truly will explode."

"And Russia will no longer be alone," Sergei pointed out. "A revolution here will keep ours alive. The party will no longer need to make compromises."

She shook her head in disbelief. "What use would India be to us? It's ten times more backward than we are!"

"All the more reason," Brady drawled. "But I think we've talked for long enough. The only thing left to decide is what we do with you."

MCCOLL WAS A SHORT STEP away from the barely open door, trying to pinpoint each man's position from the sounds of their voices. He still had no idea where Chatterji was, but he might wait forever for the Indian to speak.

He pushed the door wide, took in the frozen tableau, and let the aim of his revolver come to rest on the Indian, whose hand was inches away from the gun on the table.

"Push it away from you," McColl told him in English.

Chatterji did so.

"You," McColl said to Piatakov in Russian, "back against the wall."

"Jack McColl," Brady said, a grin spreading across his face like a mask. "I should have guessed. Are you working for the Cheka, too, or has Caitlin here joined British intelligence?"

"Neither," McColl told him, stepping into the room.

"We're here together because we want the same thing," Caitlin told the stunned Piatakov. "An end to this madness."

Brady laughed at her. "When the Cheka starts working with the British Crown, there's no revolution worth saving. But perhaps you've been too busy sleeping with the past to notice. Why not go home, as Sergei tells you? Back to your women's business."

"Nothing would make me happier. As long as he comes with me."

"At the end of a gun?" Piatakov asked bitterly.

"If there was another way to save you from this idiocy, I would have used it."

He shook his head sadly. "I can't go back."

"So that's that," Brady said. "I guess you'll have to kill us all."

She ignored him. "Sergei?"

"Remember Vedenskoye," Brady said matter-of-factly.

"No!" Piatakov cried as Chatterji tipped himself backward.

Distracted by the Indian's movement, McColl took his eye off Brady just long enough for the latter to raise his Colt revolver and would probably have paid the intended price if Piatakov, intent on shielding Caitlin, hadn't thrown himself at the American.

McColl had braced himself for the bullet, but when the Colt boomed, it was the Russian who took it, staggering forward and then collapsing in front of his shocked-looking partner.

As Piatakov toppled, McColl fired over him, slamming Brady into the wall.

McColl fired again, blowing a hole through the side of Chatterji's head as the Indian lunged for his gun.

Caitlin was on all fours, leaning over the now-prone Piatakov. "Oh, Sergei," she whispered, but there was no answer, only a dark patch spreading on the white linen shirt.

Brady was slumped behind them, clutching his upper side, the fallen Colt beyond his reach.

McColl kept him covered, ears cocked for the sound of feet on the stairs. The other people in the house would have heard the shots, but would they do anything more than lock their doors and remind one another that white people's business was better left to them?

So far, apparently not.

Chatterji and Caitlin's husband were dead, so the obvious thing to do was finish Brady off and leave the building as fast as they could.

He looked at the wounded American and wished the man would give him the excuse he needed. It was doubtless to humanity's credit that most people found it hard to kill in cold blood, but sometimes it was most inconvenient.

He didn't think he could do it, not even when the man in question was Aidan Brady.

CAITLIN STARED AT HER FELLOW American. He had led her brother and Sergei to their deaths, and it made no difference to her that both had been willing disciples. He had murdered Yuri Komarov, whom she'd come to respect and almost cherish. Three times now, he had tried and narrowly failed to kill Jack.

What sort of monster was he? The five words that came to mind were hackneyed as hell but seemed bizarrely appropriate: an enemy of the revolution.

The gun that Chatterji had knocked off the table was lying a foot from her hand.

As she picked it up, Brady must have seen the look on her face. "No," he said, trying to rise. There was more disbelief than fear in his voice, as if he couldn't quite believe in a world without himself.

After only the briefest of hesitations, she aimed at that place where most men had hearts and firmly squeezed the trigger.

Brady's head slumped to the floor, his mouth twisting into a final snarl.

FOOTSTEPS SOUNDED ON THE STAIRS, then stopped. The shooting hadn't gone unnoticed.

McColl tried to gently pull Caitlin away, but she shook him off. Back on her knees, she closed the dead Piatakov's eyes and kissed him on the forehead.

McColl could hear voices below. Arguing, probably over what to do. "We have to go," he told her. "He didn't save you so you could end up in an Indian prison," he added when she failed to respond. "He'd want you to go on with your work."

She looked up, eyes full of tears. "I know."

"Then come on. We'll go out the way I came in."

She got back to her feet, wiping the tears away on her sleeve.

He scanned the room for anything they might have left behind, then turned down the lamp. When he took a last look back from the door, the room seemed full of corpses, but for once in his violent life, he could see no cause for remorse. His only regret was that he hadn't shot Brady himself because Caitlin seemed in a state of shock.

She let him lead her across a succession of adjoining roofs and down the rickety fire escape that a progressive landlord had provided for his tenants. As they reached the bottom, a rickshaw came out of the darkness and stopped right beside them, the boy driver beaming with pride. McColl helped her into the seat, thinking that Komarov's ghost had to be working overtime.

McColl told the boy where to take them and asked for a back-street route. Soon they were speeding down narrow, dimly lit alleys where the rickshaw often scraped along one of the walls.

"You tried," he told her, conscious of how empty the words sounded.

She just looked away.

He had never seen her like this before, but then as far as he knew, she'd never shot a man before. Nor seen a husband die.

The shock would wear off, but until it did he'd have to think for them both. Would Five and the IPI be after them? By rights they should be grateful—he and Caitlin had succeeded where Cunningham and his helpers had failed—but McColl wasn't holding his breath. He and Caitlin knew too much.

They had to get out of Delhi, but where should they go? He knew Calcutta much better than Bombay . . . He suddenly thought of Darjeeling, largely empty of Brits at this time of year, and close enough to the Chinese border should they need a place to run to. One of those hotels high on the hill with their stunning views of the Himalayas. Next morning he could go to see Mirza, tell the detective the story as promised, and ask for the help of his old railway comrades in getting them out of the city.

A glance at Caitlin's expression brought McColl back to earth. Here he was planning their future, and only twenty minutes before she'd been begging Sergei to come home. Had she been lying to coax him away from the others, or had she really meant it? Even if she hadn't, why was he assuming that she wouldn't return on her own? Because she loved him? She'd loved him in 1918, and that hadn't stopped her from saying good-bye.

They were, he suddenly realized, drawing up outside the serai. It was gone midnight, and their feet on the stairs sounded loud in the sleeping building. Once they were safe in their room, he tried to take her in his arms, and after an initial flinch, she allowed him to do so. "Thank you," she said when he let her go, but he had no idea what for.

She lay herself out on the bed and stared at the ceiling.

Things would look better after they slept, he told himself, lying down beside her. He felt exhausted but was determined not to drop off before she did.

She seemed to sense as much. "Go to sleep," she told him. "I don't think I'll be able to."

"Do you want to talk?" he asked.

"No."

IN THE HOUR BEFORE DAWN, McColl awoke with a jerk, a sheen of cold sweat on his forehead. His mind reached for the fading dream, but it was already gone, leaving only the feeling that somehow he had gotten everything wrong.

He levered himself into a sitting position and stared down at her sleeping face, shadow drawn in the dim light: the dark pools of the shuttered eyes; the strong, graceful line of the jaw. The new Russia, he thought. Humanity's best hope, where the best of people ended up as executioners.

One day maybe, far in the future.

WHEN HE WOKE UP AGAIN, the sun was streaming through the window, and she was gone. So was her suitcase and, as he quickly discovered, half of their money. She was going back to Russia.

There was a note on the table. "I love you, Jack, and that makes this the hardest thing I've ever had to do. Forgive me, Caitlin."

He read it through again, and again, examining each pencil stroke as if there was some way he could release the feelings they had imprisoned, then sat staring into space for several minutes, before running a hand through his hair and walking out onto the balcony.

"I can give myself to you," she had once said to him, "because I know I can take myself away."

Outside, the familiar sensory palette presented itself: the smells, the noise, the ache of color. Across the street a man in a turban was sitting on a stool, a cobbler's last between his knees, hammering away at a long black boot. A rickshaw went past, carrying a pasty-faced European toward the Red Fort. Above the roofs the sky seemed blue as the dome over Tamerlane's tomb.

Had he always known she would go back?

He had to admit the answer was no. The fear had always been there, but he hadn't really believed that she would.

What could he do now? Go home, he supposed, if only for his mother's sake. To a country awash with anger and bitterness, to the half-dead life he'd left behind, to grieving her loss all over again.

He walked back into the room and wearily gathered his possessions together.

The map of Tashkent he'd taken from Rafiq's room at the Hotel Lux was still in his bag, and seeing it there he remembered the courtyard of women, the flickering film on the wall, all those eyes in search of a better world.

Her place of hope. He seemed no nearer to finding his own.

THE PLUMES OF SMOKE IN the distance presumably marked the station. After she'd found a place there to change back into her Russian clothes, she would buy a ticket to somewhere. She had no idea how she would get back to Moscow and suspected it might take months, but there had to be a way. For someone like her—young, clever, and white—there would always be a way.

So why did the smoke in the distance seem too close? She had done the hardest part, done it because she knew she wouldn't have the strength to do it again. So why was she crying inside?

What in God's name was she doing?

They were passing through the Queen's Gardens. "Pull over," she told the driver, pointing him toward the curb when he turned to see what she wanted. He looked around again once they were stationary, and she held up five fingers.

He muttered something and climbed down from his seat. "More annas," he warned her, before lighting a cigarette and ambling into the garden.

She sat there, absurdly exposed, watching the palm fronds sway in the morning breeze.

Was she returning to something that was no longer there?

In 1918 she'd been closer to joy than she'd ever expected. She remembered trying—and failing—to convey the strength of that feeling in a letter to her aunt Orla. What had happened in Russia was probably a once-in-a-lifetime thing, maybe rarer than that. A sense of togetherness, of social happiness, that had left her and all the people she knew drunk on hope and fellow feeling. The world had opened up, and things that had once seemed carved in stone—the poverty and exploitation, the never-ending wars, the subjection of women—were suddenly seen to be written only in sand, so swiftly erased, so easily rewritten. And she had been part of the change, one of so many making a difference.

Wordsworth had put it well: "Bliss was it in that dawn to be alive."

The years that followed had not been so joyful—the civil war and the hardship it brought in its wake had seen to that. Some had thought victory would rejuvenate the revolution, but the opposite seemed to have happened. The magic was gone, the world closing down, the sand reverting to stone.

They found it hard to admit, to themselves as much as to one another, but all of them knew. Sergei and Komarov had railed against it in their very different ways; Kollontai was doubtless still tenaciously fighting her corner. But deep in their hearts, they all knew that the odds were against them, that the brand-new world they thought they had glimpsed was fading like a dream.

Caitlin sighed and watched as a pair of young Indian men in suits strode past, presumably bound for some office. She could go back to hers in Moscow and do that work that could still be done. Part of her wanted to; part of her thought she should.

But other voices demanded a hearing. The one that said, "Cut your losses, and find a new country where doors are waiting for someone to break them down." The one that just said, "Jack."

In 1918 she'd had to choose between love and ideals because he was a wanted man where she most wanted to be. But even then, setting him loose, she'd hoped that they might meet again, that she wasn't burning her bridges completely. And miracle of miracles, she'd been right.

If she left him again, she knew there'd be no way back.

Passionate love wasn't everything, but it sure as hell was something. And though for women it often seemed to crowd out everything else, that didn't have to be the case. Maybe winning that particular battle was the hardest thing she'd ever have to do.

HE TOOK ONE LAST LOOK around the empty room, and felt the sting of tears. Feeling foolish, he wiped them away and made for the stairs. He was halfway across the courtyard below when the street door swung open and there she was, suitcase in hand.

Seeing him there, an uncertain smile appeared on her face.

"Forget something?" he asked.

"Just you."

Historical Note

With historical fiction the question often arises as to where the history ends and the fiction begins, and I feel it is incumbent on authors to at least take a stab at explaining their own approach. The most important thing, to my mind, is that the historical context—by which I mean everything from political events to food and clothing—should be as accurate as possible. Some will disagree with my judgments—history, after all, is often a matter of opinion. Others will gleefully point out the odd mistake, and as someone prone to schadenfreude myself, I can hardly complain when they do.

The plot that forms the spine of *The Dark Clouds Shining*—the employment of communist dupes by sections of British intelligence to assassinate Mohandas Gandhi—is pure fiction, but the British sense of heightened insecurity in the face of Gandhi's independence campaign was real enough, and developments in Russia at this time were certainly inviting many veteran activists to seek out revolutionary situations farther afield. The Kronstadt rebellion and Lenin's introduction of the New (and suspiciously retrograde) Economic Policy convinced many that the Russian Revolution's progressive phase was over.

Mansfield Cumming was head of the British Secret Service from its foundation in 1909 until his death in 1923 and was often ill in the year in which this book is set.

Several well-known Bolsheviks appear in the novel, but only two play any part in the plot's unfolding. Felix Dzerzhinsky was the head of the statewide security police (the Vecheka or Cheka, later the GPU and OGPU) from its formation in 1917 to his early death in 1926. Had he lived much longer, he would doubtless have died in the purges that claimed his surviving male colleagues—Stalin of course excepted—from the original Bolshevik leadership.

Alexandra Kollontai was the only woman in that leadership and, during the early years of the revolution, was important for her championing of women's and children's rights, and for her support of the Workers' Opposition, which sought, perhaps unrealistically, a greater role for Russia's decimated proletariat once the civil war was over. Sidelined by 1923, she accepted the post of Soviet ambassador to Norway, and effectively retired from Soviet politics. Her writings on gender and socialist issues, unlike those of her male Bolshevik colleagues, remain fresh and original a century later.

Jack McColl, Caitlin Hanley/Piatakova, Yuri Komarov, Aidan Brady, and Sergei Piatakov are all complete inventions, but I hope that among them they reflect a range of human responses to that saddest of human situations—the dying of a dream.

Series Acknowledgments

First off, I must thank and praise my principal editor, Juliet Grames. She has had a huge impact on these four books, mostly by metaphorically standing at my shoulder as I write and demanding to know what the character is feeling. In this and many other ways her input has been crucial throughout.

My other editors—Maureen Sugden, Rachel Kowal, Katie Herman, Ellie Robbins and Linda Grames—have also made stellar contributions. I have often been in awe of how much they know and how much they notice.

I also want to thank everyone at Soho who has helped bring the books and myself to the market, both those I know by name—Bronwen Hruska, Paul Oliver, Amara Hoshijo and Abby Koski—and those I don't.

Writing, like most endeavors, is often all about confidence, and I must thank my agent and friend Charlie Viney for his encouragement over the years.

Last but far from least, I must mention my wife's contribution. Nancy has been busy these last few years doing a PhD and hasn't read much of the series, but her voice inside my head undoubtedly helped to write it.

—David Downing